THE DARKEST MIDNIGHT

R. A. FINLEY

ISBN: 0-9893157-2-X
ISBN-13: 978-0-9893157-2-2
eBook ISBN: 978-0-9893157-3-9
Library of Congress: TX0007999636

Published by Hickory Tree Publishing

Book Design by R. A. Finley
Cover Design & Artwork by R. A. Finley

10   9   8   7   6   5   4   3   2

Second Hickory Tree Publishing Edition

To my mom.

And to Midnight.

THE DARKEST MIDNIGHT

Fain would I climb, yet fear I to fall.

Sir Walter Raleigh

PROLOGUE

**Fiend's Fell
Cumbria, Northern England
01 November**

It felt ridiculous to fear a dead man, but as Cormac walked the cold, deserted passageways of his father's underground stronghold, he did exactly that. Habit, he supposed. But dead was dead. The only ghosts Cormac might encounter lurked not in any actual darkened corner but within his own mind. The ghosts of memory. Of fear, pain, sorrow. Loneliness.

He ducked a low, rough hewn beam as he rounded a sharp turn. Either the long-ago people who had carved these tunnels deep into the mountain had been considerably shorter than Cormac's five-foot-nine or they hadn't the time—or perhaps permission—for comfort.

His boot slipped when the passageway, slick with ice, took a steep downward slant. Rather than slow, he increased pace. With every second the air felt a little thinner, smelled a little ranker; and the walls, already close enough, seemed to push in closer still. If not for the bargain with Murphy, Cormac would never have returned to Fiend's Fell.

The temperature was icy enough to chill even an American's beer, but Cormac was sweating beneath his jacket, the cotton of his shirt sticking uncomfortably to his back. It was absurd, this anxiety. As far as his Sight could tell, the stronghold was deserted. However large its current population might be, all must have accompanied his father to Orkney, and thus they either lay dead at the Ring of Brodgar or were on the run from there. Should any seek to return, it would require more time than Cormac intended to spend.

No, there was nothing to fear here tonight from his father's *thegnas*—his followers—nor from the man himself. With the memory, the *feel* of Idris Cathmor's death but two hours fresh, Cormac ought to know better than anyone.

His hands itched, their nerves not yet recovered from being conduits for so much power; his throat burned from shouting. Screaming, if he cared to be accurate (and he did not). He had put genuine emotion on display several times already this night, which amounted to several times too many.

When he'd seen Thia about to run headlong into the deadly protection spells that kept them captive within Brodgar. And again when he had held her while her body struggled to adjust to the Cailleach's newly-introduced powers. And, worst of all, when the Brigantium had used him as a conduit to kill Idris.

That had been the most public instance, no question. Even as battle raged throughout the Ring, Cormac and his father and their dueling storms had attracted a good deal of attention. It had been then, when Idris was down with Cormac's hands wrapped around his throat that the—

He shuddered, tamped down the memory before it could fully rise.

The Brigantium had seized the opportunity to rid the world of a perceived evil. He couldn't fault their perception or their decision. It was their method that currently gave him trouble.

The knowledge that, if they hadn't taken control from him in those last moments, he might have done the deed himself did not sit too well, either.

Guilt. It didn't eat at him, as the saying went. No. It invaded, thickened the blood and turned marrow cold. Threatened to transform him utterly if left unchecked.

He had nothing against it. Hell, he deserved it, did he not? Guilt over Idris, and over Thia too.

He rubbed his chest, the unconscious gesture doing nothing to ease the ache summoned by her name.

After a sequence of counterintuitive turns, Cormac entered a hexagonal antechamber.

Disbelief hit hard.

The doors to the most secure storerooms were wide open. Every single one. The wards that should have shimmered in Cormac's Sight were gone.

He didn't need to shine the light of his electric torch inside to see that every room had been emptied, yet he did. Nor did he need to enter them one by one, yet he did.

Nothing of significance remained. And, given the lack of any energy remnants—remnants that should have overwhelmed, considering what had been held within—the rooms had been magically scoured. He braced his hands on either side of an empty niche at the back of the room and dropped his head forward, his brow pressing onto the stone. Eyes closed, he breathed in the dank, familiar smell of failure.

The Achill Bell, promised to Declan Murphy upon pain of death, was gone.

CHAPTER 1

Thia dreamt of blood.

Oh, sure, there was more to the dream than that. Ancient, lichen-covered megaliths stretching up from a storm-ravaged plain to stab the night sky. The haze of smoke, the crackle of flame. Cries and shouts. Screams. Confusion and terror and loss and the feel of a man, comforting and achingly familiar, coupled with the sound of a raven's wings.

But mostly she dreamt of blood, and every morning woke and tried to forget.

It had been almost eight weeks since the events at Brodgar. Thia no longer thought of them continuously in her waking life, yet she couldn't shake the sense of them. Couldn't shake the fear and guilt, either, no matter how much of the latter might be misplaced. She felt numbed by it all; hollowed out, and despite the supportive company of her friends, isolated. She was going through the motions of her old life while trying to understand her new. Caught between the two, she couldn't connect with either.

"You are like a pupa, yes? A butterfly in its shell," Madame Demetka had told her a few days ago at the store. Thia had waited for something like an explanation to follow, but the undeniably odd (and, undeniably, oddly psychic) woman had merely smiled and gone upstairs to prepare for the afternoon's Tarot Readings.

Well, thought Thia now, if that were true then she wished she would hatch already.

She took a sip of much-needed coffee and, hip against the kitchen counter, continued to watch morning sunlight creep across the wintry garden which, once Lettie's, was now hers.

Frost dusted what leaves remained and covered the small patch of grass. The ceramic birdbath had a thin layer of ice at the edges, but nothing insurmountable. Southern Oregon could be cold but not so severely that there wasn't the chance of a feathered visitor. And there were always ravens. The ones here never left, unlike some—or rather, one in particular.

Along with a sudden bitterness, she swallowed the last of the coffee, rinsed the mug before setting it in the drainer.

Cormac was not truly a raven, although he had taken that form when she last saw him, thanks to his being half *Sidhe,* an Otherworldly being Thia had known little about at the time.

He had been his usual self (or what she assumed to be his usual self) when she'd embraced him for all she was worth, so glad that he was alive—that they had both survived. Then he had pulled away, transformed into a bird, and left her to stand alone on what only minutes before had been a battlefield, its dead and wounded scattered all around her.

For the millionth time, Thia pushed those memories aside. No good came from thinking of that night—or of him.

She bundled herself in coat and scarf, then pulled a quirky knit cap over her shoulder-length auburn hair. Her gloves and keys were on the table in the breakfast nook. The latter looked particularly cozy with the light streaming in through the mullioned windows. She used to enjoy sitting there with coffee and toast, with Lettie apt to join her before they headed out. Now it was simpler to eat at the counter if she bothered with breakfast at all.

At the back door she paused to look the garden over with a more security-conscious eye. Even if Cassie's threats were not a constant in the back of her mind, her friends had advised her to be vigilant for additional reasons. The power she had gained would not go unnoticed, they had warned. She could expect to be visited by anyone from the mildly curious to the outright hostile. There were people, Otherworldly and otherwise, who would go to great lengths to take it or try to use it through her.

But not this morning. The small yard, so crowded with life in the spring and summer, was empty and still.

She took a slow breath and called on her newfound Sight—the strange and still-developing ability to see things outside of the usual scope. So far, she had only learned how to look for "wards," as the protective energy fields were called. It was the most basic of skills, and she wasn't that great at it; but it was *something* magical, at least, that she could do without risk.

At the property line and extending upward to form a dome, the wards shimmered, translucent and faintly colorful like a giant soap bubble. They showed no evidence of tampering, so she ought to be safe from house to garage, and from there in her car with its own protection wards, the few blocks to her parking spot behind Eclectica.

Putting away the Sight—it helped to think of it like a pair of glasses—she stepped onto the back porch. Her breath was a visible plume. Her muscles clenched with cold.

Not anxiety, she told herself before she took another quick scan of the garden and double-locked the door. Only then, feeling like an overcautious fool, did she make her way down the deck's three slick wooden steps.

At the snap of a twig high in the neighbor's cedar, she startled and nearly dropped the keys. Shadowed and obscured by the draping needles, something moved along a branch. She couldn't make out its shape or even color. With a soft flapping of wings, it took off from the far side of the tree, out of sight.

Raven? Gone, in any case.

She told herself not to dwell on it.

In her first weeks back, she had driven herself all the more crazy by seeking out Cormac at every turn. Every unfamiliar face and especially every large black bird had held a longed-for possibility. Then each time—each and every time—she'd had to acknowledge his continued absence. An absence that was most likely permanent.

It had become too painful, and so she had forced herself to stop.

Stop looking, stop hoping.

Yet that was hard, and sometimes she relapsed. Her hand went to her pendant, found it no warmer than it should have been for being against her skin. A representation of a gorgon cast in sterling silver, it was an odd-looking safeguard. And an imperfect one, as it turned out, though Thia still found it reassuring. It might not detect or ward off every danger, but it had done well against a certain individual. Also, it had been a gift from Lettie.

Thia hurried down the short path to the garage. Inside, she quickly shut the door, leaned against it a moment to recover. Her hands shook but she couldn't blame the cold.

To think she used to walk to work at all times of the day or evening with hardly a concern. Now she scurried like a frightened mouse across a fenced-in yard in order to drive.

To think she used to believe that magic was nothing more than fantasy and wishful thinking.

Sure, when she had come to set up and run Eclectica's online store, Lettie had explained certain practices: Don't allow an opened Tarot deck to be sold; make sure that the wolfsbane remained in the locked case and never went to anyone not on the approved buyer's list; and so on. Thia had thought that all part of her great-aunt's whimsy. Feel-good but essentially needless precautions, like carrying around a four leaf clover for luck and not walking beneath a ladder.

How wrong she had been.

Space in the garage was tight. She brushed against crowded shelves as she skirted Lettie's older-model Datsun to get to its driver's side door. The hinges creaked. So did the springs when she settled into the worn bucket seat. Habit caused her to reach for the button on the remote clipped to the visor. She lowered her hand, took a deep breath.

Little things, they'd instructed. Start with little things.

She closed her eyes and then worked to gather what Abby called "the energy of intention" while envisioning the newly repaired main door. White with four horizontal segments and a row of small windows along the top. A system of tracks with a cable and pulley.

Thia waited until she could feel the substance, the reality of it all—along with the uncomfortable prickle as the Cailleach's power moved from her bones to gather at her palms. Then, with a calm upward sweep of her hands, she pictured the door lifting.

Slowly.

The storage shelves along the walls began to rattle, but she couldn't risk taking a look. The door, lifting. She needed to maintain the image, the feel of it. She needed to—

The loud pop of something hitting the ground was followed by sounds of breaking glass and scattering metal. Thia's eyes flew open as, behind her, the garage door crashed down.

"No. Oh, please, not again."

More and more things toppled from shelves that continued to tremble. Glass jars of nails and screws fell to shatter on the cement floor while a toolbox rattled toward the brink.

"Ah, shit"—She hadn't called back the power. She'd lost her focus but was still sending. Forcing her eyes closed again, she struggled for calm as—by the great crashing sound of it—the toolbox dropped. Her hands made another gesture, an inward sweep this time with thumb and third finger touching, before she settled them in her lap in a meditative pose.

"To me," she said, fear and frustration turning what should have been an order into a soft-voiced plea. "In me."

Gradually the power reversed course, no longer flowing out to her hands but inward *from* them, back into her bones— where it could remain, as far as Thia was concerned, for the rest of her days, never to be called upon again.

As the undirected power dissipated, the shelving settled.

Unfortunately, she couldn't ignore the power, much as she wanted to. Couldn't hope to let it lie dormant forever. In the last couple of weeks she had become better at controlling it so that it no longer shot out at unexpected (and invariably destructive) times. But that wasn't enough. She needed to be able to wield it or she would remain a danger to everyone.

She pressed the button on the remote, stepped out of the car as the garage door rattled upward along the tracks. That was something, anyway. Last week she'd warped it so badly it had stuck halfway. She sighed and then, with cold air rushing in, crunched over nails and glass shards to where Lettie kept the broom.

The last thing the morning needed was a punctured tire. Or four.

● ○ ●

Blooms Alley, Granite Springs
He had come early, cloaked in the mist of wintry dawn, as he had every morning since magic's insistent fingers had begun to prod the blanket of his solitude.

At the time, he had been gathering supplies, stocking up for the cold months ahead. That idea (what he could recall of it) had been based upon the now-failed hope of staying on the mountain until *Gwanwyn*. Spring. He did not like town.

Fear had demanded he investigate. Self-preservation, too.

Never again would he allow himself to be taken unawares.

Never again to be taken.

He shuddered, drew his scarf higher about his face, and then returned his hands to his pockets. Several fingers of his gloves lacked tips. Sunlight's faint warmth could not penetrate the shadows between brick and metal where he had constructed a shelter of cardboard pulled from the same rubbish bin he sat behind. It and the low-level warming charm he had spell-crafted kept away the worst of the cold, but—by design—not all. Comfort lulled.

He tensed at the sound of a car.

Unmistakably hers, with its 1972 motor in need of a tune-up. It parked in its designated spot. Six meters from the back entrance to the store; three from his cobbled together blind. With the opening of its door came the awareness at the base of his skull, akin to the sensation of hairs standing on end—although, with his hat pulled low and his scarf wrapped high and tight, that was hardly possible.

The sensation was false, but the warning was not.

Power. In great concentration and carrying the too-familiar resonance of the Cailleach.

He listened to the thump of the door's closing followed by the light tread of her steps on the asphalt as she approached. The sounds of opportunity. In the span from car to the build-ing's walled terrace, she was vulnerable.

The building's rear door opened with the click of a latch and a cheery squeak of hinges. But the woman had not yet crossed the halfway point.

His senses, already straining against the leash, surged. His hold began to slip.

"Good morning." *Her* voice.

Then the one with the power. "Zoe, here, let me get that for you."

Both neared, the one coming from the car; the other, from

the building.

He held himself rigid, hardly dared breathe while the bin's lid lifted. Something landed inside. Cardboard, added to the collection.

"Thanks, Thia."

After the lid was lowered and sounds assured him they were headed for the building, he risked a look. He had the merest glimpse—of the woman with the power and *her*—but it was enough to stagger. It was as if she were lit from within. If he had but one of her smiles, the ones he had seen her give so freely to others, he would not need a spell-crafted charm to keep warm.

Less than a minute after the building's door had closed, it opened again. He knew what was coming. Braced for it. Her steps were quiet. Tentative, despite this not being the first time nor even the fifth. She had been doing this for the past week.

Paper rustled and she set something on the ground by the bin's front bottom corner. He would not risk breaking cover to look. Not at it, not at her. Bad enough that he continued to come here day after day.

Irrationally, he had decided that her knowing that he spent time in this place was not a risk because she did not know *why* he did so. Nor did she know his identity. She thought he was a transient, someone in need.

She kept leaving him food.

The door closed. She had gone back inside, into the store's café, and if her routine held, she would not come out again until late afternoon. There would be more recycling to bin. More food. A sandwich and piece of fruit, typically, although yesterday there had been a takeaway container of soup.

After ten minutes, when he was sure no one watched, he pulled in the paper sack she had left.

An onion bagel, lightly toasted. The foil covering had failed to keep it hot, but he could fix that. Two packets, a butter and a cream cheese, along with a plastic knife. Two lidded paper cups. One held the usual coffee. Its aroma cut through even the thickest of the area's smells. The other cup was heavier, warmer. He sniffed at the lid's vent, although he figured if she intended to do him harm, she would have done so before this.

Probably.

No. She didn't have it in her. She was good. Innocent.

Oatmeal. He pried off the lid, tugged down his scarf. He had not had oatmeal in...He could not remember how long. And he would not try. That would mean thinking though the lost time.

There was a plastic spoon in the bag. He used it to scoop up a mouthful of steaming, cinnamon-spiced wonder. His eyes closed on a sigh.

A woman's low, seductive voice intruded. "I believe we have something in common. Someone, rather."

Power, angry and dark. His mind spun, caught entirely off guard as malevolence began worming its way through defenses he had worked long and hard to erect since his release from *caethiwed.*

His powers were not what they had once been, what they needed to be. This was an uphill battle and he had not the strength for a climb. He did try. Would continue to try until he had nothing left. He shook as the ripples of a compulsion spell licked like the tongue of a slavering beast.

Its fangs would not be far behind.

"What is it you seek?" he managed, his seldom-used voice strange to his own ears. The cup had dropped from his hands. He would not have noticed but for the spilled oatmeal's wet heat soaking through his clothing. Steam rose like thin, sheer snakes. He looked at them instead of the woman.

He had not heard her approach. Had not felt so much as a glimmer. One moment he had been alone; the next...not.

Power in combination with skill.

He closed his eyes as the tremors increased. His breathing had become choppy, his panic like a living thing. And as his control slipped, so did his footing in the silent, doomed fight against her will.

"Walk with me," she said, her sickly sweet voice closer than before. She had slipped into the space between the bins. She bent down, level with the entrance to his shelter and looked straight at him. He felt the nip of the beast's fangs then, the compulsion spell taking hold.

"Follow." She straightened, gone the way she had come. He heard her walking away.

He stood, abandoning his refuge and the cherished gift of food.

She was halfway down the alley. A tall woman with hair in a long, sinuous cascade down her back. Swaying hypnotically, it beckoned.

He followed.

● ○ ●

Eclectica, Granite Springs
Thia felt a twinge of guilt when she hurried through the café to Eclectica. The decorative interior gate that separated the two spaces was already propped open. The mess in the garage had set her back almost a half hour. The store had already opened for the day.

The café, accessed through the rear door, kept early hours (as coffee shops did). The store's morning started later, hence the gate—the unlocking of which (along with its door downstairs on Main Street) was something Thia had recently taken upon herself. It helped her to understand that she did, in fact, own what she feared would always feel like Lettie's pride and joy.

Hugging the stair rail to make way for the people beelining

up to the café, she reconsidered her word choice. *Fear* wasn't right, since the alternative would be to lose even more of her great-aunt than she already had. She didn't want that, yet she could not feel like a stand-in forever, either.

Along with this building and the house, she had inherited most of Lettie's investments and possessions. That included a London townhouse that she had no idea what to do with. Her memories of it, and of the city in general, were not what she had hoped they'd be when she'd set out.

Thia knew what she wanted to do with Eclectica, at least: She wanted to make it a continued success. In theory, that would continue with or without her. Much of it, thanks to its manager, ran like clockwork, and it was already highly popular with locals and tourists alike. Thia's efforts with online sales had simply built on that.

But it was also, in many ways, like a living thing and therefore not meant to remain unchanged. It could not be kept as a shrine to Lettie, with Lettie's original decisions cast in stone. If it did, Thia felt, then that stone would become the store's grave marker. Eclectica needed to stay vibrant, to shift with the combined will of its customers and owner both or it would atrophy and eventually die.

That was where the fear came in. Or, given everything else Thia had to deal with, maybe "moderate apprehension" was more to scale. Dealing with the power she carried, knowing it was only a matter of time before Cassie sought revenge for the deaths of her twin brother and sorcerer-father were far scarier prospects than decisions such as which wholesaler to use for Tara Water or whether to stop stocking crystal orbs now that she knew what they could be used for.

"Good morning, Lynette," she said in passing at the bottom of the stairs and then waved at the customers the clerk was on her way to assist. The Winslows. Mother and daughter, they co-owned the Victorian inn across the alley. Both smiled, waved back.

"More ornaments?" Thia was surprised—but pleasantly so. The week before, they had bought the entire stock of glass pickles.

"We like to put one in each room for guests to take home with them," said Jeanine, the daughter. "Thanks for getting more in so quickly."

Thia felt another twinge of guilt. She'd had nothing to do with the quick reorder. "I'll let Abby know."

As manager and used to handling such things during Lettie's frequent absences, Abby had acted well within her capacity. Should Thia have known, at least, that a new order was being made? Or maybe that would be micromanaging.

Dammit, enough. Was she going to second-guess *everything* now? She pulled off her scarf, removed her coat on the way to Lettie's—to *her* office—and nearly knocked over a menorah from the special Hanukkah display. For as much retail space as the building allowed, winter holidays took up a great deal more than usual. Beautiful, though, in all its chaotic, multi-cultural glory. And the wonderful scents. Thia inhaled deeply. Usually, Eclectica held the aromas of fresh-ground coffee and scones from the café along with those of the bolder-scented of the herbs sold on the main floor. Winter had added pine boughs and pomanders of oranges and cloves.

After the office, Thia went to the counter—or, to be precise, counters. Six of them, arranged hexagonally at the center of the store. After too many close calls with last-minute groups who needed to get to their plays at the Shakespeare Festival, this was one of the changes Thia had instigated.

She found Abby there, preparing to use a bare branch in a sand-filled vase to display a new shipment of fairy figurines. Made of porcelain and silk, they were colorful and whimsical and sweet—and looked entirely harmless, which Thia now knew had little to do with reality. Most fairies (aka *Sidhe*) were the stuff of nightmares.

On second thought, should these likenesses prove accurate,

their subjects would likely turn out to not be just as violent and frightening as the rest. Appearances, she had learned all too well, were deceiving.

She handed Abby a fairy from the array on the counter. "I'm sorry you had to open without me."

"Everything all right?"

Thia was spared a concerned glance before Abby looped the fairy's ribbon over a twig. The winged figure swayed, its silk flower-petal costume fluttering gently.

"I made a mess of the garage again," Thia admitted.

"The door?" Abby climbed the two-step ladder, held out her hand for another fairy.

Thia chose a brunette with lavender wings and tiny wire-frame eyeglasses. "Survived." She steadied the branch's base while Abby worked. "I don't know what I'm doing wrong, I really don't. I'm never going to get this."

Abby stepped down, collapsed the ladder. Her unruly hair had slipped mostly free of its clip. With one hand, she swept the dark curls out of her face. "Nonsense. These things take time. And you've been given a shitload of power to deal with. You can't just expect to be thrown in the deep end of the pool one morning and swim laps by the end of the day."

"It's been weeks. Six weeks, to be exact, and I can't even lift a stupid door."

"But you haven't made anything fly off Eclectica's shelves in over a week." Abby's small smile held something Thia hoped was not pity.

"Not here, no."

"Where?" Whatever Abby's expression had held, it switched to alarm.

"The garage. This morning, with the door." Thia shrugged, then admitted the rest. "Last night it was the kitchen. I'm not trying stuff at home anymore." She wadded up the tissue that the fairies had been wrapped in and chucked it into the wastebasket under the counter. "Not by myself, anyway."

"I've got time after work tonight. How about we go out to dinner, do some exercises after?"

It was an offer Thia knew she should take. But knowing and wanting were two different things. "I'm not sure that's a good idea."

"If you're worried about damage, we could do it at my place. There's not much to break in the drying shed."

Not much property, maybe, but what about *them?* People could be broken just as easily. Sweat dampened her palms. "I don't know. Maybe."

"Come on, it'll be fun." Carrying the stepladder with both hands, Abby playfully jostled her elbow into Thia on the way past. "I'll see if Kendra can come, make it a night out. There's no way anything can go wrong with both of us there with you. Come on," she repeated, but without humor. "You need to do this. It won't be safe for you until you can—"

"—control the power, I know. Believe me, I know. It won't be safe for any of us." Because a powerful, vindictive woman wouldn't hesitate to weaponize Thia's love for her friends.

That night in the Ring, Thia had killed Cassie's brother and contributed to the death of Cassie's father. It didn't matter that the former had been unintentional or that neither would have happened if they themselves had not set the entire chain of events in motion. Cassie's final words to Thia had been of revenge, and the inevitability of that threat had hung over her head ever since. Over all their heads, really.

"It'll be okay," Abby said quietly and then went to put the ladder away.

At the jingle of the sleigh bells hung on the door, Thia put on a practiced smile. Not too exuberant or the prospective customer could be put on edge. No one wanted a pushy salesperson, and certainly not before ten in the morning.

A vaguely familiar woman smiled in return and went to the

table of boxed holiday cards. With only three days left before Solstice, and Christmas only a few days after that, she was cutting things close.

A quick survey showed plenty of available clerks should the handful of browsers need help, so Thia dropped out of sight behind the counter to organize the jumble of gift boxes and wrapping supplies. Nearly everyone wanted things wrapped lately. And why not? The season was stressful enough without the added pressure of trying to tie a perfect bow.

They were almost out of small handle-bags. She would need to get on that before the lunchtime rush. A stack of folding boxes insisted on sliding every which way, and she searched in vain for something to serve as a prop. The back of her neck tingled.

A throat cleared. Masculine and tentative rather than impatient, the sound originated above Thia from the other side of the counter. She arranged another smile and stood.

She had misjudged the man's height; her gaze was level with his neck at the collar of his beige and blue checkered shirt. She had anticipated someone a bit shorter, although why she had formed any expectations at all, she couldn't say.

On the tall side of average and middle-aged, he had clean-shaven, pleasant features. Their current expression was one of tense reserve. His blond hair was neatly trimmed.

Everything about him was neat, Thia realized, from the line of his brown corduroy jacket to the drape of his wool scarf. The tortoise-shell frames of his glasses completed the image and brought academia to mind. The slight tint of the lenses obscured his eyes some, but their irises were most definitely brown.

Thia felt flushed. Nervous. *Oh, dear.* At thirty-two she knew all too well the symptoms of acute attraction. She also knew how rare such a thing was for her. Flustered, she tried to hide it by turning up the brightness of her smile. Mistake! It felt forced. Overdone, but it was too late to dial it back now.

"How may I help you?" she asked through what might have resembled a rictus grin.

"Hello," he said, and then made a visible effort to relax. His smile was charmingly shy. "Hi."

She felt a surge of delight that was completely out of scale for the situation. And to think she'd worried that she would have a hard time getting over Cormac. "Hi," she said back.

And they proceeded to stare at one another like fools.

He must have realized it was his turn. "I was hoping you— that is, wondering if you could help me."

"Yes," Thia said, amused. "Of course."

He cringed. "Right. You already asked me that."

"I did."

His rueful laugh—a nearly soundless huff of breath—caught Thia unprepared. So astonishingly familiar, that laugh.

But this man's eyes were brown, not blue. Cormac might be able to use magic to make himself look like anyone else in the world, but due to a particular quirk, he could not change his eyes. Thia would know them anywhere.

Wouldn't she?

"I need a gift for...a friend," the man who was not Cormac said. "A Christmas gift. I'm new in town, and this shop was recommended."

"Welcome to Granite Springs."

"Thank you."

"What sort of things does your friend like?"

His expression blanked. "I don't kn—that is, I don't really know her well. It's...complicated, I suppose you could say."

Thia tried to set him more at ease. "But you want to get her something. That's very thoughtful. We've got a nice selection of jewelry—I don't think there's a woman alive who doesn't like jewelry." She tapped the counter glass. Below were several velvet-covered boards of necklaces and pins.

He leaned away in subtle but definite rejection. "That feels rather...."

"Personal? Good point. What about something decorative for the home? We have—"

"I might've seen some things over there which looked, uh, pretty." He pointed to the Glass Tower—a rectangular case near the foot of the stairs. "Could you show them to me?"

"Of course." Feeling a blush flame her cheeks, she bent to grab the keys from beneath the counter. When she straightened, she found him waiting at the narrow pass-through.

"It's just over there," she said. *Good grief,* as if he didn't know that.

Instead of preceding her, he gestured for her to lead.

She did, but he stayed close, catching up to walk beside her despite the unusually rapid pace set by her nerves. She felt profoundly self-conscious.

"Have you lived in town long?" he asked.

"Almost a year."

"And you're well?" He made a small cough. "Doing well? It certainly looks as if you are."

Arriving at the Tower, Thia went around to the back. "The store, you mean?"

She looked at him through the cabinet glass. He appeared sheepish again, his gaze darting away and back. Maybe he *did* know what the expression did for him. It made him seem... endearing. She turned the key, pulled open the door.

"I'm sorry," he said. "I'm not used to small talk. I meant— well. I meant that you seem...happy. Are you?" He let out a tense breath. "Happy?"

Oh. Thia's mind flashed to her morning disaster, and she felt her carefully crafted mask of retail salesmanship slip.

The man put his hands in his pockets. "I'm sorry—again. I'm making a mess of this. Forget I said anything, would you? That's a nice piece." One hand immediately left his pocket to point.

"The butterfly?" Thia reached for the delicate figure made of silver and glass. One of her favorites.

"Yes."

"A friend of mine—a sort of friend—mentioned butterflies to me just the other day," she said, removing it. "This one is beautiful, isn't it?" She held it out.

"It is."

In taking it, the man's fingers skimmed the backs of Thia's hands; the light touch was like an electric shock. Her heart leapt, a clumsy start to the race that followed. Her gaze automatically sought his, but he was intent on the butterfly.

His expression grave, he lifted it. The wings caught the light and took it from beautiful to exquisite. Blue became vibrant cobalt while the faceted, clear segments glinted and played with reflection, giving the impression of life caught and held within.

"Thank you," he said. "This is the one." Lowering it, he met her gaze. *Brown* eyes, she reminded herself. Not blue.

"Great!" Too exuberant. Awkward. She was such a fool.

He could have started walking to the counter to make the purchase, but as before, he waited.

"Was there something else?" She turned the key with a hand that only shook a little.

"No. No, this should do it." He seemed almost sad.

The impulse to offer comfort was overwhelming, and totally out of place. She walked past him. "Let's go ring it up, then."

On the way, she caught the clerk Lynette's attention, asked her to fetch the butterfly's box from the storeroom.

"It's a limited edition," Thia told the man as she stepped behind the counter. "The number is on the base—as is the artist's signature. Bella Smythe. She's local. The box is made specially to fit, so you'll want to hang onto it."

"Sure."

She opened a new sale on the register. "Would you like me to gift wrap it for you? We have some standard papers, or you can choose from our selection for purchase over there"—she gestured—"if you'd prefer a more elaborate design."

"No, thank you."

● ○ ●

She was nattering on about gift boxes and paper and it was all Cormac could do not to lunge over the counter. She was *right there,* so close he could grab her and hold on tight and maybe never let go. He had missed her.

He was surprised—and embarrassed—by how much.

Had she always been so lovely? Cormac had first seen her in a photograph at Leticia's London townhome (while he had been breaking-and-entering). He had noted her auburn hair, her oval face with, granted, its brilliant smile and intelligent gaze and he had judged her of having little more than average looks. It was perhaps a matter of the difference between a still image and the animated, real thing. She was much more than the sum of her parts, and at this moment, in motion and in person, every one of those parts was stunning.

He was making a hash of the conversation, he knew, but it was a miracle he could formulate words at all, let alone whole sentences. She probably thought him shy.

She would be right.

Are you happy? He couldn't believe he had blurted it out like that. Morrigan's cloak in a twist, this was not going well.

And it was taking too long. He eyed the tall, dark-haired woman who had gone into the front window display to fetch a stuffed bear for a waiting customer; Abigail Collins, he had learned since Orkney. She had fought alongside the Murphy's people and the Brigantium. Had probably helped Cormac kill his father.

Unwanted emotion crested. He let it break, crashing down like an icy wave, and allowed himself to feel nothing. What he did not acknowledge could not hurt.

Abigail, or Abby as she was known, kept looking over at him with distrust. He suspected she had a talent for empathy, and an unusually (and, to his purposes, inconveniently) large one at that.

"Actually," Cormac said, returning his attention to Thia as she rang up his damnably expensive purchase. "I'm in a bit of a hurry. Does it really need the box?"

She looked at him as if he were a simpleton. Spoke as if he were one, too, although kindly. "It's rather fragile, so it would need some sort of box, yes." She kept her hand near it on the counter as if she feared he would snatch it up and cram it into a pocket. "Will you be in the area later? I could pack it up, even gift-wrap it if you'd like, and have it here for you."

Cormac took out his billfold. Her eyes widened with something like surprise as he laid several large bills on the counter. It *was* a lot of cash to be carrying, true enough, but credit cards could be trouble. None of the ones he'd brought were in his name, but that didn't mean that someone with the right skills—and aided by the right organization—could not trace them to him eventually. He couldn't risk it.

He cleared his throat, surreptitiously wiped a damp palm on his coat. "That would be perfect. Thank you."

"No problem." Thia counted out his change. "What name can I put on the gift? In case I'm not here."

Was that a hint of suspicion he detected? He pocketed the items, decided he was being paranoid.

"Connor Michaels." If he felt uncomfortable about the lie, he ignored it. "Thanks, again, for your help. I'll—well. I'll see you later, won't I?"

"Yes. See you later." She smiled, drawing his attention to her lips. He those lips intimately. Her, he hardly knew at all.

He couldn't tell if she was being polite or if she really was looking forward to their next encounter. He couldn't tell if he had made any impact (other than financial) on her at all.

She used to be easier to read.

Or was he letting his concerns, his feelings cloud his view? Aware that he lingered overlong, he forced a smile and made his way to the door.

It took him past Abby, in discussion with the customer by a table-top display of holiday items. Snow globes, stockings large enough for a full-grown ogre, ornate peppermint striped candles, and the like. She studied him far too intently, and he made a small nod in passing—his best attempt at appearing unexceptionable.

His foolishness with the butterfly had likely rendered that impossible. At the very least, he had marked himself as a "Big Spender."

And he would have to return. It was both a problem and an opportunity: Another chance to interact with Thia; another chance to be recognized despite his disguise. He stepped out of the store and onto the main, retail-centric street.

What to do next?

Given its reported population, Granite Springs boasted an astonishing number of coffee shops, including the one inside Eclectica. But he was so keyed up already, caffeine would be a mistake. After so many weeks, to have spoken with her, to have stood so close—and then that one, jolting contact. She had looked at him directly, and he, her.

She hadn't appeared to suspect that, behind the lenses of his glasses, he wore colored contacts.

Something pinged on the edges of his awareness. Something decidedly unfriendly.

He scanned the area, saw nothing to account for it other than Thia and her empathic friend watching him through the front window.

Minor and transient.

He shrugged it off and began his walk to the hotel. Might as well take care of another bit of business sooner rather than later.

CHAPTER 2

With Connor Michaels no longer in view outside, Thia returned her attention to his purchase. It really was a lovely piece, made of finely wrought silver with wings of amazingly thin colored glass. Carefully, she removed the price.

"Who was that?" Abby asked, escorting a customer with an armload of items to be purchased. Because of that, she kept her tone casual, but Thia had come to know her well enough to know there was more to her question than that.

"Someone new to the area," Thia replied as they smoothly exchanged places behind the register. "Connor Michaels. He bought a gift for a friend."

"Oh my, isn't that gorgeous," said the customer, eyeing the butterfly. "So delicate. And unusual."

"Isn't it?" Thia held it out for the woman to examine.

"The artist is local," Abby explained, beginning to ring up items. "She has worked in stained glass for years, but recently shifted from panels and lampshades to standing figures. This is our last butterfly, but there are a few other examples in the case over there if you'd like to see."

"Some other time," the woman said with a longing glance. "I'm supposed to meet my partner at her work to talk gift list progress. This should be the last of it. I hope." She indicated the three snow globes she was buying. "There are boxes for them, right? They need to be shipped."

"Absolutely," Thia said, and was about to volunteer herself when she saw Lynette approaching from the storeroom.

"I can go back," the clerk said, noticing the snowglobes. She set the butterfly's box down and then left again.

While Abby and the customer chatted, waiting, Thia moved to an adjacent counter to work. The butterfly's box was nice, she thought, but rather plain for something intended as a gift. She went over to the for-purchase papers. If memory served, there was one that—

There. She pulled out a sheet of soft cream patterned with richly colored butterflies and flowers. On another whim, she grabbed a spool of satin ribbon.

At the counter, she laid it out, began sizing it to the box.

"Mr. Michaels bought all that, too?" Abby asked. She had finished her transaction. The customer, bag in hand, was on her way up the stairs to the café.

"No," Thia admitted, "but it goes so well." She took up a pair of scissors, sliced. "Plus it's an expensive item, and he's a first time customer. It might pay off to be extra nice."

"Thia."

She paused, found Abby watching her with concern. Probably because Thia's cheeks were red. "What?"

"Did you feel it?"

Impossibly, Thia felt her blush increase. She must look like a tomato. "Attraction?"

Abby's violet eyes widened. "Goodness, no—wait. Are you saying you—"

"What feeling did you mean?" Thia put in quickly.

"Power. I thought I sensed it a few times, which could mean he was cloaking it the rest of the time. And there was something else, something...odd." Abby frowned, shook her head.

"You were attracted to him?"

"He had power?" Thia thought back, tried to feel now what she had missed in the moment. Tried not to feel discouraged when she could not. Finished with the tape, she pulled out a length of ribbon, wound it around the box. "Maybe I mistook it. Maybe that's why he reminded me of Cormac."

Abby's profanity was no less shocking for having been quiet. Luckily, it was Stefanie's day off or else they would be in for a smudging.

"*Reminded,*" Thia said. "His eyes were brown. Cormac can't change his eyes."

Abby rolled hers. "For crying out loud, Thia. He can wear colored contact lenses the same as anyone."

"He had glasses on. Connor—Mr. Michaels, I mean."

"Sure. The lenses would make it harder to tell. When is he supposed to come back to get the butterfly? I don't want you dealing with him by yourself."

"He didn't say." Thia tied an elaborate bow, the satin ribbon smooth and cool as it slid between her fingers. Soothing, or at least it should have been. "But even if he is Cormac—and it would be crazy to think that—he's not a danger to me. He wouldn't hurt me."

"He broke your heart," her friend said gently.

"No."

"Thia, come on. I know how you—"

"No," she repeated, cutting off the argument. On the other side of the front window, a small group of pedestrians pointed at something in the display and then moved on. Thia finished the bow. "I did that to myself."

"Bullshit. Cormac led you to believe he had feelings for you. That's—"

"It doesn't matter." Much as she appreciated Abby's anger on her behalf, it didn't help. Nothing helped. "It's over. Once burned, twice shy and all that. When Mr. Michaels comes to pick this up, I'll try to tell if he's wearing contacts." She put the box beneath the counter and began cleaning up. Wisely, Abby returned to the sales floor.

If Connor Michaels *was* wearing contacts, what would Thia do? Ask him if he was the two-centuries-and-then-some half-*Sidhe* whom she had met on a flight to London and, despite herself, fallen for? She dropped the scraps of paper into the wastebasket, put the scissors and tape away.

She had been told that Cormac had murdered Lettie. She had believed him to be responsible for an attack on her in a London alley, as well as a later one on the Brigantium that had killed many and left one of their agents in a coma. And still she'd had to fight with herself over her feelings. Had she been in lo—rather, had she *fallen* for him on the flight? Or had it come later, at the Ring when he had nearly sacrificed himself for her?

Could Connor Michaels be Cormac?

She used the computerized register to remove the spool of ribbon from the inventory. The bells on the door jingled.

Did she want him to be?

The high-pitched voices of multiple toddlers caused a rush of concern, but as they entered she counted an accompanying adult per child, making for a group total of six and not liable to get into unintended trouble. Lynette was finding things to do along their browsing trajectory, making herself available to assist without being intrusive. Abby was bringing another sale to one of the other registers. This might be a good time as any for Thia to check online orders.

Why would Cormac pretend to be someone else with her? It was a ridiculous thought. As ridiculous as thinking that he would be in Granite Springs at all. What would he want?

Are you happy?

An incredible rumble started up outside, causing everyone to stop and look to the window. Glass rattled in its frames as the wooden floor vibrated, the motion traveling up through display cases throughout the store. Thia and Abby met near the door just as the unmistakable belch of a Harley Davidson sounded from somewhere up the block.

Not just one Harley, Thia realized, when the bass rumble crescendoed to a roar. One motorcycle after another zoomed by, using all three lanes of the street. Glossy paint, gleaming chrome, scuffed black leather—and more shaggy beards than she had seen at one time since leaving southern California.

Maybe they were just passing through.

Exhaust seeped in through the doorway and she grimaced, covered her nose and mouth with her hand.

Gradually, the gang moved out of earshot and as people who had stopped on the sidewalk went on about their business, so did Thia. She was surprised to find the group with children gathered on the far side of the staircase, putting it between them and the door—or perhaps more specifically, the street. Each of the two women held a child in their arms while the man cradled the back of a little girl's head while she clung to his leg.

There was more here than noise upset. There was fear.

"I'd hoped they wouldn't be back," Abby said, still watching out the window.

"They've been before?"

"Every winter. They hole up at the old Soda Mountain road-house. Southeast of town," she explained off Thia's look of confusion. "It used to be a place that catered to local bikers— motorized and pedal. Nice, friendly atmosphere. Really good pie. Then, about five years ago, those guys showed up. The Rekkrs. They're good at it."

"What do they do?" Thia noted that the group with the kids was browsing again, seeming more relaxed.

"Within city limits, not too much—mainly noise and having fun acting intimidating. Outside...." Abby shrugged. "It's best not to spend time in that part of the mountain. Not till spring, anyway. Unless you're the snow plow driver," she added with an attempt at levity. It quickly failed. "Although I don't think even they go up there."

"How can they ride when the roads—never mind." Thia had better things to worry about. "If everything is under control here, I though I'd go take care of today's shipments."

A squeal of infectious, little-boy laughter drew their attention. Lynette was skillfully entertaining the group with a Jack Frost puppet.

"We'll be fine," Abby said, watching. "She could probably run the whole place single-handed."

"As could you," Thia assured her, having detected a note of jealousy.

Abby grinned. "True."

Mood lifted, Thia headed for the office. If she remembered correctly, there were only a few things to—

"Thia."

She stopped, turned back to Abby.

Who was no longer smiling. "If Connor isn't Cormac, that's even more reason not to deal with him alone."

● ○ ●

Landmark Hotel, Granite Springs
Cormac pushed open the hotel's main door and stepped into the lobby's bright warmth. Old by American standards, the building had been tastefully modernized to maintain its Art Deco lines and fixtures while using contemporary furnishings and light, neutral colors. Beneath the proliferation of seasonal trappings were some quality oil paintings. Landscapes mostly, and probably local.

All by the same artist, Cormac determined a few moments later from the spot he'd chosen in one of several seating areas that carved up the large, high-ceilinged space. Along the wall and to the left of the entrance (and the reception desk that faced it), the plump sofa afforded the best view. The out-of-the-way area had only one other occupant: a man, seated in an adjacent armchair and seemingly engrossed in his news-paper. The other areas, set nearer to the fireplace or windows, respectively, were populated with guests conversing over cups of coffee or on phones. A cup of tea would be nice, caffeine be damned, Cormac decided and prepared to flag down one of the staff.

Before he could, Murphy appeared.

That hadn't taken long. Cormac forced himself to relax—or at least to appear so. He reminded himself that it wasn't for lack of trying that he'd been unable to uphold his end of their bargain.

In a purely physical fight, Cormac would almost assuredly be outmatched. Murphy topped his natural height by a good six inches and outweighed him by one if not two stones of solid muscle. Cormac was built for guile not straight combat, whereas Murphy had been a trained warrior. Most likely he was one, still.

In a not-so-purely physical fight aided by magick, Cormac could only guess as to the match-up. Whatever power Murphy held was as thoroughly cloaked as Cormac's was. Better, then, to credit the other man with more rather than less to be on the safe side. In Cormac's experience, only people with a lot of power made an effort to hide it, and only those with great skill succeeded.

On his approach, Murphy made the small, sweeping gesture of an elementary coercion spell. The newspaper-reading man promptly stood and took himself to a chair in one of the more crowded areas.

"Wondered when you'd get around to stopping by." Murphy sank into the vacated seat. His words carried a worn trace of Ireland. "Nice disguise you've worked out. Fool anyone with it?"

Cormac shrugged. "Well enough."

"Really." Murphy slouched, a casual pose belied by the glint of power in his eyes. A flash of bronze within the brown. "So. Where is it, then?"

"I don't have it. Yet." Cormac braced for an explosion...of temper, of power—a literal explosion. Anything, really, on the scale of furious responses.

Which meant he was unprepared when Murphy, in a voice gone icy, merely said, "You've two weeks until the deadline."

The word was meant literally. Their bargain had been made according to the Old Ways: upon pain of death.

Murphy had fulfilled his part, having not interfered when Cormac had first arrived in Granite Springs in pursuit of Thia and the Stone of Shadows.

If only Cormac had thought to renegotiate when he'd asked for aid on Orkney. Given Murphy's history with Idris, he had no doubt relished the opportunity to take part in his defeat. Cormac should have made *that* the fulfillment in place of the Achill Bell. But he hadn't been thinking clearly at the time. Idris and his people had taken over the Ring of Brodgar and Thia was being taken right to them. The Brigantium wouldn't listen to reason. There had been no one else to whom Cormac could turn. Beyond stopping his father, he hadn't considered how else to make use of the situation.

A hotel employee walked past with a caraffe, and Cormac regretted not getting that tea he'd wanted. His throat was dry.

"I was hoping"—how he did loathe that word, *hope*—"that we might adjust the bargain."

"I figured as much." Murphy flicked his hand. A gesture only, not a spell. "Let's hear it. Not excuses, mind. Explanations."

Fair enough. "I went to Fiends Fell after I—after Brodgar. Everything of value had already been removed."

Murphy's eyes widened. "By Idris?"

"At his order, or by someone with his authority." No one in

their right mind would attempt such a robbery. That it should succeed? Impossible. Therefore, that had not been a robbery.

"Was there anything to trace?" Murphy asked.

"Cleansed. Thoroughly."

"That takes more than a passing skill."

"It does," Cormac agreed.

Murphy studied him. "You have someone in mind."

"I do." There was no reason not to share. "Cassandra."

Cormac's recently-discovered half-sister, bent on revenge. If he was correct and she was behind the clearing out of Fiend's Fell, it meant she had every piece of Idris's extensive arsenal. Every collected relic, every weapon, every spell.

"She would've had to work fast," Murphy said. "You arrived how long after leaving *Innse Orc?*" The Old Irish name for the islands. The mercenary's true roots were showing.

"A few hours." Cormac grimaced. "I—well, it took me some time to get my head straight."

"So she had a bit of time, then, but not much. Not enough."

That had been Cormac's conclusion as well. An undertaking of that scope would have taken days, not hours. "Idris may have intended to clear out after the ritual. If so, he would've already made preparations."

"Or there could have been people left behind, able to assist when the *claimsech* arrived." An unflattering term, but there was no arguing that it didn't fit. "It's been weeks," Murphy went on. "Why not tell me straightaway?"

Because Cormac hadn't been able to think clearly. He had been reeling, trying to come to terms with his role in Idris's death and of finally being free. All while missing Thia to the point of obsession.

"I'm telling you now," he said.

Murphy's eyes narrowed, but he didn't press.

Cormac settled back against the overstuffed cushions. "She

swore revenge."

"That she did."

"Most of the primary players are here."

"And so here is where she'll likely to focus her efforts. That didn't escape me." Another flick of his hand called attention to the leather cuff at his wrist. "I've been at this even longer than you, remember."

As if Cormac could forget. His stomach clenched. He had witnessed a lot of horrors over the centuries, but that night....

Well. He had been young, after all. Naturally it had affected him more.

"As far as I can tell, she has gone to ground," Murphy said. "I've let it be known that I've an interest in her activities. So far, nothing."

Cormac nodded, grim. He hadn't had much result on that front, either. But he had a gut feeling. "There's quite a lot of power here. More than when I visited before."

"Sure, there's been an upsurge." Murphy shrugged. "Nothing unusual in that, this time of year. You'll have noticed the area is a bit of a gathering place."

"Hard to miss." Which made it easy enough for anyone to slip in—not secretly, perhaps, but anonymously.

"If Cassie *is* here," Cormac said, casually seizing the opportunity, "you and I can at least discuss a new time frame."

Murphy laughed, causing a few heads to turn. He made a circling gesture, and they turned back. "If she took the Bell, her being here would be convenient, wouldn't you say?"

"Goddamn it, I can't protect—" *Thia,* Cormac had almost said. He couldn't protect her while he was tracking down the bell. "Goddamn it."

"Language," Murphy chided. "But 'tis the season and all that so I'm feeling kindly. Talk to me again before the two weeks are up. And maybe—*maybe*—we can sort something out." He stood. "In the meantime, we've a few rooms open. Why don't you get yourself one. We do a lovely breakfast."

The glow of power in his eyes made it clear that he was not making a suggestion. It was an order.

Cormac didn't have to take those anymore.

"I'll think about it," he said simply to make a point.

He had made a reservation days ago.

● ○ ●

Elkhorn Park, Granite Springs

They walked the uphill path in silence. She was prepared to stop any talk should the fool show an inclination for it, but so far he had been too busy fighting the compulsion spell she had crafted. Whomever and whatever he had once been, he was now broken. The power he had was erratic, weak more often than it was strong, sometimes altogether absent.

She felt her lips curve into a smile. Did he realize yet where this was leading? He ought to appreciate it. The watcher she had assigned to him had observed that, after the alley behind Eclectica, it was his next most frequented location in town.

There was a particular bench where he would sit for hours, she had been told, and yesterday she'd ruined a pair of Saint Laurent boots scoping it out. "Wilderness trail" was a more apt description of that area than "park." It would do well for privacy and, she was betting, a state of relaxation within the man that would allow her spell to take complete hold.

Passing the surprisingly busy playground, she returned the bland smiles from two women ostensibly watching a child in a puffy pink jacket climb the wrong way up a slide. Acknowledging them would, as she'd learned over the past week, make her less memorable, not more. The people here were odd that way.

Which meant they would soon forget her but not the man walking several feet behind.

Such a strange town.

And a powerful one. What a shame she hadn't the time to find out why.

The paved path changed to bark chips and her annoyance flared again. She shouldn't need hiking gear in a bloody city park.

"Is it much farther?" came the voice behind her. She smiled at the strain in it. He would wear himself down with all that internal fighting, perhaps even before they got to the bench.

She whirled on him, sent more power into the spell. Like pulling up on a choke chain. He flinched, dropped his gaze.

Good dog.

Chuckling, she walked on. Wood chips became half-frozen dirt and fallen leaves as the path wended closer to the stream. Creek, as it was called here. Rushing water drowned out any sound from behind but she sensed when he lost his battle and resumed following. The spell allowed her a vague awareness of his location and, if she strengthened her hold, his intent.

She rounded a bend and left the path for a thin, woodland track encroached upon by dead grasses and prickly shrubs. At its terminus was a small overlook with two benches.

She knew which one he habitually chose. When he arrived, she moved to stand in front of it. Pointed to the other.

"I prefer that one." He indicated the one she blocked. His gaze darted around hers. Held.

Calling power to hand, she formed a ball of white energy: *wanfýr.* Her irises as she did so, she knew, glowed amber.

The man paled. His gaze dropped to the ground.

Yet he persisted with a faint, "Please."

She yanked the invisible leash. He gasped, stumbled a step closer, and she extended her hand to put the *fýr* inches from his downturned face. At such a range, it could do as much damage as *wælfýr.*

"No. Please," he said again. He trembled.

"Sit." She moved the *fýr* so that he could, and then vanished it when he did as instructed—on the bench she had assigned. She took the one he'd wanted.

"You said you'd tell me about her," he said.

Weak, he was, yet stubborn. She shrugged a shoulder. "So I did. And now that we're in no danger of being overheard, so I will." She sent a needling jab of energy his way.

He flinched.

"Thia McDaniel," she said. "She inherited that quaint little shop you've been spending time behind. Where that girl who leaves you treats is employed."

"She feels like—" He stopped, shuddered. "Her power feels like the Cailleach's."

Interesting that he'd picked up on that. "Because it is. Thia stole it from my father after she murdered my brother."

He lifted his head, his blue eyes wide.

Cassandra smiled. "You thought she was an innocent?"

"She does not use it."

"The power?" She increased the compulsion. "Does not—or cannot?"

His eyes closed, his teeth gritting as he fought...and lost. "C-cannot. Cannot use it. She tries. Sometimes alone. Sometimes with others."

"But she fails?"

The man gave a start and looked toward the trail as if he'd heard something.

She hadn't. Nor did she sense anything, but she prepared to disguise herself nevertheless. "Is someone coming?"

He was too agitated to answer.

The trouble with broken people was precisely that: They were broken. "What the hell is it?"

He made a small noise and rubbed his temple. "I can't stay."

"You can." She pulled on the spell, forced him to sit when he attempted to rise. "You will."

"Please." He almost made eye contact.

Such a begging tone. Such need—and so strong and clear that she finally understood.

And knew just how to use it.

"It's the power that has you in such a state, am I right? The Cailleach's power?" She kept her voice soft. Caring. And fed him a lie. "You were doing better until she came back. Until Thia brought it back."

He was breathing hard, pouring sweat. She could feel him not wanting to accept her suggestion, but he nodded.

She leaned in, compassion in her tone. Malice in her words. "Would you like to do better again? Look at yourself. A near mindless, sniveling mess. Taking charity scraps left at rubbish bins."

He mumbled something.

"What's that, *wiel?*"

"N-n-not scraps," the man whispered, eyes squeezed tight as he revealed a new, deeper weakness—one far better than any compulsion spell. "A gift. A kindness."

Cassie's voice was equally soft as she leaned in, brought his head up with a finger below his chin. "*Like* her, do you? Your little muffin girl?"

He went absolutely still. His eyes opened.

She laughed. "How delightful."

● ○ ●

He hated her, this smiling woman. But it felt all mixed up in his head.

He knew that as if told to him from far away. He knew but could not sort it out. The woman was in there now, pushing her will into him, confusing him with thoughts and emotions that he did not want to make his own. If she had tried this next year, he might have been able to fight her, but he had not yet recovered from his *caethiwed*. He should never have come into town.

Why had he? Ah, right—he had gone to stock up on supplies so he could avoid town till *Gwanwyn*. And look how that had turned out.

Had that been a lure, the sudden presence of that familiar, terrible power? Had this woman been behind it? And what about the other, the one who gave him food and coffee and made him think she cared...maybe not for him specifically but for people in general. Kind-hearted. A kind-hearted woman. Had that been a trick?

He felt a mental jab.

This one, the one with seductive smiles and cold amber eyes wanted him to pay more attention (as if he could not think and listen at the same time). He was not stupid. He had heard her say she wanted his help to rid the town of the woman with the Cailleach's power. Thia McDaniel, she had said.

That had not been a lure, then. And if this woman had not seen him behind the store and become curious, he would not be with her at this moment, fighting for control of his mind.

She had had him followed, she was telling him now, taunting him with his carelessness. And rightly so. His gaze flicked up as far as her lips. Red and cruel. Smirking. He went back to staring at his boots. Splatters of different-colored paint made different patterns, depending on how he happened to see them. A falcon formed out of green and a streak of yellow. He blinked and saw instead a cartoonish dog in a pointed hat, the kind people wore to look silly at parties. Did they still do that? Wear those hats? He had not been to a party in a long time.

Sharp pain shot through his head, another bite of the beast.

It would be perfect, the woman said. It took him a moment to understand. (Maybe he had been wrong and he could not think and listen at the same time.)

Oh. His refuge. She had gone on to say how perfect it was,

off the grid with high levels of protection already in place.

This was not about him, but about the home he had made for himself.

She had no idea who he was.

He wanted to laugh nearly as much as he wanted to rage at her insolence, her audacity. Wanted to tear her apart for her malice and paint the trees with her blood. But the blame for this was his. He should not have come into town or taken so long to decide what to do about the woman with the power. Thia McDaniel.

Too slow. He had been too slow. Slow to think, to decide.

Slow to act. *Stupid.* How many times had his stepbrothers called him that? He had always denied it, always fought back.

Maybe they had been right after all.

Was that thought part of the compulsion? A side-effect of its beastly fangs digging deeper, ever deeper?

Or was it the godforsaken truth.

"Yes," he heard himself say. She wanted him to nod but he resisted. It took nearly everything he had but he resisted. He would not—

He nodded.

And wanted to die. Or kill her.

Both? Both could work. He searched his boot for the image of the dog in the birthday hat but could not locate it. Had it been on the left or the right?

He cringed as the next words entered his mind. "You and yours are welcome in my home," he said. It was little comfort that the lie sounded as forced as it was.

Even so, the woman beamed, the white of her teeth nearly blinding. "Excellent." She uncrossed her long legs and stood. Her arm swept smoothly out, the manicured fingers of her hand unfolding like a fan to direct him not back towards town as he had expected but ahead, where the park trail ended at Elkhorn Road. "Shall we?"

He was aware that he got to his feet but the movements felt unreal. Consciousness had been pushed to a cramped, far away place. He had become trapped, imprisoned in his own mind.

It was like before.

Also like before, his own carelessness—his own stupidity—was to blame.

CHAPTER 3

Having closed out the last register, Thia put the deposit for the bank in the zippered pouch. As she stepped back from the counter she caught sight of the wrapped gift on the shelf beneath. Connor Michaels hadn't come back for it. Why she should find that so disappointing, she didn't know. Well, no, that wasn't true: She knew; she just didn't want to admit it. She had wanted to find out if he was Cormac. Wanted to see him again even if he wasn't.

Maybe especially if he wasn't. It would be nice to think that she could feel that same spark of attraction for someone else.

It would be nice to think that her heart wasn't broken.

Deposit in hand, she turned out lights and went to double-check the front door locks.

Cormac had been so charming and she had been so damned attracted when they'd first met on that London-bound flight.

She frowned, considering. She'd since had time to reflect on every event of that chaotic time and had begun to wonder if they might not have met the night before. There had been a man outside Lettie's home, and Thia had felt a strange pull—she wouldn't necessarily go so far as to call it attraction, but she had felt drawn. And, in the next moment, that had been literal. He had grabbed hold and tried to pull her over the picket fence.

If that man had been Cormac in disguise, then he had been entirely *un*-charming in their first meeting. He had, in fact, assaulted her.

Her memory was that their eyes might have been similar—the man's and Cormac's—but lighting and her own fallibility made it difficult to say. She hadn't asked Cormac about it. She would need to, should she get the chance.

Not that he could be trusted to tell the truth, Thia mused on the way up the stairs. He had misled (if not lied outright to) her more than a few times.

For his benefit, mostly, but not always. It would be easier if Thia could think of him as entirely selfish. Yet at Brodgar, his deception about the knife hadn't benefitted him at all. Only her. He could have bled to death—*would* have if not for his regaining the power that had been taken from him and which enabled him to heal the wound. He had put himself in grave danger for her.

And that hadn't been the first time.

Yet in the end, when that night's battle was over and there was the possibility of something between them, he had left.

In the café, Thia found Abby chatting with Zoe, its manager and chief baker.

"Hey," the latter greeted and headed for the light switches. She was small in stature, nearly a foot less than Thia's five-foot-eight, and prone to bright smiles and quick motions, the better to showcase her collection of Bakelite bracelets.

"You okay, Thia?" Abby asked, all too perceptive.

Thia forced a smile. "Just thinking some things over. How did we do up here?" she asked Zoe.

"Great," Zoe replied, turning off overhead lights. "We had a run on the new chocolate biscotti. I took advance orders for two dozen tomorrow." She tipped her head toward where the café's deposit pouch lay by Abby's elbow on the counter.

"Wonderful," Thia said. "I'm sorry I missed them." And she was, too. Zoe was a phenomenal baker.

"I had one when I came in." Standing, Abby picked up the pouch. "It was all I could do not to go back for more."

"Thanks." Zoe laughed, held open the door. "It's the butter."

"The chocolate didn't hurt," Abby said, going outside.

"True."

Thia stepped past them both into the garden patio. "Save me one tomorrow, would you? And I promise, I'll be on time."

"Like I mind what time the boss comes in?" With another laugh, Zoe closed the door, got out her key. The wind ruffled her wispy, white-blonde hair. "I'll set aside two."

"Brilliant."

While Zoe locked up, Abby went to the vine-covered arbor of the patio entrance and peered out. Being protective of the store's nightly deposit or was it something more?

Joining her, Thia shoved the unsettling thought aside. Tried to, anyway. "We're meeting Kendra for dinner," she told Zoe. "You're welcome to join us."

"Oh, thanks." Zoe dropped her key into her vintage clutch and walked toward them. "I'd love to, but I need to pick up a few things for tomorrow's menu. Plus all those biscotti to prep."

"You're sure?" Abby asked.

"Yeah. Regrettably." Zoe exited into the alley.

Quickly, Thia used her Sight to ensure that the wards were in place, shimmering at the property line. They weren't easy to see, being the weaker of the two sets.

Because Eclectica depended on a high level of traffic, there was one set of basic protections during business—enough to keep out anyone intent on doing harm—and a much stronger set after hours.

Cassie had been specifically warded against. No matter her

intent, no matter the time, she could not get through.

"Have you ever seen our transient?" Zoe asked casually and shut the gate.

"Who?" Concentration blown, Thia's enhanced vision went out.

"Our what?" Abby looked equally shocked.

"I'm pretty sure there's a guy taking shelter back here." Zoe pointed. "Behind the dumpsters."

Abby was already halfway there.

"No," Thia called out. "Don't—"

"He's not here," she announced, checking behind.

"Only in the mornings," Zoe said. "Really, I don't think it's a big deal. He seems harmless—not that I've actually seen him. I think he's too shy to come out."

Abby straightened. "We can't have someone—"

"I'm not even sure he exists. I shouldn't have said anything. It was just a feeling I've had...and the food I've been leaving there has been disappearing."

"Food?" Thia asked. "You've been leaving food?" If someone was taking refuge behind the dumpster, that was terrible and something needed to be done to help; but not by facilitating his presence.

And why there, anyway? When Granite Springs had several well run shelters and just as many programs to help people get back on their feet, why had he chosen Eclectica's dumpster?

"Just leftover food. Mostly." Zoe bit her lip.

It was an answer to Thia's spoken question and maybe the unspoken as well: He might have chosen this location for its kind-hearted café manager.

"You need to stop." Abby used a piece of the chalk she had pulled from her purse to write on the dumpster. "It's not safe. If he's here tomorrow, you come get me and we'll deal with it. There are good places. Programs," she said while she chalked.

"I'm giving the address of a meals program."

"You're right." Zoe sighed. "Of course you're right. I wasn't thinking. It just felt as if....No, never mind. I'm too used to the Usuals"—a reference to the organized panhandlers who congregated along Main Street and around the Shakespeare Festival—"that I didn't see how this was different. I'm sorry."

Not for the first time Thia wondered if she and Abby were making a mistake by keeping Zoe out of the loop.

But, as had been Thia's situation not long ago, not everyone in Granite Springs practiced magic or understood that things like leyline travel and glamouring and warding were possible. To tell Zoe everything would mean destroying what, in Thia's experience, had been a comfortable obliviousness. Why do that unless absolutely necessary?

"It was stupid," Zoe said.

"No," Thia argued, "it was kind. Transiency, if that's what is going on here, is a complicated issue. Especially here." In a town where it could be so profitable.

"You'll be sure to let me know tomorrow," Abby said and in a rare gesture set her hand on Zoe's shoulder. "It'll be okay."

"I will. Thanks." She hugged Abby and then, pulling away, gave Thia a smile before backwards-walking down the alley. "I *am* sorry to miss out on dinner. I'll be sure to make the next one."

Thia shook her keys to untangle them. "Wouldn't you like a ride?

"No, no. I'm not far." Zoe gestured toward the next block up. "A friend on Pike lets me park in his driveway."

"You're sure?" Abby pointed to the two cars, her white and black Mini Cooper beside Lettie's brown Datsun. "It's dark and cold and we're both right here."

"I'm two minutes away, tops. See you tomorrow!" With a wave, Zoe rounded the corner, going out of sight behind the bed and breakfast.

Abby's expression gave Thia pause so she asked, "Are you sensing something? Should we go after her?"

With a small shake of her head, Abby turned toward the cars. "It's the same feeling I've had all day. Just a vague sense of *potential*, I guess is the word. Like a gathering storm."

That didn't sound good. Thia unlocked the Datsun's driver's side door and then, after getting in, leaned over to pull up the stiff passenger-side lock. "We can drive along Pike before going to the bank," she told Abby, opening the door.

"Sure."

Thia started the engine, adjusted the choke. "She'll be fine."

Abby got in. "Just two minutes away, she said."

They were both worried, obviously. Thia took the turn out of the alley too fast and then accelerated up the steep slope to Pike.

"Which way, do you think?" she asked, braking sharply at the stop sign. To the left was dark. Lights on the residential streets tended to be few and far between.

"There."

Thia looked right. Zoe was halfway down the block, headed up the inclined drive of a single-story house. Thanks to the parking garage opposite—shared between the theater, hotel, and anyone willing to pay the hourly rate—lighting was much better that direction. Thia turned the car.

When they drove past, Zoe had her car door open. A glance in the side mirror a few moments later showed her getting inside. Thia felt tension leave her shoulders. Beside her, Abby blew out a quiet breath.

"To the bank," Thia said, and took a right toward Main. A staircase down to the Park lay behind and to the left while the Festival straddled the street. It was odd to see the buildings dark and obviously empty after being packed with people and events for so many months, but its season had finally come to a close in November. The next would start soon enough in

February.

"Kendra was hoping we could eat at the hotel," Abby said as they passed the building in question yet again. The front this time. "Something about needing to sample the proposed Solstice menu. Her treat—probably because it won't cost her anything."

Thia laughed. The Landmark's restaurant was world-class; being a guinea pig wouldn't be any kind of hardship. "I'd be more than happy. What about you?"

"Kendra promised *he* won't be around."

There was no question as to whom Abby referred: Murphy, the rather mysterious owner of the Landmark. For reasons never explained, they did not get along (often with disastrous results). Out of loyalty to her friend, Thia was inclined to lay the blame on Murphy, but since he had come to the rescue on Orkney, she was also inclined to cut him some slack.

● ○ ●

Pike Street, Granite Springs

Zoe should have been more concerned that the interior light did not come on when she opened the car door. She should have at least glanced in the back seat before getting behind the wheel. But she hadn't, and a hand came around to hold a sickly sweet cloth over her mouth.

She tried to scream but couldn't get the sound past the cloth and then something—rope—dropped down from behind to wrap around her arms and chest, holding her in place. Shock and terror reached up to swallow her whole. She couldn't get enough air.

The passenger door opened and someone reached in, pulled the key from the ignition.

Zoe felt...really weird. Distant, as if she was about to pass out. Her vision wavered.

"Do we take the car?" The voice of the man holding her.

"No. Better to leave it." The woman at the passenger side leaned down. Looked in. "We'll take her."

Everything was out of focus and swimming in Zoe's mind; everything except the white of the woman's smile.

Her eyes closing, Zoe again tried to scream.

● ○ ●

Landmark Hotel

With the whole of the rooftop garden behind him, Cormac leaned his arms on top of the chest-high wall and studied the populated street below. The heavy, thermal-lined coat of his disguise served well enough against the cold of the plastered brick, but it was the warming spells cleverly cast from patio "heaters" placed throughout that kept the frigid night air at bay.

Granite Springs, admittedly, didn't lack for charm. With yuletide greenery twisted around streetlamps and strings of white lights hung on buildings and otherwise bare trees; and shop windows filled to bursting with colorful, well-intended offerings, it would be easy to fall under the town's spell.

Cormac considered his choice of words: charm, spell. Was that sort of magic at work here? Aside from the more obvious draws (entertainment, scenery, dining) and the less (common magical interests, leyline smuggling to name but a suspected few), was there a grand spell woven beneath it all?

The serene beauty of the valley's snow-dusted foothills and the comfort that seemed to emanate from the surrounding mountains could not come entirely from illusion, of course, but their effects could be augmented. Heightened. Such scale would require an enormous amount of power, yet it could be done.

He was about to close his eyes (the better to use a different kind of Sight) when a sputtering roar ripped through the night air like something let loose from the mechanized bowels of hell.

There, in the area called The Plaza, roughly twenty riders attempted to fire up their motorbikes, with varying rates of success.

The noise was nearly intolerable by the time they got them all running—and then they set off and it got so much worse. With much bellowing and waving of fists, they twice circled the Plaza before speeding down Main Street.

People on the pavements stopped to watch, and from what Cormac could see, reactions ranged from disgust to outright fear. He found himself in accord. Dark energy swirled around the riders. Whether they possessed it within themselves or merely carried it in bespelled weaponry or armor, he couldn't tell. But its presence was enough to give him a chill.

Nearly all the riders were men, and large men at that, but there were a few women (also large). Everyone wore a black leather jacket emblazoned with an emblem painted in silver: Thor's Hammer and the word, "*Rekkr.*"

Intentional misspellings were popular in the realm of rowdy biker gangs, but with that particular pairing? Chances were slim to none. Which meant that was not a misspelling of the English word "wrecker," but the accepted modern spelling of the Old Norse for "warrior."

The insufferable roar dimmed to a low rumble as they left the area.

"Mr. Sykes?"

Pushing aside his unease, Cormac turned to face the hostess from the hotel restaurant. He pitched his voice to the gruff baritone used when he made the reservation. "Yes?"

The young woman smiled politely. "Your table is ready. If you would please come with me?"

"Of course." After one last look at the taillights fading into the distance, he followed her inside.

● ○ ●

Alchemy Taproom
Landmark Hotel

"Sorry, sorry. I'm late." An obviously frazzled Kendra slid onto the barstool next to Abby. "Pasquale changed his mind about the menu being ready, so the tasting is off. Again, actually." Her hands fisted on the bar top. "This is the third time he's pulled this." Something like anger flashed in her eyes, briefly turning them from mossy green to emerald.

Either Thia had failed to notice such things before she was "let in behind magic's curtain," as Madame Demetka phrased it, or her friends were more comfortable with showing them in her presence.

"I'd call him out on it," Kendra continued with an impatient flick of her long, coppery hair, "but we're lucky to have him. And if he throws a tantrum and quits this close to the Holidays...." She shuddered and then made a visible effort to shift moods. "So, ladies, what's it to be? Our regular menu or would you prefer to go somewhere else?"

"Doesn't matter to me," Thia said, which left Abby—

—who shrugged. "We're here. And *he* isn't."

Kendra laughed. "Okay, then. Here, it is." Waving off their tab for two lavender sodas, she bid the bartender goodnight and led the way the lobby elevator. It sat empty and waiting, its doors conveniently (or perhaps magically) open.

"Things didn't go so well this morning?" she asked as they sped smoothly to the top floor.

Thia sighed. She'd managed to shove all of that to the back of her mind. "Broke a bunch of jars, scattered stuff all over the floor. Thought I'd wrecked the door again, but it rattled along okay."

Her friends exchanged a look.

"That's not so bad, really," offered Kendra.

Thia snorted.

"No, no—I mean it," Kendra persisted. "The door worked!

That's a definite improvement."

"I could've imploded the whole damn garage!"

"You don't know that."

"Everything—and I mean *everything*—was shaking," Thia said, incredulous. "I'm amazed the shelves didn't come down. I can't control the power." Maybe she never would.

"Nonsense," Abby said.

Thia stepped up to the doors as the elevator slowed to an easy stop. She didn't want to get into this now. Her failures and inadequacies; how overwhelmed and disheartened she felt—these were not things to discuss in public. Or tonight at all. She wanted to relax. Was that asking too much? She was first out when the doors opened, and so led the way down the short hall to the restaurant.

To the left of its entrance were doors to the garden and salt-water pool, and Thia caught a glimpse of twinkling lights and people out enjoying the evening before her attention went to exchanging greetings with the hostess at the podium.

"Hey, Sam." Kendra came up behind Thia. "I believe you're holding table seven."

"I am." The elegant blonde pulled three menus from a ready stack. "Want an escort?"

"No, I got this." Kendra took the offered menus and Thia and Abby followed her into the busy room. To take advantage of the daytime views, one of the long sides of the rectangular room was made of floor-to-ceiling glass (the other hosted the bar). Tonight it was all about the garden, decorated with what must have been a zillion tiny lights. It was like looking out on a fairyland.

The kind of fairyland Thia might have previously imagined, anyway, as depicted in cartoons and storybooks: all whimsical beauty and innocent fun. She had no idea what a real one might be like. Terrifying, probably.

The table Kendra took them to was one of five set along

the glass wall. As they settled, she handed out the menus. "Is this okay?"

"It's perfect."

Abby had yet to look away from the view. "How much is your electric bill?"

"Gorgeous, isn't it?" Kendra's pride was well-deserved. "We should take a walk later."

"Sure. But seriously—how much?"

Amused, Thia grinned. "Thinking of doing this at home?" Abby's house sat on a fair amount of acreage in the mountains northeast of town. What she hadn't left as natural woodland, she had landscaped beautifully.

"Some of it, maybe. My coven might hold this year's Beltane gathering there. So, please—how much?"

Kendra shrugged. "More than November's. But we've got a bank of solar panels. And Murphy got a deal on some strings of bespelled crystal."

"Bespelled?" Thia repeated. "They glow on their own?"

"Kind of like solar."

Eclectica's customers would *love* something like that. "Are they a lot of work to set up? Which ones are they?" Thia tried to pick out differences in the arrangements.

"They're easier to spot outside," Kendra said. "And, no, I think they're good to go straight from the box. Don't bother asking your next question," she added lightly, "because I don't know the supplier's name. I'll have to get it from Murphy."

Thia tore her attention away from the window, found her friends both laughing silently at her. To Abby, she said, "Come on. You know they'd sell like crazy."

"They would." Abby broke into a grin. "Including to me."

Kendra's smile shifted to a smirk as she teased, "I could call Murphy now and ask—"

"Don't you dare." Abby's good humor vanished.

A waiter arrived and began filling glasses from a pitcher of ice water.

"Hey, Danny," Kendra greeted. "Everything going well?"

"Busy, but smooth so far," the young man replied. Ice pinged cheerfully. "Some really good tippers, too."

Kendra arched her brows. "We'll try not to disappoint."

"Oh, no, Ms. Ross, I didn't mean—"

She laughed, waving away his concern. "What shall it be, ladies, wine? Beer? Cocktails?"

They decided to share a bottle of local pinot gris and were then presented with a selection of specials that included an unusual white salmon. While Danny went into detail about the preparation, Thia found her gaze drawn to a man seated across the room, near the entrance. Alone. For a moment, she thought he might have been watching them—and that it was the same man from the morning. Connor Michaels.

She was mistaken on both counts. His focus was entirely on his meal; and while he and Connor shared a similar build, this man was older and had salt and pepper hair. She looked away before he noticed her staring and was in time to catch Danny's departure.

Kendra leaned back in her chair and fixed Abby with an interested look. "I thought things with you and Murphy were better. You managed to get through the entire transatlantic flight without incident."

"I was feeling generous."

Thia took a drink of water, then: "And that generosity has worn off?"

Abby shrugged and took a drink of her own.

Back with their wine, Danny pulled the cork with a skilled flourish and then poured Kendra a taste. She swirled it in the glass, sniffed. Sipped. Nodded. As the bottle was poured into three trendily oversized glasses, Thia's gaze drifted across the room again.

The man took up his knife to slice a bite of steak. Was there something familiar about his hands? Not Connor this time, but Cormac.

She needed to stop looking for things that simply were not there. It was cruel, really, what she was doing to herself.

"Have you decided on your selections," Danny asked, "or do you need more time?"

Thia hadn't given them any thought at all. Nor did she need to. "I'll have the fried chicken," she said in turn. Her usual. Not that there weren't other temptations, but it was *so damn good* every time. Crispy and juicy and accompanied by buttery mashed potatoes and green beans and a delicious, rich gravy.

After Danny left, Abby passed around a basket of rosemary bread hot from the oven. "For tonight, Thia, I thought we would try a few focusing exercises. There's one that—"

"Is that really the problem, though?" she interrupted, a rush of nerves threatening her appetite. "It wasn't like my mind wandered or anything until things started breaking. I let go of my focus because I had to. Everything was falling apart."

"And you got scared."

"Of course! Who wouldn't?"

"You thought you were losing control—so you did." That, from Kendra.

"Huh?"

"Before you started," Abby asked, "were you worried about losing control?"

As Thia thought back, she caught sight of the lone man as he accepted his check. He said something to make the server laugh as he put cash into the payment folio, and then handed it back with a charming smile.

"Probably," she said at last and located her wine glass for a much-welcome drink. Swallowing, she cringed at her friends' knowing expressions. "Okay, I was. You know I was. I always am."

"And so you always do," Kendra said gently.

She blew out a resigned breath. "What are you saying?"

"The problem might not be the power." Abby's violet eyes were dark with concern. "The problem might be *you.*"

And didn't that make it all worse.

"What am I supposed to do about me? I can't *not* be afraid." Thia set her glass down clumsily. "I've seen what the power inside me can do—just *some* of it—and it's terrifying. I can't just snap my fingers and have that knowledge disappear. And I can't meditate the fear away. I'm scared, plain and simple. I can't fix that."

She looked over, met the man's gaze. He *was* familiar, she realized. Not just his hands, but his whole bearing. His whole being. Her vision tunneled. The rest of the room fell away.

"What is it?" Abby turned in her seat. Her voice seemed to come to Thia from a greater distance than that. "Dammit."

"What?" Kendra's voice was no closer.

The man stood and turned to leave. With his table so close to the entrance, it wouldn't be long before he reached it.

Abruptly, Thia's senses cleared. Sound rushed in and the whole room snapped into sharp focus. "It's nothing," she said, sorry to have gotten her friends worked up. "I think I must be hungry, that's all." She forced herself to look away from the man. "I got light-headed or something."

"'*Or something'* is right," Abby said, and pointed. "Is he what's had more than half your attention since we got here?"

That was most certainly an exaggeration. "I only noticed him when—"

"Power," Kendra said, staring after the man. "He's masking. A lot, if he's bothering to do it in here." She frowned. "And he's using a glamour."

"You're sure of that?" Abby fairly vibrated with tension, like a hunting dog on point.

The man stepped into the hall, out of sight.

"Yeah." Kendra stood, flung her napkin on the table as she moved off. "That's a glamour, alright."

Thia stood as well. "What are you doing? You're not going after him," she said helplessly. Kendra was already halfway to the exit.

"Stay here," Abby said, pushing her chair back. She sprang to her feet, quickly caught up with Kendra. They passed a startled Danny as he approached with their meals.

No way was Thia going to sit while her friends...while they did whatever it is they were going to do.

"We'll be right back," Thia told Danny as she joined chase. "I think."

She hoped.

CHAPTER 4

Landmark Hotel, Granite Springs
18 December

"Excuse me. Sorry." Thia narrowly avoided a woman who was also leaving but at a much more reasonable pace.

"No, no—*I'm* sorry." Without turning, the woman stepped aside. She had light blonde hair cut into a short-backed bob and held a cell phone to her ear. She sounded British.

Thia managed to catch up to her friends at the elevator. The call button was illuminated and the digital indicator detailed the car's descent. Presumably, the man rode inside. Kendra was on her cell while Abby closed the door to the adjacent stairs, apparently deciding against using them.

Mindful of the phone call, Thia mouthed a silent, "What is going on?"

To which Abby shook her head in a "not now."

Thia forced down a swell of frustration. Yes, she had only a fraction of the knowledge her friends did when it came to a lot of things lately, but she was sick of being left out of the damn loop. And this loop in particular felt like a mistake.

"About six-two, one-seventy," Kendra said to whoever was on the other end of her call. "Graying hair, slicked back. Dark three-piece suit with a candy-cane striped tie. Yeah, red and white." She paused, listened. Then, "Really? No, just watch him. I'll handle it."

Thia noted the flashing number above the door stayed at seven for several seconds before counting back up. Reversing course—which she believed they ought to do as well. Forget whatever it was they were doing and return to the restaurant.

"All he did was eat dinner," she pointed out.

Abby shook her head. "He's concealing his identity. And his power. We need to know if he's a threat. If he is, then we need to put a stop to it."

Put a stop to it? Talk about threat. Things were on a fast track to getting out of hand, and for nothing more than her friends' protective instincts had been triggered.

"It's probably Cormac." There. She said it. She should have said it sooner.

Except Abby didn't seem at all surprised. "Yeah?" she asked sharply. "And what if he isn't?"

Thia had no answer for that. Hadn't considered, really, that they might be chasing after anyone else.

Abby cast a quick look toward Kendra, still on the phone, before leaning in to say quietly, "First the guy this morning, and now this one. It could be a coincidence or it could be part of something. But even if both are Cormac, I wouldn't trust him any farther than I can throw him, and I doubt that's very far at all. So I intend to find out what that man is up to, no matter who it is."

The elevator chimed its arrival. Kendra and Abby darted in as soon as the doors allowed—and then blocked Thia's way.

Exasperation became more like anger. "If you won't let me," she said, her jaw tight, "I'll just go after." She pointed up at the digital display.

Kendra moved aside.

Thia entered. "Thank you."

Abby jabbed the seventh floor's button and then repeatedly hit "close" for doors that already were doing so.

"Whomever he is, he's a guest," Kendra said, taking a quick break from her call. "He wouldn't have access to the seventh floor if he wasn't registered. What's that?" she asked into her phone. "Still got him?"

The elevator began to slow, and Abby eased in front of Thia. "Let us go first," she told her. "Or better yet, stay here."

"I'm coming." But Thia wouldn't bother arguing the other.

"Have you considered that you're projecting?" Abby asked gently. "That you're seeing Cormac today in places and people because you want him to be there?"

"Of course I have." Thia was about to add that she wasn't a fool...but when it came to Cormac, that wasn't true.

"Which room?" Kendra asked into her phone as the elevator came to rest. Chimed. "Great. Thanks, I'll—"

The doors opened. Murphy stood waiting.

Taking advantage of everyone's surprise, he stepped inside, reached past a furious-looking Abby to press the button for the top floor. She closed what little distance remained to get in his face. "Hey, we're not—"

He put his back to her to speak with Kendra. "Security told me you've taken a particular interest in one of our guests."

"We have," she agreed. "Who is he?"

"An acquaintance."

Kendra crossed her arms. Glared. "I can get his name from registration."

"You can."

With Abby seething behind him, he and Kendra engaged in a staring contest that had Thia ease herself toward the back corner, as far from them as space allowed.

Abruptly, Kendra's shoulders sagged. "I *can* but it won't do me any good. It's a fake?"

Murphy merely lifted a brow.

"Dammit, this is important." Crowding him, she pulled the

emergency-stop button. The elevator came to an abrupt halt. "Thia's safety beats whatever deal you've made with—"

At the mention of her name, Murphy turned, found her in the corner. He nodded in greeting. "Thia."

Nonplussed, she nodded in return. "Mr. Murphy."

"Ah, such formality." He pressed a hand over his heart in a playfully theatrical gesture. His smile flashed with surprising charm. "Wound me, you do."

Abby inserted herself between them. "For goddess sake, is everything a joke to you?"

The energy level in the small space spiked so fast that Thia's head swam. Lights flickered and the elevator began to shake, bringing to mind some of the words used to describe what tended to happen when Abby and Murphy argued. Words like volatile, explosive.

Not good words.

"Hold it down, Abs," Kendra said softly.

"About this guest now, Thia," Murphy said, focused on her as if nothing of interest was going on around them. "Are you thinking he's a threat to you and yours?"

Considering, Thia looked from one friend to the other. She knew what they thought she should say, how they thought she should feel. But she couldn't lie.

"No," she said. "I'm not."

"Thia." Abby sounded like she was chewing nails.

But at least the elevator stopped shaking.

"What did that man do that should worry me?" Thia asked. "He reminded me of someone, that's all. Someone who has no reason to mean me any harm. Someone, remember, who saved my life—several times over."

"And if he *isn't* Cormac," Abby said, "then he's someone who is hiding who or what he is. Why? Maybe he's a harmless spy the Brigantium sent to keep tabs on you, but he might just as well be working with that bitch Cassie to—"

"What he *is*," Murphy said, "is a guest of this hotel. And as such, he is entitled through explicit and legally binding terms to privacy." He honed in on Kendra, his veneer of charm slipping to reveal something cold and fierce. "Should a guest be run to ground by an employee and her friends without cause and subjected to questions and accusations, the consequences to that employee's career would be dire. Disastrous, in fact, and quite out of my hands."

By the time he finished, Kendra had gone white. "Oh, God. I didn't—"

"—think. Aye, so I'd figured." Murphy reset the emergency button. The elevator resumed its upward journey.

"Did security alert you because of what I was doing? Or was it because they already had orders where he was concerned?"

Murphy smiled. "Yes."

"So we weren't the first to take a...a particular interest?"

"Safe to say."

Abby crowded him again and thrust an accusing finger at his chest. "And you didn't want us messing up whatever it is you've got going, right? Whatever deal you've made is more important than—"

Kendra laid a hand on Abby's arm. "Stop. I screwed up, Abs. He's right, what he said. We enter a contractual bargain with every guest. What I was doing—what I would have gone on to do would've been in breach of that."

The elevator arrived at the roof. The doors opened.

"Enjoy the rest of your evening, ladies." Murphy moved so as to allow them to pass.

"What? You expect us to just—"

"Time to go." Thia snagged Abby's arm on the way out and with Kendra taking hold of the other, they moved her along with them.

Kendra gave her boss a backward glance. "Who else has taken an interest in this guest? Anyone we should know?"

The doors began to close. He blocked one with a firm hand, exposing the leather cuff worn around his wrist. "Were I you, I'd focus my concern elsewhere. Should our man on Seven do anything actionable, shall we say, it will not escape notice."

Abby tugged free, turned. "And you'll tell us?"

Pulling his hand back, Murphy inclined his head. "As you wish. Abigail."

The doors closed on what might have been a smirk.

"Boss?" Danny hurried out from the restaurant. "Is everything alright?"

"Yes, thank you," Kendra said unconvincingly. "Fine."

"I didn't know—that is, I had your food taken back to the kitchen to be kept warm. Should I bring it to your table?"

Thia couldn't imagine sitting down to dinner after all that. Not here, anyway.

Nor, apparently, could the others.

"My place?" Abby suggested.

It meant a bit of a drive, but maybe that was a good thing. Put some distance between them and whoever that man was.

"Sure," Thia said. "Sounds nice."

Kendra made the decision unanimous. "Box it all up, please, Danny—and put it on my account. Thank you." Her smile was shaky but wry. "I think you'll be pleased with the tip."

● ○ ●

Moments Earlier

"Beatrice Meriwether here."

The cellular connection was not the best. Slowing her pace, Edith wove together a clarity spell in her mind, snapped her fingers next to the phone held to her ear. The static cleared. "Assistant Director, it's Edith Wilkinson."

"I know, dear. Caller I. D."

Edith cringed. "Of course. Right."

Sensing someone approaching from behind her, she stepped to the right before—

"Excuse me, I'm sorry," said the woman, rushing by.

"No, no, *I'm* sorry," Edith said automatically—to none other than Thia McDaniel, leaving the restaurant for the hall.

Bloody hell. She should have tried to disguise her voice. Made it more American, at least. Then again, this was a hotel in a town geared for tourism; Edith's couldn't be the only English voice around.

"Who was that?" the Assistant Director asked through the phone.

Before answering, Edith put herself close to the wall and ducked behind a topiary trimmed in festive silver bows and tiny lights. "Thia McDaniel."

"Is she gone now? Did she suspect anything?"

Edith watched the woman in question join the two at the lift. All were clearly concerned about something but it hadn't to do with her, Edith decided with a measure of relief. None of them looked her way. "No. I don't think so."

"Good. See that she doesn't. We want her safe. We want to know what she does. We do *not* want her feeling smothered."

"I understand." She'd been told it often enough, hadn't she? Of course she understood. But it was harder to do than she had anticipated, blending into the sidelines of someone's life, watching her and those around her without drawing notice.

The three women hurried into the lift, and Edith waited for the doors to close.

"You were not scheduled to report till later," the Assistant Director said. "What's happened?"

"There was a man in Eclectica." Edith left the impromptu blind to approach the lift. She needed to see what floor the women wanted. "And tonight, she and her friends are chasing after—well, I think it's the same man. Only different."

In the pronounced silence which followed that, the display

counted down the lift's progress.

"Explain," Assistant Director Meriwether said at last. And something in her tone gave Edith chills.

● ○ ●

Tributary Road, Granite Springs
It was easy to get caught up in internalized chaos when there wasn't much to see but silhouettes of trees against a moonlit sky and road reflectors brought to momentary life by head-lights. When one's companion was no more inclined to talk than Thia was, it became inevitable.

After collecting their boxed dinners, Thia had driven Abby back to Eclectica so they could switch cars. It had seemed a lot of bother, but now she saw the merit. Given how scattered her thoughts had become, she was glad she wasn't the one behind the wheel. On this road especially, lack of focus could be deadly.

"Do you think that was Cormac?" Abby asked, breaking the silence as she held the Mini to a long, tight curve.

The clutching of Thia's stomach might have had to do with how close the steep drop-off was and the absence of safety barricades, but she had driven this road countless times since November. (What better place to try to get a handle on her new powers than Abby's isolated property?)

She fidgeted, careful not to kick the bag of carry-out boxes by her feet. "I'm really not sure."

Abby's gaze flicked her way, then back to the curve. "You sure you're not sure?"

"For a moment, I was. Sure that he was Cormac, I mean. But now?" Thia sighed. "I'm too confused."

"Twice in one day."

"My being confused? More like hundreds of times. Today and yesterday. And the day bef—"

"Two men, I meant," Abby cut in, unamused. She steered

into a brief straightaway. "Two men that caught your interest, so to speak."

"Oh." Thia cleared her throat. "Yes, well. That's true."

"Which is why both could have been Cormac."

"But why *would* they be?" Uncomfortable, Thia tugged at the belt across her chest. "Why would he come to town in disguise—well, okay I can understand that. Maybe. Beatrice told me he has something of a checkered past." No surprise there. "But to not tell *me* who he was? To pretend he doesn't know me? Why would he do that?"

The possibility of that not only hurt, it infuriated. Because she couldn't see it as anything other than some sort of game. Or worse, a prank. Was he laughing at her?

The mirrors caught the lights of Kendra's Audi, following so she could return to town on her own later.

"If it is him," Thia said with another tug on the belt, "he's going to be sorry. He can't just come here, make a fool of me by pretending to be other people, and expect me to...." Words failed as her anger abruptly dropped.

Expect her to *what*, exactly? She had no idea what Cormac might expect her to do. What he might want from her.

She knew all too well what she'd wanted from him, though. The intensity of it had pushed her toward a dangerous line: The line between wanting everything and being desperate enough—needy enough—to settle for anything.

Anything...such as a five-minute anonymous transaction in Eclectica. Or a two-second gaze held across a restaurant.

It was awful how much she missed him.

"Maybe he has good reason," Abby offered quietly. "Goddess knows I'm no fan of his. And you know I think you would be better off if he stayed out of your life. But I suppose it's not inconceivable that he's thinking of your safety, trying not to attract attention your way."

"Then why come here at all?"

When no answer followed, Thia realized Abby's focus was divided between the road ahead and the rearview mirror.

"Abby?"

"Someone's back there. Behind Kendra."

Thia twisted to look. The headlights—the annoying, super-bright kind—were easy to spot.

"Following?" Thia asked. "Or just going the same way?"

This was the main road through these mountains, and a long one at that. Anyone could be using it, and for any number of perfectly innocent reasons.

Still, Thia worried. And Abby hadn't responded.

"Maybe it's Cormac," Thia tried. "Again." He had followed her before, when Matt and Cassie were driving her to what they had planned to be her sacrificial death.

Or maybe it was Cassie, come to make good on her promise of revenge. Thia fumbled for her cell phone. "Should I call Kendra, let her know about the car?"

It was, in retrospect, a stupid question. Of course Kendra was aware. She'd probably noticed those damn xenon head-lights before Abby had.

They had never spoken about it, but Thia suspected Kendra had a military past. She wielded all manner of weaponry as if she'd been born to it and was equally adept in hand-to-hand maneuvers—as revealed recently when she'd tried to acquaint Thia with self-defense that went beyond the basic "shout and run" Thia had relied upon previously (with varying levels of success).

"I wonder if I should turn off," Abby said with a glance at the mirror. "Or slow down, see if they pass. But that might be what they want."

Thia had her phone in hand. "I could ask Kendra."

Abby's lips compressed into a tight line and she increased speed. "Yeah. Do it."

Again looking back, Thia dialed.

Kendra picked up immediately. Her new car had hands-free capability. "I see it."

Thia put her on her speaker, held the phone so Abby could ask, "What should we do? Try to make them pass, or—"

"That might be what they want," Kendra replied.

"Mm. I wondered about that." Abby accelerated out of a horseshoe curve. "So, what—"

"My scanner can't get a read into it," Kendra spoke over her. "It's warded. Typical Brigantium stuff, but that doesn't tell us much anymore." Cassie and a fair number of Idris's followers had been members.

Thia hadn't considered using her Sight. Something like that should have been instinctive.

Her instincts were crap.

She used it now, saw the faint sheen of protective magic around the car. How specific qualities could be seen in it, she had no idea. She could no more differentiate one soap bubble surface from another.

"We should continue on, right?" Abby was asking into the phone. "They probably already know where I live, so that's no matter. And we can better defend ourselves."

"That's my take too," Kendra said. "But we should push it. They're gaining."

Abby stomped on the gas and they whipped around a turn. Thia quickly faced forward, then banged against the door's plastic paneling when Abby almost immediately cranked the wheel the other way. They zoomed past a squiggly-arrow road sign.

As the Mini continued to zig-zag, Thia gripped the handle mounted overhead. This was Abby's daily commute. She must be familiar with every bit. Maybe this was her normal speed when she didn't have passenger-anxiety to consider. A sharp curve taken too fast bumped Thia into the door again despite her braced hold.

"Almost home," Abby said, locked on the road ahead. Her knuckles stood out from gripping hard. "Nothing to it."

Right, Thia thought, but stayed silent.

In the side mirror, Kendra's headlights moved in and out of view. She had dropped back a little, likely not as comfortable with the speed. The other car had fallen back considerably.

"What the hell?" Abby's shocked question grabbed Thia's attention. In the oncoming lane, a long line of single head-lights snaked toward them. The rumble of engines became audible, then quickly increased to a roar.

Motorcycle after motorcycle zoomed past.

"Good grief." Thia shielded her eyes against the strobing effect of the lights. There had to be at least thirty. "Are these the same guys from town?"

They had to be, right? But she hadn't realized the gang was that big.

"Assholes," Abby grumbled when one after another flashed their brights. When the line shifted, attempting to crowd the Mini toward the road's edge, her language worsened.

Then they were gone, the red of their rear lights snaking on down the road.

Thia blew out a breath, relieved despite the car that still followed them. "That was crazy," she said before noticing the sign ahead. Her hand reclaimed its overhead hold.

"Here we go," Abby said, and then began to murmur under her breath. Amidst the slide and pinging crunch of dirt and gravel, she forced a tight turn onto the unpaved drive to her property.

Momentum and the confusing whirl of tree trunks and road reflectors proved to be too much. Thia shut her eyes, waited until the car straightened before opening them again.

Complete darkness.

Panicked, she jerked upright, the seatbelt digging painfully. "Where are the headlights?" She couldn't see anything—how could Abby? Why didn't Abby stop?

"I did a night vision spell."

Some warning would've been nice, Thia thought, and then noticed the absence of light behind. "Kendra too?"

"I assume so," Abby said. "She's back there...and clear of the gate." She pressed a remote that had been affixed to the dash.

Thia looked back and again used her Sight. The faint flicker of the wards reassured, and against them she could make out the dim silhouettes of Kendra's car and the property's steel gate. She faced forward again, tried to trust that Abby really could see where she was driving.

Of course, with the right skills or even just the right tools, any ward could be broken. Nothing was guaranteed, Thia had come to learn. In magic, especially.

It was why, she supposed, those who held the most power often sought to gain more. It was why Idris Cathmor had gone after the Stone of Shadows, and why his twin son and daughter had joined his terrible scheme.

What of his other son, though? Was Cormac driven by that same need? He had gained a great deal of new power thanks to Thia, when he'd siphoned some of what had been forcing its way into her from the Stone.

She had sensed at the time that she could not cope with the full amount, that it would tear her apart, and had instinctively felt that Cormac had saved her by doing what he did. Yet by her own admission tonight, her instincts might well be crap. Had she been mistaken about his motives? Had he acted out of self-interest after all?

In that case—assuming he *was* in Granite Springs—was it because he sought to take the rest of the Cailleach's powers from her?

Abby pulled onto a narrow, sloping track that wove through a stand of native fir. Her single-story ranch house and gardens lay ahead; the other drive led to the ramshackle barn used for her various craft projects.

Craft, not as in needlepoint or macrame, but as in witch.

If Thia could be assured that she would survive, should she consider letting Cormac take all her powers? They brought her nothing but danger. To herself and to those around her.

Mine.

Something fierce shivered through her bones, momentarily robbing her of breath.

She had felt this come over her before, when she had first taken up the Stone, thinking it a gift from Lettie. Nearly a week before she inadvertently misdirected Idris's ritual.

Had the powers claimed her even then?

Abby stopped the car, set the parking brake. "I think we lost them back on the main road," she said, "but we should hurry just in case."

She was out of the car and on her way to the front porch before Thia had recovered wits enough to undo her seat-belt.

CHAPTER 5

Landmark Hotel, Granite Springs
Later

His mug of honeyed tea had long since gone cold but Cormac continued to hold on. He sat at the hotel window, the compact room dark behind him, and stared out at the festive town below. The lights, the groups of revelers...Midwinter in Granite Springs was anything but bleak. Yet that was exactly what he felt.

Tiny flakes too small and far apart to be considered snow in his estimation, drifted lazily downward. His gaze shifted to a particular house, partially visible between trees and other, taller homes. The small colored lights fixed to its eaves shone brightly; the windows did not. Thia had gone out.

Would she stay the night?

He wondered where, exactly. If he examined the hills to the right, would one of the lighted windows belong to the room she was in? Or perhaps he should look to the valley, nearer to where the creek joined the river.

Was she with one of the two friends from dinner or had she met up with someone else? Someone who was more than a friend? That was a possibility he had to allow, and one to which he had no right to object.

And yet he did.

He half-wished he could blame the failed enthrallment he had tried to use on her in London. He had believed it would be an expedient way to get her to lead him to the Stone, but something had gone wrong. He still hadn't sorted out what. Somehow, somewhere during the binding kiss he had lost the threads of the spell.

For several days afterward he had believed she'd managed to twist them onto him instead. He'd had no other explanation for his increasing attachment.

It had been a damned amazing kiss. Colors like fireworks, a flood of energy—and adrenaline...and for a moment, he had thought—

No. It was too laughable. One didn't touch souls. Especially not his. He had too many protections in place for that.

Never in all his years had he known anything close to that moment with her—so, naturally he had blamed the spell and, for a time, Thia for manipulating it.

Then, at the Ring, when it had seemed that they were both doomed, she kissed him again. And it had been like before. Stronger, even. Without a single spell involved. Nothing more than Thia herself. That had been what—chemistry?

Cormac set the mug down on the adjacent table. He really should stop this pining but, truthfully, he didn't know what to do in its place. He had spent the day alternately keeping an eye on Thia and searching for signs of Cassandra or anyone potentially associated with her. He'd achieved nothing more than rubbing salt in his wounds when it came to the former and coming up empty with the latter.

Thia seemed content in Granite Springs with the store, her friends, and anyone else who might be in her life. Cormac had come because he'd worried that she wouldn't be, or that her friends could not protect her. Now that he'd seen for himself that she was and that they could, he should leave. Go back to sorting out his own life.

The Achill Bell wouldn't find itself.

He sank lower on the seat, tapped steepled fingers against his grimly set mouth. Adept at telling lies, he could almost tell them to himself. Unfortunately, he was equally adept at detecting them.

Concerns over Thia's well-being and Cassandra's threats... those were not all of the reasons he had come. Much to his dismay, he had missed Thia and wanted to see her.

He had thought that a moment would be enough.

How was it possible, then, that after each encounter today he missed her more, not less? And how, in a life spent alone more often than not (and preferably so), was it that he now felt so...damned if the word he was looking for wasn't *lonely.*

Cormac pushed to his feet, picked up his keycard. Enough of this. If he was lonely, there would be plenty of company to be had in the bar off the lobby.

And he might pick up some useful information as well.

● ○ ●

With a nervousness not felt since Kendra's first months on the job, she arrived at Murphy's office and took a deep breath outside the closed door. Held for a two-count; released on a six. She raised her fist to knock.

The lock disengaged before her knuckles made contact. Of course he'd known she was there.

She opened the door enough peer around it. Unsurprisingly, her workaholic boss sat behind his desk. He didn't look up from the paperwork arrayed before him in messy stacks.

"Do you have a moment?" she asked, and cursed her nerves for making her sound timid. Hell, she was *acting* timid with the way she was using the door between them like a shield. (A completely ineffective one, as she well knew.) She stepped past it, closed herself into the room.

The sound of the lock re-engaging surprised her. He'd never

done that before, not in all of their meetings.

"It's late, Ross." His pen scratched across paper. "Did you get your friends all squared away?"

He sounded more tired than annoyed, thankfully. Unless he intended to lull her into a false sense of security.

"Thia is spending the night at Abby's," she said, cautiously sitting in one of the two chairs before the desk. Impersonal objects, his furnishings; pieces of a mass-produced set. Good quality but generic. Her office had the same. But while she had brought things from home to liven up her space, Murphy might well have replicated a catalog photo. (Or, more likely, had the hotel's decorator do it.)

There was one notable exception. On the wall behind him hung an unsigned painting in an ornate gilt frame. A moody and well-executed landscape, its perspective put the observer atop a hillside of lush green grass to look down toward what might have been a farm or small settlement nestled among large trees. Beyond was a meandering lake and a succession of mountains overhung with clouds.

Kendra assumed the scene was Irish, as Murphy was. She had never asked about it. Nor had she asked about any of the others that, throughout her time, had found their way onto the hotel's walls. All unsigned, all of a similar style but varying in subject and tone. She had her suspicions but because she loved her job, no matter how much curiosity burned, she had never so much as mentioned them. Something about it felt personal.

Murphy did not take well to personal.

"Has better protections than Thia's own home, does it?" he asked abstractedly, head down as he continued to write. His dark hair looked as if he had been running his hands through it.

"Probably not after what we've added to Lettie's wards," she said, and fought the urge to get up and pace. "But he knows to look for Thia there."

"Cormac, you mean?" Murphy's gaze flicked to hers, then back to his work. "And you think he doesn't know where to find Pine Meadow?"

Kendra worked to cover her surprise that he knew Abby's name for her home. "He might have tried. A car was behind us for awhile, but it didn't stick past the turn off Tributary."

"It wasn't him." Murphy set aside one number-filled sheet of paper for another.

"You're sure?"

"I am."

He must have told Security to keep an eye on things. That was moderately reassuring, but, "Is Cormac here?" she asked. "Was that him in the restaurant?"

Murphy didn't look up. Didn't, apparently, intend to answer. And Kendra found herself furious.

"Dammit, can you at least confirm or deny that he may or may not be in town—hell, in the state, if that makes you feel more comfortable?"

His head came up at that. Or maybe it was in response to the emotion-triggered power that swirled through her like a rising tide.

His own power flared, dark and angry. "Flattered I am, to be sure, about your thoughts for my comfort, Ms. Ross. And sure, I'll be pleased to confirm that to the best of my knowledge, Idris Cathmor's son is indeed in the state." Blue threads of energy licked along the pen in his grip.

Here, Kendra recognized, was the man she had expected to find when she had first approached the door.

"With that," he went on, "and since you seem to be needing every bleeding detail laid out for you on a platter, I repeat my advice." The threads crackled softly. "You would better serve Ms. McDaniel by directing your attention elsewhere."

Kendra worked to tamp down her power. Not easily done,

since it was reacting to the inherent threat of his now added to the inner fury that had triggered it. If anything, she was *more* upset than before. But he had answered her questions. She had to credit him for that. Closing her eyes briefly, she shrugged tension from her shoulders.

Calmer, she met his gaze...and felt her mind catch on one of those bleeding details he'd referenced. "Elsewhere. You did say that before. In the elevator."

"That I did." He set his pen aside. She felt him set aside his anger, as well—and more quickly than she had managed with her own. Or maybe he was just better at concealing it.

"You've heard me use the word *claimsech* often enough to gather its meaning?"

She frowned at the apparent change of subject. "I think so."

"Does anyone come to mind?"

Curiouser and curiouser. "Well, Abby—no, I didn't mean it like that," she said at his delighted grin. "In the elevator, Abby called Cassie a bitch."

"Did she?"

He knew very well that she had. Devious man, telling her things without telling her things...and thus keeping himself out of trouble with the hotel's contracts and whatever other arrangements he had going.

Looking smug, he leaned back in his chair. "Although, come to think of it, I've heard that the woman near the head of the Brigantium can be a right terror as well."

"Beatrice Meriwether is here?"

"Not to my knowledge." He raised his hands in disavowal. His shirt cuffs slid, exposing the leather ones habitually worn at each wrist. "Yet with the Holidays, as you know, it's near impossible to track all the comings and goings in the vale."

Yes, *but,* Kendra thought, adhering to the strictest meaning of his words. (And how interesting that he had said vale, not valley. He gave the impression of referring to the region as a whole, but might refer only to the area up in the mountains where a leyline portal was located.) "Wouldn't she most likely stay here?"

The Brigantium had connections all over the world, sure, but the Landmark would best suit. Security and luxury. Just what the exclusive and well-moneyed group would be drawn to. She said as much to Murphy, flattered his ego a bit with it in the process—and for good measure gifted him with her best impression of awed subservience.

She may have overplayed the innocently arched brows and wide eyes, because he grimaced.

"That's more frightening than all your shows of power."

Kendra batted her lashes, making him laugh outright.

He then waved her off. "Stop, I beg you. I'll not be telling you what you want to know." He leaned forward, still smiling, and once more took up his pen. "Now leave me be. I've got all this to get through before dawn."

"I had to try," she said pleasantly and stood. The door's lock disengaged on approach, and she set her hand on the knob. Damn. She couldn't *not* say it. On a hard breath, she turned back. "Murphy."

He lifted his head, no longer smiling. Wary. "Aye?"

"Thank you again. For before." Kendra struggled to get the words past her usual guards. "My career, it—well, it means a lot to me. I could have lost it if you hadn't stepped in."

"'Tis a fine thing to be thanked for one's own self-interest." Murphy returned to work. "You're a good manager. One the Landmark would suffer to lose in any part of year. With the Holidays upon us? You're damn near indispensable." He shot her a look beneath his brows. "As you well know. Now get out. One of us needs to be rested and alert tomorrow and it isn't likely to be me." He pulled over a calculator.

"I owe you, anyway." She stepped out.

He grunted, tapping on the keypad.

She was closing the door when his voice made her pause.

"Should Beatrice Meriwether ever seek accommodation in this fair city, one might suppose she would ask around in her organization for recommendations."

Kendra tried to understand what Murphy was getting at. Or rather, what he was guiding her to. "Would they speak well of the Landmark?"

"Had they the occasion to stay here, certainly." His mouth quirked as he shrugged. "The third floor could be very much to their taste."

Ah. Kendra smiled. "Thanks—again. For the help."

"Earlier?" he said, a deliberate misunderstanding. "Think nothing of it. A slave to self-interest, I am."

Kendra wasn't so sure about that. "Good night, Murphy."

He flicked a hand over the paperwork. "If you say so."

She laughed, closed the door. The lock clicked.

● ○ ●

Pine Meadow

Knees pulled up to her chest, Thia sat on the guest room's iron-framed bed. The decor was what she termed "country cute:" A worn rag rug on a light pine floor; curtains printed with pastel checks and trimmed in eyelet lace; tatted doilies on the dresser and bedside table.

It didn't seem Abby's preferred style. The rest of the house was done in darker wood and bolder colors.

Since Thia had found herself unwilling to turn out the lights and (inconsequently) unable to sleep, she'd had plenty of time to contemplate the oddity.

Contemplate but come to no conclusion.

As with so many things.

Had that been Cormac? Prior to the chase to the elevator she had been nearly certain. But, gradually, more doubt had crept in. She dropped her head to her knees, thunked it a few times for good measure.

What would it mean if it had been?

Easy. It'd mean that Cormac didn't care to reveal himself to her, that's what.

She wasn't being fair, she argued with herself. Again. It was possible, after all, that he couldn't reveal himself because....

After several attempts to fill in the blank, she gave up. But just because she couldn't supply a reason, that didn't mean he didn't have one.

Then again, she might be making excuses.

Unnecessary excuses since she had probably been mistaken, anyway, and Cormac was neither currently nor would would he ever be in Granite Springs. Abby could be right; Thia was projecting, seeing him where he was not because she *wanted* him to be there. She was going to drive herself crazy.

So, then what was the deal with Connor Michaels?

CHAPTER 6

"Another day, another dollar," Abby said, and then set the Mini's parking brake.

Thia managed a good-natured grunt as she stepped out, her limited brain power more focused on her car in the adjacent spot. It seemed to have weathered the night okay. All four hubcaps. No notable scratches that hadn't been there before.

She hadn't slept well, and Abby had been out of coffee. Hope of the café's locally-sourced blend propelled her toward the patio's closed gate. She would treat herself to a waffle, too. Topped with three-berry compote or maybe spiced apple.

Mulling the choice, Thia opened the gate. Only then did she think it strange to find it closed. Usually by the time she arrived it was propped open for the café's morning business. She finished doing just that while Abby went through.

"Seems quiet."

It did, which Thia should have noticed immediately. Sounds from the café tended to carry to the alley, and there wasn't a single one. There was however, sound coming from the alley behind her. Someone was running toward them.

Thia straightened as Megan, the café's assigned clerk, came to a stop by the open gate.

"I couldn't get in," the girl said, out of breath. "I didn't have my phone with me so I waited around, then thought maybe you might use the front door. So I've been checking, going back and forth. Did Zoe call in sick or something?"

Before Thia could process all that, two young women came up behind Megan.

"Have the hours changed?" one asked, continuing to step in place. Both wore designer exercise gear, their hands encased in plush winter gloves. "We came by on our first lap and it was closed up. Are you opening soon?"

Thia looked to the café's dark windows. The "closed" sign inside the glass of the door where Abby was using a key in the locks. Bewilderment mixed with anxiety. "I'm sorry," Thia said, "I don't really know what—"

"That's okay," said the second exerciser. "We'll check back after our loop through the park." With that, the two headed out, their arms bent and pumping vigorously.

"Didn't Zoe say she was going to get an early start?" Abby called out, opening the door.

Megan went over. "That's what she told me yesterday when I left."

"Maybe she meant an early start at home," Thia suggested, following them into the unmistakably empty café. Only the minimal, overnight lighting was on. She flipped switches by the door to bring on the rest. The room brightened but the uncomfortable feeling of absence remained.

"I'll start setting up." Megan went behind the counter, got out an apron.

Thia had met with a similar atmosphere in Lettie's London townhouse: The sense of a space waiting for someone that would not return. And wasn't that a ridiculous connection to make? Blaming lack of caffeine, she re-locked the deadbolt to keep out the customers they weren't yet ready to serve.

"Doesn't she do most of the baking there—at home?" Thia

asked in support of her work-at-home theory, and went into the small kitchen as if somehow it might offer a clue. But, considering how rarely she laid eyes on it, of course it didn't. How would she know if it looked different from any other day? Maybe different was typical. Maybe there was no norm. Maybe Megan would know. Thia returned to the café proper.

Abby had joined the clerk behind the counter, her phone at her ear. "I'm calling Zoe's cell."

The door rattled.

Thia looked over, hopeful, but saw only confused strangers outside. She gave them an apologetic shake of her head.

"We could open," Abby told her. "I can help Megan with coffee and simple espresso drinks, at least. And sell day-olds. Six rings, then to voicemail." She lowered the phone, tapped something on its screen. "I'll try her home."

The door rattled again.

Thia went to turn its lock. Then, opening it just enough to poke her head out, she addressed the growing crowd. With the gate open, people were streaming into the patio area.

"We're running a little behind this morning. If you give us a few minutes, we'll be able to offer basics, at least." She had hoped to thin them out a bit, but nearly everyone stayed put, their breaths pluming in the cold.

Thia closed the door. "We should let them in even if we're not set up."

"Yeah." Abby set down the phone, her expression a forecast of her next words: "No answer at home, either."

Thia felt a chill unrelated to the cold which seeped through the gaps between the old door and its frame. She had called Lettie in much the same way...unaware that Lettie had been murdered several days prior.

But Lettie had been doing something dangerous: Hunting down the Stone. Zoe was doing nothing more than running a café.

As far as Thia knew.

She worked to shake off her anxiety, managed to loosen it enough so she could concentrate on the crowd outside. The morning regulars were putting their schedules at risk out of loyalty (or addiction coupled with routine).

"Thanks for your patience," she said as she let them in. "We can do espresso drinks and whatever food is in the case right away. Brewed coffee will be a few minutes." Once she got it started. She hurried behind the counter. Abby handed her a filter loaded with freshly ground coffee and then returned to prepping the espresso machine and an array of milk pitchers. The pass-through to the kitchen showed Megan was getting the crepe station up and running.

After starting two roasts of coffee and taking payment for enough orders to get Abby and Megan off to a good start, Thia excused herself and went downstairs. Eclectica needed to open in five minutes.

Lynette and Stefanie waited outside. Thia let them in and quickly relocked the door. "Zoe hasn't arrived yet," she told them, "so if you would both go help in the café after we open, please, I'll handle things down here."

With the Shakespeare Festival closed for the season, retail mornings tended to be slow. That made them an optimal time to receive new stock, process online orders, and take care of general housekeeping. And it meant that, unlike for the café, no crowd awaited. Not so much as an interested passerby.

The clerks quickly filled out their time cards and began to set up the registers. Thia—determinedly not thinking about the giftwrapped box beneath the counter—started the music.

As the light, cheerful notes of a hammered dulcimer played through the speakers, she went to switch on the rest of the overhead lights and do a walkthrough to check for an damage wrought by the automated vacuum.

A suspicious lack of the latter made her wonder if the thing had gone out at all.

A tendency to shirk its programmed duties was one of its many quirks. Getting trapped beneath items it had toppled onto itself was another.

"Is Thing on his base?" she called over to Stefanie, still behind the counter. The clerk bent down to look.

"No, Ms. McDaniel," came the reply, and Thia tried not to cringe at the repeatedly unasked-for formality. "Should I look for it?"

"Yes, please."

If only she could send the clerks to look for Zoe as easily.

Thia checked her watch. Time was up, rogue vacuum or no. She flipped the window sign and unlocked the door. Then she neatened a well-perused display. In the lead up to the holiday parade, candle lanterns and garland supplies were increasingly popular.

"The rush tapered off," Abby said, coming downstairs. In her hands were two large mugs with scones balanced on top. "I'll check in a little while, but I think they'll be fine."

"Did you hear anything from Zoe?" Thia asked, hurrying to assist her friend with—oh, who was she kidding—hurrying to get her coffee. She removed the scone and, temperature be damned, took a long draw. French Roast, nice and dark, with two sugars and a good dose of cream. She swallowed, closed her eyes to savor the effect. When she opened them, things were clearer. Sharper. She sighed. "Thank you."

"You're welcome." Abby took a long drink of her own, then, "I didn't. And I've got a bad feeling."

Thia's stomach clutched. "A bad feeling like anyone might have, or something more?"

Abby neither confirmed nor denied when asked if she had psychic abilities. But sometimes she did "know" things. Or at least suspect.

"More," she answered on the way to the counter. "Hit me

about five minutes ago. It's probably been there all morning but I've had so many other things going on—and it's not like these things are ever clear, anyway."

"What should we do? What can we do?" Thia set her coffee and scone down. Her appetite had fled, and fear made caffeine extraneous if not an altogether bad idea. "Should we call her family? Ask if they've heard from her?"

When unable to reach Lettie, Thia had called other family members to ask if they knew anything. It had been a lot of trouble for little to no result, but maybe this time, with Zoe....

"None of them are local," Abby said, "and the only other number we have is for her mother in Ohio. We'd only freak her out, I think, and not help anything." She pulled out her phone. "I'm going to try her again."

"What about her friend?" Thia asked. "The one who lets her park. He might know where she is." Zoe might not have driven away last night after all. She could have stayed over.

And what, overslept? Not likely. Besides, that wouldn't call for one of Abby's Bad Feelings.

"I'll run up to Pike, see if I can talk to him," Thia said as Abby shook her head—no answer, still, on the phone. "Maybe she had a family emergency or something and had to leave town." And for whatever reason had told her friend but not her work. Sure.

"Found him!" Stefanie's voice came from the back left. "He got into the garden section and managed to suck up half a Tibetan prayer banner. The rest dropped onto his sensor so he couldn't see to move on." She came into view holding the vacuum, a squat sort of squished cube with a curved front and wheels. From it hung a cord strung with squares of colorful fabric. "It's really jammed in there."

Setting aside her phone, Abby held out her hands for Thing. "Go ahead," she told Thia. "I got this."

● ○ ●

Somewhere in the Mountains

Zoe became aware of herself gradually, waking from a deep, dreamless sleep—a state so comfortable she was reluctant to leave. But the strange sounds and unfamiliar smells persisted. She couldn't place the odor of damp wood and cement. Heavy feet clomped on what she came to realize was a wood floor overhead. Whatever she lay was both soft and lumpy, while a scratchy, musty blanket covered her from toe to chin.

Finally awake enough to wonder about it, she opened her eyes...only to discover they already were.

Had she gone blind?

She jerked upright and pressed her hands to her face. She knew she did that because she could feel them there. But she couldn't see a thing.

"No," she whispered, a sort of prayer. "Please, no."

Rubbing her eyes, she saw kaleidoscopic patterns of color. Was that possible for someone who had lost their sight? Or was she simply in a pitch-black room?

Where *was* this, anyway? And how had—

"Oh, God." Memory returned. She had been attacked in her car. She had been *taken*. "Oh, God. Oh, God."

"It's better if you stay quiet," came a soft voice in the darkness. A man's voice. Zoe would have screamed had her throat not closed off in shock, her breath trapped in her chest.

"That way," the voice continued, "they might not know you are awake."

Try as Zoe might, she couldn't see anything. She thought the man sounded some distance away. Not necessarily a safe distance, but he was giving her advice, wasn't he? He wouldn't do that if he were a threat. She relaxed a fraction. Maybe he had been taken, too.

"W-where are we?" She hardly recognized her own voice for

all of the fear in it. "What's happening? What do they want with me?" She had more questions, but stopped to give him a chance to answer.

None came. Zoe heard only the continued footsteps overhead and voices so muffled she couldn't make out words.

"Hello?" She leaned forward. Her senses strained.

Nothing.

● ○ ●

Pike Street, Granite Springs

There in the driveway sat Zoe's car. Thia sprinted across the street only to turn around and scan the block from the new angle. Maybe Zoe had just parked and was taking a different route to Eclectica than Thia's. She could be arriving at that very moment. Thia half expected her phone to ring—Abby telling her to come back, Zoe was there—so strong was her hope that this was a simple matter of running late.

That made sense, didn't it? Zoe hadn't answered her phone because she had been driving.

But because Thia had come this far, she climbed the steep drive, laid a cautious hand on the hood.

Icy cold.

So much for that hope. The car hadn't been driven, probably not for several hours. Perhaps not since yesterday.

The idea that Zoe had spent the night at her friend's might have merit after all. The car had been parked for a long time; it could have spent the night—ergo, Zoe could have too.

Thia approached the single-level home. The typical 1970's construction was unusual in an area of Victorians and Craftsmans. Inside, curtains had been drawn across all the windows. The light in the recessed doorway was still on. Behind the warped metal-framed screen door was a plain brown slab of wood with a round knob, deadbolt, and peephole.

She rang the bell, a glowing plastic rectangle mounted below crooked brass numbers. The chime sounded faintly, and she waited. Cobwebs collected dirt and dead plant matter: Pine needles, tiny bits of dried leaves. She had ample opportunity to study them.

No one was coming. She was wasting her time.

She rang the bell again.

Behind her, downtown was coming to life. People walking, driving to work or a leisurely breakfast out. She wished she could be one of the latter, although she knew better than to assume their lives were any less difficult than hers. One never knew, truly, what was going on with people.

The door opened.

If this was Zoe's friend, he was a scruffy, groggy young man dressed in a Shakespeare Festival t-shirt, striped boxers, and a ratty, mostly beige bathrobe. His feet were bare. He blinked a few times, held up a hand to shield his squinted eyes.

"Yeah?" He sounded like he had swallowed gravel.

Thia tried for cheerful so as not to cause alarm. "I'm Thia McDaniel—from Eclectica, where Zoe works?"

The man crossed both arms over his barrel chest. "Okay."

No name offered. She pressed on. "Have you seen her today? Or heard from her? I'm sorry to...intrude, but she's late and isn't answering her phones."

The man frowned, slightly more alert. "That's not like her."

"Do you know where she might be?"

He scratched the scalp beneath his curly blond hair, tipped his chin toward Zoe's car. "That was there when I got home last night. Around one, I think. Yeah. I ran into some of the crew from the Cabaret and we shot the shit for awhile about this season's panto. I walked home, saw it parked, and figured she'd gone out too, maybe found her own way home—if she wasn't still out, you know? She's done that before. Not often. I mean, she's no party hound."

"Her car has been here all night?"

They both stared at it as if it held the answers. Maybe it did.

Thia walked over. "But she got into it yesterday. Abby and I had invited her to dinner, but she said she was going to the grocery store and then home. We saw her get in."

"No shit?" The man asked, following.

"Yeah." Thia bent and, careful not to touch the glass, peered through a side window. Things seemed normal enough: Papers stuffed in a cup holder; feathers and beads dangling from the rear view mirror; a sweater and umbrella placed in a neat little pile on the center of the back seat. She straightened.

Zoe's friend had returned to the doorway. He held a phone to his ear. "Anyway, Z, if you could give me a call when you get this, that'd be great, okay? I'm a little—well, it'd be great, that's all. Okay. Hope you're...okay." Lowering the phone, he met Thia's gaze. "Straight to voice mail."

Something about that nudged the back of Thia's mind but she brushed it away. Calls went straight to voicemail when a phone was out of range, and service throughout town could be problematic. In very rural areas, it ranged from spotty to nonexistent.

"What can we do?" the man asked, clearly more than a little worried. He immediately answered himself. "Beth Ann. I can call Beth Ann. They're real tight." He dialed.

At a loss, Thia pulled out her own phone to call Abby, who picked up after a couple of rings. "Thia? Any news?"

"No." She moved to the end of the drive so as to not interfere with the man's conversation. "Her car is here. Her friend doesn't know anything about it. He's calling another friend." She plugged her other ear in a vain attempt to focus past the café noise coming through Abby's end of the line. "He called Zoe, too, but it went straight to voicemail. He left her a—"

"Wait, what? Straight through? It rang several times when I called. Six, actually."

Thia gave Abby the same reasons she'd given herself; service and location.

"But her car is there," Abby countered. "How did she get outside the service area without driving—unless maybe she's with someone? Why would she miss work, though, and why not contact us?"

Hope sagged like a worn-out balloon yet Thia tried, "Maybe she turned it off."

"Or someone else did."

The balloon deflated altogether. "Abby."

"I know. I know. Look, come back and we'll figure this out. You shouldn't be out alone if—"

"Okay." Thia was scared enough without hearing the rest of the warning. "Give me a few minutes here first. I promise to hurry." She hung up on Abby's protest.

The man had finished his call. He hurried over. "She's going to call around, go over to Zoe's place. Beth Ann, I mean. Have you met her? Shit." He tried to catch his breath. "You don't think anything has happened to her, do you? To Zoe. Should I call the hospital? The police?"

"I have no idea," Thia said honestly. "I'm sorry, I don't know your name."

"Todd. Todd Wikowsky." He ran a shaky hand over his face. "You said your name. I—I was pretty out of it. Can you say it again? I'm awake now. Christ, am I awake now."

"Thia McDaniel." This time, she offered her hand.

Todd clasped it, held on. "From Eclectica."

She could feel the tremors before he let go. "That's right."

"What can we do now, Thia?"

Like she knew?

"We can hope we're overreacting," she said and had to look away from the fear that was so easy to read in his widened eyes. Morning light played over the snow-dusted mountains on the other side of the valley. Wisps of fog hung between the steeper foothills.

"And we stay calm," she added. "There's probably nothing to worry about. Although...maybe it would be a good idea to call the hospital."

Should she tell him what she feared might be happening? About Cassie and her threats? About magic and power and evil sorcerers and secret societies and Cormac—half-*sidhe*—possibly being in town but pretending to be other people but maybe they weren't him at all...No, she'd only sound insane.

"Hospital," Todd said, nodding. "Okay. Okay. I can do that." His eyes squeezed shut. "I should have called her when I got home so late and saw her car. I should've known something was wrong."

"We don't know that anything is. You shouldn't blame yourself, in any case. Like you said, she's left her car there like this before. You had no reason to think anything of it."

They came easily, those reassurances. Kindnesses, really, to try to relieve Todd of the guilt he so clearly felt. Too bad Thia couldn't do the same for herself.

If she hadn't driven away so quickly, if she'd waited until Zoe had driven away—or at least started backing out—would it have prevented whatever might've gone wrong? Thia couldn't help wondering, but wondering wouldn't help.

"I need to get back to Eclectica." She gave Todd her card. It had her cell number. "Please call when you hear back from Beth Ann."

"What do we do if there's nothing? If we can't find Zoe, do we call the police?"

"Let's hope it doesn't come to that."

"Yeah." He put the card into a robe pocket. "I'll see if I can find where she might've gone last night. I'm, uh, pretty tight with a lot of bar staff."

"Great idea."

She was a few steps down the drive when a thought struck.

She stopped, turned. "Todd? It's probably a good idea if you don't touch the car." She eyed the ground beside the driver's door where they had both walked, and she'd stood for some time. Shit.

It was probably too late, but: "Or walk around it much."

● ○ ●

In raven form, Cormac had observed Thia and Abby's arrival at Eclectica. He had been deciding what to do (also known as procrastinating) when Thia had come back out looking tense. The decision had made itself. He had followed.

He'd taken care to avoid her sight-lines, but he needn't have bothered. Thia proved to be preoccupied to the exclusion of all else.

After eavesdropping on her conversation with the bedraggled man with too much hair, he understood why. Someone in her employ was missing.

Another decision—the one he'd weighed all morning—had made itself. Or at least could be put off awhile longer. Cormac would not be leaving Granite Springs. Yet.

Presently, he flew to a secluded spot up Pike Street where what might have been intended as a neat little hedgerow had grown into a towering wilderness. He made himself as much "Connor Michaels" as he could manage (no time for colored contacts) and emerged unnoticed.

Thia neared the corner on the opposite walk.

He lifted his hand in greeting, found his voice. Or, rather, *Connor's* voice. "Good morning."

Thia stopped, located him across the street. Her expression was bafflingly neutral.

A peculiar silence ensued as she did nothing but stare and Cormac found himself uncertain how to proceed.

Two not-quite-strangers with so much more between them than just bit of roadway. And so much more than that simple distance, too, separating them. Whether Thia realized it or not.

They spoke at the same time.

His: "Is everything all right?"

And hers: "Are you on the way to Eclectica?"

When he said nothing more, she added, "You didn't pick up your gift yesterday," and thus avoided his question altogether.

"No," Cormac said, "I...had things to do." He felt distinctly uncomfortable. Being on different sides of the street wasn't helping. He jogged across and, armoring himself in feigned nonchalance, hopped the curb to stand with her. "I can get it now. May I walk with you?"

She peered intently at his face—his eyes, specifically.

The lenses of his glasses had darkened automatically in the sunlight, yet it was a struggle not to squirm. He should have taken the extra time to put in the damn contacts.

Abruptly, Thia turned and resumed walking.

Toward Eclectica, Cormac figured, and went alongside.

"You mentioned you were new to town," she said. Suspicion clung to each casually uttered word. "How new, exactly?"

"A day or so," he hedged. Tucking his hands into the pockets of his brown wool jacket, he hunched his shoulders against a sharp breeze. "You didn't answer my question. Is everything all right?"

"Of course. Why wouldn't it be?"

She may have gotten better at concealing her emotions, but she remained an endearingly poor liar.

"Oh, I don't know," Cormac said. They rounded the turn into the alley. "You seem...frightened."

Thia stopped. He did as well, and waited anxiously for what she would say. Only, she didn't. With a shake of her head, she walked on.

He pursued. "What?"

She slanted him a look. "Nothing."

Why was she lying? And what had made her not say whatever she had been about to?

They reached the entry to the café patio. Before she could step inside, he set a hand on her shoulder. "Thia—"

"Don't," she snapped, jerking herself away to turn on him with shocking vehemence. "Don't you touch me."

He held up his hands. "Forgive me. I didn't mean to—"

"Is this some kind of game?" Anger roughened her voice, came off her in waves. Her hands fisted at her sides.

Maintaining his pretense was surprisingly hard.

He made a little shrug. "Sorry?"

"Who are you?" Thia's eyes were bright with power, turning the hazel brilliant, like sunlight reflecting off gold.

He admired the beauty of it—how well it suited her—even as fear began to dance along his bones. She hadn't come near to mastering her abilities, he knew, and anger could cause a loss of control in even the most skilled.

"Who are you?" she repeated and took a step toward him. "What are you doing here?"

"Connor Michaels." Cormac held her glowing gaze but took a matching step back. He kept his hands lifted. "I'm here to collect the purchase I made. I didn't mean to upset you. More than you already are, that is. Please. There's no game here. No threat." He formed an awkward smile, the epitome of bashful innocence. "I enjoyed talking with you. Very much. But I've never been able to—that is, it's been awhile since I've tried to make a...a friend. A long while. I suppose I might be a little nervous. A bit awkward going about it."

Heart surprisingly in his throat, he forced out a chuckle.

● ○ ●

Were her eyes glowing? Thia thought they were, what with that hard-to-describe pressure she was feeling in them. But

Connor Michaels wasn't acting like someone confronted with anything out of the ordinary.

So maybe her eyes weren't glowing.

Or maybe Connor Michaels (assuming he *was* a man named Connor Michaels and not someone else, pretending) didn't consider glowing irises to be out of the ordinary. Abby had sensed that he carried power.

Could someone do that unknowingly? Thia didn't think it likely. The power was bound to flare up, assert itself as hers tended to do.

So, again...maybe her eyes *were* glowing. Which meant that Connor Michaels was acting like nothing was wrong. *Acting,* and doing a fine job of it.

As Abby had said, just because he wore glasses didn't mean he wasn't wearing contacts. Today it didn't matter; the lenses of his glasses were too shaded.

And that train of thought would not lead anywhere Thia needed to go, not while Zoe was unaccounted for. No, where Thia needed to go was Eclectica.

But first she needed to get herself under control so her eyes would stop glowing or worse. Not everyone would react as well to weirdness as "Connor" here seemed to, and she didn't want to risk an incident like in the garage this morning.

He continued to observe her with suspicious patience.

Given enough time, she supposed, she could find everything about him suspicious. It was that kind of day.

"I am frightened," she finally admitted. "But not of you."

Fairly sure her eyes had dimmed, she turned for the patio. He stayed with her as she crossed to the door, and she shot him a glance. "Then again," she said, "I'm also not thinking clearly."

By the lack of change in his expression, he hadn't caught the implication—that if she *were* thinking clearly, she *would* be frightened of him.

Although if he *was* Cormac, that meant he was a master at hiding his reactions. And thoughts. Feelings. Hell, he was a master at hiding, period.

But he wouldn't have any reason to harm Zoe. He might even have reason to help.

At the door, Thia made her decision. "A friend—the woman who runs this café—hasn't shown up for work today. So far, we haven't been able to reach her. We don't know where she is."

"Have the police been called?"

"Not yet. We're hoping someone knows where she is. That's what I was doing on Pike, actually. Talking with a friend of hers. She—Zoe—parks her car at his place for work. It was still there from yesterday, which makes no sense. Abby and I saw her get into it last night."

"Abby?"

He was clever, she'd give him that. Connor wouldn't know the name. "Eclectica's manager. And my friend."

"You have many friends."

Did she? Oh, she knew she had two very good ones in Abby and Kendra, the kind that would—and had—put themselves in harms way for her sake. But she was a relative newcomer to Granite Springs and wasn't close with many other locals.

Friends from Thia's times in other places...well, she hadn't kept in touch with any of them since October. Not even on social media. Could she consider herself their friend if she couldn't make the least bit of effort?

A sudden breeze blew her hair across her face and she realized she'd been lost in thought. Again. She shoved the strands back, saying, "I'm afraid that this is my fault. Whatever has happened."

Connor stepped closer, intent. "Why would that be?"

There was no answer she could give. Not to a stranger. She shook her head, shrugged.

"Are you in some kind of trouble?"

Yes. Probably. "I don't know."

He studied her, as if measuring the truth of that, and then: "You said you saw Zoe get into her car last night?"

"After we closed. Abby and I asked her to join us for dinner, but she said she had errands to run." Remorse was a painful, shifting weight. If Thia had pushed harder to get Zoe to join them, then maybe none of this would—

"But her car never left the drive?" Connor frowned into the distance, up at the bare branches of trees on Pike, their tops visible above the patio's back wall.

"It seems that way."

"So whatever may have happened, happened there."

Remorse and fear tangled. Thia could only nod.

He turned to her. Held out his hand. "Let's go see."

"What?"

"I want to check out her car." Not waiting, he took hold of her arm.

"What good will that do?" Too startled to think better of it, Thia let him pull her back toward Pike. "And if it *is* a crime scene, it can't be disturbed. Not until the police go over it."

"I won't disturb anything."

"Then why—"

"There are things I might be able to read from the area."

"What things?" She tugged against his hold. "What do you mean 'read'?"

"I have...certain talents." Looking both ways, he jaywalked her across Pike.

"Magical talents?"

"If you like." He wouldn't make eye contact.

That answered that, then. Yes, he held power. Yes, he was aware of it. And, yes, he could use it.

Did he even know where to go? Thia pointed, said, "That's

it there."

As they neared the driveway, Connor released her to then stand and survey the area. He gestured to cars parked along the curb. "Do you remember if these were here?"

"No," Thia replied, feeling useless. "It was dark, and I was only watching Zoe. Wait." She closed her eyes. "There weren't as many, maybe. There were open spaces. Why?"

She opened her eyes, found that he had walked halfway up the drive. Todd was nowhere in sight.

"If they knew she was to return to her car," Connor said, scanning the block from the higher elevation, "they could've lain in wait. The closer the better."

Thia hurried to catch up. "You think somebody did something to her?"

He turned from his study of the ground by the driver's side door. His eyebrow lifted, a familiar gesture on an unfamiliar face. "Don't you?"

She did. Of course she did. But, "I'd rather not."

"As would I." His mouth grim, he set a hand on the roof of the car and bowed his head.

Thia felt the hairs on the back of her neck lift, a tingle of awareness that had her reach for her Sight. Fear and curiosity, both.

Whatever he was doing, it caused energy to swirl around him, shimmering like heat on summer roads. He shuddered suddenly, frowning, and Thia instinctively reached out—only to pull the gesture back when he slammed his hand onto the car and swore.

"*Damnad.*"

A chill arrowed through Thia. She had heard that foreign version of a common word before, spoken in that same way. She had been trying to keep Cormac from bleeding to death at the time.

"We need to go," he said now and, coming toward her, he

reached for her arm.

Correction. *Connor Michaels* reached for her arm. His voice held no hint of the British Isles. Was Cormac that good of a mimic? Or perhaps there was a spell for accents, too.

Thia dodged with a quick back-step and held up a hand.

He stopped.

The strange, hard look on his face made her wonder what he saw on hers. She never was good at hiding things, and from him in particular.

"What did you learn?" she managed, struggling to keep her thoughts in line. Zoe was the issue here. Zoe needed her full attention.

"Nothing good." He gestured impatiently. "We can talk on the way, but we need to get you someplace safe."

A good idea, Thia figured, and promptly headed down the drive. At Eclectica, she would be safe from all sorts of things, present company included.

But when she would have turned right, he stopped her by taking a firm hold of her shoulder. "Not the store—Sorry," he said when she shook him off.

He then moved in front of her to block the way. "The store is protected, but not enough."

She hated that he was right. Eclectica's stronger protections wouldn't kick in until after business hours.

But just because he was right didn't mean she had to go easy on him. Whoever he was.

"How do you know?" she demanded as they headed left on Pike. "Is that one of your talents? You can see wards?"

"Yes."

"Why the hotel?" The intended destination was obvious.

"I have a room there. Security is excellent."

Fresh suspicion—the man in the restaurant last night, he'd had a room—struck like a hammer. When Thia would have paused to absorb the impact, he took hold of her arm and ushered her along as before.

They were halfway across the street before she recovered what she hoped was her cool. "A room? Well. Isn't that nice."

He glanced over.

"I mean, it's such a nice hotel," she went on, her certainty building along with her temper. "I stayed there a few weeks ago. The view from my room was fantastic. Do you have a good one from the—which floor did you say?"

He hadn't, and it was a rather clumsy effort on her part, but he was distracted by a car that had turned off Main onto First and was coming their way.

"Seventh," he answered absently.

It was as good as confirmation. She stared at him, unable to look away. Unable, even now, to reconcile his appearance and voice with the truth.

Past doubts and fears abruptly resurrected themselves. He had helped her before, yes, but things between them hadn't begun that way. She slid her hand into her pocket. A disguise was one thing; why not reveal himself to *her?* Unless whatever he was up to involved her too.

"The hotel director is a friend," Thia said with forced light-ness. "Kendra Ross. Have you met?"

"I don't believe so." His grip on her arm was tight.

Master manipulator that Cormac was, he undoubtedly felt something was off.

"I can call her, have her meet us in the lobby." Thia held up her phone. "You understand, of course, why I would feel better with her there."

CHAPTER 7

"**O**f course," Cormac said, afraid that he understood Thia all too well. Somehow, she knew. Perhaps not so as to be certain—she'd confront him directly if she were, wouldn't she? But she certainly suspected. Reluctantly, he removed his hand from her arm.

While she placed her call, he went to the hotel's side entry, slid his room card through the scanner. The lock released. He held open the door for her.

"Yeah, we're coming in now." She breezed past, speaking to her employee-friend. "The private entrance on First. See you in a minute."

Cormac followed, secured the door. The lobby was to the right; to the left, a banquet room getting ready to host a craft faire. Woodwork, yarn, jewelry, ceramics, soap—standard in these things the world over, it seemed. Vendors were smiling, chatting amiably while they put the finishing touches on their booths. The atmosphere buzzed with positive anticipation.

That of the vendors, undoubtedly, made up of their hopes for good times and success ahead. It had a light, silken feel, their anticipation. Cormac's, on the other hand, was dark and jagged—comprised of expected trouble, fear, and inevitable pain.

He performed a quick glamour to prevent his glasses from transitioning to clear indoors, and then he went after Thia, already several steps into the lobby.

Putting her mobile phone away in her pocket, she raised her free hand in greeting to a tall redhead dressed in an executive uniform. Her friend Kendra, entering from the wide lobby's opposite side. The woman did not so much walk as she did march: long, bold steps that conveyed a strength that boded ill as far as Cormac was concerned.

The guests from earlier had mostly cleared out, but a few lingered in the seating configuration nearest the fireplace and its cheery flames.

Sunlight streamed through the abundant windows. Maybe he needn't have concerned himself about his lenses and take the risk of the glamour—ah, but too late now. A few feet from Thia, Kendra stopped, her attention snapping to Cormac like that of a hunter sensing prey.

Sensing the glamour.

She gave him a sharp-eyed stare before Thia reclaimed her attention, hurriedly closing the distance.

Cormac, a short way behind Thia, spoke before either of them could. "You need to send people up to fifty-three Pike Street," he told Kendra. "A woman has been taken against her will."

Thia pivoted to face him. "That's what you saw?"

Kendra moved in close. Protective. "Thia, what—"

"Zoe didn't come to work this morning," Thia told her, and asked him, "She's been taken? By who—"

"Send people." He ignored her for Kendra. "Now."

With a glare, the latter crossed to the reception desk and began speaking with the man on duty.

The energy remnants at Zoe's car were weak and would only get weaker as time passed and more people walked by—or, worse, *through*—the scene. And Cormac couldn't say that he'd felt Cassandra Swinton's presence unless he wanted to arouse more suspicion. (He did not.)

But Murphy's people were capable of identifying her energy patterns and, with any luck, were more skilled than Cormac in detection and location. She was somewhere in the area and needed to be found before she could attempt whatever else she had planned.

Abduction was only the start; he had no doubt.

At least Cassie and whatever associates she had managed to pull in had no idea who was behind Connor Michaels, which meant that it was worth maintaining the pretense. Publicly, at any rate. But surely he could drop it with Thia.

Just as soon as he got up the nerve.

"What did you see? Is Zoe all right?" she asked him now, effectively backing him against the round oaken table set as the room's central focal point. On it was a towering mass of bare, twisted branches decked with ornaments and bundles of mistletoe. Thia didn't appear to be aware of those, and he was tempted to change that.

His sense of self-preservation warned him off.

"Oh, God," she said, and he recalled that she had asked him something. Apparently, she'd moved on. "I need to tell Abby. And the police. I should've called them right away. Dammit." She took out her mobile. "I've wasted so much time—"

"Wait a bit on that one." He put his hand over the phone's screen. His fingers curved around hers. The contact sparked, warm and familiar. Cormac could have kicked himself for his carelessness.

Thia's hazel eyes widened with what could only be absolute, furious recognition. He watched with fascinated dread as her stare hardened and her bow-shaped lips pressed into a thin line. Forcibly holding back her tongue, he imagined.

His own felt thick. "Let Murphy's people have a go at the scene first," he said, and willed her to let him continue with his masquerade. He contemplated using a compulsion spell, so deep went the need. Ah, hell, he could admit it: the fear. But he'd had trouble enough before with her on that front thanks to a protective charm she wore. And now there were her newly absorbed powers to consider. No telling how they might respond or how she might wield them against a magic-based threat. And *then,* even if Cormac succeeded, her friend Kendra obviously had some skill with detecting spell use. She was close enough to notice.

Slowly, Thia extricated her hand from his.

"Please," he said, "I can explain, but not now. Let me—" He broke off at the flash of barely contained power in her eyes.

"How *dare* you."

The floor trembled beneath his feet. A slight vibration that rattled the ornaments in the branches overhead but did not seem to be affecting the rest of the room.

Because it was Thia. She was bleeding power. He moved in, grabbed her wrist. Held on when she would have yanked it away.

"Thia." He stood so close he could feel her breath, smell the sweetened coffee she must have had not long before. He kept his voice low. "Do what you will to me later. I deserve it. But not now. Not here. Let it go."

Cormac loosened his own protections just enough so that he could draw on her surfeit of energy. A small current jumped to him, used his nerves as pathways. Muscle tingled. Marrow heated.

So pure, the power Thia had received—and, astonishingly, it had remained so. Cormac had siphoned a good portion from her at Brodgar, but it had adapted, merged with what other power he already possessed. Thia's remained unchanged. He didn't know what to make of that, or what it might mean for her.

"Let go," he repeated.

She had tensed at his initial draw but hadn't tried to pull away. Nor did she fight him when he took more. He wasn't after a lot. This was not for his own gain but to help her to regain control.

Her eyes stayed bright but the floor's vibrations ceased.

Carefully, Cormac released her wrist, let both his hands rest at his sides. There was nothing for it now, no getting around who he was. "Thia, I—"

She jabbed his chest. Hard. Two fingers, directly onto his sternum. She might have regained emotional control, but she was no less furious.

"What are you doing here?" she said tightly, leaning close. "And why aren't you...*you?* No, wait. You're right. Now is not the time. I'm too upset. Too unstable." She spun on her heel, stormed over to reception.

And left Cormac standing like an idiot, his mouth agape, his thoughts scrambled. He rubbed the bruised spot. Not too far, as irony would have it, from his heart.

Kendra was no longer at the front desk. After a quick, lost look around, Thia took out her phone.

"Wait." He started toward her.

Scowling fiercely, she put the phone to her ear. "I'm calling Abby. If that's all right with you." She put her back to him before he could so much as nod.

Movement above caught his eye. *Ah.* Kendra, grim-faced, stood on the second floor's railed overlook. She pulled back, out of view. Headed his way, he didn't doubt.

Soon enough, the lift chimed and opened its doors. Kendra walked straight for him, demanding, "What did you sense?"

The abduction, not what had just happened with Thia, was to be the priority, apparently. He felt a measure of relief.

Not that he didn't need to take care with what he might reveal about himself and his identity. Never mind that Thia could unmask him in a second—if she hadn't already. With her back to him and speaking too quietly for his ears without an augmentation spell, she could be giving him up right then to Abby. To anyone. He had no way of knowing who might really be on the other end of her phone call.

Ah, hell. Cormac settled on simply, "Transportation spell."

The ability to interpret type from energy remnants was not an unusual skill, therefore not much could be inferred from his answer.

"And you can tell it involved a—quote—'woman against her will?'" Kendra's skepticism was palpable.

"A logical assumption." Adopting a casual pose, Cormac slid his hands into his pockets, shrugged. "A woman is missing. If she had gone willingly, she wouldn't leave her friends and coworkers to wonder, would she? She'd have found a way to tell them not to worry."

Thia finished her call, looked over to Kendra. "I let Abby know I was with you."

"Good," her friend said and, leaving Cormac, crossed to her with one arm outstretched. Herding. "Let's go to my office. You can tell me everything that happened this morning." She tossed Cormac a dismissive, "Was there anything else?"

Of course there was. Too much else and all of it nigh on impossible for him to disclose.

Granted, emotion clouded his thinking; but it was for Thia's sake—and, by extension, the sake of everyone around her— that he'd adopted his damn disguises. Cassie, among others, could not know he was here. Could not be allowed to suspect that he cared.

Yet surely now that Thia knew the truth, he could go with them and privately explain himself.

His pulse pounded as his chest grew tight. To explain, he would have to delve into things far too personal. Things he did his damnedest to keep locked well away.

Thia would ask why he'd left her that night. Why he hadn't

contacted her since.

Why he was here now.

She already had asked that one, hadn't she? Then told him quite definitely that this was not the time.

Kendra was eying him with distrust. As was Thia, and then some. That it should affect him was...surprising.

He couldn't do this. "Not at the moment, no."

"Good," Kendra said, and resumed walking.

Thia remained, her face pale. Cold.

"If you need anything," Cormac began, his voice rough, "the hotel here has my num—"

"Thia?" Kendra called from the edge of the lobby.

"Coming." And yet she didn't move. Cormac thought for a moment she was going to say something more—to him—but she soon thought better of it. Her mouth firmed and, without a word, she strode after her friend.

He watched her go.

Why was it, he wondered, that doing the right thing where she was concerned often felt so terribly wrong?

When she was out of sight, he blew out a breath and stared contemplatively at his shoes. The shine of patent leather; the contrast of their rich black against the floor's light granite. He needed a plan. What was Cassie's? There must be a way for him to stop her without involving anyone else. Thia, most particularly. His reputation for preferring to work alone was not undeserved.

He would return to the scene. With Thia safe in the Landmark, he could go back, couple his Sight with some targeted spells to try to divine where Cassie had gone with her victim. Thia's friend.

Thia had a lot of friends. He had said as much to her earlier, and meant it. He couldn't count even one for himself. It had always been safest that way for all concerned. Friends could be used as leverage. Friends became a liability.

He'd taken two steps toward the door when his mobile rang. He stopped, took it from his jacket pocket. The number was not recognized.

"Hello?"

"The view from the roof is quite fine at the moment, Mr. Michaels," drawled the man Cormac didn't particularly want to deal with. "Do join me."

He did not mistake Murphy's statement for a question. Nor did he bother with a reply.

Returning his phone to his pocket, he headed up.

● ○ ●

"Who is he?" Kendra asked, turning one of the chairs by the desk to face Thia, seated on the small couch that had been set against the wall. For a compact office, it managed to hold a lot of furniture without feeling cramped. Kendra sat, fixed her with a formidable glare.

Thia would have to be truthful; Kendra would see through falsehood in a blink—and not only because Thia was a terrible liar. Kendra might not have Abby's gift of insight (or whatever it was), she hadn't become the director of a prestigious hotel without being adept at reading people.

But in this case, there were several truths to choose from.

"He was a customer at Eclectica yesterday," Thia said, going with the easiest. "I ran into him while I was looking for Zoe, and he volunteered to help. We went up to where her car was parked, and I guess he was able to pick up on what happened. I don't know. I couldn't."

"It's early in your training. You'll get there," Kendra said, dismissing that worry. She leaned forward. "But, really, who *is* he? What do you know about him? I saw him with his hand on you just now. He was drawing power—and you let him."

"I was losing control. He helped me get it back."

"Thia." She sat back, clearly distressed. "You can't just let strangers take power like that. I was there—or close enough. You could've let me know you were having trouble. I could've helped you with it. But you knew that." A curious look came over her face. "You knew that...and still you let him be the one. Who *is* he? And don't give me that crap about his being a customer. He's more to you than that."

So much for the easiest version.

Thia sighed. Braced herself. "He's Cormac."

Kendra swore. Profusely. And then shot to her feet to pace the narrow stretch of carpet between her desk and the door. "Of course. Ah, of course, sure. There were similarities. The masked power, using a glamour. Dammit, and I let him go." She pivoted, lunged for the doorknob.

"Wait, no." Thia stood. She didn't want to deal with Cormac right now, and she knew it wouldn't be a good idea for Kendra to, either. Not with emotions running so hot. "I don't think he'll be too hard to find later. If we need to. He has a room here." And a purchase yet to pick up at Eclectica. (Although she wouldn't count on that.)

Kendra gaped at her. "A room? Under what name?"

"Connor Michaels, maybe. On the seventh floor," she added with reluctance. But Kendra would find out soon enough.

"The same floor as the man from last night."

Thia cringed. Nodded.

"Dammit," Kendra said again, and dropped into her chair. "Thia, what the hell is going on? What's he trying to do here? Why the disguise?"

"Yeah, wouldn't I love to know." Thia sat. "He isn't a part of whatever happened to Zoe."

"No?"

"It wasn't an act, up at her car. Whatever he saw rattled him. Next thing I knew, he was all but dragging me here. Because I'd be safe. His words."

Kendra rubbed her hand across her mouth—a noted habit

when she was thinking hard, and one reason it was good she didn't wear a lot of lipstick. "What makes him think *you* need protecting? Other than the fact that Zoe works for you, what makes him connect something happening to her, to *you?*" She drummed her fingers on her lips, then, "Maybe he's just being overprotective—which, honestly, I'd agree with. Better safe than sorry." She frowned. "But I'm more inclined to think he knows something and isn't sharing."

Knowing what she did of Cormac, Thia had to agree. "They *are* connected, aren't they." Not a question. "Someone is using Zoe to get to me."

"Unless Cormac has proof," Kendra said, crossing her arms as she leaned back, "we can only assume—and you know the saying about assumptions and asses. To play devil's advocate for a second, was Zoe into anything dangerous? I've only met her a few times in passing. I have a hard time picturing her being into anything close to illegal, but last year a restaurant got shut down for running a black market operation out the back.

"Those guys seemed squeaky clean, too. Right up until the cops hauled them away in cuffs." She shrugged. "Might Zoe have ticked somebody off? Have trouble with an ex?"

Thia's mind was still hung up on the mention of the black market bust; it took her a few seconds to track the questions that had followed. "I can't imagine the first two—dangerous activities or ticking someone off. As to the third, she's never mentioned anything like that."

"Would she have?"

Another good question. "Maybe. Maybe not. We get along well. I might call her a friend of sorts, except I hardly know anything about her. If I've learned one lesson in the past two months, it's how much I can not know about people. Even the ones that I think I know well enough," she added pointedly but without malice.

If she had known then what she did now about Abby and

Kendra—about so many people in Granite Springs (and the rest of the world, for that matter, but who's counting)—how much would have happened differently? Would she have gone haring off to London like she had?

Would she have believed that she couldn't turn to anyone for help?

She might still have acted alone: "Tell no one," had been the paramount instruction. But she wouldn't have *felt* so alone. And she wouldn't have been so thoroughly unprepared for all that she encountered.

"Abby couldn't tell you everything," Kendra said with care. "Not without...." She made a gesture of helplessness.

"Not without shattering my false understanding of reality?" Thia supplied. She hadn't known the truth of the world in which they—and she—lived. In which *everyone* lived, whether aware of it or not. That magic was real and its benefits and dangers were all around.

More benefits in Granite Springs than dangers, from what Thia knew, until last October. It had been her fault, although indirectly, that danger had come then. Less than two months later, it seemed to be her fault again.

"We meant well," Kendra said. "Abby said you made such a point of wanting a 'normal life.' Especially after your broken engagement."

"Ugh." Thia winced. She hadn't thought of Stewart in what felt like ages. "I did want a normal life. Or thought I did—but that's the trouble. I didn't understand what normal truly is."

Normal was the ability to wield magical power and perform spells. Normal was evil sorcerers and the *Sidhe*. Or, more to the point, a half-*Sidhe* who took up more of her mental and emotional space than he likely deserved.

"I'd rather live with the truth of things," Thia insisted. "Not the illusion."

Kendra's cell phone rang. She slid it from her back pocket,

answered with a terse, "Yes?"

Thia could hear a voice speaking on the other end but not well enough to make out the words.

"You're sure?" Kendra asked after a time, and then closed her eyes briefly at the response.

Whatever the news, it wasn't good.

"Right." Kendra's troubled gaze came to rest on Thia. "Yes, apprise Murphy of the situation. She's got reason enough to go after us all." She ended the call.

Thia was tired. Of being scared, of being overwhelmed by new things she barely understood (and could barely believe). She had fallen down a rabbit hole that had nearly killed her, and she hadn't reached bottom yet. She had no choice but to face whatever trouble had come—again. But the thought of having to made her want to cry.

"That was Murphy's guy up at Zoe's car." Kendra told her. "He says there wasn't much to read, and he's one of the best there is. If we're to believe Cormac about his reading of the scene, he's got quite a knack."

Thia didn't care about his talents at the moment. "Do we believe him? About someone doing"—she recalled the term he'd used— "a transportation spell?"

"Yeah, we do. Barton detected faint traces. Something old and dark."

"Could he tell where Zoe is now? Is she okay?"

"He's still working on it. The call was because he thinks he knows who cast it and needed to warn us."

"Who?" Thia asked, but she knew. It had been in Kendra's response on the phone: *She.* "Cassie?"

Kendra nodded. "It's starting."

Revenge.

● ○ ●

As the only other person in the rooftop garden, Murphy was

easy for Cormac to spot. And he had told the truth: The view was quite fine. It was also cold. What had been a soft, wintry breeze at street level was a sharp wind that many more storeys up. Neither the patio heaters nor their spells were activated.

He crossed to stand to Murphy's left. He didn't receive so much as a glance.

Together they looked out across the hotel's rear lot with its overflow parking. Several people in hotel uniform made their way to the street above. Pike. The house with Zoe's car was well within view.

Cormac flipped up his jacket collar then returned his hands to the side pockets. "Cassandra took her."

"Where?"

"I couldn't tell."

At last, Murphy slanted him a look. "What *could* you tell?"

"Not much." Cormac took a frustrated breath, blew it out. "She had help. Two, possibly four people. It left one hell of a mark, transporting so many like that. There's a lot of mess from other spells, too—something to subdue the girl, another to conceal their presence beforehand. They didn't bother to clean up after. Maybe your people can do better."

Murphy grunted. "Or there's nothing to be found that the *claimsech* doesn't mind us knowing. Including that she's here. Does she know *you* are?"

"I suspected she was. So she might suspect the same of me."

"Especially if she knows you have feelings for the lovely Ms. McDaniel."

Cormac went still. He hadn't been so obvious, had he? Hell, how could he when not even *he* could say what those feelings were?

Reading into the silence, Murphy grinned. "She'd be a fool not to suspect."

Cormac didn't waste time arguing about feelings he might or might not have. "And Cassie is no fool. Mad for vengeance and power, but no fool."

"It wasn't only to her that I was referring." And with that cryptic remark, Murphy turned and walked away, toward the hotel door.

Cormac remained, his gaze on the scene playing out around the car. Murphy must have meant Thia; that she'd be a fool not to suspect—suspect *what?* Feelings that Cormac himself couldn't define? Or simply that he'd be in Granite Springs?

What a mess, and much of it his own making.

"I'm after making a call to our mutual acquaintances in St. James's." Murphy's voice carried from the door.

The Brigantium, he meant.

Cormac supposed it was inevitable. And probably in everyone's best interest, much as that pained him to admit. But he didn't have to encourage. "Up to you."

"So it is." Murphy's expression was wry. "We might as well make use of them, seeing as they already have someone here."

They did? *Ah, hell.* Of course they did.

CHAPTER 8

In the second-level basement of the Brigantium's primary base of operations, Beatrice Meriwether and Quentin Reynolds were well into the third straight hour of barely tolerating one another's company. To Quentin's mind (and he presumed to Beatrice's as well) it was a situation that had become far too frequent since the society had been found compromised by followers of Idris Cathmor.

The Closet, as this newly relocated supply room was called, was in actuality the size of a two-car garage. It only felt like a closet for being dark and overcrowded. Beggars, however, could not be choosers. Relocation had been an urgent matter of security, and this was all the space Archives had to spare within its subteranean network of rooms, itself being nearly at capacity.

"This could work to advantage," Beatrice said, not for the first time. She opened the glass front to one of several herb cabinets.

The proposal for Quentin to travel to Granite Springs had been fast-tracked; if the new systems were working as they should, the necessary approvals would await him by the time he finished here.

He, not they. Beatrice's input in this was neither welcome nor required.

"Only you would find a positive in the vengeful actions of a madwoman," Quentin said in response. Ignoring the glare his less-than-respectful tone received (really, she ought to be grateful he'd held his tongue *this* long), he carefully set a vial of belladonna into his traveling case.

"Constant negativity such as yours must be trying," she said after a moment. "But even you must see this is an opportunity to sway Thia to our side."

"It isn't a matter of sides," he said, displeased to be dragged into the same discussion they'd had numerable times already. "She wants to weigh her options. That isn't active opposition. She doesn't trust that we're the best place for her at this time. Given our current instability, you can't possibly blame her."

"We can keep her safe." Beatrice closed the cabinet door only to open the one adjacent. "Remind her of that. Whatever is happening in Granite Springs would not happen here."

It was such a patently ridiculous statement that Quentin found himself rendered speechless.

As his silence lengthened, she turned. Her shrewd, pale eyes widened with apparent bewilderment. "What?"

"Surely you aren't that naive," he said incautiously. "We are weeks from completing the 'interviews,' as you prefer to call them. We could still—and undoubtedly do—have traitors in our midst. And yet you're willing to make such claims as to the safety of someone like her?" Temper sent his lower back into spasm, and he shifted more weight onto his cane. "There is no way of—"

"Thia could stay with me." Beatrice turned away, rose onto her toes to examine a high shelf. The move brought her into a weak shaft of light; her braided hair gleamed silver.

The same color he presumed his own would turn when—or if—he reached her age. Mature gray as opposed to the darker, premature version he'd sported since...Well.

Since.

"The grounds are well protected, and I've certainly got the room," Beatrice said.

Quentin refused to rise to the bait and instead checked the contents of his case. Nearly done.

Beatrice apparently thought otherwise. "There ought to be more tincture of goldenseal here," she said, and proceeded to root behind the bottles and boxes to either side of the shelf's vacant space. "Did you already take some?"

"Yes." He glared at the back of her head. It was his mission, damn it all. His packing. "Six."

"Ah. That's fine, then," she said blithely, already on her way to another cabinet. Doubtless she'd seek out something else he had already considered. "I would hate to think we still had problems with theft."

"Not since the new systems," Quentin said, turning to get an extra packet of basil.

The theft-prevention spells should have been put in place long ago. Even if there hadn't been the concern of wide-scale treachery, many of the Closet's items were rare and carried a tempting price. Thankfully, it had not been difficult to speed approvals, either on the spells or the costly tamper-detection alarm that he'd designed. All of that had gone smoothly and, thus far, without complaint.

The computerized checkout, on the other hand, had been trouble from the moment he had propsed it. There was no more efficient way to manage the myriad spellwork supplies, especially as the recent increase in demand coincided with a staff shortage—but bloody hell, had membership resisted. That the damned program had been so unpredictably glitchy hadn't helped. Thus far, more supporters had been lost than gained.

But glitches could be fixed. Or so the programmers assured

him. Repeatedly. They had an update in the works...which he needed to check on before he left. He pivoted away from the shelves, sucked in a sharp breath when his hip protested the abrupt move.

Beatrice had come to stand opposite him at the table and rummage in his case, changing his arrangement. "You aren't taking any sweltered toad venom?"

He ignored her. And, because she watched him closely, he endured his hip's ache when he could have eased some of it by shifting his stance. He had learned long ago to never show weakness in front of Beatrice Meriwether.

"You never did have a taste for the Natural Arts," she said with an indifference he knew to be an act. Some of her most poisonous darts were thrown offhand, yet she seldom missed.

And sure enough, as if summoned, memories of mandatory childhood practice intruded. As she had doubtless intended. Countless hours spent learning to prepare the ingredients for vile elixirs and potions. Beatrice at work over her home fire. Her cauldron and the godawful smells.

"No," he said with little intonation, "I never did."

To avoid her smirk, he moved to the crystal cabinet. He had already what he wanted from the wide, shallow drawers, but he had been thinking about getting Thia a wand. Something to assist with focus and direction.

"Such a shame," Beatrice said—too casually this time, and he braced himself. Bottles clinked as she continued to poke about. "But I suppose it couldn't be helped. You do take after your father so."

Well. He hadn't braced for *that.* "Do I."

"Goodness, haven't I mentioned that before?"

Oh, she knew very well that she hadn't. Almost at random and with motions stiff and furious, Quentin selected a short, crystal-tipped wand and then wrapped it in purple velvet.

"Perhaps I've forgotten," he said, and made his way back to

his case. He dropped the wand inside and shut the lid. The latch secured with a sharp click. He didn't bother doing up the lock; there was the new procedure yet to go through.

He took up the handle, prepared for the imbalance when he hefted the unwieldy thing to carry it at his side. His bad side. Really, he ought to get a nice modern one with wheels and a tow handle. But this antique made of leather and wood had been a graduation gift from his uncle. Quentin had intended to use the whole of a lengthy career.

He was loathe to let go of any more of those youthful plans than he had already, no matter their insignificance.

"All finished?" Beatrice peered at the watch suspended from a ribbon on her jacket. "Perfect."

Quentin gestured for her to precede him to the check-out, not so much out of courtesy but as a sop to his pride. His gait could be described as uneven at the best of times. With the heavy case, it could only be called awkward.

In the outer room, the clerk got up from his chair to meet them at a narrow counter. "Find what you needed, Madam? Sir?" he added at Quentin's foul look.

Hamish MacGillicuddy, middle-aged father of three, darts champion at his local, with a strong interest in Druid lore and a high tolerance for solitary sitting.

"We did," Beatrice said, gifting him with a believable smile. She hadn't risen to the top without picking up a few tricks. Winning people over was perhaps her best.

On occasion, however, she couldn't resist her true nature. Her smile turned wry. "Whether it is in *there*"—she gestured to Quentin's case—"is another matter altogether."

Hamish froze like a man who sensed the danger of getting caught up in a private argument. No fool, he.

Quentin set the traveling case on the counter. "This should do it. Thank you."

While Hamish registered the contents with the aid of the

new system's barcode scanner, Beatrice put him back at ease with light, textbook-perfect conversation. Quentin tuned it out, considered instead his various options for getting Thia into the society's fold sooner rather than later.

Charm was out: he no longer had any to offer. Besides, that had been Beatrice's tack, and all it had got them was Thia's obstinate, "I need time."

Coercion was out: not only could such an approach make an enemy out of Thia, but also of her friends. Powerful friends such as hers would make powerful enemies.

Fear was...potentially useful.

Thia's hesitation to join them had fear at its root, didn't it?

All hesitation stemmed from fear. Fear of making the wrong choice. Fear of the unknown. Fear of danger. Of disaster. Of pain. And, where fear already existed, it was a simple matter of giving the right encouragement (the right fertilizer, if he cared to continue the analogy) to make that fear grow. Thrive, even. Then Quentin could step in and promise protection.

What ironic rot.

"I'll undo the anti-theft spells now, ma'am, if you'll pardon my change in attention," Hamish said to Beatrice, in essence ending her inane chatter. He took a long, ornate key from a secure drawer and then proceeded to touch it to every item. The contact broke the spells that would have locked down the room and summoned armed guards had a still-protected item been taken past the door.

The process was intentionally tedious as a matter of safety, and rather theatrical in the choice of prop...because Beatrice had insisted. And, damn her, she'd had a point. Keys had long been symbols of power and responsibility, and clearly Hamish took pride in the implication that he was a man in possession of both. Any object could have been made into the precondition of the spell's unraveling, but would he have felt the same about a paperclip?

Hamish returned the key to the drawer and then tapped the system's touchscreen, sending an itemized list to the printer. Quentin would need to sign it, and a copy would go in his file.

Was fear the key to winning Thia over? She wouldn't need to trust the Brigantium completely (after all, Quentin did not). But if she trusted them *enough,* she could be swayed.

The situation in Granite Springs could be very useful with that.

His hand clenched on his cane's chased silver knob. He did so hate it when Beatrice was right.

● ○ ●

Eclectica, Granite Springs

Three coffee urns, the plastic kind with the high spigot and large pump-button in the top, sat on the café's battered sideboard along with spoons, napkins, and a variety of sugars and sugar substitutes. Dark roast, medium, light, decaf. Thia filled a hand-thrown mug with dark, followed it with two packs of sweetener. This was Officer Briswell's third cup.

For the past forty minutes, as café business went on as best it could around them, she and Abby had been telling the city police officer all they could about Zoe and her disappearance (minus the magical elements). Downstairs, Kendra and few associates she'd brought in were posing as customers in case of additional trouble.

To Thia's mind it was not going well—the interview, that was. She assumed things downstairs were fine.

The officer was amiable enough, interested enough, but in Thia's opinion wasn't concerned enough. There was no sense of urgency no matter how much she and Abby tried to convey one. It would be easier if they could tell him about the energy readings et cetera, but if he wasn't a believer, that could do more harm than good. He might write them off as New Age weirdos and even charge them with wasting police time.

Thia stirred in enough half-and-half to turn the coffee tan, and then took it to the table. She set it before him, retook her place beside a glowering Abby.

"Right," he said after downing half the coffee in one go. "As I was telling Ms. Collins, there isn't enough here for a missing person case. She hasn't been out of contact long enough. And while you say she isn't the type to neglect her responsibilities and she said she'd be in early—she could have changed her mind." He drummed his notepad with the capped end of his pen. "People can and do take unexpected, seemingly out of character actions for any number of reasons. Or none at all. Things happen."

"They do," Abby said. She leaned forward, both hands tight around her own mug of coffee. "*Bad* things happen. Maybe not as often here as other places, but they do happen. It *has* happened." Unexpectedly, she slammed a hand on the table. Liquid sloshed. "A bad thing has happened to *Zoe Forbes.*"

"I understand that's what you believe, Ms. Collins, but do you have proof? Anything that suggests she's in danger?" He sounded sympathetic but his gaze was impersonal as it moved from Abby to Thia and then back again. "I'm not saying your feelings are wrong here—Lord knows I've been saved by gut instinct a time or two. But I'm bound by procedure."

"You're saying you can't do *anything?*" Abby's fair complexion was a perfect canvas for anger. Red bloomed high across her cheekbones.

"No, ma'am, that's not what I'm saying. I'm saying that it's a problem not having anything concrete to—"

"Ah, Officer Briswell." Murphy's voice sounded from behind Thia, startling them all. He must have come in through the store. "I was hoping to catch you."

"Mr. Murphy." The officer sprang to his feet. "Good morn—afternoon. Y-you've been looking for me?"

"Looking? Not at all." Strolling into view, Murphy appeared bored. "Your Chief kindly gave me your last known location.

By now these ladies must have told you where their Zoe was last seen, so naturally it's surprised I am to find you still here."

Officer Briswell opened his mouth to speak, but Murphy's attention had moved on. Giving Thia and, surprisingly, Abby a brilliant smile, he set his hand on the back of the officer's vacated chair. "May I?"

"Please," Thia said, more than a little confused.

"Oh, yes, do," Abby seconded. "We can't offer much of the menu, since Zoe isn't here. But we've plenty of—"

"An espresso would be lovely." Murphy sat. "Thanks for the offer."

With a sound very like a growl, Abby got up. She went to place the order with Lynette at the counter.

Officer Briswell cleared his throat. "You spoke with Chief Nash?"

"Not more than ten minutes ago," Murphy said. "He assured me that every available resource is to be put toward resolving this terrible situation. To the highest level of satisfaction."

"He said that?"

"Indeed. Ah." Murphy's attention shifted as Abby returned, and he adjusted his posture so she could set the small cup and saucer near his left hand on the table. "Ta, love. That looks just the thing."

Abby sat down, crossed her arms in belligerent silence.

"Every resource," Murphy emphasized to Officer Briswell. "The state lads from Forensics Services are keen to go over the young woman's car."

"They are?" Briswell fumbled his notebook and pen, nearly dropping them.

"Already on their way, I should think." Murphy took a sip of espresso, then, "That's very nice, it is. A local supplier?"

"Yes," Thia said while Abby continued to fume. "University Roasters. On the boulevard."

"Very fine. I might have to see if they—" He turned as if surprised to find Officer Briswell still there. "Is there something more you need in order to get started?"

"N-no, I think…I think I've got everything." Unsteadily, the officer tucked away his notebook. "Thank you."

"Certainly." Murphy lifted his cup, tossed back the rest of the espresso.

"Ladies." Officer Briswell hurried to the back door.

After he'd gone, Abby leaned hard on the table and fixed Murphy with a glare. "What the hell was that?"

He set his cup on its saucer with a sharp, porcelain clink. "What that was, Collins, was my assistance." Each word was spoken with precision and hard, like pebbles picked up and thrown. "You're welcome."

"Thank you, Murphy," Thia said hastily. "However you got the police to move on this, we appreciate it."

"Money, that's how," Abby said with scorn. "And his weight as a big, important businessman. He threw both around and of course everyone jumped to do whatever he asked."

Thia couldn't understand the anger. "What he asked was for help finding Zoe."

"Yeah, and what's in it for him?" Abby pointed an accusatory finger. "Come on, Murphy, you never do anything that's not in your own interest. What is it this time?"

Murphy's dark eyes were wide, his tone mocking. "I can't be interested in a young woman's safety for her own sake?"

"Not even if she were your sister," Abby snapped, only to suck in a shocked breath.

Silence dropped around them like a bell jar, heavy and thick. Chatter continued at other tables but sounded muffled. The hiss of steaming milk grew distant, as if the few feet to the counter had quadrupled.

It was cold, too, in their silence. An icy, unnatural cold that, Thia realized with dread, had Murphy as its source. He sat as still as stone. His lips were pressed into a thin, harsh line. His eyes, always dark and difficult to read, appeared nearly black.

"Have you a sister?" Abby's voice was hoarse. Stricken. "Ah, hell. Declan, I didn't—"

"But of course you have the right of it," he said abruptly, his brogue particularly thick. "Sure, I'm only ever after my own interests. When Idris's *claimsech* of a daughter swore revenge, she included me in it, or don't you recall? And so I merely sought advantage in setting the forces of law on her trail." He stood, nodded to Thia. "Ms. McDaniel, good day." His dark gaze flicked to Abby but didn't settle. "Ms. Collins."

Wordlessly, they watched him exit the way he'd come, down the stairs to the main floor. The cold went with him. Ambient sounds resumed at full volume.

"Abby," Thia murmured when he was out of sight. She felt horrible. And horrified. What sort of power was that, to make the air go cold? To mute sounds?

"I know, I know." On a moan, Abby covered her face with her hands. Thia struggled to make out the rest of her words. "He makes me so crazy, I don't know half the shit that comes out of my mouth."

"I've seen you keep it together with even the most obnoxious customers. Why can't you with him?"

"He starts it. Mostly." Brushing back her flyway curls, Abby lifted her head. "I can't read him. With most people, there's something, some emotion that comes across." She shrugged. "I can't say that's comforting, since it isn't and sometimes I wish I didn't pick up on it. But it's something I expect, maybe even rely on. Imagine if you suddenly didn't have any visual or verbal cues to go by—how would you gauge a customer's mood?"

"Intuition?" Thia suggested, but for all she knew, that was the product of visual and verbal cues.

"When someone is sad," Abby said, "I might feel it as if it's my own. Anger, excitement, joy. Depending on the strength of the emotion, I might also pick up some of what's *behind* it. The cause." She stared at the empty espresso cup. Murphy's cup. "He's an emotional dead zone. But instead of feeling like nothing, it's aggravating. Like shards of glass, poking at me. Slicing."

"So you poke and slice back?"

Abby nodded, sadness or perhaps guilt drawing down her face. "Until I feel something from him. Any emotion at all. Anger is an easy one to get."

"Is that what you got this time?" Thia asked, dubious. She hadn't Abby's gift, or talent, or whatever it might be called, but she knew anger well enough. Anger was hot. Anger lashed out. This had been the opposite. Cold and directed inward, like a vacuum.

"No. Goddess, no," Abby said. "Give me shards of glass any day."

Thia was inclined to agree. "That was awful."

"You felt it too?"

"I felt something. Cold, mainly. And everything got quiet. It was a lot worse for you, I bet."

Abby made a noncommital noise.

When nothing more followed it, Thia asked, "What made you say that, about not even if Zoe were his sister?"

"I have no idea." Abby's eyes were wide. "It just came out. I don't know. I must have picked up on something without realizing it. But I shouldn't have said it. I'm so used to being pissed off by him that I didn't think...I mean, he's not a good person. You've heard the rumors about what he does."

"Mercenary stuff." Thia couldn't exactly fault him on that. If he hadn't brought an armed force charging to the rescue on Orkney there was no telling which way the battle would have gone.

"Mercenary stuff isn't rumor." Abby leaned back. "I meant

his business dealings."

"Ah." Thia hadn't heard any of those rumors, then, but she wasn't going to ask now. There were so many more immediate things to worry about than how Declan Murphy might run his hotels.

"When I asked him if he has a sister," Abby said, frowning thoughtfully, "he didn't answer. But he was still...broadcasting. I could read him. That much, anyway."

"And?"

"He doesn't. Not anymore." Abby crossed her arms over her chest as if cold. "He did, though. What I felt—what we *all* felt—was loss."

● ○ ●

Brigantium Headquarters, London

While Quentin's opinions of the Brigantium might vary given the day and his own mood, those regarding the building the society called home remained constant. He loved it.

How could he not? It had been designed to evoke that very response.

Neoclassical, it was a grand contradiction: conservative in form; unabashedly opulent in style with its marble and carved wood, its crystal chandeliers and sconces, its polished brass and gold leaf. Here was wealth, the building proclaimed. Here was power. Stability.

Whether the current crisis would prove it all to be a mere façade, only time would tell, Quentin mused darkly as he and Beatrice passed through the entrance hall to the main doors.

He had first set foot here as a small boy—brought by the same woman walking beside him tonight—and he had been awed, exhilarated that he should one day make his life within such a setting; where history was palpable and the thrill of momentous decisions and truly important goings-ons was in the very air one breathed.

He was much more jaded now, much more embittered, but no less awed. No less exhilarated, truth be told. And didn't Beatrice know it, and use it to her will.

A young man with a manila envelope clutched in his hands trotted toward them, his oxfords making loud, rapid slaps on the floor's black and white mosaic. Their paths crossed near the central medallion, and wordlessly—breathlessly—he held the envelope out to Beatrice.

She took it with a brusque, "Any instruction?"

"No, m'um," he managed.

"Very good." Beatrice dismissed the young man with a flick of her hand and, as he bowed and backed away, she lifted the flap to withdraw an immediately recognizable gold chain and pendant. It dangled from her aged fingers, swayed slightly to and fro, calling to Quentin as it played in the light.

Studying it, Beatrice told him, "Eben and his team believe they've managed to craft a spell which takes into account the discovered vulnerability." She extended it to him, an offering he couldn't refuse. "I thought you should have yours back."

He quirked a brow. "With the new spell, of course?"

"Of course."

No sense of humor, had Beatrice. He shouldn't have let it bother him, but they had spent far too much time together today and his temper was short. He spoke without thought: "How nice to think you care."

He regretted the words immediately.

Beatrice's face drained of color, then flushed as something akin to fury burned deep within the narrowing black of her pupils. "I have always cared, Quentin Sigmund Aloysius," she said sharply. "The evidence is in every breath you take. You are my—"

"Yes, I am, aren't I," he snapped, chagrin making him behave even more the ass. Wedging his cane between his upper arm and side, he snatched the protection charm from her hand to examine it on his palm. A nice way of avoiding eye-contact, that.

It looked no different than it always had: the stylized face of a gorgon; fangs, disproportionately large eyes, and all.

It felt the same, as well, apart from a strange chill. Not one of temperature, although the metal would warm slightly when worn. No, it seemed...hardened somehow. Closed. An interesting reflection of the change the Brigantium must undergo, he supposed, and moved his hand to his breast pocket. He let the chain and bespelled pendant drop inside. He'd put it on eventually.

Beatrice reached into the envelope and took out another set. The design was the same but done in silver. The usual choice for a woman.

He was surprised. When they'd discussed replacing the one Thia had been given by Leticia—her old novitiate's pendant, and equally vulnerable to threat from someone wearing either version, novitiate or full member—Beatrice had come down against it. She had argued that Thia was neither and, besides, wasn't that a nice carrot to dangle?

"You've changed your mind?" Quentin asked.

Beatrice frowned. "Changed my—Ah. Not at all. This isn't for Thia, but for Edith. It wasn't ready when I sent her, and since you'll be working with her, I'd appreciate it if you'd—"

"I'll be what?" He nearly dropped the traveling case.

"Working together," his infuriating mother said. Her brows lifted in fake innocence above smug, amused eyes. "Didn't I mention?"

"No, Bea. Somehow you neglected to mention you felt the need to saddle me with one of your damned meddlesome—"

She clucked her tongue. "Careful now, dear, before you say something else you'll regret. You've done enough of that for one day, have you not?" Her free hand took hold of his coat while the other dropped the silver charm in with his gold one.

She gave the outside fabric a pat, smoothed the lapels. Then she resumed the walk.

It took Quentin a moment to rein in his temper; he caught up with her outside, atop the set of steps down to the street. He handed his case to one of the attendant guards who then transfered it to the sleek car waiting below. Exhaust plumed from dual pipes while the engine purred.

Above the heart of London's Clubland, thick clouds pressed close, the city's electric glow turning them a vague, eerie shade of peach. The night air was cold enough, sharp enough, for snow. Traffic congested to the left on Pall Mall, likely having trouble merging onto Cockspur Street. Quentin stifled a sigh.

His hesitation here beneath the portico, his disinclination to begin this journey, was instinctive and within reason. Only a fool stepped unreservedly into danger.

"Arthur sends you his best," Beatrice said into the prolonged pause.

Quentin snorted. "Does he."

Neither looking at the other, mother and son stood stiffly, close enough so that their arms nearly brushed. She was much shorter than he, and thinner than he remembered from any time before.

"He would have come to see you off, of course," she added eventually, "but for his meeting with the Lord Mayor."

"Of course." Quentin wondered why she bothered. Setting his cane's ferrule on the next step down, he prepared his hip for the task. "I'll be off, then."

"I'll leave you here." Something in her tone—a gentleness, unfamiliar and unexpected—gave him pause.

He looked over, found a matching and equally rare concern in her expression, and he had the shocking thought that she would embrace him. Yet her arms remained fixed at her sides. Ah, yes. Waiting for him to make the first move. When of course he would not. She knew that.

"Well," she said, likely relieved, and then held up a hand in blessing. "*Sumite vires ex lumen.*"

Take strength from the light.

Quentin bowed his head. When he lifted it, she had already turned away to re-enter the building.

"Resolve this quickly," she ordered without looking back as she crossed the threshold. "There remains much to do here." The door closed behind her.

Alone at last, aside from the expressionless attendant. And the men waiting by the car.

Time was wasting.

Quentin blew out a held breath and began making his slow, careful way down.

Much to do here. As if Quentin weren't the one taking on the brunt of the reorganization and review of the entire membership. Everyone who remained was putting in extra hours and energy as they sought to maintain normal operations in the midst of utter chaos, but they hadn't Quentin's vision and all it entailed. They weren't kept up most nights, plagued with memories not their own.

His feet on level ground, he felt some of the tension leave his spine. Stairs always presented a challenge.

With a nod to the security agent who held open the rear door, Quentin climbed into the car, settled himself with relief on the padded bench seat. The door closed, saving him the trouble of doing so. The car rolled forward. Since there was no need to communicate, the privacy glass between him and the driver was up.

His traveling case sat near his left ankle. He nudged it, then laid his cane across his lap.

Outside was the twinkly, exuberant bustle of London during the winter holiday season. Inside was the near-silent dark of a posh sedan—complete with a small liquor cabinet. Figuring on at least a twenty minute ride to the leyline access point,

Quentin dropped two cubes of ice into a crystal tumbler and then drowned them in Talisker single-malt.

CHAPTER 9

Business in the café had dropped considerably after the lunch rush, and Megan was more than capable of handling drink orders with an occasional waffle or sandwich by herself. But just in case, Thia had brought her laptop upstairs. She had caught up with online orders and was working to expand the website's listings. It was tedious, adding descriptions and images for each item the physical store had to offer, but rote enough so as to be nearly mindless. A good thing, that, since her mind was incapable of focusing on any particular subject for long.

Was it possible to get mental whiplash? With the way her thoughts leapt from one worry to another and then back again within a matter of seconds, Thia had begun to wonder.

At the sound of someone coming up the stairs, she raised her head and was surprised to see Kendra. "I thought you'd left."

"We need to go."

"Okay," Thia said, thinking Kendra referred to herself and those who'd come with her. "Thanks for staying as long as you did. I really appreciate—"

"Um...no," Kendra interrupted. "I mean *we* need to go. You. Me." She gestured between the two of them. "Now."

"We do?" Thia still didn't understand. "Go where?"

"The Landmark." Kendra rested her hands on the back of the chair that held Thia's computer bag. "I talked it over with Murphy and he gave the okay. There's a room on one of our high security floors with your name on it. Free of charge." She picked up the bag, held it open expectantly.

If not for the hotel inarguably being the safest location in town, Kendra's herding behavior might have been annoying; as would her assumption that Thia would take no issue with whatever plans had been made for her without her input. *Had* she been asked, she would have said she'd prefer to continue working at Eclectica and go home when the day was done— as usual.

But "usual" had gone out the proverbial window well before Zoe's abduction. So had "normal."

Thia thought she had come to accept that, but clearly she hadn't. Not fully. The routine of the past weeks had lulled her into a false sense of normality. Of security. The illusion that she knew what any given day might bring. How did that saying go? "Expect the unexpected." That's what she should've been doing. That was her true normal now: the unexpected.

Oh, how she missed normal.

She closed her laptop. "Better safe than sorry, right? Thank you," she said, getting up. "And thank Mr. Murphy. I would like to pay *something,* though." As Lettie's main heir she could afford a night or two. Probably. She slid her computer into the bag Kendra continued to hold. How much did a high security room like that run?

"No need," Kendra insisted. "It was scheduled to be part of the January remodel. We're just closing this one early."

Thia knew the hotel got booked solid around every holiday. But she'd do better talking to Murphy later about rates and payments than arguing things now.

One of the men Kendra had brought with her came up the

stairs, an anxious look on his face. "Ms. Ross?"

"We'll be right there, Baxter."

He returned down the stairs, and just like that, Thia had second thoughts. It all felt so confining.

"Can't this wait?" she asked. "We're open until six, and then we need to close down the registers and make the deposit."

"Abby can handle all that, can't she?"

Before Thia could reply, the person in question came up the stairs and proved her hearing to be in perfect working order.

"I absolutely can," Abby said, coming to a stop at the table. "Things are slow this afternoon. There's no reason you can't take your office work to the Landmark."

Yes, there was. But it was an emotional one that she didn't want to get into, and it wouldn't hold up against two people determined to keep her safe, anyway. "I can't stay cooped up twenty-four seven," she said instead.

"It's the best way to protect you," Abby countered.

"We don't even know that I'm in danger. *Zoe* is."

"And you could be next," Kendra said, temper flaring in her moss-green eyes. "Are you willing to take that chance?"

Thia gestured helplessly. "It could just as well be *you*. Or you, Abby. If you close alone," she continued over their protests, "how is that a good idea? We've been closing together every night for weeks. Why should tonight be any different?"

"I can protect myself," Abby said, but at Thia's glare, she huffed out a breath. "Fine. So I'll take someone along."

"Why not me? I can—"

"I'll see if some of the crew can stay on downstairs," Kendra said to Abby.

"If they can," Thia pointed out, "why can't I stay too?"

Abby shook her head. "That's not—"

The café door opened with a bang. In unison, they turned toward it and braced for attack.

It was only Madame Demetka, her arms wrapped around a battered file box. A great jingle-jangling could be heard from it as she rushed in.

Behind her, the door drifted gently shut.

"I have come as soon as hearing!" With a resounding thunk, the town's most popular Tarot reader set the box on a nearby table. "So terrible, this missing of our Zoe!" She began lifting out items—a fat white candle, an all-too-familiar feathered turban, a bundle of sage.

Thia felt the bewilderment that so often accompanied the unusual woman. "Madame Demetka, you aren't going to hold appointments here, are you? You'd be much happier in the Rowan Space." Located down a short passage to the left of the café from the top of the stairs, the room was available for readings, meditation sessions, craft classes, and whatever else might be of interest; sometimes free of charge, sometimes (in cases of fee-based events) for a small percentage.

"No, no, no." Madame Demetka waggled her crimson-nailed fingers with barely a pause in unpacking. "I will tell my client we read only after Zoe is returned to us. This, it is complete priority." Three chunky stones with the colors and sheen of peacock feathers, a silver-chained amethyst pendulum, and a beaded velvet pouch joined the table's growing array.

"I'm sorry, *what* is complete priority?" Thia looked to her friends. They appeared equally confused.

"Finding Zoe! Is obvious!" Madame Demetka straightened. Then, in a near-instant shift of mood, she clucked her tongue, waved both hands as if fanning herself. "I am sharpish. Please forgive. Is stress."

Abby stepped hesitantly forward. "Madame Demetka, who told you Zoe was missing? Was it your guides?"

"Them? Bah." She shook a fist ceiling-ward before rooting around in the box once more. "No help, there. Not yet." She lifted out a large crystal ball, held it against her side while she searched for what turned out to be its brass stand. "When I get here first time, I talk with the men poking around your trash bins." A quick tilt of her head indicated the alley.

"There are men out back?" Thia hurried to a window, but the alley's bins proved impossible to see from that angle. The patio wall was in the way.

Joining her, Abby said, "I don't think anyone is there."

"I'm going out," Kendra declared. "Wait here, both of you." With stealthy movements, she slipped out the door, moved toward the propped-open gate.

"Men in suits," Madame Demetka said as she flicked a white cloth, draped it over the crystal ball. "And one lady. In British accents, they tell me of poor Zoe and ask questions I cannot answer. It is good I come early, no? I had time to return home for my things."

Thia had stopped listening after "suits" and "British." She pulled open the door before Abby could stop her.

"Wait," the latter said, following her out. They soon caught up with Kendra, who sprang into some sort of attack pose, a wicked-looking knife gripped in her hand.

Her stance immediately relaxed. "Fucking hell, you guys. I told you to wait." She tucked the knife into one of her knee-length boots. "They're not here, anyway."

With half of Thia's mind caught on the fact that Kendra carried a knife—and in her boot, no less—she said, "Madame Demetka says they wore suits and sounded British. Sounds like the Brigantium."

"Brigid's blessed whistle," Kendra muttered. "That's all we need. Academics."

Abby shrugged. "They fought well at the Ring."

"Yeah, okay," came the grudging concession.

"But why were they here?" Thia asked, feeling the end of her figurative rope slip from her grasp. "Not just Granite Springs, but *here* here?" Her gesture toward the dumpsters went a bit wild. She couldn't do this. Not now. "Forget it."

She headed back to the café. "There's enough crazy going on without trying to figure out the damned Brigantium."

She pulled open the door to find the café's overhead lights had been turned off, and a surprising number of people were gathering. With light continuing to enter through windows and the store beyond, the space was only dim, not dark, but it was difficult to see details, especially along the room's edges.

By the table with all her unboxed things, Madame Demetka was speaking to a bookish, middle-aged man. "—will need to reschedule, Mr. Gregory. You understand?"

The white candle had been lit. The flame looked alarmingly high.

The man nodded enthusiastically. "Of course. Of course I do. Such a lovely, kind young woman. What is being done to find her?"

"This, Mr. Gregory," came Madame Demetka's proud reply, complete with grand sweep of her arm. With those sleeves, she was a fire hazard. "*This* is being done."

Before Thia could decide whether she might be better off outside, Madame Demetka caught sight of her and beamed.

"Ah, *miri mora,* here you are." She patted the back of a chair she'd pulled out, the one in front of a deck of cards. "Please take seat. We are almost ready!"

● ○ ●

From his place in the shadows between the outer wall and a growing crowd of onlookers, Cormac watched as the erratic, kaftan-garbed woman used an amethyst suspended on a silver chain to dowse ineffectively behind the coffee bar. Now and again she would concentrate on a specific area and, with eyes closed, mumble phrases cobbled from Romany and gibberish. The crystal would either spin a lazy circle or it wouldn't, yet either way the result was the same: the woman would cluck her tongue, frown at the ceiling, and move on.

The performance had been going for about twenty minutes and Cormac had run out of patience in half that time. But the curiosity that had impelled him to follow her into Eclectica in the first place also compelled him to stay.

He'd seen her with Brigantium agents behind the café while he was overhead, exploring the town in his raven form. With her flamboyant, clichéd costume and ridiculous array of New Age gewgaws, she was undoubtedly a charlatan. She was also immediately recognizable. She had been visiting Thia at home the night he'd first come to Granite Springs.

It had amused Cormac to call down a storm for his arrival, and when the woman—what was the name she used, Madame Dementa? No, not quite so obvious...Demetka. That was it. When the Demetka woman had left the protection of Thia's home, he had targeted her with strong gusts that had turned her voluminous garments against her. All in good fun. Mostly.

Then had come his first person-to-person encounter with Thia, not that she'd known it. He hoped that she still didn't; that she hadn't thought back and seen through the disguise he'd used.

At the time, he'd suspected she knew what Leticia had done with the Stone, and he hadn't been nice about it. Should Thia ever figure that out, it would be one more mark against him.

He risked a look at her, seated at the table cluttered with Demetka's miscellany. She was watching the woman's efforts with such rapt attention that she hadn't noticed Cormac—or, rather, Connor Michaels. Nor had the two friends standing by her side; but then, he was making an effort to not be noticed.

It became easier as more people wandered in from the store or patio. Unfortunately, that made it harder to see what the Demetka woman was doing.

"Ah!" came her sudden exclamation from somewhere near the espresso machine. Her multitude of bangles and bracelets jangled as she raised her hand high above her audience's heads.

She held a wooden spoon.

"This!" She waved it about like a flag at a parade. "This is the key!"

There was a smattering of tentative applause.

Carrying the spoon aloft, Demetka left the counter for the cluttered table. People repositioned themselves both to let her pass and to get a better view. Cormac moved as near as he dared. He couldn't see her face once she sat down, but he could see her hands and most of the tabletop.

She laid the spoon on a square of burgundy velvet dotted with gold stars. A grand sweep of her hand brought her sleeve dangerously close to a lit candle. Thia, from her seat opposite, gently nudged that out of range.

"This spoon knows well our dear Zoe," the supposed psychic announced in her bizarre accent. She was no more Romany than Cormac was; he'd stake his art collection on it. Hell, he'd stake his whole house.

Demetka's hands hovered over the spoon. "Zoe's energy is much infused here. I call upon my guides to focus upon it, to use it to locate our absent friend."

Well, *that* was interesting, Cormac thought, feeling a faint buzz run down his spine. Something genuine lay beneath the woman's nonsense after all.

"Please, everyone, to focus also upon the spoon. My guides have difficult work ahead."

The room filled with tension as people tried to do as asked, whether they knew how or even what was meant. Someone cleared his throat only to be angrily shushed by another. Thia stared at the spoon with a sad, almost lost look.

Cormac found himself unaccountably angry.

No, not unaccountably. Thia shouldn't be involved in this. In any of this. That was Cassie's doing. Cassie—which meant, technically, the blame could be traced back to Idris. Even in death, the man continued to hold sway over Cormac's life. Would he never be free?

"Dude, chill," came an irate whisper. Standing to Cormac's left, a youth with a goatee and feathered cap shot him a glare. "You're messing with my vibes."

Dammit. Tamping down the power that had flared with his ill-timed thoughts, Cormac glanced around to see who else might have noticed.

Kendra looked directly at him, her green eyes alight with what he supposed was meant to be a warning.

How amusing. The woman hardly had any power. She'd be no match at all. He returned his gaze to the spoon.

Ah, why not? He set his focus. Not a spell, not exactly. But he fed the intention placed on the spoon, and any possible connection to the missing woman. It wouldn't do much, of course, unless—

The Demetka woman clapped her hands. "I have received something! Yes, something!"

Loathe as Cormac was to admit it, she might. She carried no discernible power, her rituals were as nonsensical as her speech, yet there *was* something to her guides, whatever or whomever they may be.

This might lead somewhere after all.

● ○ ●

Lake of the Woods, Oregon

When painfully bright light was directed at Zoe's face, all she could think was: Thank God, I'm not blind.

Then she couldn't think much else at all.

It was as if she were half asleep, ideas and feelings drifting away almost as quickly as they popped up.

She didn't struggle when the woman grabbed her arm and hauled her to her feet. Didn't think to ask questions or resist when she was led up a shaky set of stairs and into what turned out to be some sort of rustic lodge.

She didn't even wonder at the bonfire visible through a set of windows, or the motorcyclists that circled it, yelling and throwing things. Their voices held such intense anger; their faces such glee.

Such obvious love of violence should have been frightening, and yet Zoe didn't feel afraid.

She didn't feel anything.

"You are not difficult to coerce," the woman said, sounding like a graduate of RADA. Alan Rickman, Fiona Shaw, Diana Rigg. Tom Hiddleston. Round vowels, rich tone.

The woman's teeth were a perfect white between smiling, glossed lips. She was beautiful in a way that literally stunned. Zoe was numbed. Stupefied.

"Quite unlike the others." The woman's eyes were a brilliant amber. "Have you met Avery?"

Zoe hadn't known anyone else was there. But sure enough, a man stood nearby, out of the light. His head was down so he could stare at his scraped and paint-spattered boots. Lank brown hair hung like a curtain before his face. Behind him was a wall of shelves that, amazingly, held jar after jar of glass marbles. The kind kids used to play with in the old days.

"Up." The woman snapped her fingers beside his exposed ear. "Let her get a good look at you."

With obvious reluctance, the man lifted his head. *Good* was a relative term. His features were half-concealed by a scruffy beard. Shadowed, blue eyes looked out from beneath worried brows.

"Well?" The woman gave Zoe's arm a squeeze. "Is he at all familiar?"

Zoe wracked her memory, came up empty. "I've never seen any of you in my life. Please, whatever it is you think I know, I don't, okay? I don't know anything about anything."

Rather than making an apology and promise to let her go,

the woman laughed and Zoe's arm was given another ungentle squeeze. "We are well aware of that, my dear."

"Then why am I here? My family isn't wealthy. They can't pay you."

The man went back to staring at his boots.

"Come." The woman pulled Zoe along. "Your lack of funds is of no interest."

They entered a kitchen large enough for a restaurant, but inefficiently set up and the appliances looked to be at least thirty years old. Two women in drab robes unloaded groceries from a number of boxes set on scarred, woodblock counters.

Zoe's muscles locked. A cult. She'd been taken by a cult. A hard push sent her stumbling to the center of the room.

"Renée and Clara," the woman said from behind Zoe, and the two others stopped what they were doing to stand in a kind of subservient attention. "Meet the new chef."

They bobbed their heads. "Pleased to meet you," they said in unison.

Zoe. They meant Zoe. She waved her hands. "No. No, no, no." Her mind felt clearer, and she knew she didn't want this. Any of this. "There's been a huge mistake. Please, I just want to go...home," she finished lamely.

"That is not possible." The beautiful woman smiled. "So you might as well make yourself useful. I am sorry for it," she said, clearly not sorry at all. "But you see, Avery has an attachment to you. And since I need him—and this fascinating home of his—it seems that I have need of you, too."

"I don't understand."

"Don't you? Poor dear. It's really quite simple." The perfect smile hardened. "Avery doesn't want to see you come to harm. I need you to be where he can see exactly that. Or exactly *not* that, if you take my meaning."

"You're using me...to get what you want from *him?*"—Zoe looked to where the man in question cowered in the doorway.

"If he doesn't do it, you'll...you'll *hurt* me?" She felt dizzy. "I don't understand this. I don't even know him!"

With another laugh, the woman turned her malicious smile on Avery. "Would you like me to tell her?"

Though Zoe wouldn't have thought it possible, he shrank even further into himself.

"Ah, shame," the woman mocked. "It seems he doesn't want you to—"

The lighting in the room turned orange.

"What the hell is this?" The woman spun toward Avery. He flinched and grabbed his head as if pained.

"Alarm," he whispered.

"I gathered that, you idiot." The light did strange things to her eyes, making them look as if they glowed.

Avery turned to the window. Outside, the motorcycle riders were still circling and throwing things into the fire, causing it to send up great flurries of sparks.

His eyes appeared normal enough, Zoe thought, and risked a glance back at the woman to compare.

Yep, definitely weird. Maybe it had to do with the color of the iris in the first place. Avery's eyes were grayish while hers were a kind of amber—so it made sense, didn't it, that they would be made more intense in orange light?

"Something touched the shields." Avery continued to stare in the window's direction, but it seemed to Zoe that his focus was elsewhere. Inward.

The woman made a rude sound. "Like what, a bird?"

Avery's gaze dropped to the floor and he took a step back. The woman matched it, staying close to jab a finger at his chest. "If we're to put up with this every bloody time a bird flies through the—"

"Not a bird. Energy with intent." Avery's hands fisted at his sides, and Zoe felt a moment's fear for him. For herself, more. If there was to be a fight, she didn't want to get caught in the middle.

"Explain." The woman lowered her finger.

Avery touched his temples. His eyes closed. "Something is searching." He cocked his head. "Someone? Yes. Someone... is searching for...someone. Searching for—"

His eyes shot open, his gaze landing unerringly on Zoe. She felt her own eyes widen as everyone turned toward her.

"Searching for *you*." The woman lunged, grabbed Zoe before she could evade, and backed her up against the dishwasher.

Zoe knew she wouldn't win a struggle, not even if there had only been one of them instead of two (or four, counting the two in cloaks; or upwards of twenty, with the riders outside). Was she smart to not try, or cowardly? She didn't know.

"Can they feel her through the wards?" The woman asked Avery, and began towing Zoe back the way they had come. Fingernails dug into the tender skin of her wrists.

"She is sought specifically," Avery said from behind. His hands pressed between her shoulder blades. Urged her along. "Some sense of her might leak through."

If they hadn't sounded insane before, they sure did now. Zoe locked her knees, refused to take another step.

It didn't matter. She'd stopped on a small rag rug; with the woman pulling and Avery pushing, it simply bunched around Zoe's feet and slid with her across the wood floor.

"Please," she said. They were taking her back to the basement. "Not the dark."

The pressure from Avery's hands lessened and she felt a tiny hope. But all too soon, he pushed again.

"I can't," he said softly. "I'm sorry."

Zoe wondered if he meant it.

"Could they sense me?" the woman asked. Either she hadn't heard them, or didn't care. "You should have mentioned this. If I were to be the target of such a location attempt, would some sense of me leak through?"

The man said nothing, but that seemed to be an answer in itself. The woman shot him a look over her shoulder of such loathing that Zoe shuddered.

They arrived at the basement door. The woman stepped to the side, let go of Zoe's wrists to give her a hard shove.

"No, please!" Zoe stumbled onto the tiny landing. Darkness reached out, surrounded her utterly when the door slammed shut.

"I thought I did," she heard Avery say on the other side.

The floor began to shake, the walls too, like at the start of an earthquake. They were rare in the area but not unknown. Zoe dropped to her hands and knees and pressed herself against the door. To stand inside the jamb itself would be better, but she doubted they'd let her. They didn't seem concerned about their own safety, let alone hers.

"Fix it," the woman was yelling. "Fix it so everyone here is hidden *specifically*. Do it now, or I'll take it out on her."

Zoe wondered who that might be...and then remembered. How in the world had she come to this? How could she be used against some man she'd never met?

"I will need something from everyone," came his muffled reply to the woman's threat. "Something that has picked up their essence."

So much of what they'd said this whole time made no sense to Zoe. Wards? Energy? A person's essence? If she had known before that Granite Springs was so popular with occult-type people, she would have gone to the University of Washington instead. But no, she had been dazzled by Southern's theater program and the proximity to the Shakespeare Festival.

After graduation, when her auditions went nowhere and her part-time job turned full-time, she had never thought to try her luck somewhere else. Instead, she had taken over the café when the original manager wanted to move on. It had been too sweet a deal (literally, with her love of baking) to pass up.

Huddled on the floor while the entire world shook around her, she promised herself that if she got out of this, she would move. Portland, maybe. Yeah, that sounded nice. A lot of her classmates had moved up there.

Amidst the noise of the quake, she didn't hear the click of the locks being undone or the creak of the knob turning; the door simply opened. Her support gone, she tumbled out only to be yanked to her feet. Everything remained cast in orange. The woman's eyes were such a bright amber that Zoe could barely make out the pupils.

She held Zoe's upper arms so tight bruises were guaranteed, and there was no point in struggling even if Zoe wanted to. Her mind was dulling again.

"It's not safe here," Zoe blurted. "The whole building could come down." The tremors were not massive, but given how rundown this place was, it might not take much. She looked to Avery, but he merely shook his head. Slowly. Slightly. His gaze dropped to the floor.

The woman laughed, then let go of Zoe's arms to grab hold of her right hand. Roughly, she pulled off Zoe's class ring.

"Hey, no, that's—"

Zoe was pushed back into the basement. She fell over the jamb, landed hard on her right hip.

"Here," she heard Cassandra say as the door slammed shut once more. The locks engaged. "Do her first."

Avery's reply was muffled.

The quake was passing. As the building stilled, Zoe could hear better through the door. Someone, a man, was singing. Avery? The tune was odd, the execution shaky, but his voice was pleasant. Whatever the language was, she didn't know it.

The light that managed to make its way beneath the door lost its orange color.

"It worked?" the woman asked. "Good."

Avery's reply, if he made one, was too quiet for Zoe to hear.

She pressed her ear to the door only to jerk back at a hard impact against the wall. Glass crashed, shattered, and something like hail pinged and rolled along the floor. The marbles. Hundreds, thousands of marbles. She scooted to the far side of the landing, near the hinge where it would take light the longest to reach should the door open. She drew her knees up, hugged them.

"I should do more to you than that," the woman said on the other side of the door. Anger did more to project her voice than volume. "But there isn't time. Get up. You'll sort me out next."

Zoe heard the scrape and shuffle of someone—must have been Avery—getting up from the floor.

"Have you experience with Druid Fog?" The woman's voice faded along with the sounds of their footsteps, moving in the direction of the kitchen. "No? Well. You're about to."

Zoe dropped her head to her knees. The finger where her ring had been throbbed. She massaged it absently. The skin felt raw. That particular ring had such a tight fit, she usually used soap.

Had there been an earthquake or not? And had Avery really made the lights change color by singing?

Portland, she promised herself. Portland.

● ○ ●

Eclectica, Granite Springs
"Bah!" The Demetka woman slammed her hands on the small table, threatening the objects on it. Hot wax splashed as the candle rocked and guttered.

"I thought—ah, shit," she said in a calm and quite different voice. The pseudo-European accent had been replaced with one with origins in the deep American South. She covered her face with her hands. "It's gone."

Thia's reaction to the shift was curious. While her friends

showed an astonishment which verged on alarm, she seemed merely confused—the same response she'd shown for much of the production that came before. As if this abrupt change was no more (or less) odd as any of Demetka's prior behavior.

"Is the show over?" asked someone from the far edge of the crowd. Someone else attempted to start a round of applause but was quickly shushed.

A man whom Cormac had seen speaking with the women earlier came forward. "Madame D, are you all right?" When she didn't respond, he looked to Thia. "Is she alright?"

Hesitantly, Thia asked, "Madame Demetka—Sally?"

No response.

"Should we do something?" the man asked.

Kendra stepped in, smoothly linked her arm with his. "She'll be fine," she said, leading him toward the stairs. Her voice carried. "Everything is fine."

"I'd had an appointment," the man remarked as they moved through the crowd, "but instead got this. Exciting, wasn't it? And at no cost. I'd like to reschedule as soon as possible."

The crowd, with the excitement over, began to disperse. If Cormac (rather, Connor) wanted to stay, he needed to find a way to avoid notice.

He turned to the wall at his back and feigned interest in the artwork displayed there. The first piece, a watercolor of a unicorn grazing in a woodland glade, wasn't half bad. Not to his taste, but not lacking in skill. He moved on to the next. His goal was the recently-vacated armchair in the windowless corner, the darkest part of the room while the overhead lights remained off.

Less than a third of the crowd remained. He glanced over his shoulder, located Thia at the counter. In one hand she held a water pitcher; in the other, a glass. Several people gathered by the cash register to place orders. When her gaze began to travel, he quickly turned away.

He needn't have worried; she only sought assistance. Out of the corner of his eye, he watched a clerk hurry over, soon to be joined by Abby. Together they began handling the customers, and Thia took the glass of water to Demetka. Cormac seated himself in the armchair and picked up a dog-eared magazine from a nearby rack.

The cacophany of grinding coffee beans and steaming milk soon predominated in the small space, but Cormac's hearing was excellent (especially when aided by a small spell).

He had no trouble hearing Thia's question as she arrived at Demetka's table: "Did you get anything?"

Air currents in the old building being what they were, the flame of the candle atop the table flickered madly. Light and shadow alternated, distorting and disguising as it moved over Thia's face.

Cormac wove a quick spell, cast it with the subtle flick of a wrist behind the magazine. The flames steadied; their light brightened.

"Thank you, sugar," drawled the former Demetka. Reaching for the glass of water, she fixed Cormac with a startlingly alert gaze. Thia, thankfully, was preoccupied with sitting down.

Demetka-Sally looked away, taking a long drink.

Cormac waited, tense. She'd sensed something about him, but would it matter? Would she mention it? Call attention?

"Maybe I got a little something," the woman said, putting the empty glass down, "but not enough to go by. A slight tug to the North, into the mountains."

She pulled off her turban, tossed it onto the seat of an empty chair. "There was a sense of trees. Water...maybe. But Christ knows there's plenty of both up that way." Unexpectedly, she tipped her head to glare at the ceiling. "Excuse me? Tell her *what* is here? The *storm?* Lord love a duck, y'all make no sense sometimes."

Her gaze leveled and she made Thia an apologetic shrug.

"They want me to tell you the storm is here."

The windows offered views of a clear blue sky outside.

"I don't understand," Thia said.

"You and me both, sugar. You and me—What's that?" Her attention returned to the ceiling. "Ah. Yes. This I see."

Her accent was shifting, reverting. "My Guides, *miri mora,* they remind me of the night in October when the storm came to your house. *That* is the storm they mean."

Cormac swore inwardly and considered whether he could get to the stairs unnoticed.

"That storm, he is here now," Madame Demetka said, her gaze skimming the café. Oddly enough, she avoided Cormac's part of it. Intentionally, he had to think.

Instead, she locked on Abby at the espresso machine. "Ah, *miri kushti,* if I could please have a Café Piedmontese? Many times, thank you." She smiled at Thia. "I do love the mocha with the orange. Even though the zest, it gets troublesome." She mimed pulling something from her teeth.

CHAPTER 10

Plenty had not been an exaggeration. After several hours spent exploring the vagaries of Madame Demetka's professed "tug" to the north mountains, Cormac considered *plenty* to be a vast understatement. Most all of the higher elevations was dense forestland marbled by a network of brooks, ponds, lakes and such—frozen and hidden beneath thick snow, which made anything short of a river or lake that much harder to detect.

Cormac's raven form was well adapted to cold, and he had cast himself a warming spell; nevertheless, the time spent in the mountains was not without cost. And then there was the tedium of the flyover, made worse by the nagging feeling that there was something (if not several somethings) he ought to be doing instead.

Still, his devious half-sister did need to be found. Until he came up with a better way, he had only this needle-in-a-hay-stack search based on "feelings" which he could not disclaim (much as he might like to) as either the lies of a charlatan or the confusion of a woman full of good intention yet devoid of talent. Demetka-Sally might be all of those things, yet her link to the Other was real.

Cormac had felt the connection in the café, but hadn't got

far with his attempted trace of the energetic thread. It had been too thin and fragmentary.

Distance, environmental conditions, lack of power—there was no shortage of natural causes for that. But it might also be by design, as a way to hide the source's identity, for good reason or ill. Protection. Deception. If trickery were the aim, then whatever Demetka's supposed guides "revealed" could be intentional misdirection that would lead straight to a trap.

Cormac had set out on his flight with such potential danger in mind, but so far he'd risked only boredom, cold exposure, and wasted time.

At least the scenery was of interest. Tall, snow-dusted pines unlike anything back home. High plains and winding, rocky gorges and a dramatic peak whose near-perfect conical shape proclaimed its volcanic origins while a low thrum of energy warned it was not dead but, rather, dormant in the way of a hibernating animal. Not a threat while it slumbered through its winter, but not a place to be near in its springtime.

Whenever that may be.

He took a final pass over its southern base and then headed back toward town. He couldn't shake the sense that *something* was there to be found, but damned if he could hone in on it. Someone could have crafted a damned good cloaking spell— one so good that it left no trace of itself. Or perhaps the odd feeling was an effect of the area in general.

The confluence of three mountain ranges and several major leylines made for unusual energy patterns and an ocassional pocket of very high levels. Never in all of his years had Cormac encountered so much power within one geographical region.

● ○ ●

It was like something out of science fiction serials, Quentin mused. The reduction of the human form to its most basic state—namely, a confusion of atoms and awareness—that was then transported along a kind of "beam" from one location to another. Except, unlike in television and movies, the travel took longer than an instant. So did recovery.

Oh, and there wasn't always a convenient spot to arrive.

Dropping out of the leyline, Quentin's form coalesced and landed him face first in a snowdrift.

If it hadn't been so cold, if he hadn't got a nose and mouth full of snow, he might have appreciated being stationary for a time. The journey from one side of the globe to the other was not...pleasant. But his newly materialized body demanded air and warmer, drier surroundings. He pushed himself up on his hands. Icy wet trickled into his leather gloves at the wrists and soaked into the linings. When he figured his equilibrium wouldn't be jeopardized, he straightened the rest of the way so that he was kneeling, and took his first look around.

He was in a large field. That it was covered in snow came as no surprise. He brushed off his coat while he delved a bit deeper. The energy of the area was potent and complex. No wonder Leticia McDaniel had chosen it for both business and home. Spells and charms would take substantially less effort, although the unusual resonances could yield equally unusual results.

It would make for a fascinating study on locational effects.

Some distance to his right, an engine revved. A black four-by-four flashed its brights. His ride awaited.

Closer would have been nice.

Holding out his left hand, he called for his cane with a quick flex and splay of his fingers. The ebony and silver stick rose from the snow several feet away to fly into his impatient grip. He stabbed it into the drift, levered himself up.

His hip was not pleased to say the least, and only the cane prevented a fall.

Beneath the knee-high snow, the ground was quite uneven. If he had been able to see it, he'd have managed better. As it was, he couldn't predict the depth or security of one step to the next. It made for rough going, and there was no bloody way he could do it while carrying his traveling case, let alone his suitcase as well. Someone else would have to play fetch.

The same spells that had allowed his luggage entry to—and accurate exit from—the leyline also triggered faint tracking beacons. He spotted his traveling case on the way to the car. His suitcase must have landed farther afield.

Snow melted into his wool trousers and wicked its way up to his thighs.

By the time he reached the road, his muscles were locked with cold and his teeth threatened to chatter. A hot shower, he promised himself. Dry clothes. The hotel had better not be far.

He limped up to the Mercedes—the ride would be comfortable, at least—and watched as the front passenger-side door opened. The woman he had been saddled with stepped out.

She seemed happy to see him, which he knew had nothing to do with him, personally. She often seemed happy, even in the most taxing situations.

He found it infuriating.

"My things are back there." He didn't care how brusque he sounded. "Two cases." He yanked open the vehicle's rear door, then promptly lost his balance and tumbled into the heated interior. His hip landed hard on the seat. He stifled a groan.

Edith closed his door and walked around to speak with the driver. She pointed in the direction of the traveling case. "Do you mind, Rick?"

Given the charming smile she flashed the man, of course he didn't mind. He set off immediately.

Edith opened the rear door and, ignoring Quentin's scowl, slid in beside him. She flashed him that same smile. "How was the trip?"

His jaw locked from trying to stop the chatter of his teeth. He felt as if half his muscles were cramped, and the vehicle's warmth barely penetrated. He considered using a spell to dry his clothes. Usually, he avoided magic use so soon after leyline travel. Things could be a bit unstable yet.

Edith waited, that damn smile continuing to light up a face already too pretty. Good looks, he had found, made certain people too sure of themselves. As if getting one's way in life required only a simple show of teeth.

At least her glasses dulled the effect somewhat.

"Far," Quentin said when he remembered she'd asked him a question. Out in the field, the driver lifted the traveling case from the snow and looked around in confusion.

"Oh, dear," Edith said, as Quentin kept much cruder words to himself.

The spell on his suitcase must have failed.

While the beam of the driver's torch glided across smooth, undisturbed snow, Quentin stewed. His clothes had been in there. Toiletries. He would have to replace them all. What a ridiculous waste of time.

The driver turned back to the car. He held up the traveling case, shrugged as his free arm swept out to indicate his failure to find the other.

"Was there anything important in there?" Edith asked.

Quentin heard pity in her voice. He abhorred pity.

● ○ ●

Pure luck placed Cormac in the sky above the vale to witness that. He finished his loop and turned south toward Granite Springs. A direct line of flight would get him there well before the Brigantium. Presumably Quentin would be staying at the Landmark. The others were. It posed yet another problem.

Was his arrival coincidental? As part of a strategy to bring Thia into the Brigantium, perhaps. Cormac knew that was a goal of theirs. Or was this in reaction to the abduction? Did they suspect who was behind it?

● ○ ●

Lake of the Woods

Dinner had been a total nightmare, Zoe thought—now that she could *have* thoughts again. In the pitch-black basement, her mind gradually returned. She tucked her legs up, wrapped the blanket more securely around herself.

Cassandra. That was the awful woman's name. While Zoe had been made to perform as a sort of mindless robot, she'd learned that much, anyway.

People had surrounded her, watched her at all times. They had even limited the kitchen tools she'd been allowed to use. What they thought she could do with salad tongs, she had no idea, but she had a sudden memory of a scary moment when she hadn't set them down quickly enough after use.

And the people themselves, good Lord. She trembled at the rush of images, all too vivid in the dark. At least she hadn't had to serve many of the bikers. Most had turned down food to roar off on their motorcycles instead. "The Rekkrs." Spelled wrong on purpose, of course, to prove how super rebellious they were.

Yet Zoe didn't doubt the name was accurate. She'd bet they wrecked a lot of things.

They'd come back from their ride not long after she and the two creepy girls from the kitchen finished serving Cassandra and her bunch of gray-cloaked...Zoe didn't know what to call them. In a brief moment of clarity, she had asked the girls if this was a cult, but all Renée had said was that talk was not permitted. So, yeah, Zoe was thinking cult.

Engines revved outside, enough of them to vibrate through the stone wall at her back. She shifted away.

While she had loaded dishes into a washer older than her mother, the Rekkrs had added to the bonfire from a heap of broken picnic benches and tables, and then gathered around it to shout profane things and, as far as she could tell, drink their dinner. Too drunk to know how cold it was outside.

The gray-cloaks hadn't joined them after dinner, but they *had* gone somewhere. Wherever Cassandra had, maybe. She'd left right after her specially prepared meal (no simple stew for her, oh no). When Zoe had been taken back to the basement, she'd gotten the impression that the building was empty.

Maybe they were all out with the Rekkrs now, but if stew was too common for Cassandra's tastes, Zoe doubted she'd think much of drunken partying. More like they were somewhere doing their own weird cult things.

Was this her chance to get away? But they'd taken her coat. Her slacks and sweater wouldn't keep her warm past a couple of minutes, and her 1950's-style ankle boots weren't intended for wilderness treks (or any treks, really) in any season. It was a toss-up as to which would happen first: break a leg or freeze to death.

"I'm sorry," a man said quietly—startling and so close.

Only inches away, it seemed, and Zoe lurched back, bumped her head on the stone wall. "Stay away! Stay away from me!" She kicked and struck out blindly. Nothing connected, but she kept trying. "Don't you dare come near me. Just stay away. Go away!"

Eventually she realized that she wasn't so much protecting herself as she was wasting energy. Beyond the one sentence, and an apology at that, the man—Avery?—hadn't said or done a thing. As far as she could tell. Was he still there?

She hadn't heard him leave, if he had. But she hadn't heard his approach, either.

She tried to get herself under control. She was shaking. Not from cold, but she felt around for the ends of the blanket she had dislodged anyway. Her hand landed on something cold. Metallic. She jerked her hand away, then reconsidered. Cold, smooth metal. Cylindrical. A flashlight.

She picked it up, quickly turned it on and shone it around the cluttered basement. She would explore in detail later, but for now she only cared that she was alone.

● ○ ●

Avery slipped out of the Lodge through the fourth of seven escape routes. This one used the basement's main room and terminated at a panel cut in the side of the porch behind a sprawling rhododendron. An illusion hex he had carved into the wood siding further shielded the access from view.

He had frightened her. He had made her cry.

Had he meant to? It was difficult to think while the other woman's influence poked at him all the time. And the gods-damned Rekkrs with their noise and their violence. For over an hour they had been tearing around their *coelcerthi*—made from tables that had taken a full week to build. They threw liquor bottles into it and shouted, gunned their engines.

Posturing. The actions of...of...His head hurt. He reset the access panel and crawled out from behind the shrubbery.

The *swynwraig* and most of her followers had gone into the barn. Whatever ritual they were performing there generated considerable energy. It prickled him, made him itchy. Edgy. It likely joined with the alcohol to fuel the Rekkrs's lust for mayhem, whether that was the intended result or not.

Too much energy.

Moving away from both the *coelcerthi* and the old barn, he skirted the property to the West, covering his tracks with a spell as he went. That took concentration. Snow was not easy to manipulate. Not like water. He was better with—well, of course snow *was* water, but frozen. Frozen was tricky.

The lake was gone.

He stopped, frowned at the strange whiteness where there should have been shoreline. Eight paces from where he stood, thick white mist stretched high into the sky, much taller than the trees that should have been there, too, alongside the lake. All of it swathed as if in living cotton.

He had forgotten about the Druid Fog.

The *swynwraig* had compelled him to help with it. That was why he had not remembered. He did not remember a lot of things done under compulsion.

He had frightened the woman—the other one, the one in the basement. Zoe. He had frightened her and made her cry.

Had he meant to? Had that been compelled? He shook his head, as if memories were stuck and needed to drop into the right places.

When nothing did, as usual, he sighed and stared out where the lake should have been. Where it still was, even though he could not see it. He *did* remember what it looked like. After so many nights spent just like this, standing and staring, those memories were set.

Druid Fog to conceal the whole of the Lodge and its land. An excellent security measure, but distasteful. A cruel, selfish trick. Whoever went in would become hopelessly lost, even inside a small area. Distance and direction were so distorted, circling and backtracking could turn ten paces into ten miles. And the longer the exposure, the stronger the effects until time itself became a contorted, erratic mess.

Keeping threats out was one thing. Harming innocents was unforgivable.

But what was he to do?

● ○ ●

Landmark Hotel, Granite Springs

Finally. Thia pushed open the thick glass door, stepped into the rooftop garden. Her triumph was twofold: Not only was she getting to do what she'd hoped to do the night before, she had managed to get some time to herself, out from under the watchful but claustrophobic gaze of either Abby or Kendra (or as it had been throughout dinner, both).

She was supposed to spend this hard-won time in her room. There had been a kind of promise involved, but she'd taken care with her phrasing. "Hotel," she had said; and while technically the garden *was* outside, a walk within it could not be considered "leaving."

Thia was most definitely on hotel property, and even the most basic use of her Sight assured her that the Landmark's protection wards extended far overhead—at least twenty feet up—and went out a full ten beyond the building's perimeter. Ten feet as of the second floor, anyway, she saw after peering over the edge. That width wouldn't do at a lower level, since it would put the wards over halfway into the sidewalk.

She pulled back, put away her Sight, and simply appreciated the moment.

Heat lamps flickered along paths made by raised planters and cozily-arranged patio furniture. People had placed themselves throughout, either in seated groups to enjoy drinks and shared plates; or in pairs to take leisurely, arm-in-arm strolls beneath the clear night sky.

She set her attention elsewhere, not wanting to intrude, but also to discourage the wistful direction of her thoughts. She hadn't come out here to think. Not about her problems with magic and anxiety, not about Zoe—and especially not about Cormac. Not about anything. She had come out here to *not* think.

Once she focused on the lights, that was surprisingly easy to do. They were amazing, and not just the ones in the garden.

Main Street in its December glory rivaled the Vegas Strip. White lights outlined every building, every window. More ran up poles to encircle colorful, oversized wreaths that had been placed around the usual lamps, while still more outlined the bare trees.

The streets beyond were dotted with houses that were just

as decorated. White lights, multicolored lights, animated or still, and an occasional glowing Santa or snowman inflatable attached to a roof.

Several blocks above Pike Street, at the top of the steep hill, someone had used fat yellow bulbs to outline a giant peace sign, while nearer in, a giant redwood tree had been draped from top to bottom in vertical strands. How, she had no idea. A crane? Or, no, given what she now knew, she might better think along different lines. If she was expected to use magic to raise her garage door, she had to think that someone else could use it to hang Christmas lights.

Something fluttered in. A soft, feathery disturbance of the night air, like a bird coming to land on the wall behind her.

The nerves along the back of her neck went on alert. Her spine stiffened. She did not turn. She would not.

"I know it's you," Thia said, although she more than likely spoke to nothing and no one. Empty space or an owl, maybe. Barn owls roosted near the top of the hotel's elevator shaft, she'd been told, as well as in the outdoor theater only a block away.

But the other people in the garden were either too far away or too engrossed in their activities to notice a woman talking to herself, so what did she have to lose?

Even if they did notice, would it matter?

"I don't know why you're here," she went on, "or what you think you're doing by pretending that you aren't you, but I'd really rather you stopped. Pretending, I mean. At least with me." She took a breath, blew it out. "After everything, can't you trust me that much, at least?"

A breeze tousled her hair and sent the flames in the patio heaters into a frenzy.

"I meant what I said, you know. On Orkney." She was afraid she still did. Like a fool. She wrapped protective arms across her chest. "When you left like that, so abruptly, after...It hurt.

It hurt a lot. But I understood. I think I did, anyway. I'd like to understand this." She uncrossed her arms to make a broad gesture.

Two people by the fire pit looked over, their faces puzzled. They probably thought she'd waved.

Thia gave them a small smile and decided to leave.

Even if she wasn't talking to herself, she might as well have been. If he hadn't responded by now, he wasn't going to.

"I'm in Room 84 if you want to talk," she said, her throat tight. "About anything."

There was nothing left for her to do but walk away.

So she did, one forced step at a time...while determinedly not looking anywhere but ahead.

Would he reveal himself? Would they finally, really and truly talk?

Was he there at all?

She opened the door with a shaking hand. If her heart were made of glass, that was when the first crack would've formed. The second would've been after she was inside, moving slowly down the hall, and heard the door click shut.

No other sounds behind her.

The cracks deepened, multiplied. Her room was only one floor down; to take the elevator would be silly—and she didn't think she could stand the wait. She took the stairs.

It seemed she had gotten her questions answered, and each with the same, clear response:

No.

● ○ ●

As the rooftop door closed, Cormac wondered what would happen if he went after Thia. If he caught up not as Connor Michaels but as himself, what would he say? She was easy to lie to, and he happened to be very good at it. But he felt sick at the thought of trying. So what did that leave? He couldn't tell her the truth.

He didn't know the truth.

Still in raven form, he dropped off the wall and strutted the short distance to a vacant, outward-facing settee. Springing onto the seat cushion, he double-checked sight lines and, all clear, cued the shift.

As it took, he slouched, became a man reclining on an over-stuffed piece of outdoor furniture and trying to come to grips with the mess he'd got himself into.

Ah, but what else was new? He'd always been in a mess of some sort.

Thia said she understood why he had left, but she couldn't possibly. He had killed his father and chief tormentor. He had seen Thia barely escape death several times over. She couldn't possibly understand how consumed he'd been by fear.

He'd barely been able to breathe while she looked at him. When she had embraced him, he had thought he might stop altogether.

I love you, she'd told him earlier that night when it seemed likely that they—and more definitely he—would not survive. What was Cormac supposed to do about that when, as it had turned out, they had *both* survived?

What was he supposed to do about it *now?*

Room 84. To talk. He sat up, pushed to his feet.

He got as far as five steps when he caught sight of the head-lamps of the Brigantium's Mercedes. It pulled over to stop in the loading zone. Quentin stepped out, skidded on a slick patch on the walk. The silver tip of his cane emitted a wave of heat, melting a safe path ahead.

Careless, to employ magic with so many potential witnesses about, but Quentin looked to be a man past caring. Cormac could sympathize; he'd had a rough time traveling those same lines back in October.

Cormac also couldn't help being amused.

A man hurried out from beneath the marquee and into view. Finding himself too late for the car door, he changed course for the boot, presumably to assist with luggage. The driver, getting out, waved him off while the blonde woman emerged with a small case.

"Shall I carry this?" she asked the still-fuming Quentin.

He snatched it from her with a sharp, "Is my room ready?" as he limped beneath the marquee. Out of Cormac's sight.

"You'll need to sign some things at Reception," the woman called after him. She was smiling.

The door must have closed on his response, if he made one. The woman rolled her eyes.

The man who had tried to be of assistance joined her. "He's a right basket ain't he, Edith, love?"

"No comment," she said with a chastising shake of her head. Then ruined the effect by laughing.

The driver sighed. "I suppose we're to go back now, as his nibs so kindly requested, and hunt his luggage some more? Or can it wait till morning, seeing as we won't find it no matter what time of day or night? Nothing more than that case came out with him."

So the Brigantium still had trouble with leyline transit, did they? No real surprise, Cormac supposed. The magic involved was arcane, its intricacies held upon pain of death (or, rather, pain of extreme torture and then, if one were lucky, death).

Control of a line or network of lines meant control of the traffic. It was an immensely profitable, intensely dangerous business, both for what and whom were conveyed along the lines and because of those who did the conveying. Disputes were frequent and violent, with some dating back millennia.

Traditionally, control was familial and tended to have ties to the Otherworld, but blood feuds had taken their toll—pun intended. As particular clan numbers dwindled, leaving their portal holdings vulnerable, new groups had moved in.

That the portal near Granite Springs had no tollkeeper—no clear territorial association whatsoever—seemed improbable to the point of being troubling. But as it had nothing to do with Cormac, he wasn't going to waste time worrying about it.

Below, the woman named Edith shrugged. "I know it's lost. But *he'll* know if you don't try. Better to get it over with."

The driver grumbled but got in. His door slammed.

The other man had paused halfway into the front passenger seat. "You aren't coming?"

Edith shook her head. "Believe me, I'd rather."

"Until tomorrow, then." He closed his door.

With a wave as the agents drove off, she belatedly followed Quentin into the Landmark's lobby.

A motorbike engine fired.

Cormac tracked the sound across the intersection, watched as a Harley Davidson, its headlamp *not* on, left the car park at the corner to follow the Brigantium's Mercedes.

Granted, the street was one-way, so there was no choice but to follow the Mercedes, and the surroundings were so well lit that a headlamp could easily be forgotten.

But if the rider's behavior wasn't enough to raise suspicion, his Rekkr-emblazoned jacket was.

Cormac stepped behind a large planter and ducked down as if to tie his shoe. Instead, he shifted back to raven form and took flight.

At the end of the next block, the Brigantium drove through as the signal changed from amber to red.

The motorbike accelerated with a noxious belch of exhaust, intentionally running the light. Sure, being a Rekkr, the rider likely had an anarchist streak, but it also kept him up with the Brigantium's—

Metal tore through Cormac's left shoulder with a force hard enough to knock him off course. His wing useless, he spiraled into an out-of-control drop.

CHAPTER 11

Seconds from impact, Cormac shifted out of raven form. His native bone and muscle mass were less fragile, and with flight out of the question, he would run a damn sight faster as man than bird. Even if he couldn't currently manage much beyond breathing. Tucked up where he had somehow rolled against the main unit of a convoluted central air system, he tried to rise above the shock and spreading pain.

The roaring noise was not in his head.

Right, he'd been following a motorbike. But this sound came from the wrong direction. Circling back?

Cormac pushed so he sat, braced on the compressor.

There wasn't much light on the flat commercial roof, only what that cast by the moon and the Landmark a block away. His best estimate put him one or two shops past Eclectica. That made things easier. Thanks to the slope of the hill at that point, what was two stories on Main Street was only one on the alley behind. The leap wouldn't be pleasant, but he'd made worse.

With a rough exhale, he looked down at his chest, touched careful fingers to the blood-soaked fabric of his jacket. The end of a crossbow bolt jutted from the juncture of collarbone and shoulder.

Someone yelled above the idling engine. "What'd you get, Ronny?"

"Looked like a raven," Ronny (presumably) yelled back.

Ifrinn. There had been more than one Rekkr around. Using his good hand and the frame of the ventilation unit, Cormac pulled himself to standing and pushed off for the back of the building.

"No shit?" The engine stopped, making it easier to hear the two men—whose volume remained high. Damaged hearing, no doubt. "Why'd you do that?"

"It was following you, man."

"A bird? A bird, following me?"

"That's what I said, isn't it?" Ronny was on the move, his voice's point of origin changing angle, coming closer.

Cormac dodged a steaming vent and cut right. If he could get onto Eclectica, it would be an easy drop from the veranda and give him a straight track down the alley.

"That's some weird shit, dude. Is it dead?"

"How do I know? It hit up there. Get off your ass and help me find it." Heavy boots pounded up the side street toward the alley.

Again relying on his good arm, Cormac vaulted over the low bricks of Eclectica's eastern parapet. He hit the roof at a run, pain screaming across his chest.

"Where we goin'?" Out of breath, the voice came from the left—inside the alley, maybe two buildings away.

"We're goin' looking for the fucking thing, Hedge," came the frustrated reply.

Cormac stopped. If the Rekkrs kept to that side, he'd have to climb down to Main after all...or run the roofs the entire length to First Street to take what was probably closer to a three story drop.

"I swear to *Vánagandr,* dude, I'm gonna fucking shoot you one of these days."

"What? What'd I say?"

Cormac nearly smiled. In a fight, if it came to that, it would be one on one plus an idiot. Favorable odds even with the bolt interfering with his left shoulder, but he'd rather not test them.

He'd rather not have to deal with whatever reinforcements they might call, either.

"*Blatqnn,*" Ronny snarled, his second use of Old Norse in Cormac's hearing. Who the hell were these guys? "Just help me look for a fucking way up."

"Okay, man. Okay. You want it for a trophy or something? Is that what we're doing?" They passed Eclectica.

Would its protection wards engage if Cormac were to do a low-level concealment spell while on its roof?

"I want my bolt back, that's what," Ronny said. "And Skati will want the bird when he gets back."

"Why? He didn't kill it."

"Magic and shit, man." Ronny was some distance away. "He collects the things. Here. Up here." Boots clanged on metal.

Careful of the sightlines, Cormac peered over the rear edge, scanned the alley. At the second building in from First Street, the two Rekkrs climbed a set of metal stairs to the third floor. The giant with the mountain man beard, Cormac recognized as the rider who had set off after the Brigantium's car. The other one, by no means small, was rotund and had a thin, light colored braid flopping down the back of his jacket.

"Hell, Ronny," that one scoffed. "Birds can't talk."

"You don't know shit, man. You really don't."

They eyed the top of the building from its narrow landing.

"Are you sure you can reach that?" asked the one who wasn't Ronny.

While their attention remained fixed there, Cormac eased himself lengthwise on the bricks that topped Eclectica's back wall. The veranda of the garden patio was only two feet down.

Excellent. Even with a pain dampening spell, he wasn't sure his left arm could take the weight if he had to lower himself from the parapet instead of simply go over.

"Come on," Ronny said. "Give me a leg up."

"How?"

"Get up here."

Amidst the rattling which followed Ronny's order, Cormac rolled off, landed in a crouch on the veranda's ridged plastic roof. The timing turned out to be excellent, coinciding with a terrible bang from over at the stairs.

"Fuck, man," Ronny bellowed. Boots stomped on the metal stairs. "What the fuck!"

"Sorry. Thought I had you. I got it now."

Grateful for their ineptitude, Cormac skulked to where the veranda met the garden wall near the rubbish bins.

"You sure this fucking time?" he heard Ronny ask.

"Yeah, man. On three."

Cormac sat at the edge, pushed off to come down between wall and bin. The impact sent fire racing along injured nerves. His vision wavered. He made sure he was outside Eclectica's wards and then wove the dampening spell. It took its time to kick in, and still left him with a good deal of discomfort...and unsteadiness. He wondered how much blood he'd lost.

Enough to rule out the tempting idea of simply waiting out the two Rekkrs.

With a quick look to the stairs—empty, so they must have made it onto the roof—Cormac set off. He kept low, using the shadows cast by the bins, until he reached the alley proper. To turn right would put him in the open past the men currently clomping along the roofs. Not that they knew they were now looking for a man.

To the left, although indirect, would allow him the cover of Eclectica's garden wall.

He went left.

Traffic sounds had increased over the past several minutes, and when he reached the side street he found it full of cars. Two lanes, moving in opposite directions—barely—as drivers searched in vain for parking. The spaces on both sides of the street had been filled. So had the lot across the way. But that didn't stop drivers from going in, only to have to make their way out again, past another car making the same mistake.

Before joining the stream of pedestrians headed down the short, steep block to Main Street, Cormac worked a glamour to conceal the dart's protruding shaft as well as the blood. His left shirt and jacket sleeves were saturated; he kept his hand in his pocket to keep from leaving a dripping trail. Until the dart was removed, he couldn't do much to heal the wound.

Pedestrian chatter concerned an event at one of the retail shops. People were excited about special pricing, raffles, and a gingerbread contest, whatever that entailed.

Rounding the corner, Cormac and the others merged into an even more populated stream. One, thankfully, that would take him in the direction he needed.

He noted the two motorbikes parked in front of Eclectica: the one he had intended to follow plus one he should have spotted while doing so. Its rider must have been positioned there. Later he'd need to consider the why of that.

A jovial group stopped to admire Eclectica's festive window display. Cormac smiled in the vague way the townspeople had and joined them. "Lovely, isn't it?"

There were seven in all, ranging from young adult to senior. Multiple generations of one family, he decided, when half of the faces which turned his way sported similar features and matching smiles.

"Have you been inside?" the eldest of the women inquired before turning herself and her wheeled walking frame back to the window. She seemed particularly taken with a collection of woodland-themed glass ornaments. "Is it as wonderful as it looks from here?"

"I have," he said easily, "and it is. Are you new to the area, then?" He took slow steps onward, subtly drawing the family along.

"No," said a middle-aged man. His arm was linked with that of a petite woman in a colorful knit cap. "We're down from Salem. Thought it would be nice to spend Christmas together in a new setting. My sister passed a couple months back," he added quietly, and the woman briefly laid her head against his arm. "It's been hard. On my parents, especially."

"My condolences on your loss," Cormac said, surprised by a pang of genuine emotion. His experience with family was the stuff of nightmares.

This one couldn't be more different.

It was obvious in the looks they gave one another, the way they walked together. They were individual parts formed into a whole. The loss of one would cut deep.

"How about you?" asked the elderly woman, behind. "You live here?"

Cormac weighed a lie, tossed it away. "No."

What an interesting notion. He liked his place in Cumbria, but for obvious reasons he hadn't made an effort to befriend anyone there, so it could feel rather remote; and there was... something to Granite Springs. Or perhaps he was confusing the town with one person in it. But the idea of spending time here, of letting it become familiar, held a striking appeal.

What was this? For Morrigan's sake, he'd spent the better part of his long life alone. And "better," in that case, was both quantitative and qualitative. He had been better off alone.

Blood loss was making him melancholy.

He had put an awkward pause in the conversation. As they crossed First Street, with the Landmark in all its festive glory ahead, he filled it. "Have you seen the hotel's rooftop garden? There's a brilliant view, and table service."

"Oh, dad, come on." A woman in her early twenties tugged

the middle-aged man's coat. "We should do it. Do they have desserts?" she asked Cormac. "Have you—hey!" She wheeled on the young man who had playfully elbowed her side.

"Desserts, Jess?" he teased. "Don't you mean drinks?" In a loud aside, he told Cormac, "She just turned twenty-one and is looking for any chance to get carded."

It took a moment to translate that as a reference to what must be legal age in the States.

"Ah," Cormac said. "Congratulations."

Jess, her cheeks already rosy from the cold, flushed bright red. "Thanks," she told Cormac and then, frowning, she gave the young man's shoulder a not-so-playful jab. "Thanks a lot."

They had reached the portico.

"I'm staying here," Cormac said, angling toward the lobby doors, "so I'll bid you a good night. If you'd like to give the garden a try, speak with reception there." As he gestured with his good arm, he sent out a tiny mental nudge.

"Dad?" The middle-aged man looked to the eldest, who had been walking silently in the rear of the group. It was almost as if the same man had aged thirty years, the resemblance was so strong. He looked to the woman with the walker.

"I do love Irish coffee," she said.

"That you do," he said with a chuckle. He gave Cormac a bright smile. "Thank you, son—we'll give it a try."

Cormac barely managed a nod in return. The old man likely called every male he perceived to be younger, "son." A verbal habit that meant nothing. But Cormac had never before been called that without scorn.

They entered the lobby as a group and then, amidst wishes of good nights, Cormac left for the lift. His reluctance to do so must have been an effect of his injury and his dread of what he next had to do.

But he did admire them, a family touched by sorrow but determined to find joy together. They gave him one last wave as the elevator doors closed.

By the time it arrived at his floor, he felt decidedly unsteady. He fumbled for the keycard in his jacket as he negotiated the corridor.

The room's damned electronic lock took a couple of tries, and then he was home free, so to speak. He let the door close on its own behind him.

The maid had come and gone: The bedside lamps were on; the comforter, folded back. Cormac wondered if she had done more than the usual turn-down—not that he had anything to hide. He staggered to the bath, turned on all its lights with a held mental intention and flick of his hand.

One-armed, he struggled out of his jacket, dropped it to the floor on his way to the combination tub-shower. An adjacent shelf held a stack of fresh towels. He grabbed one, knocked two more to the floor for easy reach before he climbed into the tub.

His breath hissed when he leaned back on the cold enamel and fresh agony shot through his shoulder. The dampening spell was breaking down, unable to withstand the effects that the continued presence of iron-based metal had on his body.

And to think, he had yet to begin.

Gritting his teeth, he surveyed the damage. Blood soaked his shirt, sticking it to his chest like a second skin. The bolt protruded a good two inches. Given the type, that meant at least two more inches were imbedded. Fabric had been driven into the wound.

He positioned his hand at the shaft.

He hoped the walls had excellent sound-proofing.

● ○ ●

The Ogham Room, Landmark Hotel

Thia was supposed to be meditating. About twenty minutes earlier, Abby had insisted that she join her in one of the event spaces so they could work on Thia's skills (or lack thereof).

She hadn't wanted to, but it would be more productive than wallowing in negative emotion alone in her room. She needed to learn to control her power. If Connor-aka-Cormac hadn't helped her that morning, things could have gone very, very badly.

So there she sat, cross-legged with her palms upturned on her knees while she tried to focus her mind on nothing and oneness instead of the ache setting into her left ankle or the one-sided conversation she might have just had with a raven (or herself alone, if she was wrong about his being there) or how badly she could fail in the exercises Abby had planned.

If she damaged anything in the room, could she afford to pay for it? What if something went really, *really* wrong? Thia's breathing sped up. She worked to slow it.

But because her heart rate had also sped up, her effort to limit the breaths her body thought it wanted only created a sense of confusion and thus more anxiety...and a faster heart rate.

She opened her eyes, darted a glance at the room's art deco clock. Twenty-two minutes gone, eight more to go.

Abby sat about five feet away, directly opposite. Her pose was a model of stillness; her expression, of perfect serenity. Truly impressive for someone whose nature seemed to be so emotionally charged. Quick to anger, quick to laugh. Clearly, Abby could meditate.

Whereas Thia could not. It should be so simple. Think of nothing. Just be. Couldn't she just *be?*

Maybe if she tried to—

"I can feel you thinking from all the way over here," Abby said with quiet calm. Her eyes stayed closed.

"I'm sorry. I can't clear my mind." Thia let her spine slump. "It's just that I—I'm not sure about this."

"The meditation?"

"No, about tonight. Practicing."

Abby's eyes did open then, dark violet in the low light, and her fingers released their mudras. "What's the worry? It's all stuff you've done before. We're just practicing. Exercising."

"I don't want to wreck the Landmark."

An antique crystal chandelier hung overhead. The walls and ceiling had elaborate plasterwork and crown moulding. The artwork was oil—actual paintings, not prints. Repairs would be difficult if not impossible, depending.

Pine boughs and bolts of fabric and boxes of supplies had been set around the room in advance of an upcoming event. All of it flammable.

"Oh, come on," Abby said. "You aren't going to wreck an entire hotel." She checked her watch, closed her eyes again. "Even Murphy and I didn't do that much when we had that disagreement."

"You totaled the ballroom."

Abby grimaced. "Because it wasn't set up to withstand that sort of thing. This room *is*. Kendra assures me it can take up to a hundred times more than we're going to deal with. It gets rented out for weddings and initiations all the time. What do you think all those decorations are for?" Blindly, she waved a hand at the supplies. "The guests who rented this room plan to perform high magic. You and I are only going to play with a little candle flame and some water and levitate a few spheres. Stop worrying."

"Okay. Okay." Closing her eyes, Thia took a deep breath, let it out. She could do this.

But what if she couldn't get herself calm enough?

What if she couldn't keep her focus when she was calling on her power and she lost control? She didn't have a great track record.

Abby was with her, which usually meant things went better than when Thia went solo, but what if she lost her grip on the power altogether? There was so much of it, what if it literally overpowered Abby?

Magic could go horribly wrong. Not just property damage. Magic could maim. Magic could kill. She had only to consider a rumor heard about Quentin. That some years back he had been gravely injured when the group he'd been working with had tapped into more than they could handle. No one else had survived.

The power Thia carried was as old, or perhaps older, than the Celtic goddess who had wielded it. Vast age and potency made it tricky for modern practitioners. Unpredictable. Abby likened it to a folk song. Thia had an early version while most everyone else knew only the result of centuries of iteration. The basic tune might be the same, but here and there a note might have shifted. Sometimes the differences didn't matter. Other times, they did.

What if this was one of those times?

What if her power killed Abby?

"I can't do this." Thia untwisted her legs and sprang to her feet. "Not tonight." Not ever.

Abby sighed. "Thia."

"No, I mean it. I can't do this."

"All right." Abby held up a placating hand. "We can try these exercises tomorrow if—"

"No. I'm done. The Cailleach's powers came out of a crystal sphere, and they can damn well go back into one. When I first got to the Ring, Cormac was going to bleed to death because Idris had bound his powers the same way. So it's possible."

Thia's gestures had become over-animated and she sounded crazed, maybe, but she didn't care. "We can find someone to bind mine, put them in something like the Stone again."

"And then what?" Abby asked. "Assuming we find someone who has that ability—and assuming they can be trusted not to take the power for themselves—what would happen next?

How would you keep this new Stone safe?"

"Drop it in the middle of the ocean."

"Okay, sure." Abby's agreement...wasn't. "But you'd have to get it there in order to do that. And if you think things are hard now with the Brigantium interested in using you, think about how worse it would be if the powers were back in such an easy-to-handle form. Imagine how many more people and groups would be involved."

Thia didn't want to. It had been bad enough the first time.

"Right now," Abby went on, "there's an unstable, dangerous woman who by her own vow is more interested in revenge than getting the Cailleach's powers out of you. And there's the Brigantium, which at best only wants you to join, but at worst want you as a weapon. And, yeah"—she didn't let Thia interrupt—"the potential exists for more.

"There are a lot of power-hungry people and organizations in this world. But the fact that the powers are *in* you is both a deterrent and protection. If you put them into another Stone of Shadows, it'll be October and Orkney all over again. Everybody going after the object with the powers and you an easy, much more defenseless target."

Abby was right. Thia was stuck on this path with no way to go but ahead. Into the dark, dangerous unknown. "This way I'm still a target...but a harder one."

"And if you'd work at it," Abby said, pointing to the dreaded box of supplies, "if you learned to wield the Cailleach's power, you could become a next to impossible one."

If she didn't accidentally kill everyone in the process, Thia thought, and forced herself to sit.

● ○ ●

Room Seventy-Nine

Cormac's fingers slipped, of course. Several times. It was the blood. And the pain. When he did succeed, the bolt clenched in his unsteady fist, he was barely conscious. But, at last, he could get the full effect of his spellwork. Already the pain was lessening; and the wound, closing over.

He pushed himself up to stand, and then braced his good arm on the tub-shower's acrylic wall until his head settled.

The tub was a literal bloody mess, as anticipated, but easy enough to clean. He laid the bolt on the towel rack, shucked his shoes and clothes, and pulled shut the curtain.

The tap was one of those long-handled twist affairs. Cormac cranked it, pulled to direct the flow to the shower. Hot water immediately sluiced down his chest, carrying away the blood. He toed the stained towels until they were directly under the spray.

Pink-tinged water swirled at his feet before gurgling down the drain. He'd do a cleansing spell if he had to. Better that than having housekeeping set off an alert.

He prodded his shoulder. Already, the wound had knitted, the skin over it angry and new, so he broke the healing spell. His *Sidhe* heredity would speed the rest of the process along, and with the worst of it done, he'd be wise to conserve what power he could. That there would be more violence to come, more threats to face and in short order, was a given.

As the spray beat down, he tested his left arm. Rolled his shoulder and neck.

He wasn't a fighter by choice. It was a matter of survival. Idris had been his first teacher, and perhaps the earliest and most lasting lesson had been one of endurance. Next he'd had to learn how to respond to other threats: locals who attacked first and asked questions of his presence later; intruders who wanted what he had. And sometimes *he* was the intruder after what *they* had.

Bowing his head, he let the water massage the back of his neck. The deep tension remained. The anxiety.

He shut off the shower, grabbed the remaining clean towel

to dry himself. On his way out of the tub, he picked up the bolt. His mobile, he retrieved from his jacket pocket.

He was laying out fresh clothes when Murphy answered.

"This had better be—"

"Is Thia safe?" Cormac interrupted, pitching his voice at his phone on the bed while he pulled on a pair of plaid boxers.

"What? Of course she is. She's in my damn hotel, isn't she? Meeting up with her friend and risking untold damage to the Ogham Room with some fool practice session—"

"We need to talk and I'm not up to going anywhere just yet. You know the room number."

"Of all the bloody cheek, giving orders to—"

Cormac ended the call and then reached for a pair of black trousers.

By the time Murphy knocked and then almost immediately flung open the door, Cormac was fully dressed and slouched in one of two chairs by the room's single window. The drapes were closed. Murphy stormed the rest of the way in, closed the door with a flick of power. It clicked softly shut. Even in his anger, it seemed, he had a concern for his guests.

Or their potential complaints.

"Well? What is it then that couldn't—" This time, Murphy cut himself off. His gaze went unerringly to the bolt on the table. "Did you leak that all over my hotel?"

Blood had dried in smudges on the otherwise shiny metal.

"Tried not to." Cormac's shrug wasn't as nonchalant as he'd intended, thanks to the wince that accompanied it.

"*Mac conlón.*" Murphy used his mobile to place a call, telling someone to: "Check the lobby and front entrance for marks of a red, liquid nature. Discreetly, mind you. Also the lift"— he looked to Cormac, who nodded—"and corridor on Seven. And send up a first aid kit. The likes of which you or I might require from time to time. Right."

Pocketing the phone, he bent to examine the bolt. "How

did you get it?"

"I was tailing the biker who was tailing the Brigantium's car. Got shot down. Near Eclectica. Not long after Quentin had been dropped off outside." Murphy had to already know the man was a guest.

"Shot *down*, was it?"

Cormac ignored that. "By a second biker. Stationed there, presumably. As far as I can tell, he shot for sport. When he and his *marrer* came looking, it was for the bolt and a trophy for their boss. No name mentioned, but it's not Cassandra. They said 'he.' And called him *skati*."

Murphy frowned at that but seemed to file it away for later. "So they didn't know what—or rather, whom—they shot?"

"No. And probably still don't." Not after all the care Cormac had taken. He shifted in his seat. Wounds like this one had a tendency to become more painful the closer they were to full healing. Had to do with repaired nerves. "The one called Ronny liked to curse in Old Norse."

Murphy picked up the bolt.

"Watch it," Cormac snapped. "There could be prints."

Shit. Sure, there were prints—prints all over the thing—and every single one at this point would be Cormac's. He hadn't thought beyond getting the damned thing out.

Oblivious to Cormac's realization, Murphy studied the bolt. "Even if I could gather prints, there'd be no way to identify who left them. I don't have access to the kinds of databases that—"

"The Brigantium might." Not that Cormac wanted them to try. As far as he knew, they didn't have his prints on file; he'd prefer to keep it that way.

"They might." Murphy returned the bolt to the table, stuck his hands in his pockets. "Our uncomfortable alliance seems to be forming again."

Cormac eyed the bolt. He never should have said anything

about prints.

"I'm no happier about it than you," Murphy said.

Ah, hell. Forget prints—Cormac's *blood* was on there. What the Brigantium could do with that made what remained in his veins run cold. His hand was out, taking, before he'd thought.

But Murphy hadn't made a move to stop him. Instead, he nodded toward the bathroom. "Soap ought to do it, aye? No magics, but wipe it well."

At Cormac's questioning look, the man shrugged. "It's not as if I want them to have *my* prints, either. Hurry, would you?" He again pulled out his phone. "I can't avoid this, no matter what either of us would prefer."

As Cormac took the bolt to the sink, he heard Murphy ask to connect with room Thirty-two. He let the water run until it was scalding, and then set the stopper. The basin began to fill.

"I'll have to let Kendra Ross in on this before long," Murphy said from the doorway. Cormac met his gaze in the mirror. "Nothing short of a blood oath will keep her from telling the other two."

Cormac soaped a washcloth and began to scrub.

"Aye," Murphy said, as if he'd heard the profanities that ran though Cormac's mind. "But she'll find out soon enough, and is liable to murder me ten times over if she believes she's been left out." His attention went to the phone still held by his ear. "Quentin? Murphy. You'll be wanting to head down to Room Seventy-Nine. I've a little something of interest. No need to bring your friends."

Cormac rinsed off the soap, dried the bolt as Murphy ended that call and then placed another.

The knock on the room door startled them both. A phone's faint ring could be heard from the other side. Murphy moved as if to open it.

Quickly, Cormac glamoured himself into Connor Michaels,

drawing on energy that would otherwise go toward healing. He put in his back-up pair of colored contacts and then gave the results a hasty once-over in the mirror. Not his best work, but it would have to do.

He walked out to see Murphy open the door to a visibly angry Kendra Ross. She held up her still-ringing phone. "This is you about to tell me why you have Jonah cleaning up a blood trail that goes from the lobby to this door, is it? And why you asked Tina to bring one of our special kits?"

"It was." Murphy tucked his phone away.

Kendra's stopped ringing. "Good."

As she stormed past him into the room, she caught sight of Cormac—Connor. Her expression registered surprise before moving onto something more like disdain.

"I'm not sure why you bother," she said to him, and Murphy chuckled. Everyone was a critic.

Short notice, wounded—Cormac bristled but said only, "I'd rather the Brigantium not know," and went to retake his seat.

"Naturally." Murphy still looked far too amused.

Cormac let his irritation show in his eyes. It was a challenge he'd rather not follow through on, given the odds. But sometimes a threat was what it took to make people see reason.

Murphy's eyes flashed in response—challenge met—but he merely shrugged. "Fair enough. Is that the kit there with you, Ross?"

She set a worn, embroidered bag on the table next to Cormac. "I took the liberty of relieving Tina." Lifting the bag's flap, she extracted a small wooden box. Her motions were almost reverent as she placed both hands atop it. "Are you sure?"

As second after second passed in silence, Cormac began to wonder if the question had been directed at him. But Kendra hadn't looked away from the box. Nor had Murphy.

"There's no harm in it," Murphy said at last.

Kendra appeared none too pleased but she lifted the top of the box.

A ripple of power danced along Cormac's skin.

CHAPTER 12

"**D**o you need any topical remedies?" Kendra asked. "I understand your mother was full *Sidhe*."

Cormac tried not to react at the mention. "She was."

They were using the wrong tense. As far as he knew, she was alive and well in the Otherworld with the rest of her family. Cormac's birth had been her ticket home.

He slid fingers beneath his collar. Sensitive nerves burned as he traced the raised, slick scar. By morning there wouldn't be so much as that. He withdrew his hand. "And it's fine."

"That must've been a nice gift to have around Fiend's Fell," Murphy said from where he'd made himself comfortable on the bed. He referred to Idris's tendency for sadism—about which they both knew far too much.

"It was." In addition to that tendency (yet not unrelated), there had been periodic rituals that required Cormac's blood in rather significant amounts.

Kendra removed three small crystals from the box, dropped them into a silk pouch that she then tied with a green cord. "Here."

After a quick look with his Sight (Cormac might be willing to trust, but that didn't mean he did) he took it. Energy shot up his arm and set fire to his shoulder.

"Morrigan's cloak," he gritted out as his muscles spasmed. Agonized, he forced his fingers to close more tightly around the charm. At this rate, he'd be healed long before morning. He should have paid more attention. "What's in this?"

"A little this, a little that." Kendra shut the box with a sharp click. It went back inside the bag, which she slung over her shoulder. She shot him a glare. "You're welcome."

"My thanks, then." And Cormac *was* thankful. It was her animosity he resented.

He wasn't well liked—he preferred it that way—and anyone would be a fool to think him a reliable ally. But he hadn't done anything to Kendra, personally.

And he would have thanked her unprompted...if he'd been able to think more clearly past what felt like actual flames using his collarbone for kindling.

"I'm not the enemy here," he told her. "You might consider cutting—"

There was a knock on the door.

"Play nice, children," Murphy said, and snapped his fingers. The door opened.

Kendra, her posture suddenly alert, took two steps back to place herself against the wall.

But the man standing in the corridor presented no threat. Not currently, at any rate. And his present state of dress made it difficult to imagine he ever could be.

In place of his bespoke suit were track pants and a green "I Heart Oregon" hoodie. His short-cropped gray hair stuck every which way and appeared several shades darker for being wet.

"I was in the shower," Quentin said by way of greeting and limped inside. "This had better be good."

Murphy waved the door closed. "Unusual choice of attire for you, isn't it?"

That earned a black look. "This was all your establishment could provide while my suit is laundered. There was a slight problem with my luggage." He lowered himself into the other chair by the window.

Across the short table, Cormac braced for discovery, and the accusations which would naturally follow.

Quentin's eyes narrowed, studying him, but he asked merely, "Shoulder wound?"

Cormac made a brusque nod.

"Bullet?" Quentin's hand went out.

"Bolt." Cormac from his pocket. He would've placed it on the man's palm, but that was withdrawn at the last moment.

"On the table please."

"Misplace your gloves, did you?" Murphy chided.

A muscle clenched along Quentin's jaw. "They were wet."

"Surely you could have dried them in a flash. Literally."

The Brigantium's man muttered a rude Latin phrase. Head bowed, he held his hands an inch above the bolt. "I'll get on with this, shall I? Unless you'd rather we chat some more?"

Cormac shot Murphy a warning look—only to see Kendra doing the same. The response to both was an amused shrug.

Silence fell like a shroud as Quentin closed his eyes. Power began to wreathe around him, rising strong enough to needle Cormac's skin.

"Careful, *a mhac,*" Murphy said quietly. His eyes held a faint glow. As did Kendra's. The power was affecting them all.

It was an odd power, Cormac thought, repulsed. Cold and... *dead* was the word that came to mind. Usually he felt power as something, well, if not exactly solid then at least substantial.

This was not that.

This was the tangible absence of that. Instead of substance there was a hungry sort of nothingness, as if the air itself was being displaced—its very molecules consumed—by cold fire.

It called to mind images of the Ankou and *bean sidhe* and the Wild Hunt, and Cormac wondered at some of the rumors heard about the *de facto* heir to the Brigantium throne: How every soul who had been with him at a midnight ritual gone wrong had not lived to see sunrise.

If anyone other than Quentin knew how he had managed to survive—and become more powerful for it—they weren't talking. They weren't even guessing, as far as rumor went.

Cormac could hazard a few guesses now that he'd felt the power firsthand. And, he realized belatedly, he had felt once before. It wasn't a memory he relished, so it had been slow to surface.

Orkney, in the Ring of Brodgar. The Brigantium was using him as a conduit. His hands were still on Idris's throat. And in the blink of time between the lethal magic shutting off and the departure of Idris's life, he had felt this same...absence.

That had been Quentin's contribution.

Cormac inched his chair back a bit from the table. It didn't help. No one in the room could escape the discomfiting chill.

Then Quentin picked up the bolt.

● ○ ●

The Ogham Room

Thia watched as Abby took a fat red candle from her supply box and set it on the floor between them. Scattered throughout the same area were spheres made of different materials: wood, stone, metal, glass.

She couldn't help but continue to think this was a bad idea.

"The room is strongly protected," Abby said, "so there's no need to cast a circle. Magic can't get in or out."

It hadn't helped Thia's nerves when she'd heard it the first time, and it didn't help now. "Great, but I still don't think I should—"

"Light the candle." Abby made an abrupt gesture. The room

went dark.

Anxiety shifted into overdrive. "I don't know about this."

"I do." Abby's voice, hard and steady, cut through the dark. "You've done this plenty of times. You'll light the candle and we'll work on levitating the spheres. Nothing will go wrong."

"You're sure?"

There was a slight pause. "I'm sure."

"Were you just checking? Sensing things out?"

If Abby hadn't picked up on any Bad Feelings, then maybe Thia *could* trust herself to do this right.

"Just light the damn candle, Thia, would you?"

That was *not* an answer. But the frustration Thia had heard was enough to get her to reach down and call to the power within. She'd done this before—plenty of times, as Abby had said. It was only one little candle wick. She wasn't alone, so even if things got out of hand, they wouldn't get far. She was being paranoid when what she needed to do was simply relax and be confident.

She could do this.

In her mind, she envisioned the red candle as it sat only a few inches away. Then, as usual, she startled at the tingle that was the Cailleach's power coming awake. One day she'd be used to it.

Pretending this was that day—night, rather—Thia coaxed the energy toward her right hand, held palm-up. The gesture would be unnecessary if she were more adept; it served like a set of bicycle training wheels. If she truly knew what she was doing she could simply spark fire where she wanted it to be by will alone.

When her hand grew hot, she added a flame to her mental image and snapped her fingers.

The candle flared to life.

Thia jerked, shocked. The flame shot up, reaching twice the height of the candle.

"Oh, God." She waved her hands as the flame continued to grow. "What do I do?"

"Stop feeding it power," Abby said, calmly enough, but she sat forward. Tense.

"Am I?" *Argh,* yes, she was. Thia could feel it, rushing down her arm. How stupid. And the longer she let it, the higher the flame stretched. "Sorry."

"Don't be. Just fix it."

Thia forced her eyes shut, worked to block the energy that continued to flow down her arm. Like turning off a tap, she told herself, and bore down.

The power resisted.

"Thia." Abby no longer sounded calm.

"I'm trying."

But the harder she tried, the harder the power pushed back. Her whole arm was hot with the energy while the rest of her went cold with terror. She couldn't stop either one. She was a self-fulfilling prophesy of disaster and there was nothing she could do about it.

"Thia, just relax."

The unusually high register of her friend's voice did *not* help. If Abby was scared, then—

"Thia. You need to relax."

"Tell me something I don't know," Thia snapped. Her eyes opened—shit, the flame was a foot high and fluttering wildly. The room was protected against magic, but what about fire?

She was going to burn down the Landmark.

Forget controlling the power, they needed to put the flame out. For Thia to do it alone, she needed to draw the energy into herself. But since she couldn't make it stop flowing out, that wasn't going to happen. "Abby, please, can you douse it with something?"

Melted red wax streamed down the candle's sides to form a

spreading pool on the wood floor. Thia considered tipping it over, smothering the flame in the wax. But what if that didn't work? She was trembling, her muscles locked with the effort of trying to put the out-of-control genie back in the bottle. Sweat ran down her face. "Please? Do something."

"I'm trying," Abby said tightly. She was holding her hands out, palms down.

"No," Thia said, "I mean something physical. There has to be a fire extinguisher." Because Abby's magic wasn't working, either.

An orange-red glow surrounded—no, emanated from Thia's right hand. *Shit.* She clenched it into a fist, tucked it into her lap. A useless move, she knew even as she made it. Physical gestures were merely tools and therefore only as good as the person who made them.

Since Thia completely sucked, her gestures were useless. It would come down to intention and strength of will and focus and ability and a bunch of other things she couldn't manage.

"Never mind the candle," Abby said suddenly.

"What?"

"Levitate the wooden sphere."

"Are you kidding?" Stupid question. Of course Abby wasn't kidding. "You want me to try *more* magic?"

"Concentrate. Use the power for something other than the candle. Redirect it."

"Oh. Right, maybe...." Thia focused on the wooden sphere, imagined it lifting from the floor.

She watched it shoot up and hit the ceiling hard enough to break off bits of plaster. "No, no, no!" She waved frantically, helpless as the ball sped back down—toward Abby, who made a sort of sweeping motion and somehow sent the ball veering left. It crashed into a mirror and, amidst a shower of broken glass, dropped to roll along the floor.

The room vibrated an airplane in flight.

"Abby," Thia said, terrified, "I'm losing control. Please, get help. I don't know if—"

"*Focus,* dammit. The outer reflects the inner."

Thia just wanted this to be over. "I'm too scared. Please. I can't think."

"Focus on the spheres."

Oh, fuck this. Fuck all of this. Anger, unexpected and immense, roared up from somewhere deep down and, for a moment, overrode fear, overrode everything. For a moment only, but a moment was all it took to go to hell: The spheres, candle, and a number of other objects from around the room leapt into the air to whirl about like a cyclone.

Abby cried out, ducking too late. Something clonked her on the side of the head and she toppled to one side.

"I'm so sorry!" Thia started to go to her but the hollow glass sphere crashed nearby, exploding. A hot blob of wax splashed down on the back of her hand. She shook it, reacting to the searing pain, only to then see the candle with its high flame sail across the room to strike the wall in a splatter of molten wax and fall onto a stack of boxes. She ran toward the cardboard as it caught fire.

The doors burst open, and as people rushed in a tidal wave of force slammed into Thia and she went down. The landing was strangely gentle, like falling onto a mattress.

A woman aimed the nozzle of a fire extinguisher—Thia had been right, there *had* been one handy—at the burning box. Anything airborne immediately dropped.

Voices were muffled as if coming through a thick wall. She tried to sit up. Couldn't. She was trapped in something, but nothing was there.

The fire was out.

The woman set down the extinguisher, conferred with two of the men who had accompanied her. Thia couldn't see more, couldn't so much as roll over.

"Abby!" Her own voice was loud, especially in contrast to the others. "Abby, are you okay?"

"I'm fine." Her friend's voice was as muffled as all the others and came from behind.

"Thank God. I'm so sorry." Thia's muscles were cramping. She felt like they would tremble but for being frozen in place. "I can't move. Why can't I move?"

Abby came around to kneel where Thia could see. Her face was pale—except for the red mark on her forehead, courtesy of whatever had struck her. "You're in a containment spell," she said. "Have you got the power under control? If you do, they'll release you."

"They?"

"Hotel security. Alarms were triggered when power started pushing against the room's protections."

"Oh. Good." Thia tried to take a deep breath but the—what had Abby called it? Containment. The containment was too tight. "I think I'm okay now."

"You're sure?" Abby's violet eyes held a mix of concern and, if Thia wasn't mistaken, fear.

"Yeah." She could feel the power moving beneath her skin, but it was retreating. Sinking in rather than flowing out.

Abby pushed to her feet. "I'll let them know."

● ○ ●

Room Seventy-Nine, Landmark Hotel
Despite Quentin's preparations, the first moments after he grasped the bolt were a struggle, a chaotic assault of sensory fragments. He had yet to discover a way of opening himself to them that wasn't akin to turning on all the available radio stations at once. Then he had to sift through the noise until he found ones that might be of use. The most intense were not always the most recent nor the most pertinent.

It was inefficient and tiring, but it wasn't as if the ability had come with a training manual.

He flinched, suddenly seeing with almost painful clarity as he flew through the night sky above a brightly lit street. He (or rather, the memory) banked slightly left and he felt his wings stretch out, slicing through the cold air. The freedom was exhilarating. The power of it, and the absence of—Pain tore through his shoulder. He fell, shifting before impact.

Ah. Quentin had sensed the injured man in the hotel room was using a glamour. Now he knew why.

And who.

"What'd you get, Ronny?"

"Looked like a raven."

Quentin focused on those voices, tuning to their specific frequency so as to pull out similar fragments and push away those that didn't match.

A new memory. Someone else. He lay on his back, staring up at branches loaded with white blossoms. Apple...perhaps pear. The dying man didn't know, and neither did Quentin. He'd never been in an orchard before. He might make a point to visit one in spring. Beautiful. Too bad the fragrance was marred by the sharp, awful scent of blood.

A shadowy figure stepped into view, blocked out the petaled canopy as it bent over Quentin's face. A scraggly, ginger beard parted to show wet lips and discolored teeth. The rest of the face was in shadow beneath a black leather hat.

A cowboy hat, Quentin thought dimly, fighting the pull of the remnant he had tapped into. The band was finished with a brass medallion of Celtic—no, of Norse design. The wolf Fenrir.

"Deyr sjálfr ið sama," the warrior said, and then stepped on Quentin's chest and pulled out the bolt.

There. He shoved away the figment of someone else's agony and latched onto the essence of the man holding the bolt.

Ronny, with the poor dental hygiene and Fenrir on his hat.

He was all over the place. Too many moments, too fast.

Flashes of roadside scenery. Asphalt and clear blue sky and blurring guardrails. Gears and exhaust pipes. Leather boots and jackets.

Rekkrs. A motorbike gang...and so much more.

Stained floors, stale smoke, unwashed bodies. Alcohol and drug haze. The faint scent of pine woods. Sawdust and peanut shells.

A bar with a broken mirror.

In the disjointed reflection, a neon advertisement for Mack Pilsner flickered on the wall beside an open door.

Outside, just visible, was a faded wooden sign. The lettering was reversed, a portion of it too faded to make out.

Quentin concentrated, grappled with the image that otherwise would have flowed by, one tiny part of an unending flood. Something was ringing.

The last two letters were clearly "la." In the middle, "lh." Could it really be that simple?

More ringing. Two phones, two voices answering. Upset.

Present time and place intruded, scattering memories like drops of scalding water.

Quentin blinked, disoriented. He let the bolt drop from his hand. It struck the table and rolled. Where didn't matter. He shivered, then gritted his teeth when nerves in his hip socket pinched.

"Uncontrolled magic in the Ogham Room," Murphy said, his mobile at his ear as he strode toward the already opening door.

"Thia." Murphy's assistant hurried after him. "I told Abby to work with her there."

The man across the table sprang up to follow.

With a sigh, Quentin called his cane, used it and the table to stand. He was always so damned cold after these things.

A cold that seeped into his bones and made them that much harder to move.

CHAPTER 13

Thia didn't look hurt. Standing in the corridor looking in, Cormac took a deep breath of relief. He had run flat out, imagining the worst.

Whatever the danger had been, it had passed. It must have stemmed from Thia; she lay bound in an unfamiliar variation of an entrapment spell. Abby sat with her while several hotel employees conversed by a charred stack of boxes at the left-hand wall.

"Bugger me," Murphy said as he arrived. With Kendra, he brushed past Cormac to enter the room.

Thia wasn't fighting her magical bonds, so Cormac couldn't assess how effective they might be against a less willing and more adept subject, but the design was intriguing. The base spell enwrapped, restricting movement and was then interwoven with protection wards turned inside out. Rather than block the subject's power, the wards contained it. Simple, yes, but clever and excellently done. He stored the details for later consideration.

Abby left Thia to join Kendra in speaking with the hotel staff. Telling them what had happened, Cormac could safely assume. Her frantic gestures painted a picture of chaos.

The wallpaper behind her had been scorched black nearly

to the ceiling. Drops of what Cormac had first taken to be blood dotted the floor, with a sizable pool in the center of the room. A more careful look proved it to be red wax.

Sure enough, the stump of a red candle lay near a toppled chair by the far wall.

Bits of broken plaster and mirrored-glass were everywhere; the culprits might have been a set of balls that looked to be part of a levitation training kit. Stone, wood, metal. Only the glass one was absent—ah. Cormac spotted its likely remains at the base of a table. The things were notoriously fragile but this one had been pulverized, more dust than glass.

What exactly had gone wrong?

"I'm so embarrassed," Thia said, her voice sounding as if she were speaking through cotton. Murphy waved over one of the hotel security guards.

After a quick consultation, the guard pulled a wand from where it had been tucked in his belt. A quick slash followed by a twist and two flicks, and the spell around Thia released. Cormac stepped farther back into the corridor, less liable to be noticed.

"Oh, God." Thia sat up. "The room. Look what I did. This is horrible. I'm so sorry."

Taking another step back, Cormac fought the impulse to go to her—and do what, console? She wouldn't welcome that. Wouldn't welcome *him,* despite her earlier words on the roof. Those had been an invitation to talk. What he wanted at the moment had nothing to do with conversation.

Besides, she didn't need him. She had her friends. Even as they stood at a distance, they kept looking over, checking in. Making sure she was all right.

And she seemed to be, if a bit pale. She got up, walked to where Murphy stood looking down at the wax. "You have to let me pay for this," she told him.

"Do I now?"

"Yes."

"No," chorused her friends, going over.

Footsteps and the muted tap of a cane on carpet heralded Quentin's belated arrival. Cormac tensed. What had the man learned from the bolt? And what might he do with that.

"Did I miss all the fun?"

Cormac shrugged. "We all did."

"Pity. I should like to see her in action." Quentin limped into the room, pitched his voice toward the group. "Candle lighting, I presume?"

Thia's distraught expression lifted, conveying surprise and pleasure as he joined them. "Quentin," she said, and reached out to briefly touch the man's arm. Cormac, along with his wound's lingering burn, felt a fierce sting of jealousy.

"When did you get here?" Thia asked the man. "Have you heard about our café manager?"

"First things first." Quentin's attention wandered the room. "Candle lighting followed by levitation of cardinal elements." He poked the wooden ball with the tip of his cane, gestured with the knob toward the bruise Cormac had already noted on Abby's forehead. "All this is the result?"

Thia looked crestfallen. "I lost control."

"That, my dear, is an understatement. But don't take it to heart. It's easier to learn to fly a two-seater than a jumbo jet. I've some things which might help. We can talk tomorrow." Without waiting for a response, he began making his return to the corridor. Cormac ducked out of sight.

"Here, I can take that," Thia said. To whom and about what, he could no longer see.

After what felt like an age, Quentin exited the room. He raised a single, condescending brow. "Is that disguise fooling anyone?"

Cormac's jaw clenched. "Cassandra and her people."

Or so he hoped.

"Ah. Well, then." Quentin moved on, pushed the button for the lift.

After it took him away, Cormac went to call it for himself. There was no purpose to his lurking about, and as much as it pained him to leave, his shoulder pained him more.

The benefits of his *Sidhe*-inherited healing process were not without cost. The charm Kendra had given him helped repay some of that, but so would time spent in nature.

The rooftop garden would have to suffice. With the Rekkrs potentially out and about, searching, to leave the hotel would be an invitation to risk.

● ○ ●

It had happened again. Thia couldn't believe it...yet of course she could. It was as she'd feared. "I'm so sorry."

Her umpteenth apology.

Everyone had stopped listening to them, but Thia couldn't seem to stop making them. Maybe because no one treated the damage like the big deal she felt it to be. *Knew* it to be. She'd lost control so badly she could have burned down the Landmark—a building whose very name suggested how significant it was—and endangered everyone inside.

She'd already tried with Kendra and Murphy, so while they spoke with Abby near the main blob of wax, Thia approached the trio that was sorting through the burnt boxes. Salvageable stuff went into one pile; ruined, into black plastic bags. When they didn't acknowledge her, she felt another stab of guilt. It was late on what had to have been a very busy day, given the impending holidays, and she'd made more problems for them to deal with. She cleared her throat. "What can I do to help? Please."

The three paused for a fraction of time; enough for them to glance in unison behind her—toward the center of the room, Thia could assume, to take their cue from either Kendra or Murphy. Two of them returned to their work. The third, an older man with thinning hair and ruddy cheeks, said, "We've got this in hand, I should think, ma'am. But thank you."

"If you're sure." Guilt felt a lot like an acid stomach.

He flicked another glance over Thia's shoulder. "Yeah," he said. "I'm sure. Thank you."

"Alright." There was nothing for it, then. Thia walked away, at a loss. She'd caused all this damage, surely there was something she could do to—*ah*. She picked up the wooden sphere from Abby's kit. There were several deep scratches and dents that hadn't been there before, and a coating of plaster dust. She rubbed it on the leg of her pants.

"Don't worry," Abby said, coming over. "They're designed for hard use."

"That one wasn't." Thia pointed to the powderized remains of the glass sphere.

"No," Abby acknowledged. "But it's easy enough to replace. There's a store just up the street—maybe you've heard of it— Eclectica? I happen to know they have six more in stock. Plus I get an employee discount."

"How can you joke about this? Abby, look what I did." Thia flung her arms wide.

"I was here, remember? I know."

And had the bruise forming on her brow to prove it.

Thia grimaced. "Are you sure you're okay? I'm so—"

"If you apologize one more time to me or anyone else here tonight, I will send that sphere at your head. In fact"—Abby snatched it from Thia's hand. "It's late and we've got Hecate-knows-what to deal with tomorrow. We should call it a day." She carried the sphere to her supply box. It sat miraculously unharmed, right where she'd left it.

"Ready to go back?" Kendra walked up. "We can order room service, relax with a movie."

Thia didn't see how she could relax ever again. "I think I'm too tired. Honestly." And she *was* tired. Exhausted, if she let herself think about it. But more than that, she needed time alone. "And like you said, who knows what we'll face next. We should all get some sleep."

Try to, anyway.

"You sure?" Kendra pressed. "The on-demand selection is terrific. So is the chocolate-drizzled caramel popcorn in the minibar."

Across the room, Abby pried the metal sphere from where it had lodged in the wall.

"I'm sure." Thia had to get away before she cried.

Kendra's smile faded. "I know it might seem wrong to think about enjoying ourselves while Zoe is in trouble, but we've got people working on finding her. So does the Brigantium. In my experience it's important to take what good life has to offer, however and whenever you can."

Box in her arms, Abby came over. "But if you really are too tired, we understand."

"I am," Thia said. "Thank you, though. I appreciate it." She gave Abby a quick side-hug, avoiding the box. "Goodnight. I'll see you—" She let it go at that. She didn't want to get into a discussion about whether she'd be allowed to leave the hotel for work in the morning. She hugged Kendra. "Goodnight."

"Sleep well. Don't worry about this. I'm not."

"I'm not either," Abby said. "When you've mastered your powers, you'll look back on tonight and laugh."

"Yeah, right."

Like she could ever master her powers.

Inside the elevator, Thia let go of the act she'd put on for everyone, her friends especially. Her shoulders drooped, and she covered her face with her hands. She'd been holding back so many tears that her head ached.

A convulsive sob escaped, and she quickly pulled her hands away. Not yet. Not until she got to the room. There could be people when she stepped out.

The temptation to return to the roof had been strong but pointless. And so, when the elevator doors opened, it was on her floor. She paused, toyed with the idea of going instead to the seventh.

Equally pointless.

She stepped into the hall, heard the doors sliding closed as she moved on, feeling her pockets for her keycard.

If she didn't want the company of her friends, why did she want Cormac's?

On Orkney, she was sure she loved him. But she had been caught up in extraordinary circumstances. (Put another way, she might not have been thinking right.)

What *was* that "love" she'd felt, anyway? Attraction mixed with admiration and gratitude? Fine. Thia could feel all that and also not have anything more to do with him. People could feel things for one another...while moving on with their lives.

Never mind that at times if felt as if he were true north to her inner compass; that when they were together, no matter the difficulty (including outright terror), it felt as if she was home.

Never mind all of that because more often than not he was misleading her. Disguises, misdirections, obfuscations. Lies.

Thia didn't know Cormac; she knew what Cormac chose to present. Which meant that her feelings for him were based mostly on fictions.

What was the reality? Cormac was a known thief with a bad reputation. Thia had witnessed some of what he was capable of—the violence, the sorcery. The darkness.

Lost in thought as she rounded a corner, she nearly walked into a group of people coming around the opposite direction. Fast reflexes and lucky guesses as to side-step direction got her through.

They were dressed for a rugged time outdoors: all-weather gear, heavy boots—the works. She would have pegged them as Sierra Club if not for the immense and elaborately carved staffs they carried. Far too cumbersome for an efficient hike.

The usual excuse-me and sorries were offered (thankfully, Abby wasn't there to hear Thia's), along with several cheerful, "Blessings to you."

"And to you," Thia said, arriving at her room.

Inside, she flipped the deadbolt. Courtesy of the staff, two of the lamps were on low. She flung herself onto the turned-down bed, her face narrowly missing the wrapped chocolate that had been placed on the pillow.

● ○ ●

Rooftop Garden, Landmark Hotel

At the sound of the door opening, Cormac checked his pose, made sure he appeared relaxed. He had selected a patio seat near the outer wall, not too close to the door but not too far, either. He could see it out of the corner of his left eye. He wasn't facing it directly.

Wouldn't want to be obvious.

The person who walked into the garden wasn't Thia.

Cormac felt a jarring pang of disappointment—his fifteenth so far: one for each new arrival. And he had to admit, finally, what he was really doing.

Energy of the kind he could draw upon to replenish his own was minimal despite the proximity to nature. The setting was too urban. Basic sleep would benefit him more.

He went inside to do just that...

...so it made little sense that a few minutes later he found himself at Thia's door instead of his own, with his hand raised as if about to knock.

He really shouldn't.

Besides, he didn't know if she was there. She could still be in the Ogham Room with her friends. Worse, her friends could be inside *this* room with her. Cormac certainly didn't want to face them *en masse.*

He lowered his hand.

She wouldn't welcome him, in any case. More likely, with all that lay between them, he would only upset her more.

● ○ ●

Room Eighty-Four

Thia thought she might've—finally—cried herself out. It felt similar to surfacing after a deep dive. Abrupt and welcome and a bit disorienting. She pressed fingers to her closed eyes, squeezing out the last of the tears. The queen-sized bed was littered with tissues. She was incredibly thirsty.

She was on her way to get a wastebasket and a glass of water when a shadow disrupted the line of hallway light that shone beneath the door.

Someone was there.

Her breath stalled.

She knew she was safe, physically. Access to the room floors was for guests only, and the rooms themselves had additional security measures beyond the multiple locks.

More to the point, maybe: if someone intended to do her harm, they wouldn't just stand there.

Thia knew who it was. She had invited him, hadn't she? She waited for the knock.

Watched the shadow move away.

For an excessive length of time, she stared at the unbroken line of light under the door. Then she went to clear the tissues off the bed.

● ○ ●

Room Thirty-Two

Quentin entered his room to the ringing of both his mobile and the landline. He ignored the former, left on the bureau in his haste to dress from his interrupted shower, and went to pick up the latter. He had a good idea who was on the other end of both calls, and she could bloody well afford the charge without eating into his minutes.

"Hello, Beatrice," he said into the hotel phone's receiver.

Distinctly angry silence came over the line.

His mobile stopped ringing.

He propped his cane against the nightstand and gratefully sank his weight onto the mattress.

"You didn't call," Beatrice said, her voice low and clipped. "I had to learn of your arrival—your *safe* arrival, mind you—from Edith." She launched into a scold.

Quentin listened with only half an ear while little by little he changed position on the narrow bed. Turning, bringing his legs up, leaning back until at last he was fully reclined.

There were two rows of pillows. First the overstuffed and impractical kind with decorative cases. Next the simpler kind intended for actual sleep. Anticipating things slightly, his eyes closed.

"You've always been this way, even as a child. For the life of me, I don't know why I put up with such—"

Enough. "I meant to call, Bea. There was a...distraction."

"Your luggage. I have been made aware—"

"More than that, actually." Quentin explained about Thia's uncontrolled event. It was interesting that the news hadn't travelled to London already, and spoke volumes on the hotel staff's ability to contain problems even under watchful eyes.

Of course, it also suggested that those eyes had not been as watchful as they should have been. His fault, perhaps.

"Where were our people?" Beatrice demanded. "Why was someone not present—or at least near at hand?"

Because he had sent them out to find his luggage. Because he had been frozen through and unable to think of little else than a hot shower. Because he had been brought to consult in regarding the urgent matter of the bolt.

"I only just arrived," he said, unwilling to volunteer any of that. "If you would like to give another lecture on someone's failures, why don't you ring up Edith? She was in charge here." Technically only until Quentin had landed in the snow, but she could damn well stay in charge until morning.

"You may be assured that I will be speaking with her. One moment," Beatrice said, and put him on hold.

He hated when she did that. Last year she'd gotten it in her head to add a music track, as if thirty seconds of Vivaldi on repeat would improve the experience. He had come to loathe The Four Seaso—

She came back on. "Is there nothing more to tell me? What of the girl—what's her name? The missing one."

"Zoe Forbes."

"What of her?"

"I only just arrived," Quentin repeated. "It's quite late here, remember? There's nothing more I can tell you that can't wait until a decent hour."

"Decent for you, you mean."

"Of course." As if she didn't stay up till all hours. And in any case, if he called her first thing Pacific time, it would only be early evening, hers.

She made no reply. Instead, she began speaking to someone else, her voice muffled as if her hand covered the mouthpiece.

"If you're finished with me," he muttered while he figured she wasn't listening, "perhaps you would be so kind as to ring off and let me sleep?" He was so tired, he could probably drop off regardless. Shifting his grip on the phone, he considered chucking the overstuffed pillows to the floor to make proper use of the functional ones.

"You have a visitor," came Beatrice's unmuffled, unwelcome voice at his ear.

His eyes opened. "What?"

There was a knock on the door. He sat up too abruptly for

comfort.

"I've sent Edith," Beatrice informed him. "I want you to go over everything with her. You should have done so already. In fact, you should have alerted her as soon as you learned of Thia's crisis."

Quentin gritted his teeth and stood. Anger and pain, such a frequent combination. Ignoring his cane, he hobbled to the door, yanked it open.

Edith stood across the threshold, a phone held to her ear. She was pale, her eyes large behind her spectacles.

"Goodnight, Bea." Quentin ended the call, then tossed the hotel phone carelessly onto the bed behind him. He regarded his uninvited guest. Uninvited by *him,* that was.

Edith's phone call had ended as well. She looked up from tucking her phone into the outer pocket of her faux-leather satchel. "Assistant Director Meriwether told me that Thia—"

"It's late," Quentin said, shutting the door in her too-pretty face. He caught a glimpse of her shock, her mouth opening, and he suddenly felt like smiling. The latch clicked. He kept his hand pressed against the door, as if it might reopen on its own. Or he might reopen it. "We can do this in the morning," he told her, and then before he thought better of it, "Meet here. Eight o'clock sharp. We can order in."

As he set the locks he might have heard her say something unflattering. It had been quietly done, however, so he couldn't be certain.

He counted to ten before he looked through the spy-hole to see that she had left.

● ○ ●

"Son of a bitch," Edith said, and then recalled exactly whom he was the son of. She could get written up for that.

Still, the man was...any number of names she shouldn't utter while standing outside his room in the corridor of an upscale, anyone-could-happen-along-at-any-moment hotel.

Mustering her dignity, she spun on her heel and proceeded to walk away. Chin up, shoulders back, head held high.

Unruffled. Undaunted.

The Assistant Director had told her enough about what had happened tonight with Thia. By morning, Quentin's version would be redundant. Even better, Edith would be able to tell *him* a thing or two.

She had all night to discover them.

Rick and Marcus were still on their search for luggage that would never be recovered. Their company would have been welcome, Edith thought as she rode the lift to the second floor; but she could handle this. With the various factions, as it were, united against a common enemy, she should have no trouble gaining entry to the Ogham Room. She'd examine the evidence with her equipment and some new apps she'd been wanting to try. She'd conduct interviews. And then high-and-mighty Quentin Reynolds could go get stuffed.

The lift opened and she marched out. He thought he could shut a door in her face, did he? Well. She'd show him what—

"Will you open Eclectica tomorrow?"

Sounds of a hushed conversation ahead broke through her pique. She slowed to a stop at the juncture of two corridors. As tasteless as eavesdropping was, sometimes it yielded more results than direct inquiry.

"That's up to Thia," Abby replied to Kendra's question, and Edith peeped around the corner. The two stood outside the closed doors of the Ogham Room. No one else was around.

Well, except for Edith, of course. But they didn't seem to realize that.

Abby faced the other way, so Edith couldn't read her expressions, but her posture and voice held tension.

That same tension was in Kendra, whose expressions Edith *could* read...but only while risking discovery. She pulled herself back behind the wall.

"Eclectica has to open," Abby said. "Last-minute shoppers count on us. People will be upset if we don't."

"Upset enough to hold a grudge?"

"It's a risk we shouldn't take." Abby paused, then, "I'm sorry about the damage. I had no idea it would go that badly."

"You didn't have a feeling?"

"Actually, I did." She sounded bewildered. "I expected it to go well."

Edith had read the files the Brigantium had put together on Thia and all her associates in Granite Springs. Some files had been larger than others.

Abigail Collins's was one of the smaller, reading more like a *curriculum vitae* than a true report. Majored in business at a middling university, then went on to hold a series of retail jobs. Respected member of a local coven. Prescience highly suspected but unconfirmed. Edith closed her eyes to better focus on vocal nuance.

"Is that usual, being so wrong?" Kendra, worried.

"When I get a clear feeling like that? Never. Well"—Abby, rueful—"almost never. I don't understand how things got so flipped. Except that maybe Thia used too much power at the start. I hadn't expected her to panic about it, but she did.

Then things went wild.

"She's been doing so well, you wouldn't think a little rough start would freak her out." There was a brief, fraught pause. "Or that her emotions would have such an influence."

"It's unpredictable, what she has," Kendra said. "We knew that."

"But not how much. This was insane. If your people hadn't come when they did, I don't know what might've happened."

Edith's eyes opened at that. Did Quentin know how badly the situation was before hotel staff intervened? The Assistant Director certainly hadn't made mention of it.

"Do you think she'll be able to control it?" Kendra had gone so quiet that Edith had to strain. "Maybe we aren't the right teachers."

"Who else is there? The Brigantium?

"Yeah, right."

Their scorn resurrected Edith's pique. How dare they? The Brigantium might be going through a difficult patch, but it was an honorable institution whose research and discoveries had made vital contributions not only to the field of magical studies but to the world at large.

No one spoke for an odd length of time. Too late, Edith remembered that along with prescience, Abigail Collins was suspected of possessing heightened empathetic sense.

Sod it. Edith gave brief consideration to banging her head on the wall. Being so close, it wouldn't make much noise.

"It's late," Abby said, sounding a forced kind of casual. "I should head home if I want to have any hope of getting the lantern-making supplies ready for the coven to pick up. Walk me to my car?"

They were coming Edith's way. Quickly, she headed back to the lift. If no one had required it in the interim, it would still be there.

No, on second thought, she wouldn't take the chance. She'd use the stairs. They were closer. She'd be out of sight by the time the women rounded the corner.

"What about Zoe?" Kendra was asking, her voice drawing ever nearer despite Edith's haste. "Is she okay?"

"I've got nothing," Abby said. "It's like she's in a dead zone."

Edith jerked at that, alarmed. Apparently Kendra's reaction had been similar, because Abby quickly added an apologetic, "I don't mean that literally. At least...I don't think so."

At the stairs, Edith pushed the door open as quietly as possible. Thank Brigid for well-oiled hinges.

"I hope not," Kendra said from what was probably only two

steps from view.

Edith eased the door shut. If Thia's friends suspected they'd been watched, they would see the lift hadn't been engaged and check the stairs. The inclination, Edith knew from training, would be to look down—the direction which would lead to escape into the outside world. She ran up.

And hoped she was right.

• ○ •

"Thanks, Silvio." Kendra put away her phone. "It was one of the Brigantium agents. Edith Wilkinson."

"What was she doing?"

"Watching you and me talk, apparently. They'll check the tapes, but it doesn't sound like a big deal."

Abby nodded but didn't look relieved. "I should've picked up on her sooner."

"You and me both," Kendra said, and pressed the elevator button. "Today has been too long—and tomorrow will come too soon. Do you really have to prep stuff for your coven?"

Abby sighed gustily. "Yeah, I really do."

• ○ •

Lake of the Woods, Oregon

The temperature inside the barn was freezing, but the people working within didn't mind. Cassie made sure of that with a simple bit of mind control. Childsplay. As was the warming spell she had worked upon herself.

From her position at the hayloft's rail, she allowed herself another minute or two of watching them—her *thegnas*, to use her father's term. Most of them had been his to start, but she had managed to pick up a few of her own. She had a deft hand with the more coercive magics. And she did enjoy them so.

Below her, the gray-cloaked men and women were a flurry of activity, an efficient assembly line that would bring Cassie's plans for Granite Springs to fruition. She'd had to part with a few choice objects from Idris's collection in order to acquire so many snowflakes. The carved quartz sparkled in the lantern light, the reflections they shot back growing stronger as they passed from hand to hand, progressing through the stages.

First the careful unpacking from the salt barrels. Then came several potion applications and incantations until finally, they were laid in boxes lined with morning glory vines.

Being wintertime, those too had cost a pretty penny.

One of the women toward the end of the line broke off her chant and swayed. The snowflake she'd been holding dropped to the scarred wooden floor.

Pulling her hands from the pockets of her anorak, Cassie clapped for attention. "You!" She pointed to one of the men along the wall. "Replace her!"

She then shifted her gaze to Avery, cowering near a stack of finished boxes. "Take her crystal back to the beginning and get her from my sight."

It was frustrating, having to rely on the weak.

But, then, the weak never argued and were easily replaced.

Confident that her orders would be carried out, she turned away, stepped up to the disgustingly basic altar she'd created at the back of the loft.

She slowed her breathing, forced her mind to clear. In the center of the narrow table and between two purple tapers in matched silver holders sat a wide onyx bowl. The oil within trembled as she held her hand above it and concentrated on the man she needed to contact.

She was making use of his Rekkrs, after all; and while she might resent the implication that she was not fully in control, she did allow that he was entitled to an occasional update.

That didn't mean she would tell him everything, however. Doubtless he wouldn't like the destruction she had planned—not when he had plans, himself, for the region. But she would deal with his wrath later to take advantage of what she had now: Opportunity.

She circled her hand counterclockwise. The candle flames fluttered, sizzling on their wicks. Their reflections danced on the oil's otherwise black surface. She stared into it, felt her gaze go soft. Distant.

Inward.

«*Make it quick.*» His voice sounded in her head. A pressure built, like a too-fast change in altitude. «*This is not a good time.*»

Despite her warming spell, Cassie shivered—and endured a rare moment of doubt. This was not a man who would take deception lightly.

She had come too far in it to turn back.

CHAPTER 14

When Lettie had hired Thia, it had been to expand her store's online presence and sales capability. Because there was only one office, in a way it had been fortunate that Lettie had been absent much of the time, off on her "buying trips" (and, as it had turned out, covert missions for the Brigantium).

It had been unfortunate in another: the mail. So much mail. Each week had added another stack of product catalogs to await Lettie's perusal, with very limited space in which to do so. Then there were the unsolicited products, the invariably bulky samples that companies sent in the hope that Lettie would find them to be the best new things ever and wonder how Eclectica had survived without them.

It wouldn't be such a bad gamble, Thia supposed, if only the senders had done the tiniest amount of research beforehand.

Yes, the store offered a wide variety of products, but solar powered battery chargers fell well outside that range. As did scented placards meant to hang from a car's rearview mirror, and talking doormats.

Thia stared down at the latter and contemplated sending it to her brother as a joke. A nudge with her foot prompted a stilted, electronic greeting. Best not. His rambunctious sons would turn her joke into cruel and unusual punishment. She rolled the mat up and stuck it in the box destined for charity. It proceeded to greet her again.

One box would not be enough, she discovered, somewhat amazed that while she had worked the entire morning, she'd hardly made a dent, there was that much stuff.

True, though, it didn't take much to overload the eight-by-eight room. And she hadn't been the most focused worker, or the most energetic. What little sleep she'd gotten had been marred by unpleasant dreams.

There had been a convuluted rehash of October's events, as usual. She had some variation of that almost nightly. Mixed in with it this time had been a strange, anxious replay of recent events. And then there had been parts that…Well, she hoped those were just her imagination run amuck.

Prescience had better not be one of "gifts" the Cailleach's power had to offer.

She shuddered, recalling the scene of darkness punctuated with explosive flashes. Terror and sorrow and loss. And something to do with Santa Claus and a Christmas tree.

The computer chimed, alerting to a new email in Eclectica's account, and Thia went to check. It was important to process orders and respond to inquiries immediately to avoid overselling an item through the brick and mortar store.

If only she felt the same impetus toward her personal email. She could answer a question about the finish on a rosewood wand with no stress at all, but could hardly face dealing with chatty emails from family and old friends. They all asked how she was. How could she possibly answer that?

She sat down at Lettie's desk—her desk now, whether it felt like it or not—and clicked on the bobbing email icon, found a new order. She smiled, pleased that not only was her website working well, but that someone had found something which filled a need.

In this case, fourteen bundles of locally-sourced mistletoe

tied with string dyed using traditional, organic methods. Thia printed the order form, made special note of the request for express shipping, and sent an "in process" notification to the customer. She was about to go fill the order when someone knocked.

"Come in." She expected either Abby or Kendra, since she'd had a hard time convincing them to let her leave the hotel. It had taken a promise to not set foot outside Eclectica without the company of one or the other.

She would like to think she had finally won them over to her point of view (that she needed the distraction of work so she wouldn't go crazy with worry), but she knew it had more to do with Kendra stationing some of the Landmark's security team in the store.

But instead of one of her friends come to check on her, it was Quentin.

"Am I interrupting?" He asked, approaching the desk. His cane was in his hand but hardly seemed necessary; the limp that Thia had often observed was absent.

The door closed smoothly behind him.

Thia wondered if she said yes, he *was* interrupting. Would he leave? Somehow she didn't think so.

"I came to see the place and was told you were in here," he said smoothly, and sat in the chair opposite her desk. "Saved me the effort of tracking you down to ask how you're faring today. After last night."

"Ah. Thank you." She winced inwardly at her awkwardness. But, truthfully, Quentin Reynolds made her a little nervous. She'd been relieved to see him yesterday, after everything, and was glad he was in Granite Springs to help with the current situation...for the same reasons. He was intimidating. She had seen him use his cane to direct a white-hot current very much like lightning into clouds above the Ring of Brodgar and from there into Cormac, and from Cormac to Idris Cathmor—who had then died. Quentin was formidable. Terrifying, maybe.

His eyes were a disconcerting gray, light within a dark, outer ring; and gave the illusion of clarity, like light reflecting off an icy lake. The corner of his mouth lifted. "So, then. How are you faring?"

"I'm doing okay." A knee-jerk response, more out of habit than thought. "I'm worried about Zoe, of course, but—"

He set the tip of his cane on the floor, abruptly pushed to his feet. "I understand there's more than a café upstairs. You have a room for practitioners?"

"The Rowan Space, yes." Perplexed by the abrupt shift, she rose with him. "It can be used for all sorts of things."

"Show me?"

"Of course." She proceeded him out. "Tarot readings and rune castings are the most popular, but there are also guided meditations. And on Saturday afternoons we've been hosting a series of lectures. Last week was on setting a circle."

"Ah. Did you attend?"

"I did." Single file, they passed between two heavily laden Christmas trees. Traditional folk ornaments from around the world on one; Granite Springs souvenir ornaments made by local crafters on the other.

"It was interesting," Thia added. "I'd no idea there were so many different ways."

Truthfully, until recently, she'd had no idea there were *any* ways. She hadn't known what a circle was in terms of rituals and protected space.

"If we'd used one last night, maybe things would have been better contained," she said.

They reached the base of the stairs.

Quentin gestured. "Ladies first."

"Thanks." She headed up. "Abby had said the Ogham Room could contain much more than we'd be dealing with, but you saw what I did to it. A circle would have protected against all that. Wouldn't it?"

"Not necessarily." His voice sounded strained, and Thia felt bad. The century-old building had no elevator and no viable way of installing one. Those who needed to avoid the stairs had to go around the block to enter through the patio.

"Why not?" she asked. "If a circle keeps unwanted energies out, couldn't it keep unwanted one *in*, too?"

"Magic needs to breathe. It won't tolerate a chokehold. And that wouldn't have helped you in any case. You lost control. You would have lost control of your circle as well."

"Oh."

Arriving at the top of the stairs, Thia was surprised by how empty the café was for midmorning, and how heavy the quiet felt. What few customers there were sat at the tables along the wall, where their computers could make use of electrical outlets along with the free WiFi.

Abby stood at the counter with Todd. He looked wrecked, with pasty skin and bleak eyes.

"Would you excuse me a moment?" Thia left Quentin at the entrance. "Todd, how are you? Is there news?"

"That's why I came in," he told her in a scratchy voice while, mutely, Abby shook her head. No news. "I was hoping maybe you'd heard something. I haven't. Not since yesterday."

"Oh, I'm sorry," Thia said. "No. We haven't, either."

She hadn't thought to keep him informed. Not that there was much he could be told, but still. He was Zoe's friend and he was hurting, and she hadn't thought of him at all.

"Yeah, so Abby was telling me." Todd's eyes filled with tears. "I just don't understand who would do this. Who would do such a thing."

"Here." Thia guided him to a nearby chair. "Let me get you something—tea? Coffee?"

Seated, he stared up with a dazed expression. "Can you do chai? I know"—he paused for a difficult breath. "I know it's on the menu, b-but that's Zoe. She knows all the drinks. She makes it look easy, but maybe it isn't. I've never had it from anyone else here. Maybe she's the only one who knows how."

Abby was already pulling the box of pre-mixed liquid from the refrigerator under the counter.

"We can make the chai," Thia assured him. "Maybe not as well as Zoe, but when she's back, she can tell us her secret."

"You believe that? You believe she'll be back?" With a sniff, he dragged the cuff of his sweater beneath his nose.

"Of course." She went to grab a stack of napkins from the sideboard. "With so many people looking for her? Of course she will."

After handing them over, she turned away to give him a bit of privacy—and herself a bit of distance from the sounds that followed.

She had neglected Quentin, and he had apparently tired of waiting. He arrived at the counter as she did. "I'm sorry, there was—"

"Quite alright."

The espresso machine's steamer sputtered as Abby startled, then recovered. She didn't turn, and so it was to her back that Quentin gave a politely neutral, "Good morning."

Thia wondered if they had spoken beyond the encounter at the Ring, when Quentin had been set to take power amassed by a group (Thia and Abby among them) and Abby had argued on behalf of his safety.cHe had not appreciated that, to put it mildly.

Last night, Thia hadn't seen them get within fifteen feet of one another.

"Like a bad penny." Abby shut the steamer off with a hard twist and then poured the heated chai into a tall, clear mug. "Should have expected you'd turn up."

"Indeed," Quentin said evenly. Thia couldn't tell he'd taken offense. He made a slight gesture toward where Todd sat with a napkin pressed to his eyes. "Who's the distraught fellow?"

"A friend of the café manager," Thia supplied. "The woman who was—"

"Abducted," Quentin finished. And Thia finally put two and two together.

"*That's* why you're here." She felt slow. "When I mentioned it last night, you already knew all about it."

Abby set the metal pitcher down with a bang. "Those were *your* people hassling Madame Demetka yesterday." She turned to face him. "How long have you had spies in town?"

"Shortly after threats were made against Ms. McDaniel," he replied easily. "And her friends."

Tempting though it was, Thia left the intrusion-of-privacy, you-have-no-right argument for another time. "Do you think Cassie is behind this?" She's the one who made the threats he was talking about.

"Of course. Don't you?"

"It's the general consensus." Feeling hollow, she sat on the last in the counter's short line of stools.

"Does that include the police?" Quentin seated himself on the first, propped his cane against the second.

"I have no idea." Idly, she straightened a pile of promotional fliers. "It's been tricky, trying to tell them what they need to know without telling them things that...well. You know.'"

Too damn many secrets, that's what. Sometimes she wanted to scream. She looked to Abby. "Would the police have found the same sorts of things Murphy's people did?"

Dammit, she couldn't even pose a simple question without worrying about who might overhear. She had to cloak plain speaking in clunky generalities and hope to be understood.

Abby didn't seem to. "Things?"

Thia checked their surroundings. Todd stared morosely at the wadded napkin in his hands. Customers appeared to be engrossed in whatever was on their laptop screens. Even so, she kept her voice low. "Magic-type things. Energies and residues and whatever else I don't know enough about yet. How much do the police know about those kinds of things?"

"I have no idea," Abby said after a moment. "I don't know anyone from the department. Murphy does, obviously. The chief."

Thia remembered how he had used that to intimidate the officer the other day. "We should ask Kendra to ask him if—"

"No matter," Quentin said with a casual glance at his wristwatch. Gold and leather. "I'll ask him myself at our meeting."

Abby bristled. "Can anyone join, or are we to be kept out of the loop now that the illustrious Brigantium is taking an interest?"

"No loop intended." Quentin sounded bored. "We arranged to share our findings, that's all, when they return."

Thia frowned. "When who returns from where?"

"Did your Ms. Ross not tell you?"

At Thia and Abby's blank looks, he shrugged. "I suppose it's early yet. Late for me. I wouldn't mind one of those, myself." He indicated the chai, cooling on the counter.

"Oops." Thia grabbed Todd's drink, took it over to him.

Abby poured fresh mix into the metal pitcher. "So, then— what did Kendra not tell us?"

● ○ ●

"I can't possibly know what someone has *not* said," Quentin told them, amused. "But were I to guess, it would be that she did not tell you that she and Murphy planned to visit the den of a gang of motorbike enthusiasts."

"What?"

It wasn't often that Quentin could say he'd baffled someone. But that was clearly what he had done to Thia.

Her witch friend, Abby, set his chai nearly out of his reach on the counter. Subtle but intentional. Still bothered about

Orkney, apparently.

He stretched for the mug, brought it in. Even through his leather gloves, he could tell it was too hot. Also intentional, he didn't doubt.

Thia looked from him to her friend and back, fairly buzzing with anxiety. "Why would they do that? The visiting, and the not telling?"

"I can't speak to their motives regarding the latter." With a knowing smile, he raised the mug to Abby as if in a toast. But instead of cheers, he uttered an invocation, *"Defrigesco."*

With his smile hidden, he took a lengthy swallow of the no longer scalding liquid. Caffeine and spices worked their own, welcome kind of magic as he put down the mug, rotated it so the handle pointed away. "As to the former, I believe it has to do with a crossbow bolt pulled last night from an interested party."

"Someone was shot?" Thia exclaimed, causing several of the café's patrons to look over. She cringed, mouthing, "Sorry."

Quentin took another drink of chai while they waited until attention shifted away.

"What the hell is going on?" Thia then asked in a whisper.

Conflicted interests, habitual secrecy, unclear motives, and distrust, Quentin almost replied. But ironically, it was *because* of those things that he said only, "Our mutual enemy appears to have recruited the Rekkrs. Perhaps you've seen them?"

"We have." Abby perched herself on a tall stool behind the counter. "They winter here."

"Who was shot?" Thia pressed. "Was it Cor—someone we know? Are they okay?"

She wasn't fooling Quentin any more than, it seemed, she had been fooled by the half-*Sidhe's* disguise. That was to say, not at all. Clearly she knew Cormac was in Granite Springs, and just as clearly—whether by intuition or a lucky guess— she'd correctly assigned his role in last night's events.

Quentin took pity on her. "No ill effects."

"Really?" Her hazel eyes were wide, endearingly fearful on behalf of someone who didn't deserve such a gift.

Quentin felt an odd pang. Not envy, exactly. Certainly not loneliness. Yet he did wonder what it might be like to be the focus of such concern. He, too, was one of the undeserving. He had given up on the possibility some time ago.

Both women watched him curiously. And no wonder.

He covered his lapse with a long drink. Set the mug down. "He's fine. And on his way with—"

He broke off as blur of gray, ivory, and brown entered the left of his visual field. He turned toward it, conscious of Thia and Abby doing the same.

Edith smiled warmly, sounding only slightly out of breath as she came to a stop by his side. "Sorry I'm late." Cheerful as a songbird. "Don't mind me, please."

But Quentin did mind. How had she approached so quietly? The floor was wooden. Every chair shift, every step produced some type of response, and yet here she was, unannounced by footfall, vibration, or creak.

He cleared his throat to perform the introductions. "Althia McDaniel, Abigail Collins. Edith Wilkinson, my...assistant."

"Of sorts." Edith smiled, good-natured as always, and shook hands with the others, who insisted she call them familiarly. Thia. Abby. "Thank you. And please call me...Edith" she said with a light laugh. "A few people do call me Edie, but I'm not sure it suits me much anymore."

Moving to the stool on Quentin's right, she took up his cane and he felt his blood run cold.

"Not that it doesn't suit me when I'm with them," she said, bewilderingly, as she leaned his cane against the counter. As if it were an object of no significance whatsoever. "But, please. I'd meant to be here sooner," she said, oblivious to Quentin's shock, and seated herself beside him. "Let's continue. Where were we?"

He forced his jaw to relax. "*We* were not anywh—"

"*We*," Abby challenged, "were just hearing how a crossbow bolt connects a biker gang to our friend's disappearance, and that other friends and acquaintences of ours have decided to head out to—where was it you said, Quentin?"

"I didn't."

She returned his glare. "No, not yet you hadn't."

"Is there some reason they shouldn't know?" asked Edith.

She radiated warmth. Close as she was, Quentin could feel it, like a light touch down his side. Reminding him how cold he was. Ever since that night, so cold.

He steeled himself against that warmth. "They've gone to one of the Rekkrs's known haunts. A roadhouse, I believe you yanks call it."

"Which one?" Abby asked.

Edith answered for him. "Valhalla."

"Really." Abby didn't seem surprised.

"You know it?" Quentin took a drink, considered her.

"By reputation."

Thia shifted on her seat. "I haven't. Where is it?"

"On the old highway into the mountains south of town," Abby said, and then pinned Quentin with a particularly sharp gaze. "How did things get from a bolt to a specific location? Did someone follow the shooter there?"

"No." He was surprised by an impulse to break eye contact. Normally, others looked away from him.

"He read it," Edith volunteered, and Quentin felt his face go slack. She couldn't...She wouldn't...Yet she had.

"Read what?" Thia asked.

"The bolt," Edith said to his continued horror, and had the temerity to *smile* at him. "He's brilliant at that."

Abby eyed his gloves. Within, his hands itched to be pulled

from from view. He left them where they were, one clenched on the mug, the other flat on the counter.

She looked up. Calculating. But it was to Edith she spoke. "You must have heard about the reading Madame Demetka did here."

"Yes." Edith very carefully avoided looking his way.

Suspicion began to bud. He had been too stunned to stop her, initially. Now it seemed he was too late to stop where this was headed.

"She used something of Zoe's," Thia said. "A wooden spoon. Is that what you did with the bolt?"

"Yes." No point trying to lie. Edith—damn her—would only call him on it. She was as bad as Beatrice. Scratch that: She was worse. People genuinely liked Edith, and that made them all the more pliable.

"Could you try with the spoon?" Thia's hope was a tangible thing. Like a prod.

Resigned, Quentin took up his cane. Excluding their little group, he counted five people in the café. "I'd prefer not to have an audience. Might I have use of that room we were on our way to see?"

Presumably it had been designed to buffer the surrounding energies of the people and objects in the store. Hopefully it also buffered what he suspected came from the building itself.

"Of course." Thia hopped to her feet. "Abby, what did we do with the spoon?"

"It's in the kitchen. Hang on."

They waited while she went into the next room.

Edith stood too close for comfort. "I don't take kindly to manipulation," he told her.

"Well, certainly," she said, all innocence. "Who does?"

Oh, yes, she was much worse than Beatrice. He could almost believe that she hadn't just successfully manipulated them all.

● ○ ●

Outside the Rowan Room
Several Minutes Later

"There you all are," Todd said, coming out of the café. One hand held a wad of napkins; the other, his chai. "I looked up and you were gone. What's happening out here?"

"Not out here. In there." Thia gestured down the short walk to the Rowan Room with its closed door. "A man we know is doing a reading, trying to locate Zoe."

"Really?" When Todd would have rushed forward, Thia and Edith moved to block. He stopped but stayed on the balls of his feet. Eager and ready to move. "How's it going? Has he come up with anything?"

"We don't know," Thia said. "He's been in there awhile." She had already asked Edith if they should check on Quentin, but Edith had been adamant that opening the door so much as a crack would be disruptive.

Abby made a small sound and straightened away from the wall she had been leaning against. She'd been so still, so quiet that Thia had almost forgotten she was there.

"You okay?" Thia asked, concerned. Abby looked dazed.

"Fine." But the odd, drifty look persisted.

Edith leaned close, asking Thia, "Is your friend on a Sight Journey?"

"What's that?" Todd asked, joining them to form a strange little cluster.

Edith's smile was indulgent. "It's a kind of inward exploration of—"

"Fuck." Abby jolted and took off for the room. She hit the door full-out, shoving it open. Thia raced after her.

"Is it over?" Todd called after them.

The windowless room was pitch dark except for the shaft of light cast through the doorway. It fell across Quentin, face down on the floor. One arm was outstretched, the wooden spoon gripped in his ungloved hand. Nearby, his cane lay at an angle, the silver glinting with what Thia would later recall as an unnatural brightness.

She and Abby rushed to him, knelt down. Blocked the light. Their shadows fell across him, merged with the black of his coat.

"He won't thank you," Edith said from the door. The words might have been meant to discourage action, but the worry her voice carried spurred Thia on.

"Someone turn on the lights, would you?" Thia's hands were inches above Quentin's back and prepared to shake him...and yet she hesitated. He didn't like to be touched, to be helped. Edith was probably right.

Abby was having the same misgivings. Her hands were no closer than Thia's.

But Quentin wasn't moving.

"Is he all right?" Todd asked as the overhead lights came on. "I-I could call 911. Should I call 911?"

"No," came Quentin's low reply. Or perhaps it was a moan.

Thia's breath went out on a grateful rush. "Quentin?" Still unsure about her hands, she placed them in her lap.

"I'm all right." He didn't sound it.

Thia met Abby's concerned gaze above the expensive fabric of Quentin's suit coat. He shifted slightly, released the spoon as he drew in his arm. Nothing of his face was visible. Thia wondered if he had fallen directly on it. That had to hurt.

"He's fine." Edith stepped away from the light switch. She had her phone out, but not like she planned to make a call. She proceeded to wander the room with it, moving it over the walls. "These numbers are phenomenal. Has anyone ever mentioned a presence here?"

Thia struggled to make sense of that. Failed. "What?"

Muttering invectives, Quentin worked to push up onto his

hands.

"Stay down," Abby ordered. "Give yourself a minute." She placed her hand on Quentin's back—to hold him down, Thia thought—but snatched it away when he swore and dropped flat again. Looking shocked, Abby cradled it to her chest.

At Thia's inquiring look, she shook her head in a clear, "Not now." Or perhaps that was a, "Not ever."

And perhaps Thia didn't want to know after all.

"We're bound to attract notice," Abby said a moment later, and stood. "I'll close the door."

Not only that, she locked the knob.

With obvious effort, Quentin rolled onto his back. His eyes were closed. Blood was drying beneath his nose. He touched it cautiously with his ungloved hand. Grimaced. "Damn."

"Broken?" Thia asked.

"Not this time."

She frowned. How many times had there been?

Todd brought over several napkins (fresh, thankfully). Since Quentin continued to keep his eyes closed, Thia took them.

"Here." She touched one to his hand. "For your nose."

"Thank you." He slid it from her light grip, pressed it to the blood.

"Did you see Zoe?" Todd asked, leaning down anxiously. He looked to Thia. "Does he know where she is? Is she okay?"

One thing Thia knew about the Brigantium was how much they valued secrecy, whether warranted or not. She stood, laid a guiding arm across Todd's back. "Why don't you wait for us in the café?"

Abby unlocked and held open the door. "We'll be right out, I'm sure."

"Okay," Todd said blankly, turning as he stepped out. "But is Zoe okay? Did he find her?"

"Just a few minutes, please, Todd," Thia said. Abby shut the door.

"Right," he said through it. "I'll be—I'll be out here, then."

"Okay," Thia said, as Abby rolled her eyes and re-locked the knob. They turned back to the room.

Quentin was sitting up, wiping his face. Edith continued to move her cell phone along the walls.

"What is she doing?" Thia asked Abby as they walked over to Quentin.

"No idea."

"Levels and frequencies," Quentin answered. He stuffed the bloodied napkins into one pocket, pulled a leather glove out of another. "It's a pet project of hers." He put the glove on. "A bit of an obsession, really. As you can see."

Setting his cane firmly, he levered himself up. "Thank you, I'm fine," he protested when Thia would have helped.

"Stubborn, much?" Abby's tone was biting.

Rather than taking offense, Quentin flashed her a pained grin. "Indeed." He limped toward a stack of chairs at the back wall.

Thia got there ahead of him and pulled a chair down from the top. "What went wrong?"

"Thank you." He lowered himself into it. Gray eyes looked up into hers. "What makes you think anything did?"

It took her a moment to realize that his response was not an example of dry English humor. "You expected that?"

"Magic carries a cost," he said with a chilling calm. "Surely you understand that by now?"

Thia should have. Had believed she did, after the times she had been told. Her throat had gone dry.

"Do you?" he asked gently.

She couldn't answer.

Quentin sighed. "Anyone can learn to work magic. It's the cost that makes the difference." He propped his cane against his thigh. "More so even than belief. Very few are prepared to pay what is required."

"What was required of you?"

"No." Abby stood in the center of the room. "Don't."

His laugh was unpleasant. "Very good, Ms. Collins. Sensed that, did you?" His gloved fingers tapped on the cane's knob, calling attention. "Yes, that's part of the price I pay."

Thia was tired of people talking riddles around her. But that was a fight for later.

She was making quite a list.

"Did you find Zoe?" she asked him.

"In the present? No, not a bit. In the past, however...." His eyes closed. "Much cooking. She was particularly happy with refinements to a biscotti recipe, and concerned for a specific person. She didn't think he ate enough. And hoped he would like the oatmeal."

"If you didn't get any sense of Zoe *now*—'in the present'— does that mean she's...." Thia couldn't say it.

"Dead?" Quentin's eyes opened. Pale. Hard. "No. I touched on that possibility, shall we say. More likely she's somewhere extremely protected. It's blocking all sense of her."

"Is there a way to use that? You mean *magical* protections, right? Is there a way to detect the magic and, I don't know, hone in on it? Madame Demetka said she got the feeling Zoe was to the north. Somewhere with a lot of trees, maybe near water."

"Ha," Edith scoffed, drawing their attention. She had made her way to a distant corner and was moving her phone along the baseboard. As silence stretched, she looked up, seemingly surprised to find them watching. "Sorry, but that's incredibly vague, isn't it? Trees. Water. And in an area that's full of them. Oldest trick in the book."

"Not *quite* the oldest," Quentin drawled.

Edith grinned. His lips twitched.

Abby made a sound of frustration, spread her arms. "So, all this was for nothing."

"We know Zoe is alive," Thia said, grasping for figurative straws. "That's something."

"I've given you more than that," Quentin said, and planted his cane. He used it to rise. "The bins—I assume they're out back?"

"Your people have already been over that whole area," Abby said as he began to move stiffly toward the door.

He shot her a look over his shoulder. "First, I am not those people. Second, they were focused on locating Ms. Forbes."

"And you're not?" Thia asked.

"Not at the moment."

CHAPTER 15

A frigid wind gusted through the alley. Thia huddled deeper into her coat while the fringed ends of her tartan scarf fluttered. To Abby, beside her, she murmured, "What are they doing?"

"Got me," her friend said with a shrug.

Thia didn't bother asking Todd, standing to her right. The three of them formed the front (and only) row audience of the Brigantium Show, as performed by Quentin and Edith.

Heard, not seen, he was behind the dumpsters and making muffled observations while she stayed out front to act as an assistant of sorts, dictating into her phone. "Basic cardboard shelter," she'd say after him. "Splattered oatmeal. Bootprints, size ten and a half, British measurement."

Occasionally she would sweep the phone over a dumpster or the ground below and then, without comment, tap something on its screen.

"We have all this on file," she told Quentin. She had said it three times already in Thia's hearing.

From behind the dumpster, there was the sound of sliding cardboard followed by a loud bang.

A moment later Quentin emerged, brushing himself off. He

ignored Edith to ask Todd, "Did she ever talk about who she thought to help here? Or when it had begun?"

Todd shifted uneasily. "Not to me. I didn't know anything about it, but that sounds like her. She's caring like that." His voice broke. "I should've asked her. I was always talking about myself. I should've shown more interest— no, I should have *been* more interested. Oh, God, I'm an awful friend. An awful person. I suck."

No one argued with his harsh verdict. It would have been the usual, polite thing to do, but Thia didn't think Todd was looking for, or even able to hear, reassurances just then. And, really, who was to say he wasn't right about himself? None of them knew him, for one; for another, there he was, looking at Zoe's terrifying situation in terms of himself.

Thia wondered if maybe she, too, might suck as a friend.

As an employer, too, since she should have been aware that someone was lurking by Eclectica's trash and recycling. She should have known sooner that Zoe was leaving food out.

Granite Springs was such a relaxing, welcoming place that a person could be lulled into believing life was without risk. Despite knowledge to the contrary, it became easy to think that bad things couldn't happen there.

Todd huffed out a sigh and, with a toss of his head, flung back the curly blonde locks blown across his face by the wind. "Hey, man, can't you just touch stuff and, like, get a read?"

Quentin slanted him a look before directing Edith to a place to photograph. She joined him in the narrow space between the dumpsters to do so.

"Come on," Todd insisted. "The homeless dude had to have touched the dumpster at some point. You could use that."

It seemed that Quentin wasn't going to respond, but after Edith finished her camera work and moved away, he turned. His expression was so cold, with his eyes such a flat, harsh gray that Thia couldn't blame Todd for taking a step back.

"I could," Quentin told him, "if I were willing to pay the cost. I'm not. But what of you?"

"Huh?"

"You claim to regret not being a better friend. *You* could pay what is required. If you're willing."

Thia felt a chill of apprehension. Beside her, Abby had gone eerily still.

"Um." Todd blinked, wet his lips. "W-what would that be? The, uh, cost."

Quentin's smile was predatory. "That all depends, you see. Imagine how many people, how many things, have come in contact with these bins. Even if we presume only a fraction of them left behind a lasting remnant, the number could still be quite large, yes?" He leaned more weight upon his cane. "Each and every remnant would carry a cost in direct relation to its strength."

"Y-you can't, like, pick out which ones you want to read? In advance, I mean."

Abby broke her stillness to step around Thia and face Todd. "It doesn't work that way. It just...happens. All of it, coming at once."

"The lady is correct." Quentin gave her a nod of what might have been respect.

Todd's anxious gaze flicked from one to the other before settling on the dumpsters. He flipped his hair back again. A nervous tick. "The cost would be high, huh?"

"Very." Abby was terribly grave.

"Would I die?"

Neither she nor Quentin said a thing.

They didn't have to.

Todd paled. "Shit. That's...Jesus." He scrubbed at his scalp. "Zoe. I-I don't—Aw, shit, man. I can't. I can't do that."

Wide eyes fixed on the dumpster, he took a step back, and

then another. "I mean, if it's her only hope—God. I still don't know. I don't know." Having increased the distance by a good two feet, he stopped. "I just don't know, man."

"What if we share it?" Thia surprised herself by asking.

All eyes focused on her.

"I assume energy is the form of payment, right? Power."

"Whatever you're thinking," Abby said, "it isn't a good—"

"What *are* you thinking?" Edith seemed intrigued. Eager.

"I'm not sure," Thia said. "On Orkney we combined power so Quentin could use it. Could we do that for this?"

Edith grinned, clearly in favor.

"I didn't know there was a way to put the cost on someone else," Abby said.

"There isn't," Quentin said dully. "The cost would be mine. No getting around that. But if I were given...." He closed his eyes, pinched the bridge of his nose as if fighting a headache. "It would not be without risk."

Thia regretted having said anything. What was she doing, sticking her nose in places where she knew next to nothing? *Dangerous* places, where "risk" could mean "chance of death." She had no business suggesting things she didn't understand.

But...Zoe. They needed to find Zoe, and to stop whatever Cassie planned. *That* was the biggest danger, the biggest risk.

"How much would we need?" Thia asked as the wind picked up. "How many people?"

Quentin turned to study the dumpsters once more. The line of his shoulders slumped almost imperceptively. "How many can you get?"

● ○ ●

Green Springs Highway

There would be snow, Cormac knew, in the higher elevations, but here in the foothills east of town, winter seemed more a matter of cold slumber. The car sped past hillsides of frosted, dry grass and bare trees beneath a hazy sky.

"How much farther?" He sounded like a petulant child on holiday. Relegated to the rear seat, he *felt* like a petulant child. He wasn't accustomed to riding as anyone's passenger.

It chafed.

Kendra interrupted her tedious conversation with Murphy, driving, to blandly reply, "A few miles more." Then it was back to the mind-numbing minutiae of hotel management. Linen suppliers, banquet seating arrangements, guest services, and the like, *ad nauseum*. Cormac sighed. His shoulder was stiff, but otherwise fine. He should have flown ahead.

"Did I hear it right that the Retreat altered their menu at the last minute?" Murphy accelerated into a turn, with barely a change in the engine's luxurious purr.

Cormac wasn't in the market for a new car, but this one was tempting.

"They did," Kendra said. "They pulled the same thing last time, so we were ready."

"What was it they wanted?"

"Plum pudding."

"You're joking."

Kendra laughed. "No."

"How very Dickensian."

Cormac considered jumping out. He figured he'd have time to shift into flight before hitting the ground if he leapt high to start.

"Ah." Murphy slowed the car slightly as the road entered a grove of trees. "There we are, coming up on the right. I'll give it a drive by, find a spot up the way."

Adjacent to the road was a blocky wooden sign, the paint of its letters faded and flaking. Several in the middle were hard to make out, but there was no question as to this being the right place. The question, Cormac decided as he engaged his Sight, was how recently anyone had been by.

There was no car park to speak of, only a wide strip of dirt between the road and the Valhalla Roadhouse itself, set back among pines and cedars.

Kendra echoed his thoughts. "Looks deserted."

The wood siding was as worn as its sign. The windows were cracked, with some smaller panes wholly absent.

Yet, bits of color glowed softly within the darkness inside as electricity continued to feed neon signs ubiquitous to liquor establishments. And some ruts in the dirt out front looked recent. Or recent enough, Cormac judged, by their not being iced over like the rest.

"It isn't warded," he remarked as they drove by. He assumed Kendra and Murphy could see that for themselves, but it was surprising and therefore something to consider. And, besides, they were here as a team, weren't they? That's what teams did, was it not—share observations? He had never been part of one before. (Although, "team" implied trust. Something they decidedly lacked.)

"Should make this easier, then," Murphy said of the absent wards, and Kendra nodded, agreeing. But Cormac suspected they weren't any more confident about the situation than he was. There was something...off about the place. Something unsettling. The word *creepy* came to mind and stuck.

A mile distant, Murphy turned onto an unpaved forest road. The car bounced over ruts and holes until out of sight of the motorway behind, maybe five or six minutes more.

"Good enough," Murphy declared, and parked.

Cormac got out, put on his gloves while the others went to the car's boot. From it, Kendra lifted a short sword in a belted sheath she then strapped around her waist. Murphy took out a battle axe, hefted it a few times as he rolled his shoulders, limbering up.

Curious, Cormac went to look inside.

A safe sat open, exposing several handguns and what looked

to be a semiautomatic rifle. Outside that were swords in their scabbards, a box of knives, a mace, and a crossbow not unlike what could have fired the bolt into him the night before.

"Quite the armory." Cormac stepped back, hoped his initial revulsion hadn't shown. The other things he didn't mind, but he hated guns.

"Just a few odds and ends," Murphy said, trading the axe for a Ruger SR. He tucked it into a holster already worn under his wax jacket. An extra clip went into a side pocket. "Care for any?"

Looking set to protest, Kendra opened her mouth but then quickly closed it. She needn't have worried.

"I've never had much use," Cormac said. Leaving them to follow, he set off for Valhalla.

The terrain looked easy despite patches of frost and ice. He abandoned the road almost immediately to cut a direct line through the woods. The others caught up quickly, and they proceeded to climb in silence, an odd trio with an odd history.

Cormac didn't detect anyone else in the area. That wasn't a guarantee, since there were ways of going below the radar, so to speak; but even animals were absent, so he thought it more likely that other forces were at work. Wise forces like of those of self-preservation, as his own were telling him to go no further.

Bad vibes, some might say.

At the top of the rise he stopped and looked down—twenty feet down—the granite scarp to the roadhouse below.

"Could be worse." Murphy's voice was wry as he studied the crumbling rock face.

Cormac concentrated on the roadhouse. "Two rooms. The main bar and something one-third its size behind. Kitchen, probably." He couldn't see details—his Sight didn't work that way. But he could sense generalities. "Plus a few small rooms. Probably storage. No occupants."

"Right. Let's get on with it, then," Murphy said and moved to position himself at the edge.

"Of course." With a rare grin, Cormac leapt off, taking raven form. He landed almost effortlessly, shifting back to himself, at Valhalla's rear door.

"Bastard," Murphy called, and Cormac laughed outright.

While the others made their difficult way down, he tried the door—locked—and pulled his basic set of lock picks from his jacket. He may not carry weapons, but he was rarely without what had long been essential tools of his trade.

There were two locks to contend with: one in a knob that was half falling off; the other a much newer, heavy duty dead-bolt. He could take care of both with a spell, but that would leave a trace. So might his picks, but anyone with an internet connection could learn how pick a lock these days. Magic would arouse much more suspicion, and could point it more quickly in his direction.

He supposed he could bust or pry open a window and get in that way—as if he were merely an amateur, someone who saw an opportunity while driving by and took it—but the options for that were all at the front of the building, visible from the road.

Having chosen to start with the deadbolt, he was raking the pick over the pins when sounds of a minor landslide intruded. He ignored them along with Murphy's, "You all right there, Ross?"

They joined him soon after. Kendra brushed dirt and pine needles from her clothes.

"Problem?" Cormac asked pleasantly.

"Not at all," she said. "You?"

The deadbolt slid out of the way with a satisfying click. He figured that was answer enough and made quick work of the knob's simple mechanism. Childsplay.

For him, it had been.

He pocketed his tools, pushed open the door.

The stench was a solid, grasping thing. Stale beer and burnt grease. Leather and sweat. Tobacco smoke.

Cormac stepped into the dank gloom.

A filthier kitchen he had never seen. His gloves meant that he needn't worry about leaving prints, but he'd do his best to not touch anything, regardless.

"Good God, man," Murphy said as he pushed by, going with Kendra to the barroom. "No need to linger."

But Cormac did linger, wondering at a fainter scent caught lurking beneath the rest. Certainly blood wasn't an unusual presence in a kitchen. Vegan, this place was not. Yet...unless they also butchered the meat they served, there shouldn't be enough to notice at all.

It was too old to belong to Thia's abducted friend, however, so he left to join the others.

The light was better there, filtering through the grimy (or broken) front windows and reflecting in the cracked mirror above the bar. A neon sign near the main door buzzed and stuttered, advertising Mack Pilsner in crimson, intermittently glowing letters. Below them, the tubing meant to represent a white stag failed to glow at all.

"This is a bloody antique," Murphy griped from behind the scarred and undoubtedly sticky bar. Glaring at its register, he pounded a key with his gloved finger. A bell chimed and the drawer shot out with a rattle of coins. "No receipts, of course. No telling when it was last used. Christ Jesus, do they not even take cards?"

No names to track down.

Kendra had been surveying the floor. "I can see prints, but that's no good. I can see prints everywhere."

Careful to avoid the obvious traffic pattern, Cormac went to look out the glass by the door. Muddy boot prints covered the shallow porch. Cigarette butts littered the entire front.

"Are there ashtrays?" he asked the others, turning around.

What tables there were had been crammed into one area, far from the door. They were bare. With few chairs available and only a couple of stools, Cormac guessed that not much time was spent seated. Quite possibly, more time was spent brawling—which would explain the dearth of lighter-weight furnishings. Splinters of wood littered the floor along with a multitude of peanut shells...and the cigarette butts that had nowhere else to go. Ashtrays were often the first things to go in a fight.

There were no trash bins evident, either.

"This was a waste of time." Kendra kicked what might have been a piece of broken chair.

"Not necessarily," Cormac said. And how rare was that, his being the voice of optimism? Yet he meant it. "I don't think Cassie has been here. If she has, she didn't do anything."

"This isn't their base of operations," Murphy said.

"Precisely."

"That's hardly anything," Kendra complained. "To come all this way—and fall down a cliff, thank you—and all we learn is that this is just where the Rekkrs come to drink and play Russian roulette with food poisoning?"

"It was more than that, before." Cormac was thinking again of bad vibes and old blood.

"Before what?"

He shrugged. "I don't know. Before Cassie."

"How do you mean, 'more'?" Murphy came out from behind the bar.

"I can feel it. Can't you? And the smell. Beneath it all."

Murphy paused. Grimaced. "It's there."

"What is?" The light from the window caught Kendra's hair, turning it into a brilliant, shimmering red. Red like the sign. Red like—

"Violent death," Murphy offered, and Cormac had a sharp, almost overwhelming need to leave.

And never return to this place.

The ring of a mobile phone cut through the quiet. Murphy twitched, hiding it well but not entirely. Cormac hadn't done any better.

Kendra's reaction was extreme—an exclamation along with a lurch. But the phone turned out to be hers, and vibrating as it rang. She pulled it from her pocket.

"It's Abby," she said shakily, reading the screen. She swiped across it, accepted the call. "Hey. What's up?"

CHAPTER 16

In the middle of greeting arrivals in the café, Thia spotted Kendra entering the patio. It was both a relief and a cause for panic. Now they could begin.

With apologies to the woman she was about to interrupt, Thia announced, "They're here," and went to meet her friend at the door.

"Wow," Kendra said of the crowd of fifteen or so. "Not bad for short notice."

"Members of Abby's coven. Those who work nearby or were in town to do some shopping before the parade. Plus some of their friends."

"Great. Let's do this."

Thia envied Kendra's enthusiasm. Mostly what *she* felt was apprehension.

It took a few minutes to wrangle everyone, but soon enough the group was forming a circle near the dumpsters. Murphy stood nearby, directing a number of the Landmark's security team into positions around the alley. How strange this was going to look to people passing by.

Or maybe not, for Granite Springs.

While Quentin and Edith, out of earshot, continued what

looked to be an intense conversation, Thia scrutinized faces both familiar and unfamiliar. Cormac had gone with Kendra and Murphy to the roadhouse...so where was he now? *Which* might he be?

Abby walked up to Murphy, gestured at the circle. He shook his head and went to join one of the security men stationed much farther down. Interestingly, she watched him for some time after. For people who couldn't stand one another, they certainly found reasons to interact often enough.

Footsteps to Thia's left.

"Hello." Cormac's voice. As if she'd summoned him.

She turned, found herself facing a portly, middle-aged man with mouse-brown hair that poked out around the bottom of a knit cap. His eyes were a mix of blues and grays and muted greens, like the waters of the North Atlantic. Cormac's eyes. They sparkled as if he were amused. His smile confirmed it.

"Oh, for God's sake." Thia pivoted away. The other side of the circle would do. She headed there.

Did he not understand how freaky that was? How *weird* it was that he could transform—or give the illusion or however the hell it worked—into a completely different person? Oh, fine, except for the eyes. Whatever. A minor detail when the rest was the issue.

Thia inserted herself between Edith and some man (Greg? Gary?) she had been introduced to only a few minutes before. He was a soft-spoken, *genuinely* middle-aged man with a well-kept beard and a mustache waxed into very thin, very precise twists.

"Exciting, isn't it?" he said, cheerfully enough, although he seemed tense.

Thia nodded vaguely and chanced a look across at Cormac.

He was watching her. His persona's shoulders had slumped. His mouth had turned down, no longer amused. His eyes no longer sparkled.

Well, too bad. If he'd thought she would find it amusing—as he'd seemed to—to have another trick played on her, then he deserved to feel disappointed. To have his feelings hurt. How did he think she felt when he played these tricks? This wasn't fun for her. This wasn't a joke.

Although, he had spoken with his voice just now. What she knew to be his voice, anyway. And, really, he didn't seem to be the joke-playing type.

Maybe he'd just been glad to see her, as she would've been to see him if he hadn't driven her half crazy with all the Connor Michaels stuff yesterday. She looked away.

Centered between the two dumpsters, Quentin stepped in line with the circle. "If everyone could join hands."

"Excuse me." A woman near the patio gate waved. "Before we do anything, shouldn't we cast a circle in salt or chalk and ask Hecate to aid us in our task?"

"No." Quentin eyed the rest of the group. "If that is the last of the interruptions, would everyone join—"

"I'm uncomfortable working without the protection of the blessed Lady of Silence," the woman said with an angry flick of the pashmina she wrapped more snugly around her neck.

"Well, I'm not," Quentin snapped. "And as I'm the one at risk, that should serve. Now, if you wouldn't mind?"

Thia thought the woman would speak again, but Abby set a hand on her arm and whispered in her ear. The woman kept silent.

Meanwhile, Thia's subconscious had latched onto the word "risk" and flooded her system with adrenaline. Her heart rate picked up and her chest went tight. This had been her idea. If something were to go wrong, it would be on her. Yes, Quentin had agreed to it—they had all agreed to it—but that would be little consolation if anyone got hurt. He knew what he was doing, didn't he? But she'd seen him that night in the Ring of Brodgar. She'd seen him just today in the Rowan Room. He didn't seem to think much of his own limits.

"What did he mean, *risk?*" Thia quietly asked Edith, beside her. "And how much?"

The Brigantium agent reseated her glasses on the bridge of her nose and then offered her right hand. "Only one way to know. Shall we?"

Thia took hold with her left, and then turned to the man on her right. Gavin. That was his name. Their palms met. His skin was cold. Not surprising, with the temperature hovering in the low thirties. Thia could feel Edith's hand losing warmth. Her own, too long from her coat pockets, already ached. But this couldn't be done through gloves.

"For those who are new to this kind of work," Edith said, unexpectedly addressing the gathering as hands were clasped all around the circle—"it really is quite simple. Relax, drop what major blocks you might have in place, and let the energy find its way. Nothing at all to worry about."

"Truly?" Thia asked under her breath.

Edith slanted her a look. "Mostly. Frequently, worry—fear, in the worst cases—can create danger where otherwise none exists. Don't give it control over your will."

Ah. Right. Easier said than done.

Quentin, at the ceremonial head of the circle, pulled off his gloves, tucked them into his coat pocket. His cane lay at his feet. He clasped hands with the Brigantium agents on either side. His head lowered as he seemed to gather himself. When it came up again, he looked straight out and said in a bold voice: *"Potestas est."*

Immediately, power ignited within Thia's bones and began making its way outward, tingling along her nerves.

"Relax," said Edith, and Thia realized she had tensed to the point of holding her breath. She let it out, reminded herself that she had done this before and under much more stressful circumstances (a full-out battle, for goodness sake). She had practiced on a smaller scale several times since, and nothing had gone wrong. Well, not that she knew of. That first time, in the Ring, she wasn't so sure.

Energy from the people to Thia's left pushed its way in to merge with what had risen within. Then, drawn by whatever Quentin was doing, the mixture flowed out through her right hand and into the man who held it...and on through him to the people to his right.

Her left received power. Her right let it go.

Gavin twitched, his eyes going wide. Thia hoped he wasn't getting more than he could handle. Presumably he had a good amount of his own or he wouldn't have been invited; and he was supposed to be giving a portion of his own away, and not retaining anything he received. They were to act as conduits. Pass-throughs. Which meant there was no danger of anyone getting more than they could handle, right? Thia's brain ached as she tried to think this through. Quentin had said the risk—whatever it was—was his. So all these other people should be perfectly safe. Except that in magic there were no guarantees.

"Relax," Edith reminded her.

Thia let out another held breath only to barely catch the next one when Quentin's eyes flashed white.

Her own eyes felt like they might be glowing, but not like that. She'd caught sight of herself once while practicing with Abby and Kendra and a scrying mirror. It had been startling and fascinating, and explained the odd, vague pressure she'd been feeling. Her irises had glowed a kind of warm gold, as if a light had shone through the usual hazel coloring. That was the norm, when it happened, from what she understood: a luminous variation of the person's eye color.

She looked around the circle. Not everyone's were affected, including Abby's. The brown of Edith's was lit a soft amber, while Kendra's green was a radiant emerald. And Cormac's... Cormac's were that deep, luminous blue Thia could gaze into for hours. She made herself look away, settling again on Abby.

And she belatedly realized that if Quentin was the end target of the circle's power, that meant he received from both sides. Abby, standing directly opposite him, was what? Dividing her power equally? Serving as an anchor?

She realized then, too, that she could watch this using her Sight...but then, one screw-up, one loss of control, and she'd endanger everyone present. She had been doing okay with it, but what awful timing if something did go wrong.

In front of the B&B, a man and woman unloaded suitcases from their car. What might they think of this? If they focused on the eccentric dress exhibited by the coven members, they might presume the circle to be part of a New Age or Hippy peace-prayer, maybe. But then the Brigantium in their much more businesslike attire might shatter that notion.

Then there was Quentin's cane, rising from the ground to float, vertical, near where his hand gripped that of the man to his right. In a coordinated move, both men let go—only to grab onto the ebony stick. Its silver knob glowed white like Quentin's eyes.

"The cane will stand for Quentin," Edith explained in a near whisper. "Watch."

As if Thia would look away.

There was some maneuvering so that the man to Quentin's left could reach. They then broke their handclasp to grip the cane.

"This reduces the risks to the circle," Edith said. "The cane will serve as Quentin's connection to us. Since he'll no longer be in direct contact, whatever he might incur will not come through."

Quentin let go.

There was a noticeable drop in the circle's flow, like when too many appliances drew on a circuit, and then the energy balanced, returning to its previous level.

In as smooth a walk as Thia had seen him do, Quentin went

to the dumpster that held the recycling. He extended his arm, laid his hand flat against the scarred metal. Immediately his spine went stiff; his head bowed.

The energy flow in the circle escalated. Thia felt a tug deep in her marrow, the demand for more. Quentin shuddered and it seemed his knees would buckle.

He recovered, set his other hand next to the first. More was called from the group. The woman who had wanted to ask for blessings cried out. She sounded more surprised than pained, Thia thought, but kept an eye on her for a moment to be sure.

She seemed all right, if paler than before.

A light tremor ran through Edith, calling Thia's attention. She, too, was pale. Her eyes had closed.

Abruptly, it was over.

Quentin took his hands from the dumpster and dropped to his knees. Energy, now with nowhere to go, reversed course, lashing the circle like a whip.

"Release hands!" Edith shouted, her eyes not only open but wide. Almost instantly, everyone let go.

Thia felt light-headed and a little wrung out, but otherwise fine. Was that it? She turned to Edith, but the woman was no longer—There she was, crouched by Quentin. He continued to kneel, utterly still, with back to the group.

Had it worked? Thia chanced a look across the circle.

Cormac-in-disguise was watching her. So he wouldn't take her interest as a signal to approach, Thia went to join Edith and Quentin. She wasn't avoiding, she was—all right, she was avoiding.

"If you get me a map," Quentin was saying in a tired, low voice, "I could point to it."

"Point to what?" Abby asked him as she came up. The circle had broken into smaller groups of animated conversation.

"Avery *ap Hywel.*"

Abby frowned. "What's that?"

"Not what. Who." He took an unsteady breath. "I need to lie down."

Then he passed out.

● ○ ●

"That's twice in one day you've been unconscious," Thia said to him a half hour later in the café. He hadn't been out long, maybe a few seconds. And he had refused help getting up— no surprise there—or getting inside. "Maybe you should stay here. Rest." She grimaced as he took another swig of what looked to be a noxiously "healthy" smoothie. Busy thanking the circle participants as they'd left, she hadn't been present when the drink was made (and for which she was very, very grateful). But it was dark green and quite thick and it smelled awful. Like garlic and vinegar and dirt.

"I'll be fine," Quentin said. "All in a day's work."

"Really?"

His mouth quirked at her skepticism. "Perhaps not. But I will be fine."

Through the window, she saw Abby leave the patio for the alley. "If you keep drinking that"—she gestured to his half-empty glass— "I don't see how."

"Don't knock it until you've tried it."

Thia felt her stomach rebel. "No, thank you."

The door opened. Edith peered around it without entering. "The cars are here," she informed them. "We're all set."

"Right." Quentin set the glass down, pushed back his chair. Thia would have waited to accompany him, but he dismissed her with a curt, "See you out there."

"I believe there's a seat for you in Murphy's car." Edith held the door open for her. "Your friends are there."

"Thank you." Thia hurried out. The day hadn't gotten any warmer as it progressed, and it would be even colder in the mountains where they were headed: a former summer camp.

It had fallen on hard times several decades back, she'd been told, and eventually shut down altogether. Entering the alley, she felt in her coat pockets for her hat and gloves. Her scarf hung loose about her neck; wind threatened to snatch it away. She grabbed both ends, held them fast as she jogged to where a sleek Maserati idled.

The sight of the man standing by the near passenger door made her falter. He faced away from her, but she'd know him anywhere. Moderate height—only an inch or so taller than her. Trim build. Dark brown hair, currently being tousled by the icy wind.

Cormac.

She sped up.

He bent as if to get in, then paused. Close now, Thia could see past him to where Abby sat on the far side. If looks could kill. He began to back out.

"Oh no you don't." Thia gave him a hard shove. He fell into the car.

"Don't mind me," Abby could be heard to gripe while Thia continued to push and prod until Cormac was all the way in.

She plunked herself down beside him, forcing him over to the middle, and shut the door. "All set," she announced, and drew the seatbelt across her chest to fasten it in the buckle between her hip and Cormac's. "Let's go."

"Aye-aye, cap'n," Murphy said from the front. The car leapt forward.

The unexpected force flung Thia back against the padded leather. Cormac grunted softly, having experienced the same.

She glanced over. "You should put on your seatbelt."

"Worried about me?" he asked pleasantly, and then grunted again when the hard turn onto the street was made without slowing. He fell against Thia as she tipped to the side.

"Dammit," Abby grumbled, righting herself from her slide onto Cormac.

Thia dug under her left thigh, pulled up half of the belt, and offered it. "It's the law."

With a curious look, he took it by the buckle. Warily. And then turned toward Abby. "Pardon me." When she shifted, he retrieved the belt's other half. The click of its fastening was loud in the otherwise quiet car. Thia could barely hear the engine through the high-end sound dampening.

"Are those snow tires?" she asked Murphy. They seemed too quiet, too smooth. Roads in the valley could get icy enough, but high in the mountains? They would be lucky to not need chains.

"We'll be all right," he said, answering the worry behind the question.

Still, a direct answer would have been nice.

The car kept to a legal, responsible speed along Main Street. Orange and white barricades had been stacked by the curbs at each intersection. Closures would soon begin in advance of the early-evening parade.

Thia had been looking forward to it for weeks, having heard great things about one of the regions biggest events. Musical groups and marching bands, dancers, acrobats, giant puppets and balloons, a terrific Santa Claus. And caroling afterward on the Plaza. It would be her first time.

Last December she had been in Los Angeles. Amazing what changes a year could bring.

"I'm furious with you," she told Cormac in an undertone. As close as they were, with their shoulders and hips touching, she felt him tense.

"You have every right," he said a moment later, his voice even quieter than hers had been.

She resisted rolling her eyes. "Do you even know what I'm furious about?"

She was all too aware there were three more people present than the conversation wanted. She wished they'd start their own and not be such a silent, unavoidably listening presence, but so far, they weren't.

Murphy signaled a turn and stopped to wait at a light.

"For everything." Cormac spoke so softly it made the gentle tick of the turn signal sound like rim shots on a snare drum. "For leaving, for not...calling, for not being honest when I was disguised, for...."

She felt a tremor run through him. "For?"

The light changed. The car shot across the intersection and sped down the rural route out of town.

"For?" she prompted again. She faced forward, which helped to prevent motion sickness as Murphy took curve after curve too fast. The limit was twenty-five. They were doing at least twice that—and right past the police station, at that. Yet no sirens followed.

"For not being honest." Cormac, too, stared straight ahead. Sometimes it was easiest to speak openly when eye contact was not involved.

That was another reason Thia didn't look at him, no matter the temptation. He was himself, finally—the version she had come to think of as him—and she wanted to look, to take in the full effect of him while she could.

Yet she didn't, because she understood how he hated to be pinned down.

"I haven't been honest with you," he went on when she said nothing. "But I can't—I can't do that here. Now." He sounded small. Lost. "I can't."

Thia continued to face forward. The speedometer was at an alarming seventy. The car practically flew over the top of a rise before a railroad crossing. The landing jarred, turning her reach for Cormac's hand into a less-than-graceful move. She slammed down on it where it rested on his knee, and he startled. There was the zing of contact—the reason he had been so careful not to touch her when he'd taken the buckle.

Skin to skin was honest.

He held himself taut. Thia worked her fingers between his until their hands were clasped.

She said nothing.

He exhaled roughly, gave her hand a tentative squeeze. She returned it, held firm as she subtly shifted her weight, letting her length rest along his.

She teetered on an emotional edge. It was a place she had been only once before—also with him, as it happened. Also thanks to him, she knew how far down the ground was, and how hard she would hit if she were to go over.

His hand was warm, the skin smooth over muscle and bone. Not a lazy hand but a strong, adept one. A hand could say a lot about a person, and so Thia concentrated on it, reveled in the gift offered with its hold. Companionship. Simple on its surface, complex beneath—and so often underrated.

The ride continued in relative silence until they were well out of town—much farther than they should have been with the posted limits. Murphy was an excellent driver, but holy hell.

"What's the plan when we get there?" Abby asked what she had probably been holding back the whole time. She did like to have a detailed plan.

"We get in, we get out," Murphy said. "Preferably with the girl."

Naturally, such vagueness didn't satisfy. Abby leaned deeply forward into the front-seat gap between Murphy and Kendra. Bickering commenced.

Thia briefly touched her head to Cormac's shoulder. Lifted it to continue watching the road. "I'm still furious with you."

"I know."

The car skidded around a tight turn, shuddered as its tires sought traction on slush. They were well into the mountains, entering a high prairie known colloquially as The Vale. Snow spread itself thickly over the flat grassland.

The road glistened in the early afternoon sun. It had been recently plowed but not salted. They didn't do that here. Thia could see the small lava rock used instead. It pinged wildly on the car's undercarriage.

"There cannot be a more specific plan of action," Murphy said in response to something from Abby. He whipped the car into another turn. "Not until we see what there is to bloody see."

"I'm just saying that we need to have a better idea of what we're going to do. General scheme of things. Contingencies. There's no reason we can't talk options and variables."

The tires lost traction on a stretch of ice and went halfway into the the opposite lane before Murphy regained control.

"Guys," Kendra said, sounding strained. "Can we not do this right now?"

"I'm fine," Murphy said, but Thia noted how the bones and tendons of his hands stood out. He gripped the wheel as hard as she did the armrest. And Cormac's hand.

"Sorry," she whispered and forced her grip to relax.

Abby was undeterred. "All I'm trying to do is what he clearly isn't capable of—"

At the unmistakable thump of a foot slamming down on a pedal, the wheels locked and the car went into a frightening, rotating slide. Abby dropped back into her seat while Thia tried not to shriek.

Almost entirely turned around, the car drifted to a stop.

Everyone took a breath and a good, long moment.

Abby broke it. "You could have killed us! What the hell was that?"

"Hey." With the hand Thia forced loose from the armrest, she reached across Cormac to poke Abby on the thigh. "Look at the fog."

She hadn't noticed it herself until they had stopped. Then

suddenly there it was, surrounding the car.

"Druid Fog." Cormac let go of Thia's hand.

"Should we back out?" Kendra asked. "Before we lose where we are?"

A car blew past them in a swerve that narrowly avoided their rear bumper. Its brake lights were on, luminous red against a field of misty white.

Murphy flung off his seatbelt and shoved open his door to launch himself from the car. The other reversed, coming up alongside.

It was the sedan—the Brigantium's car—with Quentin and Edith. The driver's window rolled down.

"Let me out," Cormac said to Thia. Kendra had her phone in hand and was telling the driver of the third car to reduce speed so as to not hit anyone.

Thia got out into the icy damp. The fog's crystals were like tiny needle pricks on her face. She pulled up her scarf, buried her mouth and nose as best she could. Cormac followed her out and strode to where Murphy spoke with Quentin through the back passenger window.

"Yes," the latter said as Thia got close enough to hear. "I can navigate it, same as on the Orkneys."

"As can I," Cormac volunteered. "It has Idris's magic in it, coming from—" He frowned, turned in a small half circle as if honing in on a signal. He pointed. "That way."

"Right." Cane first, Quentin emerged. With a black fleece hat covering his gray hair, he looked years younger if no less haggard. "We proceed on foot. Single file. I'd suggest we tie in like mountaineers but that could go poorly if we're attacked."

CHAPTER 17

Through a cloud of white and with Quentin at the lead, they walked for what felt like hours. In reality, if Thia's watch could be trusted, it had been only forty minutes. The disparity might have been caused by the curse within the Druid Fog, but could have just been from the nightmarish, freezing-cold aspects of the experience itself. Much as she feared what lay ahead, this part could not end soon enough. The temperature was so low, the skin of her face not covered by scarf or fleece hat felt burned. The rest of her ached with cold and the effort of not shivering.

As instructed, she was using her Sight, but because the mist was so thick, visibility remained an eerie and claustrophobic matter of inches. Her focus alternated between her feet (so as to not stumble) and Cormac's back (so as to not lose sight of him and thus mislead the people following her). She could only trust that he kept close to Edith ahead of him, and she to whoever was directly ahead of her.

The set-up reminded her of a team-building exercise. The kind favored by large companies with low employee morale.

In Los Angeles, she'd been made to participate in a few, and she and her fellow participants had found them so silly they'd been a source of amusement for weeks.

No one laughed now. No one so much as spoke; it was too problematic, with sound being as limited as vision. Thia could hear her own footsteps on the mix of ice and rock along what she thought was a lakeshore, and her own strained, nervous breathing. That was it.

She reached back, felt Abby's brief handclasp before pulling away. Her friend, at least, kept up. Hopefully the rest of their group did as well.

What would they find after all this? Would Cassie be there waiting? Were they walking to an ambush? Would there be another battle like in Brodgar?

Terror born of memory rose up to become even more claustrophobic than the fog, taunting her with sights and sounds that were weeks old but felt as fresh as minutes. She closed her eyes against them—and walked straight into Cormac, her nose smashing into the knitted wool of his cap and against his hard skull beneath. Her eyes open, she stumbled back.

Cormac spun, reached out as if to steady her. "All right?"

They were out of the fog.

Disoriented, Thia shied from his hand only to knock into Abby. "Sorry." She moved so the rest of the group could exit smoothly.

The formation shifted from single file to a side-by-side line with the fog at their backs.

Ahead was a shifting "wall" of protection wards set before a snowy pine forest. Somewhere within was the old camp.

"What do you think?" Edith asked. She stood by Quentin, but it was Murphy, several positions down, who responded:

"I think it's too bloody easy by half."

Beside Thia, Abby bristled and sucked in a breath, but if she had intended to argue, Quentin's agreement kept her quiet.

"The question is why," he went on. "Does Cassandra think this adequate protection, or does she *want* us to get inside?"

"We'll never know from guessing." Murphy turned to a man

by Kendra near the end of their line. "Liam, you've a knack. Do you mind?"

Short and squat with a good deal of gray mixed into his wild red hair and beard, Liam took a step closer to the wards and extended his arms, hands held palms-out. He gave a moment of consideration. "The dark will be a wee bit tricky."

His voice reminded Thia of the cereal leprechaun. Four leaf clovers and purple horseshoes.

His words, though, caused her to observe the shimmering barrier in more detail. Now that she knew to look, it wasn't hard to pick out what he meant by "dark."

Like others of their kind, the protection wards were made up of strands of energy, woven together. Threads of different widths and transparency and color, and all of them moving in a kind of animated tapestry. Magic given form. There among the colorful lines, Thia picked out dull, murky ones: Shadows woven between the bright.

"Leave those to me," Cormac volunteered with a reluctance that tugged on her unwilling sympathies. (Their closeness in the car didn't mean she wasn't still angry.)

"They're separate," he explained as he arranged his fingers in specific, mirrored poses. The tips of the first two touched that of the thumb, while the tips of the last two touched the base. "A combination of multiple threads."

"Obviously," Quentin remarked. "But how do you—ah."

Intent, Cormac traced small circles in the air with his hands posed, and then quickly splayed his fingers. As if unwinding a loop and then flinging it away.

Before Thia had gained her Sight, she'd been shown warding but had found it too strange to believe. The complex waving of arms and twisting of hands had meant nothing. Being able to see the energy patterns made all the difference.

She had watched when Kendra had strengthened the ones Lettie had originally placed around Eclectica and her home, so she'd thought she knew what to expect here. But Kendra had been augmenting. Strengthening. Liam and Cormac were trying to destroy. It turned out to be apples to oranges.

Liam would take hold of one strand, pinning that tiny part in place while the remainder wriggled as if fighting to escape. Light would emanate from his fingertips, changing hue until it matched that of the pinned strand. When it did, the strand would disappear.

He was unraveling the interwoven spells.

Increasingly, the dark strands were isolated, and Thia came to understand Cormac's reluctance.

Despite the cold, sweat glistened on his face. His mouth was a thin line of strain. His eyes were closed—she supposed to better concentrate on his Sight. He certainly had no trouble picking out the murky strands.

Again and again he did so, implementing the same sequence of gestures: Pinch, unwind, fling. And with each repetition, a dark thread would untwist, becoming many strands of color before shattering into bright fragments and vanishing.

Thia wondered at the difference between the types, but she didn't dare break the reigning silence to ask. Concentration was key, and the work hard. Standing as close as she was to Cormac, she was aware how his breathing had roughened.

When he flinched, she realized he wasn't just working hard physically, he was masking discomfort...if not outright pain. There was blood on his fingers. Not a lot. Mostly dots, welled as if from pinpricks. But one thin line of red ran down into the sleeve of his jacket from a deep slice along the base of his thumb.

Liam had finished. Only the shadow strands remained, and very few at that.

"Mind if I try?" Quentin's cane was tucked under his arm, against his side. His hands were lifted expectantly. "I believe I have the way of it."

Cormac blew out a breath. Opened his eyes. The blue glow faded, leeching his irises to dull gray. "All yours."

● ○ ●

She was coming. The one with the Cailleach's powers. Avery uncurled himself to put his ear to the door of his hiding place in the cupboard beneath the stairs. There had been no sounds for...he did not know for how long. It was as if he had been forgotten.

He cracked open the door. No one. But *she* was coming and not alone. He slipped out, left the door ajar. He would return soon.

On the way to the basement, he ticked through the mental inventory of the security measures he had designed.

He could do nothing about the ones that had been added, but when it came to his own..."*Diarfoga*," he muttered. Like flicking a switch. There would be no flashing orange alert this time.

Vaguely, he expected punishment. Not only had he acted on his own, he had sabotaged the alarm system.

Yet he reached the basement without consequence. Had he been forgotten?

He opened the door, silently descended the stairs. Used to the dark, he located her easily on the mattress he had brought for her.

His throat was dry. He needed to clear it before he could speak.

He did so.

Shrieking, she scuttled until her back was to the wall. She fumbled with her flashlight.

"This way," he said.

The flashlight clicked on, the beam shining directly in his eyes.

He closed them. "Don't."

"What do you want with me?" Her voice was shrill. She did not lower the beam.

Avery continued to see red. He covered his closed eyes with his hands. "Your friends are coming." A shiver moved through him. "Quickly. Before they get too close."

"My friends? Who do you—Tabby and Brendan? Why would they come here? Wait, how do *you* know them?" He heard her moving about. "Too close for what?"

"Not for." He lashed out, grabbed her wrist before she could hit him with the flashlight. "To."

"No!" She fought him like a mad thing, bucking and kicking. Scratching. "Let go of me! Let me go!"

He wrestled the light from her, shut it off before tossing it aside. "*Rwyt ti mewn trymgwsg.*"

She went limp. He caught her quickly, scooped her up into his arms. He had to hurry. They were here.

● ○ ●

It was too quiet, which made it easy to be too loud. For Thia, anyway. Admittedly, everyone else moved through the woods with perfect stealth.

They had spread out and were avoiding the more obvious routes from the lake to the camp buildings, and she lacked experience with stealthy, run-through-the-wilderness sorts of activities. As a result, unfortunately, she made a ton of noise.

Thia tried to keep her footsteps light, to move in a way so that her clothing didn't rustle. For a time, she would succeed. Then, inevitably, her like-new hiking boot would come down on a twig and snap it, or she'd step wrong on an unexpected patch of ice or rock (or an icy rock) and her arms would flail in order to catch her balance, and that would brush the sleeves of her coat against her sides and sound as loud as a flag in a windstorm.

Okay, it wasn't quite that loud. She was being too hard on

herself. But the woods were so quiet that even her breathing sounded like cries for attention.

And, really, how was it that to no one else made anywhere near the amount of noise?

Well ahead of her, Murphy and Kendra moved with predatory efficiency. Sleek and silent and not a single clumsy or poorly conceived action between them. Cormac, too, some distance to her right, sprinted with similar expert grace.

Thia couldn't see Abby or the three men who made up the rest of their group, but since she couldn't hear them, either, they were doing better than she. Hell, even Quentin with his physical limitations and cane did better.

Edith had stayed at the edge of the Druid Fog. If anything went wrong, she'd send word to the men at the cars, and they could get help. Thia should've stayed with them, or back in Granite Springs altogether.

She didn't belong here. And she was nearly out of her mind with fear. Why had she fought so hard to be included in this?

Because she had power. Although she couldn't wield it, she could share it so that others could.

She was a blundering, noise-making battery.

Apparently she was choosing this, of all times, to feel sorry for herself. She told herself to lighten up.

Four steps later, she managed to snap another damned twig underfoot. She stopped. Maybe it would be best if she waited here. Her noise could put them all in danger. She tucked up along the trunk of a pine and nearly rolled an ankle on what proved to be a dropped cone.

Murphy nimbly vaulted a fallen log on his sprint to a woodshed at the edge of the grove. He crouched beside it, made a brusque signal that led Kendra and Cormac to change course to join him.

This was the first structure they had encountered. Beyond it was an expanse of torn-up ground. A lone, battered picnic table suggested the area's original use. Beyond that was what had to be the heart of the camp—a multi-story log and beam structure that had seen better days. The adjacent parking lot hosted the smoldering remains of what must have been quite a bonfire. Snow and mud mixed, forming a brown slush pitted with tire tracks and dotted with charred trash and hunks of wood.

Crouched with Murphy at the shed, Cormac spotted Thia by the tree. He waved her over.

She didn't move. She felt useless. Worse, even: A hindrance. She shook her head.

Abby came up beside her—would have startled her but for the slow way she came into Thia's peripheral vision. "What's wrong?" she mouthed.

Thia's comprehension of the words was more a matter of lip-reading than of hearing.

Everything, she wanted to say. Or even, more simply, *me.*

She merely shook her head again. "Nothing," she mouthed back, and together they set off for the shed.

● ○ ●

Thia didn't look furious with him anymore, Cormac thought as she and Abby joined the impromptu gathering. She looked scared and a little sad. He angled himself so as to make room between himself and Quentin, but she placed herself next to her friend Kendra, with Abby going on her other side.

She had looked at him, though, and now acknowledged his offer with a small smile. That was something, at least. Better than when she had recoiled from him outside the fog.

With the arrival of the three men who had been bringing up the rear, their little rescue force was fully assembled.

"It's too quiet," Murphy said, stating the obvious, then, "We should split up. Liam, I want you with me while I check out the lodge."

The back of Cormac's neck prickled. Magic use. A lot of it. He sprang to his feet. "Run."

He didn't hesitate, didn't check to see how his actions and advice were received. He grabbed Thia's arm, pulled her with him as he set off.

She stumbled, struggling to come upright while his refusal to let go forced her to keep up or be dragged. Once she found her feet, she didn't resist. That was good, because the needle-pricks of warning had turned to thorns.

"For Morrigan's sake, run," he shouted back at the others. They hadn't left the shed's paltry cover. Panic had entered his voice, so maybe this time they would catch on. Did no one else feel the spellwork in progress?

As he asked himself, he caught sight of an alarmed Quentin touching a spot a few inches below his neck—where he likely wore a charmed Brigantium pendant. The things heated when warning of danger. Perhaps that would get the others to act.

The shed was small and windowless, not viable. It was the lodge or nothing.

Cormac veered toward it, yanking on Thia's arm when she didn't adjust course fast enough.

He was able to identify the spell-in-progress as one of Idris's favorite manifestation spells. That explained why he'd felt it first and so strongly. Not only was it Idris's magic, it required Idris's blood.

Blood to which Cormac had a connection. As would Cassie.

Unless she held a measure of Idris's in reserve, she would have needed to alter the spell to accept hers. Yet Cormac had still sensed it. Did that mean the two of them, as half siblings, shared enough for a discernible connection? Idris had used his blood link to maintain his hold over Cormac.

For one, it had enabled Idris to summon him at will. Could Cassie do the same?

Thia tripped. Cormac hauled her upright. The lodge was a

good fifty yards away.

Hooded figures appeared out of thin air around them while more burst from a barn at the car park's distant edge. They were concentrating on the periphery, forming a rough line, but three stood in the most direct route to the lodge. If more filled in there, Cormac and the others would be cut off and surrounded.

"Ah, sod it," he heard Murphy exclaim, undoubtedly having reached the same conclusion. "Move!"

As one, the hooded *thegnas* lifted their hands chest-high and flat-out. Glowing spheres of weaponized magic formed above their upturned palms. White *wanfýr*. Generally non-lethal at these distances, but that wouldn't make a hit any less painful. The potential inconvenience of being rendered unconscious went without saying.

One hand on Thia's arm, Cormac gathered his own *fýr*-ball at his other. But he wasn't going to mess around with *wanfýr*. He formed a sphere of blue *wælfýr*.

And he flung it without warning.

It struck the central man in the chest, knocked him back several feet to land twitching as the energy coursed through him.

To avoid the same fate, the men on either side had launched themselves in opposite directions. They hit the ground hard, tangling themselves in their robes. It opened up a temporary but clear enough path to the porch.

Cormac dragged Thia along it, skirting the now limp form of the man he'd struck. Had she not been with him, he might have simply jumped over. They ran up the steps and onto the porch.

His Sight hadn't been allowed to see inside the lodge; that changed the instant his foot touched the first tread. A scan of the front rooms showed them to be empty. He flung open the door to what turned out to be a small reception area. He and

Thia entered.

The rest of their group came after, dodging and deflecting *wanfýr* while holding back Cassie's *thegnas* with a few lobbed *fýr*-balls of their own.

Murphy, as last in, slammed the door. He directed his men—Liam, a giant named Roger, and another whose name Cormac had forgotten—to shove a heavy bureau from beside the door to serve as a barricade.

"Check the rooms," he then ordered, and they headed into the corridor that led into the lodge proper. "Secure doors and windows."

Kendra, after a quick glance at her friends, followed.

Two front rooms could be accessed from the reception area. One to the left, one to the right. Murphy trailed Abby into the former while Quentin went into the latter.

Cormac stayed with Thia. She was trembling. Pale. He had yet to release her arm. "All right?" he asked, dividing his focus between her terrified face; the front window which showed a line of cloaked men and women with *wanfýr* held at the ready; and, through his Sight, the rest of the lodge.

"Y-you killed that man," Thia said in a small voice.

Ifrinn. Cormac met her gaze and lost the other two threads of focus. Her eyes were dark, the pupils wide. With shock, he wondered, or horror. Perhaps both.

"Yes," he said.

She took a slow, deep breath, obviously thinking something, but damned if he could tell what.

"Are you all right?" she asked after a time.

His hand slowly left her arm. "Am *I*? Yes. None of the *fýr* got anywhere near."

"That's not what I meant. You killed that man out there. I wanted to know if you—" She made a weighty, helpless shrug. A sympathetic light replaced the darkness in her lovely eyes. "It's a difficult thing."

Her hand reached out and he thought she meant to touch his arm, perhaps take his hand like in the car.

His body automatically canted toward it, toward her...only to have her step back, her hand again by her side, at the sound of footsteps converging in the corridor.

People, rushing toward them from the back of the lodge.

Those who had gone to check the front rooms came out as Liam and Roger returned with a man with bound hands and, cradled in Liam's arms, an unconscious woman. The man was disheveled and kept his head down, making no visible effort to resist. The woman was small and apparently easy to carry, with extremely light blonde hair.

"Zoe!" Thia and Abby went to her even as Quentin directed Liam into the right-hand room.

"Well, well, well," Murphy said, going up to the restrained man. "Fancy you being here."

"I did not hurt her." The man's voice was hoarse. He didn't look up. "She sleeps."

Through the doorway, Cormac could see Zoe being laid on a old, worn sofa. Quentin pulled a vial from one of his coat pockets only to put it back for another. "I'm normally more organized," he told Thia and Abby. "If my luggage hadn't gone missing, I'd—"

"She sleeps. That is all," the bound man insisted.

Murphy sighed. "We'll not be getting a thing from him this way, Rog. You might as well take him in."

So the entire hallway party joined the others. Roger kept a firm hold on the bound man, who became agitated when he saw Quentin hold a vial under Zoe's nose.

"Do not wake her! She was frightened and I had to—" His legs buckled, dragging him down against Roger's hold. "Now? But not before." He shook his head, seemingly dazed. "Why now?"

Cormac, rubbing the tingling nerves at the back of his neck, went to a window at the room's far side. He lifted a drawn curtain.

The *thegnas* stood in a line, encircling the lodge. The deep hoods of their gray robes rendered them anonymous.

The *wanfýr* at their hands had changed to *wælfýr*.

"We may have made a slight tactical error," Cormac said to the room, and let the curtain drop. Quentin, having lifted the curtain of a different window, did the same.

"What do you mean?" Thia asked from near a rocking chair, a knitted blanket she had taken from it clutched in her arms.

"This was a trap," Cormac replied, and was rewarded with her full attention. He almost wished he hadn't sought it, that he'd let Quentin answer. Because now he was forced to watch his words sink in.

Fear dawned in Thia's eyes, drained the color from her face.

He had wanted to keep her safe. Why had he let her come here? He had failed magnificently. He felt sick.

● ○ ●

The blanket Thia had lifted from the back of a rocking chair smelled musty. It was a smell that pervaded and, along with the layer of dust on all the furnishings and rustic bric-a-brac, made her wonder when the room had last been used. She had never seen such thick dust on a floor before. It was even in the bare portions between rugs. She and the others left tracks in it.

"A trap?" she asked Cormac. The chintz curtain behind him swayed gently. Dust motes floated, visible even in the muted light. "Coming into the lodge, you mean?"

"All of it."

Quentin had let the curtain of the window he'd looked out fall as well. Thia hadn't been able to see past either of them. She wondered what was happening outside. How much time they had.

"Why not before?" the man muttered from where he knelt on a threadbare rug near the room's center. Murphy's man, Roger, stood behind him, hands pressed on his shoulders as if to hold him in place. "Why now?"

Without warning, he fixed an eerie, glowing-amber gaze on Thia. Her breath caught.

"Now you will know the pain you caused," he told her with all the emotion of a narrated shopping list. "Now you'll know destruction."

Thia couldn't look away. She was aware of Cormac closing in, and others. Murphy stepped between her and the man to ask him, "What are you talking about, Powell?"

"Compulsion." Quentin left his place by a window—and his cane—to limp over.

Abby looked up from her seat beside Zoe. "Is *that* what I feel?"

"You feel something?" Thia asked.

"A presence. Something or someone...not him."

"Cassie?" Thia spoke at the same time as Cormac. "It's more than compulsion," he said. "She's using him as a conduit."

Abby walked toward the man. (Powell, had Murphy called him?) She gestured to Roger. "Let him go."

Roger looked ready to refuse, but for Murphy's, "You heard the lady."

"Abby?" Thia didn't like the grimly determined look on her friend's face or the bleakness in her eyes. She moved closer, vaguely aware that everyone else had stilled. Waiting. "Abby, whatever you're thinking of doing, don't."

Released from Roger's hold, Powell remained on his knees.

"Don't fight it," Abby told him and, to Thia's skyrocketing alarm, got down on her knees before him. "Don't fight her."

She took a visibly shaky breath. Pushed it slowly out.

And then looked directly into the man's eyes.

Into the bright, honeyed amber which Thia suspected was not his own.

On a gasp, Abby's eyes went wide and then rolled back as both she and Powell collapsed.

Calling her name, Thia rushed over. Murphy got there first, scooped Abby up before she hit the floor, and carried her to a large recliner near the front of the room. He laid her gently down.

Quentin pushed past Thia and then Murphy. "Let me at her. Quickly." He pulled off his right glove, touched fingertips to Abby's frighteningly pale cheek. "Ah, bollocks." He snatched his hand away, began patting his pockets. "Where did...." His voice trailed off.

Cormac stepped beside Thia to set a hand on her back. She choked down a sob. "Is she—" She couldn't say it. Abby was so still. So pale. Her face utterly expressionless.

Three things happened simultaneously: Quentin touched a lit match to a tiny spoon of yellow powder which released a nauseatingly strong odor of rotten eggs; Kendra ran in with Nigel to announce, "They're erecting more wards. Stronger ones. If we hope to get out of here, we need to go now." And Zoe lurched up and began to scream.

It scared Thia so badly that she dropped the blanket she'd forgotten she held, and nearly tripped over it on her way to Zoe. She intended to sit with her and offer comfort, but the young woman's excellent two-footed kick landed on her hip and knocked her to the floor.

"You can't make me," Zoe shouted. "I want to go home!"

"Zoe." Thia pushed onto her elbows. Her hip burned. "It's okay. Please. You're okay." She could barely hear herself above the shrieking.

"Allow me." Going behind Zoe, Cormac bracketed her head with his hands. "*Geswefe.*"

Zoe quieted. Her expression eased and she seemed to focus

and truly see—at last—her surroundings.

Cormac let go.

"Oh." She blinked, yawning. "I'm so sleepy." Her eyes closed as she lay back down.

Asleep.

"What the hell did you do?" Kendra demanded of someone on the other side of the room. Thia rolled over in time to see her shove Quentin away from Abby. He stumbled into a side table, steadied the lamp that threatened to topple.

"Quentin didn't do anything," Thia said as Cormac helped her up. "Abby looked at him." She pointed at Powell, lying face down on the rug with Roger standing over him.

It didn't make sense, what had happened. Nor did Thia, she realized, with what she'd said. She needed to try again.

Kendra lifted Abby's wrist to check her pulse.

Oh, God no.

Thia forced herself to try again. "Abby looked at Powell"— her hand trembled as she pointed—"and then she screamed and they passed out. How is she?"

Kendra had put down Abby's wrist. She lifted first one, then the other, eyelid. "I think she's just out cold. But her pulse is slow. We need to get her out of here."

"We *all* need to get out of here," Quentin said, seated in a high-backed chair. He dragged a slow hand through his hair. Replaced his fleece cap. "They intend to attack the town."

Several people spoke at once.

He made a frustrated gesture. Sighed. "Your friend tried to read Cassandra through *him*." He used his cane to indicate Powell.

Thia hadn't remembered him picking it up. Hadn't he left it by the window?

"Before she was cast out," Quentin continued, "she caught a glimpse of the plan. Incendiary devices. Charged crystals made into snowflake decorations. Something like that has a limited shelf-life, so she intends to use them soon."

"The parade." Thia's head spun.

"It's in two hours." Kendra dug into her jacket pocket. "Can we use our phones?"

"They've completed the wards," Cormac said. "I doubt it."

The grimace Kendra gave her phone's screen suggested he was right. "Can you get through them?"

"With her *thegnas* here ready to repair—or worse—defend?"

"We could distract them," she persisted. "Keep them busy while you and Liam take down the wards."

Liam didn't look too thrilled about that.

Nor did Cormac. "Even if we assume whatever you direct at them could do a damn thing within the wards, you're talking about a full-out assault with risk of complete failure. Death. Are you prepared to risk that?"

"I am, yes." Kendra didn't hesitate. "For the sake of several hundreds if not thousands of parade-goers, I absolutely am."

"What about the lives of your friends?"

At that, Kendra said nothing.

So Thia did. She had to. "It's my fault Cassie is here. My fault she's targeting Granite Springs. Ten thousand people are expected—and Santa Claus, for crying out loud. There will be so many children."

The town's Santa, she had been made to understand, was a legend in his own right, a draw for people from all over the valley. Many were convinced he actually *was* Santa.

Cassie would take advantage of that, of something wholly good, and corrupt it to the point of evil.

"She can't do this." Thia's heart sank, heavy with dread. "We have to stop her. Whatever the cost."

"And to be sure we will," Murphy said, coming around from where he had stood, for so long silent, at the head of Abby's reclined chair. "But not by engaging her forces here. It would take too much time. Besides, we won't need to. Will we?" He nudged the still-unconscious Powell with his boot.

Or the *not* still-unconscious Powell, as it turned out. The man moaned.

In a flash, Murphy bent, hauled him to his feet by his lapels, then shoved him into Roger and Liam's hold. Between them, they kept him upright.

"We won't need to," Murphy said, "because knowing Powell here, he's made a veritable warren of escape routes."

The man's already pale face went white as his eyes took on an amber glow.

Murphy shot Quentin a look. "Can you block her hold on him?"

"Unnecessary." Grimly, Quentin laid his cane on a low table and hobbled over. To the two men acting as Powell's support, he said, "Try not to interfere," and then braced both hands on Powell's head.

Quentin wasn't wearing gloves.

His eyes flashed silver as his body went taut. Fine tremors shook him and Powell both, and to a lesser degree, the two other men. It reminded Thia of a first aid training video she'd seen on electric shock.

If any of them wanted to break contact, could they? The video had explained that with electrocution, the victim was caught, unable to move.

"Is that—" she had been about to say "normal," for lack of a better word, when from beside her, Cormac sucked in a sharp breath and lunged.

He hit Quentin in a tackle that put them both on the floor in a tangle of limbs.

Powell's head whipped up, his face a mask of terror, and the men holding him flew back as if thrust by an explosive force. They slammed onto the floor, slid to a stop. Powell crumpled, seizing.

Thia was the closest to him. That same training video had taught that the first step was to touch the victim's shoulder and ask, "Are you okay?" (More as a test of consciousness than anything. Obviously someone convulsing was not okay.) She was about to initiate that when Cormac scrambled over and grabbed her around the chest. Holding her tight, he rolled with her, then pinned her face down, his hands on her wrists.

"Don't," he said—rather belatedly, Thia thought. He could have said it before he'd knocked her down. His voice rasped in her ear. "Cassie will get to you if you touch him."

Okay, so she had overlooked the *first* first step: Make sure the scene was safe before moving in.

Regardless, "He needs help," she said, struggling.

"She won't kill him. Not while he's of use."

Other sounds intruded on Thia's awareness.

Kendra, frightened. Murphy urging someone to not do this, to hold on.

"Let me up." She struggled harder.

Rather than obey, Cormac positioned himself so Thia was *more* restrained. With her face turned into him and jammed beneath his shoulder, she saw nothing but the dark fabric of his jacket. She was in a cocoon of sorts made of hard floor and him. He smelled of pine soap and—

Something else filtered through. Something awful.

Kendra was pleading. Crying. Murphy shouted names.

The two men. Cassie might have further use for Powell, but not for Roger or Liam. Quite the contrary.

"Let me up," Thia insisted, distraught. As squashed as her face was, the words were nearly unrecognizable. "I need to help."

She felt Cormac's tension, the expansion of his chest. The warmth of his long, resigned exhale. "There's nothing you can do, *muileach*. Nothing anyone can do. It's better if you don't see. Trust me…in this, at least."

She did. Trust him. That was the problem, most of the time.

Kendra cried out, and a dreadful silence followed.

It was broken by the sound of slow, uneven steps, followed by that of an unfurling blanket. "Here." Quentin's voice. "I'm sorry. I couldn't stop her. I didn't—"

Murphy cut him off. "We none of us did. Now we do."

Tempting as it was, Thia couldn't stay sheltered forever. It had already been too long.

"Cormac." She wriggled. "Let me up."

His head pressed more heavily, a brief touch as if he, too, would prefer to stay as they were. Life, however, would move on.

For some.

He lifted from her, then helped her to stand. She took stock of the room. It felt foreign, almost as if she was seeing it for the first time. Only a few minutes, but so much had changed. She had changed.

Powell, no longer seizing, lay where he had fallen. Quentin stood by him, looking down.

"He sleeps," he said in answer to Thia's unspoken question. "We'll have to leave him. With his connection to Cassandra, it's too dangerous."

She understood—and didn't that speak volumes about how much her life had altered over the past weeks, that she could understand (at least in concept) that someone could be used as a weapon against them by someone else who was nowhere near.

Beyond that man on the floor, a rug and the blanket Thia had found for Zoe had been spread over two more.

She felt hollow, too shocked for grief or anger. Both would come later, and feed into and on one another. The ouroboros of tragedy.

That, too, she understood.

CHAPTER 18

Quentin, having plucked an escape route from Powell's mind before Cassie's lethal interruption, took the lead and directed what remained of their group into the hallway, out of earshot from either Powell and, through him, Cassie. Kendra, last to leave, closed the door. Thia left Cormac's side to go set a comforting hand on her back.

"I'm okay," Kendra said in response.

Cormac didn't believe her. He didn't think Thia did, either. The woman looked shaken to the point of fracture. And why not—the deaths of her associates had been as shocking and gruesome as they come. Burned from the inside out. He had spared Thia the sight. If only he could have spared her more. She was by nature a caring person, prone to forming attachments. Death hit her hard, no matter its cause or its victim.

Yet even in the midst of her own reeling emotions, she took those of others into consideration. She worried for Kendra. She had worried for *him* earlier.

Not only kind, she was generous. Of herself, of her time and energy. In all its forms. She had argued hard to accompany them this afternoon, risking herself not because she thought to actively assist with her power—she continued to fear and struggle on that front—but so that others could make use of what she held.

Cormac found such generosity, such willing sacrifice despite fear, incredible. Ah, sod it—*she* was incredible. And as foreign to him as that close-knit family he'd met outside her shop.

Even now, while she attempted to comfort one friend, she cast anxious looks at another, unconscious in Murphy's hold. She worried for them all.

Cared for them all.

Such depth of concern, of emotion. She had said she *loved* him, all those weeks ago. She'd held his hand in the car today, despite being justifiably furious. (Had anyone held his hand in such a way before? To comfort, and be comforted?)

He didn't know what to do with her, except keep her safe. That, he could do. Or...die trying. He felt a bit shaken himself as the thought rose from a previously unknown depth. One he had not believed possible for him to have. He was, after all, an entirely selfish creature.

Perhaps that was at the heart of it—selfishness. He wanted Thia for himself. The strength of his protectiveness was really the strength of his desire to have her. Like a possession. Yes, that made sense in a comfortable way. That must be it.

As for the love she had professed, he hardly knew what that was. If he ever thought to learn...well. He was rather old for that, wasn't he? Nearly ten to every one of her years.

"We need to cloak ourselves." Quentin's cane was tucked under his arm while he fumbled in his pockets. "Our absence might be noted, otherwise. And Cassandra could have a way to track us. We can't chance it." He studied a vial containing phosphorescent green powder and then, frowning, returned it to his jacket. His haphazard search resumed.

"In my experience," he went on, "the most effective method requires twenty minutes and a toadstool harvested from the base of an English yew under a black moon. I don't happen to have one on me, so unless anyone else does"—wry, he glanced around—"I believe we could substitute with a combination of belladonna, copal, and monkshood."

Familiar with that ritual, Cormac thought the substitution would likely succeed, but twenty minutes was time they did not have. "Or we could try a *gelýcost.*"

At the Brigantium agent's puzzled look, he elaborated. "A *doppel-gänger* illusion. A bit of misdirection that makes it seem like we're still here. Where will the route take us?"

"A tunnel to the lakeshore, about a mile from where we left Edith. It could work. What do you need?"

"Scissors. For a lock of hair. From everyone. And a bowl of oil."

"Scissors, I have. Silver." Quentin pulled a small pair from his front jacket pocket.

"There must be a kitchen," Thia said and set off down the corridor. "All of those people have to eat. Oh." She stopped. "What kind of oil? Some magical type, or would cooking oil do?"

Camellia was Cormac's personal preference, but any ought to work. "I'll come with you."

He didn't want her going alone. Besides, the search would be quicker with two.

As it happened, the kitchen was easily located—at the end of the corridor—and held few cupboards. Instead, items were lined up on counters and open shelves. Straight off, Cormac noted several new-looking bottles near a scarred behemoth of a stove. Canola, olive, peanut, almond, mineral. Not exactly food-safe, that one. He took the olive.

From the sink's drying rack, Thia took a bowl the size and depth of a grapefruit half. "Will this do? There are a bunch."

"It's fine. We only need one." Cormac pocketed a tin of bay leaves he happened to see on the way, and then waited for her at the doorway.

When she joined him, he almost reached out to comfort as

she had done with Kendra. But while he hadn't hesitated to grab and hold her down to protect her, he found he was at a loss now. Comfort should be a simple matter, and yet it tied him up in knots.

"How are you holding up?" he asked instead as, side by side, they retraced their way down the corridor.

"Oh." She spared him the briefest of glances. "I'm trying to not think about it."

"Fair enough." Bending, he picked up a playing marble he'd noticed the first time past this set of damaged shelves. Clear glass, slightly chipped from use, with interior swirls of white, red, and green. He lifted the flap of his jacket's small upper pocket and slipped it inside. "There's a number of things I try not to think about."

"Does it make it easier?"

"I used to think so."

They rounded a corner. Ahead, the group awaited. Quentin took a cutting of hair from Zoe, sleep-spelled in the arms of the hulking man whose name Cormac had yet to recall.

"And now?" Thia asked.

They had arrived. He could avoid answering if he wanted.

Quentin approached Thia, held up the scissors. "May I? Just a little from the back. No one will notice."

"Of course." She turned, offered.

As another man's fingers sifted through hair which Cormac knew to be gloriously silken, he held her gaze and solemnly shook his head: No.

Lately, his not thinking about things had not made any of it easier.

Quentin handed Thia an inch-long cutting of her hair and looked to Cormac. "That leaves you."

A member of the Brigantium with a sharp implement, given leave to stand close. Jugular, eyes...all vulnerable.

"Allow me," Thia volunteered, and traded her hair plus the kitchen bowl for Quentin's scissors.

Cormac breathed a sigh of instinctive relief, and she moved in, a knowing lift to the corner of her lovely mouth.

Too aware they were the center of attention, Cormac told the others, "All the hair can go in together. It doesn't matter if they mingle."

Thia stood close and, lifting the scissors, snipped them with faux menace. Teasing. "A little off the top?"

He hid his smile, bowed his head. Her touch was light as she worked through the hair at his crown.

"Thank you."

"Sure." The blades tugged and left. As did her touch.

He straightened.

She held up the hairs, studied them. "You know, I think I like this much better than the blond."

● ○ ●

She'd rattled him with that reference to his Connor Michaels disguise. He had recovered quickly, but she'd seen it because she had been looking.

To understand Cormac was to notice and catalog details. Subtleties of expression. Fragments. A slight lift of a brow. A minute change in tone. He held such mastery over himself, he presented only what he intended. The way to know the truth of him was to look for the rare moments when his control slipped. When he didn't present, but reveal.

Thia had set out to create one of those moments, and she had. It was meaningless in the larger scheme of things—the tragic deaths, Abby's health, the impending attack on Granite Springs, the danger that awaited outside the lodge to name a few. Yet, although small, success felt like success. After what felt like so much failure, it felt...empowering.

Hopeful.

And now, with equal parts fascination and fear, she watched Cormac pour oil into the bowl taken from the kitchen. For education's sake, she should use her Sight, but she couldn't bring herself to try. She had, quite honestly, seen enough for one day. For a lifetime, it felt like.

Yet there was so much day ahead.

An odd glow emanated from the bowl, and the sickly tang of singed hair.

"*Kele kom welo*," Cormac said. Or something like. It was no language Thia had heard before. Harsh yet musical with an unpredictable cadence. "*Exs koutino, neuje ansro neibo*."

He held his hands over the bowl and flipped them one way and the other several times, reminiscent of a "so-so" gesture.

She heard a snap like the close of a mousetrap but couldn't identify the sound's source.

"That should be good for a half hour, more or less," Cormac said with a shrug. He put the bowl on the floor. "Enough for a head start."

Quentin limped to a short, narrow closet set into the side of the staircase to the upper level. He pulled it open, gestured inside with his cane. "There's a trapdoor."

"We need to secure this," Murphy said with a tip of his head toward the front room's closed door. Both of his arms were full of Abby, cradled against his chest. Her head rested on his shoulder. Her eyes were closed, as if she were merely asleep, while her lower legs and one of her arms dangled loosely. That and her pallor were reminders of how deeply unconscious she was. "If Powell recovers enough or if Cassandra directs him to check on us, the game's up."

Cormac went to the door in question and, from his jacket, removed a small case. From it, he pulled what looked like two metal sticks.

Picks, Thia amended after he crouched down and inserted them into the lock.

"This won't stop him," he said, working, "but it might slow things up."

"As would something heavy." Kendra pointed. "How about that?"

In the middle of the hall was a glass-fronted case. It turned out to be an excellent choice. Packed with vintage National Geographics and unlidded shoeboxes full of marbles, it took everyone (minus Murphy and Nigel) to move the case in front of the door.

Cormac went into the small closet. From it came the scrape of wood followed by the thump of something heavy. "There's no ladder," he called out. A faint, flickering light shone from the doorway. "It's a ten-foot drop, give or take. Into a storeroom. About fifteen by twenty."

"No ladder at all?" Quentin's voice was tight, and Thia felt a moment's concern. Considering his reliance on a cane, would he have to stay behind?

"Ah. Wait," Cormac called. "I see it. Down below, tucked up against—hold on."

Thia inserted herself between Murphy and Kendra in time to see Cormac lower himself into a two-foot square opening in the closet floor. Then he dropped out of sight.

There was the sound of an impact and a grunt. The strange light flared again as metal rattled, clanged. The top of a ladder thrust up through the opening.

"Right, then." Murphy deftly shifted Abby's limp form into an over-the-shoulder fireman's carry.

"Be careful with her," Thia told him as he went with Abby into the closet. She needn't have said anything. That was her helplessness speaking.

As he began to navigate the ladder, she stepped in to hold her hands by Abby's head, protecting it as it lolled. Her dark curls hung loose, which meant that her knit cap had been left behind somewhere.

When they descended out of reach, Thia moved so Nigel, with Zoe over his shoulder, could maneuver onto the ladder, and then she protected Zoe's head in the same way.

The flickering light that had shone while Cormac had dealt with the trapdoor had been taken down to the storeroom. As Zoe was carried into it, Thia saw a problem. "She's going to freeze."

She should have considered it sooner. Zoe wore what she'd had on before her disappearance: Retro-style wool slacks and a cashmere sweater over a turtleneck.

"There's a load of bedding down here," Cormac said as he came into view. A ball of *wanfýr* hovered above his upturned palm. That was the light, Thia realized. He looked up at her. "Scores of blankets. Old but serviceable."

From behind Thia, Kendra told her, "Go ahead." Meaning the ladder. Nigel and Zoe had touched down and were getting clear of the bottom.

Abruptly, that seemed a very long way down.

Thia grabbed hold of the sides and stuck her leg into empty air, her foot searching for a rung. By the time she found one, she was shaking. Tiny tremors of over-adrenalized stress. She forced herself to bring her other leg in.

Two unconscious, two dead, and the crisis not nearly over.

She began to descend. For what felt like too long there was nothing but herself, the aluminum bars beneath her feet and gripped in her hands. In reality, it was under a minute.

"All clear," she said for whoever would be next, and moved to the ladder's side. As Cormac had described, the storeroom wasn't large. He'd neglected to say that it smelled funky, like wood rot and wet cement.

A couple of feet away, Murphy and Nigel had laid Abby and Zoe on a makeshift pad of wool blankets and were bundling them in more. Thia went to help. "How are they?"

Murphy tucked in a blanket corner. "The same."

Cormac brought the *wanfýr* closer. Behind him, the ladder rattled. "Zoe is under a sleep spell. I could wake her, but if she goes into hysterics again...." He shrugged. "It's less trouble to carry her."

"Abby isn't waking up," Thia said as she and Nigel finished securing Zoe's blanket-wraps.

"She took a hard, psychic hit. But she's strong."

"She is," Kendra echoed, stepping off the ladder. "We'll take her to the Retreat on the way back into town. They'll know what to do."

"Will they?" Aside from the shopping habits of its members when at Eclectica, Thia knew little about the spiritual center itself. She gave Zoe's blankets a final pat before she stood.

"If not," Cormac said, "the Brigantium will."

She looked over only to flinch at the *wanfýr* crackling above his hand, closer than she'd realized.

"It's safe enough."

The qualifier kept that from being reassuring. "Safe *enough*," she said with a roll of her eyes. She turned away. "That's great, then. Silly me."

After a pause, she felt a light touch at her back as Cormac's hand—the one not controlling a potentially weaponized ball of energy—made a tentative pat between her shoulder blades.

As attempts at comfort went, it was remarkably awkward.

She supposed that was why she found it endearing. Cormac presented such consistent self-assurance, such worldliness— Otherworldiness, too—yet a simple thing like this threw him for a loop.

Simple for Thia, anyway. With his upbringing, with Idris as his father, and the life he'd led...this could not be simple for Cormac.

She didn't have to be any less angry or frustrated with his choices and deceptive behavior, but she could empathize. She could forgive, and even credit him for trying.

Plus, she was why Cormac was involved in this mess, wasn't she? What other business could he have in Granite Springs? Unless he'd been tracking Cassie. In that case, Thia was just incidental. She could ask him about it, obviously. But could she trust his answer? Probably not.

She leaned into his hand on her back, felt the quick tension in his frame. "Thank you."

His hand stilled. "For what?"

Letting her head drop back to rest against his shoulder, she took a moment to simply breathe.

The *wanfýr* at his other hand continued to light the storeroom. It mesmerized. A spherical, ever-shifting collection of energy: Beautiful and frightening and as incomprehensible to her as Cormac's age and ability to turn into a raven. His *Sidhe* side. Otherworldly gifts. There was something more to this train of thought. Something elusive. The Cailleach was from the Otherworld, and thus so were her powers. Thia's powers now. Although she certainly wouldn't consider them a gift.

"I feel like all this is my fault," she said on a rising tide of emotion. "All of it. Cassie's being here, the deaths of those men—Liam and Roger. Oh, dammit." She was going to cry.

The *wanfýr* went out as Cormac used both hands to turn her around, pulling her against him in a tight embrace. Holding her while she feared she might shake apart with the effort of not breaking down.

"*Muileach.*" His breath brushed warmly across her ear as he spoke in a near-whispered rush. "You can't blame yourself for the actions of an unstable, power-mad woman. If she hadn't made you her target, she'd have chosen another. Me, I should think, whether we had succeeded on Brodgar or not."

His hands moved up to bracket Thia's face, and she let him tilt it up—not far; they well-matched for height. Faint light came from somewhere, enough that she could read sincerity in his eyes. Concern in the lines of his mouth and brows. His thumbs swept lightly under her eyes, brushing away the tears that had spilled despite her hard work.

"You're a good person, Thia McDaniel," he said, adamant. "You can't fathom what could—*would* have happened if they had succeeded that night. I can, and believe me, it would be a hundred times worse than anything she can do on her own. It was because of you that they failed, and that's why she is targeting you and yours. And that's why we all owe you a debt, no matter what is to come."

That was, quite possibly, the most he had ever said to her in one go. And, she had to think, the most honest. Silent tears ran down her face.

His lips touched her forehead briefly. "You stopped them."

She lifted her left hand to cup his cheek. Kept it there as she considered what he'd had to do that night. "So did you," she said gently.

He shuddered and started to pull back.

"Cormac." She took hold of his wrists before he could. "So did you. You did what had to be done."

"Yes."

She sighed out a breath. "But it isn't easy, is it." Even if she hadn't already understood that, there was the feel of his pulse, beating quick and hard under her grip as proof.

"No," he said. As if it were a terrible secret, long held and painfully divulged.

Thia didn't hesitate, didn't question the impulse to bracket his face with both hands as he had hers. But instead of kissing his brow, she found his lips. And gave him a piece of her heart.

Another piece, if she cared to be accurate. She had given him several already.

She had forgotten what kissing him was like. No, that wasn't accurate either. She could never forget what kissing him was like. But it was an experience that couldn't fit completely into memory.

And thank goodness for that, otherwise she'd spend all her time revisiting it.

She could get addicted...if she wasn't already. But right now, she didn't care. Her worry dropped away as Cormac got over his initial surprise and began to participate. His lips firmed, pulled at hers while his hands slid up her arms and around to her back.

A throat cleared nearby.

They sprang apart, found Kendra standing where the ladder had been. She held a large knife, its blade aglow with *wælfýr.*

"Time to go," she said, her tone as rigid as her expression.

"We were just—I was—" Thia sounded ridiculous, even to herself. "Okay."

"The tunnel is over there." With the glowing blade, Kendra pointed across the storeroom to a large hole in the wall.

Quentin, standing beside it, held his cane aloft—the better to shine the light coming from its newly incandescent knob. A large piece of plywood lay by his feet. The hole's cover, Thia assumed. She hadn't heard its removal. Hadn't heard Quentin descend the ladder, either. She was disoriented for a number of reasons. Murphy and Nigel were gone; Abby and Zoe with them. Already in the tunnel?

"Sorry," she said, although sorry wasn't what she was feeling. That was another thing about kissing Cormac. It had a way of overriding feelings like regret. For a time, anyway.

CHAPTER 19

This was agony. Sheer, bloody agony. Quentin bit back a whimper. A *whimper,* for fuckssake. He was maxed out on pain dampening spells—and risked the group's discovery with the use of such magic, but damned if he could go another inch without them.

He didn't *want* to go another inch. Sweat poured down his face despite the tunnel's biting cold. Biting, like the pain in his hip. Sharp, vicious, ravaging teeth. He was not meant for crawling, not anymore.

Shifting his weight to his good side, he pulled his right leg forward. His hip twinged, clicked; not much of a protest.

This was the easier part.

He paused a moment, steeled himself for what was to come. It had been getting consecutively worse and, fine, he'd admit it: He dreaded what came next. To steady his nerves, he spent a few precious seconds like that, tipped uncomfortably to one side.

The others had gotten far ahead of him. He listened to the faint—and growing fainter—scuff and shuffle of their movements through the narrow, crudely supported passage. The cold was good, he supposed. Presumably, frozen ground was less liable to crumble.

They would wait for him at the exit, but they needn't. The half-*Sidhe* could get them through the Druid Fog. Not as well, but it was possible. Quentin could stay here, not having to move until...until spring, for all he cared.

That would never work, of course. Someone would be sent to dig him out, and that would be one humiliation too far. He set his leg down and began shifting his weight onto it so he could move the other forward.

Fuel to fire.

Pain that had been smoldering burst into sudden flame—and he was barely on the leg yet. He put more weight onto his hands. He had tried that before. The results this time were no different; the change in angle brought new discomfort and no relief to his hip.

Speed, that was the trick. Like ripping a sticking plaster off a cut. He blew out a harsh breath and, teeth gritted, sent his weight to the—Oh, *Brigid* help him. Fire raged. He was only vaguely aware that he had dropped to lay flat on the ground because the contrast of its cold to the heat of his pain was so marked.

He couldn't do this.

Not without pills.

Gradually, he got one arm beneath himself to work its way into his jacket's inner pocket. The opiates would muddle his thinking and ruin him for any but the most basic spellwork. His hand froze. He might as well remain where he was for all the good he'd be once medicated.

● ○ ●

"I'm going back to check," Thia said, although how she might do that she didn't know. The tunnel was too small for her to turn around without a likelihood of getting stuck. No way did she want to risk that.

Well, okay, simple enough: She'd scoot backward, that's all.

Except Kendra was right behind her and didn't seem in favor of letting her by.

"I heard a moan," Thia said. And had heard nothing since. Kendra must have noticed the same. "He might need help."

"We don't have time. Abby needs help more."

"But—" Thia's mind balked, unwilling to accept such a stark choice. Leave him behind? In the tunnel? And not just in the tunnel, but the mountains, miles from town?

Murphy and Nigel had continued on, pulling Abby and Zoe in their protective blanket coccoons. Cormac, between them and Thia, waited. She stared at the treads of his boots, dimly illuminated by the light from Kendra's blade.

"In a fight," Cormac said, "the Brigantium agent would be of more use than your friend."

Thia's chest constricted. But...he was right.

"He's fine," Kendra argued. "He's just slow. Quentin!"

No response.

"Quentin!" she tried again. "He's too far back, that's all."

"What's the holdup?" Murphy bellowed from some length ahead. This deep underground, volume wasn't a concern.

"Quentin," yell-replied Kendra. "He's too slow."

"I think he's hurt," Thia insisted and began moving. Backwards. Kendra wouldn't actually fight her on this, would she? "I'm going to—" She stopped.

Someone was moving in the tunnel behind them.

"Here," Quentin called faintly, still a good distance away.

"What happened?" Thia asked. "Are you all right?"

"Cramp." He said after a time. "Fine now."

"You're sure?" Was it her, she wondered, or were his words a little slurred? She strained to hear his next reply.

"Yeah."

Yeah right, more like. He was lying.

Kendra gave Thia's leg a nudge. "He says he's fine. Let's go."

They did, for almost a half hour more.

The tunnel let them out at the lakeshore via a steep bank. Cormac dropped to his feet and held out his hand for Thia. She accepted it, let him help pull her out onto solid ground— or, as it turned out, ice beneath a thin layer of snow. Her feet slid as, thinking to make quick room for Kendra, she took an unprepared step.

Bracing her with an arm around her waist, Cormac brought her clear of the opening.

"Thank you," she whispered, and gave herself a few seconds to drop her head against him. The tunnel had not been easy, to put it mildly. She used his solidness, his living warmth, to steady herself.

Too many had died. Too many others might. She breathed in, hoarding memory. His hold tightened, and then as if by mutual agreement they separated.

"Ready?" he asked.

Thia nodded, although she wasn't at all sure that she was.

Several yards away, Murphy waited with visible impatience. Abby was a tightly wrapped bundle in his arms. Beside them, Nigel had Zoe draped over his shoulder while he spoke into a phone. Joining them, Kendra pointed back the way she had come.

Murphy shook his head, tipped his chin toward the Druid Fog stretched across the frozen lake. Or...*was* the lake frozen? Or was that just the shallower parts? It was impossible to see more than a foot inside the fog. At its edge, vaporous tendrils shifted in a chill breeze, giving the impression of a beckoning, living thing. Thia shuddered inwardly. If they attempted to cross here, would it take them onto thin ice? Into the water itself?

The fog cast light, making the area brighter than it should have been given the hour. The sky directly overhead was the lavender of a rapidly progressing sunset. There was less than an hour before the parade.

Behind her at the tunnel's exit came a grunt and the sound of scrabbling. Quentin began to emerge.

"Careful," Thia advised. "It's ice."

He sighed. "Of course it is." He inched himself down. His face looked pasty beneath the sweat.

Thia had been rebuffed enough times that she knew better than to offer help.

His feet touched down. He planted his cane and, with one hand on the bank, pushed himself upright. After a pause, as if he needed to be sure, he set off. His motion was deliberate... and unsteady, both.

She and Cormac followed. As on the approach, their route skirted the shore. No one wanted to chance the more direct line across the fog enshrouded lake.

A few minutes in, they were met by Edith hurrying from the opposite direction, phone in hand.

"I managed to relay your message," she told Nigel breathlessly. She looked from Zoe to Abby before quickly assessing the remainder of their group. Settling on Quentin, her gaze narrowed. "Are you on——"

"Leave off." He moved past her.

If that had been an order, Edith disregarded it. Staying with him, she asked an accusatory, "Can you navigate the Fog like this?"

"I'll have to, won't I?"

Concerned, Thia asked Cormac, "Is there a problem?"

He huffed out a soundless laugh. "Enough for a list. But you mean those two? He's medicated himself, I suspect—and so does she." As close as they walked together, Thia felt his small shrug, and when he reached into a pocket. "If he can't get us through the fog, this can. I took it off one of the cars and put a tracking hex on it." He showed her a shard of mirrored glass.

They had reached the end of the lake. The rest of the way would be forested and lead deep into the fog.

"I thought the fog interfered with everything," she said.

"It's a *Sidhe* hex," he said, as if that should clarify things. He tucked the shard away.

As the overall pace increased, the others shifted into single-file, but Cormac and Thia remained side-by-side. Their hands bumped together often enough that somehow they ended up clasped together.

"I wouldn't trust the link for anything like a traveling spell," Cormac said, "but as a general idea it shouldn't steer us too far wrong if or when Quentin does."

As the fog grew thick around them, she squeezed Cormac's hand, glad for the contact.

● ○ ●

Medicated or not, Quentin managed to lead them out. And as soon they were, Cormac informed Thia that he would get to Granite Springs faster if he flew. He'd given her a look that made her suspect he had something more to say, but in the next blink of an eye he'd become a raven and taken flight.

He was high above before she had recovered wits enough to tell him, "Be careful."

She'd had to run to catch up with the others.

As they sprinted together across the road, the young man who had remained with the cars popped out from behind a large granite boulder to open the hotel sedan's rear passenger door. The interior light came on—a welcome yet dangerous beacon. Despite the fog's glow behind them, dark had come with the sun's full setting. With the moon but a tiny sliver in the sky, that dark was very dark.

"Here." The young man gestured to Nigel, who jogged over. Together they settled Zoe inside. Nigel climbed in after her and pulled the door closed.

"Boss," the young man said, moving to hold open the front passenger door as Murphy approached with Abby. "All Nigel said when he called was that you were heading back with two injured." His confusion was painful to witness. "Did Liam and Roger stay behind?"

Murphy settled Abby in the front seat. "They're gone."

As grief overcame the young man, Thia's felt the threat of her own. She dodged it by going over to help. Activity made emotion easier to ignore. She took off her scarf while Murphy reclined Abby's seat and buckled her in. After he finished, she slid past him to tuck the scarf behind Abby's neck as support.

Her friend didn't look any worse, but she didn't look any better, either.

"She's—she *will* be okay, won't she?" Thia laid the backs of her gloved fingers against Abby's cheek, and then pulled away so Murphy could close the door.

The young man, already seated at the wheel with the engine running, wasted no time. With a spray of slush and grit, the sedan shot onto the road and sped off.

"She's a fighter," Murphy said as he jogged to his car. Shards of broken mirror crunched beneath his feet when he reached the driver's door but he hardly spared them a glance. "The staff at the Retreat has experience in this. She'll be fine." He got in. The Maserati's engine fired.

Kendra raced to the passenger side. "Nigel called and told them what's going on. If they have people downtown for the parade, they can help us there too." She closed her door and the car shot off.

Thia ran to the one that remained—the Brigantium's SUV. A middle window rolled down so Edith could poke her head out. "Take your pick," she said. "Around the other side with me or up front. Quentin's in the back having a lie-down."

"Sod off," came the man's voice.

Thia changed direction, planted a hand on the hood when

she skidded on an icy rut. The passenger door opened as she rounded toward it and she grabbed hold, used it to change her momentum and launch herself at the seat. The car began to move forward, and there were a horrible few seconds before Thia was fully inside with the door shut—and several seconds after that while she held her tongue.

Time was of the essence, she knew, but good grief.

"Welcome aboard," Quentin drawled from the back.

"Yeah. Thanks."

Seemingly oblivious, the Brigantium driver floored the gas.

● ○ ●

The familiar, terrible stench of charred remains. The familiar, terrible voice of the woman who continued to force her way into his mind. And the familiar, terrible sensation of guilt.

Her insistent prodding made Avery's eyes open.

The front room. He lay on the floor. Frowning, he set the flat of his hand on it and found it bare. What had happened to the rug?

He sat up and had the answer. Across the room, it had been laid over one of the bodies. He would never get the smells out. Or the stains, he supposed. Good thing the pattern was a dark one.

«Go look for them, fool.»

Her voice in his head. His eyes closed and he bent forward, pressing hands to his temples. He assumed she meant the rest of Zoe's rescue party. The ones left alive.

"They are not here," Avery said, and then stood because she forced him. He turned in a tight circle, taking in every angle. The curtains had been drawn over the all the windows.

"Empty," he said, but she already knew that; she could see as well as he. She used his vision, after all.

«I need to know if they're still inside. It feels…wrong.»

Impulse accompanied by a sharp jolt had him staggering for

the door. After everything, he was shaky. Drained.

The door was locked.

Panic rose up to take him by the throat. He choked, sucked in a terrified breath…and reminded himself he was in his own home. Not the other place. This room could not hold him.

"Something is on the other side," he said, barely getting the air through. "Them, yet not them."

She must have suspected they had got out. If she discovered that he had weakened some of the lodge's defenses, she would most likely kill him.

Did he care?

He pondered that while he went to the front window and opened the curtain. Her gray-cloaked minions were lined up outside, no doubt surrounding the building. Spheres of deadly *fýr* hovered at their ready hands. Avery twisted the window lock, pushed up the sash, and climbed out.

«*What are you—Oh, of course.*»

He walked along the porch to the front door and opened it. What he saw nearly made him smile. He knew that she could see, but it pleased him to tell her. "They are gone."

Instead of the people whose presence had been sensed here in the corridor, there was only a bowl on the floor. He went to it, saw oil and hair, mixed.

Trickery.

Avery heard himself laugh, and then nothing at all. He was out before he hit the floor.

CHAPTER 20

Finding downtown parking could be a challenge in the best of times. The evening of an immensely popular parade that required a seven-block closure of its Main Street route plus several side streets so entrants could assemble was definitely *not* the best of times. It was, Thia thought, quite possibly the worst.

So they didn't try. The Brigantium driver followed Murphy's car up to a line of barricades. As he shut off the motor, Thia saw Murphy and Kendra got out, ahead.

Parking tickets didn't rate very high on the list of things to be concerned about.

"I'll stay with the cars for now," said Brigantium driver. Thia was starting to feel guilty for not knowing his name. "In case anyone comes thinking to tow them. If we need them, it'd be a shame to find them gone."

"Right. I'll check with you in ten. Keep your phone handy," she said, tapping and swiping at her own. She tucked it away, looked over at Thia. "Ready?"

Her smile was probably meant to encourage, but Thia was far too anxious for that.

Outside the car, people were everywhere. Streaming in on

foot from side streets to congregate thickly along Main. The noise of it all got louder when Edith and Quentin flung open their doors.

"No." Thia doubted anyone heard her belated reply. But the question had most likely been rhetorical. And, either way, the answer didn't matter.

Ready or not, this would happen.

Was happening.

Thia got out, felt adrenaline flood her muscles as the reality of it all sank in. The sights. The sounds. The feel of the air. So many people. She hurried to join the others as they made their way toward Main.

The temperature was not as cold as in the mountains, but after the heat of the car's interior, it might as well have been. She dearly missed her scarf.

Murphy had put them near the start of the parade, at one of Granite Springs's more complicated junctions.

It was here that the Boulevard's four lanes split were split into two sets of one-way lanes. Those then diverged around a gas station and stayed at least a block apart for the whole length of the shopping district.

One of the sets—the one the parade would take, counter to the usual direction of flow—was Main. And, as if the city planners had decided the arrangement did not cause enough confusion: at the point where Main needed to be absorbed into the Boulevard's *two* easterly-moving lanes, it had *three*.

So, at the junction, that "extra" lane had been made to take a short curve, bisecting the Boulevard's generous median and taking traffic across its second set of lanes to join an inter-secting, northbound street.

This had resulted in a traffic island large enough to function as a small park.

Cormac caught up with them there, emerging so suddenly out of the mass of paradegoers at Thia's side that she startled.

"It's bad," he said as their group closed around him. A tight, still cluster in a sea of festive motion. "I went over the route. The Rekkrs are spread out, dropping the devices in rubbish bins, planters, and the like." To Murphy he asked, "I take it you alerted the Police? There's a high presence, even for an event this size. And a decided interest in the Rekkrs."

"We made a few calls," Murphy replied. "But their hands are tied, so to speak. They can't act without cause. Which is why my own people are out in it as well."

Cormac acknowledged that with a nod. "I saw them make a few...removals, let's say. Subtly done, but I was looking."

"Let's hope no one else was or there'll be hell to pay—and not just for failing to do as ordered."

If Cassie were to learn that her plans were in jeopardy, Thia imagined "hell to pay," would be about right.

"What of the devices themselves?" Edith asked, intent.

Kendra answered. "I called Gavin, from Abby's coven. They should be searching for them now and marking the locations. Members of the Retreat should be helping."

"Can we contact them?" Edith asked. "I need to see a device *in situ,* and as soon as possible. Obviously."

"Try the memorial tree." Cormac's mood shifted from grim to cheerful. An actor stepping into a role. "Why don't we give it a look? Such a lovely scheme. Some of the ornaments are particularly of interest."

Pretending to be just another bunch of people out enjoying themselves, they wended their way across the crowded park. The closer they got, the harder Tia found the performance to do. If they couldn't stop Cassie, people could—no, make that *would*—die. More memorials to add to next year's tree.

They squeezed their way past to-go-cup laden teenagers to get in close to the tree's base.

A fir of moderate height and width, its branches had been strung with multicolored lights and decorations of all shapes and sizes. Each was meant to represent (via charitable dona-tion) the life of a deceased family member or friend. Thia had gotten one of the lights in Lettie's honor.

A blue light, as happened to shine on a branch near Thia's face. Below that hung a snowflake ornament.

"This is one of them?" Thia asked, staring pointedly.

Cormac, close at her side, followed her gaze. "Yes."

"It's so...pretty." And it was. Nearly the size of her palm, its faceted branches picked up the different colors and lights. A captured rainbow, sparkling inside a snowflake.

"It is," Cormac said. "And remarkable. I've never seen the like."

"What do we do? Will it go off if we try to move it? Can we disarm it where it is?" Thia looked to everyone, but no one volunteered an answer, not to anything asked.

They were as lost as she.

"I can scan it," Edith said, taking out her phone, "and send a snap to headquarters. Someone there might know how to disarm it."

There was a disturbance in the crowd to their right, where people moved abruptly (and none to happily) out of the way of a flapping mass of red.

Not an attack, as Thia had feared—and they had all braced for—but Madame Demetka in an enormous red cloak.

"*Maw!*" she excalimed, rushing up. "My Guides they tell me I must look for you here, and so I have—ah, hell, is that what I think it is?" Sally stared in horror at the snowflake.

Quentin arched a tired brow. "That depends. What do you think it is?"

"Spelled to explode."

"So it is." He smirked. "Your guides told you that, did they?"

"Stand aside, sugar." Ignoring him, Sally pushed past Edith, who had been attempting to take a close-up of the crystal.

Cheers and energetic drumming heralded the parade's start. The lead marchers set off, creating a kind of gravitational pull as bystander interest tracked with them.

Sally lifted both hands to the snowflake and, holding them near but not touching, closed her eyes. "All right," she said in her Southern drawl. "*Fè m 'konnen sekrè ou.*"

It wasn't French, Thia knew that much from classes in high school and college. But it sounded similar and not at all like the language Madame Demetka exclaimed on occasion. That one sounded harsher, more sibilant. This was more about the vowels.

"*Fè m 'konnen sekrè ou,*" Sally repeated, and Thia caught the looks exchanged between Quentin and Edith—who held her phone toward Madame...toward Sally. Recording.

Sally's eyes opened. "Does anyone have some primrose oil?"

Edith, juggling her phone, lifted the flap of the satchel slung across her chest. "*Primula vulgaris* or *veris?*"

"Sorry, what?"

"Oh. My apologies. Common primrose or English cowslip?"

Sally looked intrigued. "There's a difference?"

"Oh, yes. But not, I think, in this case. You intend to do a revelation spell?"

"Yep."

"Fascinating." From her satchel, Edith took a cobalt glass bottle. She held it out. "In what language?"

Sally took the bottle. "Which is this, primrose or, what did you call it—cowslips?"

"Cowslip. Singular."

"Huh." Turning to the tree, Sally uncapped the bottle. She tapped a few drops of oil onto her fingertips, flicked them at the snowflake. "*Montre m danje a.*"

There was a small flash. Sally jumped back with a startled cry. Thia startled too, and bumped into Cormac. He steadied her with two hands on her shoulders. Her heart pounded.

"I thought she'd set it off," Thia whispered.

"No." His volume matched hers. "Amazingly, that seems to have been her revelation spell working."

"Sugar," Sally said, looking again to Edith, "do you happen to have anything with toadflax in that bag of yours?"

"For hex breaking?" Edith began rooting around in the large compartment. "I should think so."

Quentin smoothly offer a small vial taken from one of his jacket pockets. "Allow me."

"The more the merrier." Sally uncorked it. "Here goes."

With her arm extended fully—and her body leaning as far away from the tree as she could get it—she shook the vial. Liquid, lit by hundreds of memorial lights, splashed onto the snowflake. "*Pa fè mal.*"

There was a pop like a lightbulb burning out and the crystal darkened to a cloudy gray.

"Brilliant!" Edith closed in to better record with her phone while Quentin limped over and knocked the snowflake to the ground with a swipe of his cane.

The smoky crystal shattered on the pavement.

Thia was amazed not just by the magic but that they hadn't attracted more than a curious glance or two from the people packed in around them.

But, after all, the parade was what they had come to watch.

She hoped they got to see it all, uninterrupted. Safe.

The drummers had made it two blocks up Main to pass in front of Eclectica. Behind them, a ballet troupe performed movements from their annual production of The Nutcracker.

Coming level with the memorial tree was a group of at least thirty people dressed in diaphanous, white garments. Solemn, they carried softly glowing paper lanterns. Some were hand-held; others, suspended from poles and lifted high. *This* was why supplies had been selling so well lately. Bringing up their immediate rear was a line of giant walking puppets—also in flowing white cloth and with lanterns.

It was a stunning, vaguely chilling sight.

And there was no time for Thia to absorb it. The crystals could go off at any time...although wouldn't the best time be when Santa Claus had arrived at the end of the route?

From what Thia had heard described, once Santa went by, most parade watchers moved to follow, essentially becoming part of the parade. As many people as could fit into the Plaza did so to watch his speech and sing carols.

Scouring the line-up of entries to come, she estimated how much time they had.

A distinctive red-and-white cap drew her eye to a large float that was ten, maybe twelve groups back.

"We have tincture of toadflax," Kendra was saying. "It's part of the kits offered in the higher level suites. There should be at least a gross in the supply room. I'll have Andy bring it up, distribute it from the lobby." She began typing on her phone, composing a text. She glanced at Sally. "Are the snowflakes safe to move while armed?"

The woman nodded. "They're like grenades. Once the pin has been pulled, it's to do with time, not motion."

Thia shivered in a particularly chill wind. "And the pins have been pulled?"

"This one's was. So I'd say...yep."

"Right," Kendra said, still typing. "Until we have the stuff to disarm them, we can collect what we find. After we've got it, we can do that on the spot."

Edith held up a vial taken from her satchel. "I can do that now. But this won't last long." She shook it. "So if someone could please get more to us? Without our having to go to the hotel?"

"Yes." Finally, something Thia could do. "There's some at

Eclectica. Not as much as the Landmark, but enough to start. The clerks were to close early, but I have my key." She patted her pocket, felt the familiar outline. "I can get it all, and whatever else we might need. So...what else is that?"

Cormac took hold of her arm. "Cassie will be watching for you. You shouldn't be anywhere near here."

"Of course I should. I'm part of this."

Murphy rounded on Cormac. "Don't you think the *claimsech* is watching for us all? The time for subterfuge and avoiding risk is over. What matters now is speed."

"He's right on that one, sugar," Sally said.

And yet Cormac didn't let go, not even when she pried at his fingers with her other hand.

"Cormac." The better to fight him on this, she looked him in the eyes—and saw the fear. Details and subtleties, again. He was afraid. For her? "Ah, hell. Cormac."

Such glorious eloquence, that. She nearly rolled her eyes at herself. But she truly was at a loss for what to say.

It'll be all right? She didn't know that. (She was pretty sure, actually, that things wouldn't be.)

Don't worry about me? When people told *her* that, it never worked.

Edith, intent on Kendra, brushed past them. "We need as many people as we can get to bring the devices to the hotel— unless they happen to already have toadflax." She looked to Sally, "Does the trigger need to be in that language?"

"No. Any version of 'Do no harm' should get it done."

"Right." Edith put the phone to her ear, plugged the other as she turned away to talk.

Kendra held up a hand for everyone's attention. "We should all stock up, carry as much as we can so we can supply others."

"We should also spread out so we're not one big, clear target along the way," Cormac said, his grip tightening. He shot Thia a look. "You want to go to Eclectica? We'll go. *Now.*"

Moving faster than she could anticipate, he pulled her into the crowd. After a few shoulder-wrenching steps, she caught up to his hold on her arm. He drew her even closer against his side. As one, they wove their way around people, leashed dogs, and bloated baby strollers.

At Thia's, "Excuse us," a man with a toddler riding his shoulders swiveled and Cormac nearly got a face full of the little girl's shoes. Thia stopped talking.

Until they reached the front of the crowd—on that side of the street, anyway.

"We can't cut through the parade," she protested. "We need to go around."

"Just act like you belong."

Musicians and singers in elaborate Shakespearean dress.

Yeah, right, in her modern winter gear, she belonged.

Unrelenting, Cormac took her off the sidewalk and into the parade.

Some danced impromptu jig steps. Others, waving ribbon streamers high in the air, belted out an enthusiastic, "—night in December, no snow, no hail, nor winter storm—"

"—shall hinder us for to remember," Cormac's clear tenor joined in, "the babe that on this night was born."

Thia was so surprised she nearly tripped up the curb. They had made it across. And Cormac could sing. They crammed themselves into what was an even tighter crowd on this side of the street.

Cormac was moving quickly, darting this way and that. Thia couldn't look for snowflakes; she was too busy looking out for obstacles. She did catch a glimpse of what she thought might have been the pashmina-wearing woman from Abby's coven talking with a police officer by a lamp post.

And that might've been Gavin *up* the post and reaching into the wreath hung around the lamp.

Eclectica's door was coming up. Thia dug in her pocket for

her key.

"Ms. McDaniel!" Stefanie's voice called out from—where?

As Thia searched, the young clerk popped out ahead of her, bounced to stop at Eclectica's door.

"Hi!" She greeted Thia again and gave Cormac a wide smile that was not returned. Her cheeks were rosy from cold and excitement. Her long blonde hair cascaded from beneath the fuzzy white trim of a peaked red-and-green cap. "Isn't this so fun? I just love parades. Don't you?"

Thia, with Cormac practically glued to her side, stuck the key in the top lock, turned it. "Well, I—"

"Thank you so much for giving us the time off for this, Ms. McDaniel. Did you forget something? It'll be a shame if you miss the tumblers. They're my favorite."

Thia finished with the second lock. Cormac, reaching past her to open the door, remarked, "Isn't that them now?"

"Oh my gosh, really?" Stefanie whirled.

"Quick," Cormac muttered, giving Thia a push.

She stumbled over the threshold, heard the door close. He set the bolt.

Through the plate glass, Stefanie beamed at them. With a wave, she darted back into the line of watchers.

"Where's the toadflax?" Cormac jogged past Thia. He must have had a general idea, because he was headed in the right direction, toward the back wall. "This way?"

"Yes." Thia chased after him. "If it isn't hazardous, it'll be on the main shelves. Alphabetical order."

Passing too close to a decorated tree, his shoulder jounced a branch. A large peacock took flight only to crash on the wood floor.

Smithereens.

Thia crunched over them.

"Send me a bill," Cormac said, not slowing down. "After."

"It's not important." Downtown was about to get blown up.

Although, it was nice to think that there might be an "after" in which she would be in a position to send him a bill. A safe and sound position.

"The additional stock, where is that kept?" Cormac asked as they arrived at the shelf unit. Ten feet long and solid oak, it held hundreds of herbs from around the world. Dry, powder, extract, essential oil. To the right was the locked cabinet that held the hazardous substances.

"Underneath," Thia said in answer. The top half of the unit was open shelving; the bottom, cabinets. "They aren't locked."

Cormac located the section that held "R" through "Z" and crouched down, opened the double doors.

Thia reached over him to the toadflax on the shelf. Six small bottles made of brown glass with labels of apple-green with white print. Each held one ounce of herbal extract and came with a convenient dropper in the top.

She was about to put them into her coat pocket when what sounded like a firework went off outside.

● ○ ●

The trouble with relying on a gang which called themselves the Rekkrs, Cassie thought as she looked out over the roof's edge, was that each and every one of them loved to do exactly that: wreck.

Worse, they weren't very bright.

On the sidewalk below, another was culled from the parade crowd and put in handcuffs. Harrassing bystanders for sport while placing the last of the snowflakes, the fools had yet to notice they were being systematically rounded up.

Cassie formed a second ball of *wanfýr* and sent it into the air to explode over the street. Warning flares, if the Rekkrs had the wits to realize it.

Her *thegnas,* at least, could be counted on to heed them and act accordingly.

That bastard half-brother of hers was just down the block, inside Leticia's store with Thia. And there, cutting across the parade route in a dash toward the hotel were Declan Murphy and his red-haired associate.

Cassie could feel the tug on the threads of her slightly less-than-well-laid-plans. The threat of unraveling.

"You." She snapped her fingers for Reginald—Ronald? Oh, what did it matter. The Rekkr with the crossbow.

He left the assembled group behind her to join her at the roof's edge.

Murphy needed to witness the coming destruction. It was the least he deserved for his role on Samhain. The red-haired cow had been there too, hence she also deserved to witness what would come—but she happened to be a particular friend of Thia's.

Yes, she would do.

Cassie pointed. "There. Take her out."

"Yeah?"

"Yes. Hurry." They were nearly at the hotel.

The Rekkr positioned the crossbow. Took aim. With a click and a rush of displaced air, the bolt shot out.

A woman squealed and fell, swallowed up in a confusion of bystanders.

"Dammit." Not the right woman.

The redhead glanced back at the commotion before, along with Murphy, disappearing under the shield of the marquee.

The parade went on, unaffected—a sequin-laden bunch of acrobats doing tumbles and flips down the street—but where the woman had fallen, an energized huddle had formed, and more and more interest shifted its way.

A snapped thread, unraveling.

People gestured or took out phones. Two uniformed police

officers pushed through the crowd. A man stood, waved them in with bloodied hands. Someone screamed. Others joined in.

The *wælfÿr* formed at Cassie's hand with hardly a thought. As she turned away from the building's edge, she sent it into Roderick? Roland?—ah, no matter. His eyes went white and he dropped like the useless sack he was.

His crossbow clattered, coming to rest near his limp hand. Cassie picked it up, tossed it to the nearest, gaping Rekkr.

"I hope you can use it a sight better than he did," she said before returning to watch the confusion below. It was only a matter of time before people thought to look to the roofs for the shooter. The snowflakes weren't due to go off for another fifteen minutes. She needed a distraction.

"The police are taking in your friends," she told the newly armed Rekkr. "You oughtn't let them."

A man in a white anorak shimmied up a lamp post to pluck one of her snowflakes from its wreath.

For a moment, Cassie refused to believe it. Who the bloody hell was he? He had to be part of Thia's interfering band of friends. How the fuck had they found out about the hexed crystals?

She quickly scanned what she could see of the route. Sure enough, people were poking about in rubbish cans and raised planters. Too numerous and intent to be coincidental.

Her plan was unraveling hard and fast.

Well. She'd serve as her own distraction, then. She formed more *wælfÿr,* let it fly.

It struck the lampost climber on the back and must have spread throughout his body because, as he fell, the snowflake in his hand exploded.

Brilliant.

● ○ ●

It wasn't fireworks. Thia hadn't really expected it would be, but as she hurried to the front of the store and saw reflections of blue flashes from outside, she felt a tiny piece of hope die nevertheless.

Wælfýr.

An explosion rocked the building, rattled glass shelves and windows. She caught her balance and ran to look out. "What was that?"

"Nothing good," Cormac said, behind her, as distant sirens began to wail.

Shouts could be heard coming from the left, farther down the street. People outside Eclectica looked about in obvious confusion.

"Get away from the door." Cormac grabbed Thia's hand.

Resisting, she used her other to reach for the lock. The bag they had loaded with toadflax, its handle looped over her arm, swung wildly. "We have to go out there. Look, there's Edith and Madame Demetka." Or Sally.

Whichever, there she was across the street.

She and Edith were speaking with three women dressed in close-fitting robes of deep purple. Members of the Retreat. Their hands held a number of snowflakes.

Edith upended her bottle, dousing them, and then tossed it aside. Empty.

"Thia," Cormac said, "get away from the door."

She barely heard him. A fire engine was turning onto First Street. Ahead of it on Main, crowd movement was frenetic, with a heavy emphasis on *away*.

And no wonder. The building at the corner, the Ice Cream Shoppe...its glass front was gone, the metal frames bent if not altogether absent.

Where an old-fashioned streetlamp should have been, there was only a jagged-topped pole. The shade tree out front was half gone; its remaining branches, smoldering.

Through the chaos of people and emergency vehicles, Thia

caught glimpses of scattered debris. Broken glass, shards of metal. A red and green striped scarf. What might have been a diaper bag. She saw several people with bloodied faces, but couldn't tell how many others were hurt, or how seriously.

The fire engine parked alongside the Shoppe and shut off its siren. Its lights continued to strobe. The ambulance kept going, working its way onto Main to cross to the hotel.

What might have happened there?

"I have to go." She flipped the lock, grabbed handle.

"Whatever that is"—Cormac wrapped his arms around her and hauled her up, kicking and wriggling, to carry her several feet—"there's nothing you can do." He set her down.

More sirens could be heard in the distance.

"It might be Kendra. Murphy," she said looking past him to the windows. She felt cut off, isolated. This wasn't right—she was supposed to be supplying people with toadflax. She lifted the bag. "At least let me take these to Madame Demetka and Edith. They're just over there."

"Let them come to you."

The parade was at a standstill.

For this block, at this point, that meant balloons, floating above an increasingly fearful crowd. A cartoonish gingerbread man, a smiley-faced star, and Christmas tree with googly eyes bobbed in relative place, tethered to their teams of handlers by thin, almost invisible cords. The star's tip aligned with the roof of Founders Hall, four stories to the block's usual two.

Behind the last team was a high school marching band and beyond that, if Thia remembered correctly, Santa.

"I think I can make it across," she said, but then saw a look of alarm come over Edith's face—and her hand reach beneath her scarf in a gesture Thia recognized, having made it several times herself when the pendant had heated unexpectedly.

It did that to signal an impending threat.

"Something is happening," she warned Cormac.

Across the street, Edith shoved Madame Demetka (Sally?) into the Retreat women. Knocked off balance, they toppled into a street-side planter.

Wælfýr formed at Edith's hand and, aiming high, she flung it. The blue energy sped past the gingerbread balloon's feet, where, limited by the windows, Thia lost sight of it.

There was a sound like a crackle of lighting and blue sparks rained from above, winking out before reaching street level.

People glanced around in startled concern, clearly uncertain if that was part of the parade.

"What's going on?" Thia asked. Cormac gripped her arm as if afraid she'd try again to go outside. He looked up, toward the balloons. Or the sky.

"*Wælfýr*—Not just hers. That was *wælfýr* striking *wælfýr.*"

"An attack?" Thia pulled against him. "We have to help."

Not that she had any idea how.

"That's not a good idea—" He grunted when she elbowed his ribs. "For Morrigan's sake!" Snatching the bag of toadflax from her, he pushed her away from both him and the door. "Whatever you do, do *not* leave the wards. I'll be right back." He opened the door with a wave of his hand and dashed out.

It closed hard with an incongruously merry jingle of bells.

She wanted to follow but understood how that could make more trouble, not less. With her nose to the door's glass, she strained to see what was happening. The sheer mass of people made it difficult. She could only see parts.

Moments of Cormac as he wove between balloon handlers. Two ambulances, lights flashing, joined the fire engine at the corner. The ambulance in front of the Landmark. Nothing, though, of what might be taking place there.

Who had been hurt? And how seriously? It must be bad, to require three.

The idea of canceling the parade and clearing the area had been ruled out. It had been too close to the start time; with most everyone already in the area, sending them away could have resulted in more chaos, not less—especially once Cassie realized what was happening. They had feared she would have been pushed into an immediate, violent response beyond the timed threat of the crystal snowflakes.

But, now? Surely that was moot. Downtown needed to be cleared. Immediately.

Cormac thrust the bag of toadflax at Edith, who grabbed it and held it to her chest. He pointed to Eclectica. An invite to the protection of its wards. Madame Demetka stood and helped the two women from the Retreat to do the same.

A bystander stepped close, said something that involved a lot of upward pointing.

Asking about the *fyr*-balls seemed a good bet.

Edith shook her head and shrugged.

In blue flash, the gingerbread balloon exploded. Eclectica's glass panes were hit with a powerful gust and Thia leapt back, cringing instinctively with her hands at her head.

Outside was pandemonium as the crowd scattered.

So much noise. Panic. Adults scooped up wailing, terrified kids to carry them. Friends, families yelled to one another as they tried to stay together while it seemed like everyone was running or pushing or being pushed in every direction.

Cormac and Edith helped lift a sheet of balloon fabric while several more bystanders went to aid the handlers it had fallen upon.

The block limited escape options: left or right. Ultimately, more people were choosing left, since that meant not having to go by the remaining balloons. But that took them to the intersection at First Street with all of its congestion. It only increased as some hesitated, not sure where to go next, and others tried to reverse course.

Thia's hands were on the door. One push, and she could be out there, helping.

Wælfýr streaked down from a high angle to blow apart the metal-encased trash cans on the corner. Pieces of metal and burning refuse shot into the crowd. People fell. Others, trying to run, tripped over them.

The handlers of both the star and Christmas tree let go of their tethers, abandoning the balloons to join a frantic exodus to the right, back toward the Boulevard. In the minutes since the gingerbread exploded, that area had cleared. Two blocks down, Santa's float stood empty.

The star balloon ruptured and dropped.

Eclectica's door opened to let Cormac run inside.

"What about Madame Demetka? Edith?" Thia asked as he hurriedly closed the door again. Locked it.

"They're hunting snowflakes. Let's go." He spun her around, gave her a push toward the stairs.

"What's the plan?" she asked as they ascended. A low roar grew into something identifiable: motorcycles. A lot of them.

She and Cormac were on the mid-point landing when they heard the sharp crack of gunfire.

"Hurry," he urged. Once at the top of the stairs, he nudged her toward the Rowan Space. "I'll add protections to what's already there. You'll be perfectly safe."

● ○ ●

Cormac marked the quicksilver changes of Thia's expression and knew she was not going to go along with his perfectly reasonable plan.

"You'll have to make me," she said with a stubbornness that had become all too familiar.

He could do that. There were a number of ways. But all of them were violent. He found he couldn't do that, not even for her own good.

Instead he found himself asking, "Is there a way to access the roof from inside?"

Her face blanked momentarily but then brightened and she brushed past him. "There's a hatch. A ladder drops down."

He followed her into the café.

"You're not about to do something crazy." She darted him a concerned look on the way past the counter. "Are you?"

Cormac had spied his half-sister on the roof two buildings down. Yet, as much as the idea of confronting her tempted, he wasn't suicidal. Plus he had the feeling Thia wouldn't let him go it alone. No, she'd chase after him and get herself killed.

"Just a quick bit of reconnaissance," he said.

He really should get over his reluctance and shut her in the Rowan Space.

She turned left at the sideboard and went to the end of the short hallway. "There."

A two-foot square hatch in the ten-foot high ceiling.

While he checked the wards—nothing that would prevent his going through—Thia brought over a pole with a hooked end. She used that on a small metal bar set into the hatch and pulled.

The mechanism was hydraulic, smooth and nearly silent.

As cold outside air rushed in, so did sounds that had been muted by the brick exterior. Gunshots, explosions, shouts—some enraged, some maliciously joyful, with others more in the "cease and desist" category.

Thia used the pole to bring down a ladder.

Cormac thought back to his previous experience on these roofs and decided a small, dark profile would be best.

"Wait until I give you the all clear," he told Thia.

He had no intention of giving it.

She nodded, looking so terribly grave that he couldn't help himself; he pressed a quick kiss to her surprised mouth.

Then he backed up, took raven form, and flew through the opening.

Her hushed, "Be careful," followed him out.

CHAPTER 21

"It was meant for me," Kendra said to Murphy as they crossed the lobby. She couldn't shake the sight of that woman, struck down beside her. The sound of the bolt hitting flesh. Bone. "That could have been me."

"But it wasn't."

The elevator pinged, opening before them so he could enter without breaking stride. He must've summoned it the instant they'd come in from the street.

She moved to follow but he turned, blocking the way, and held up a staying hand. She stopped. "What, you want me to wait for Quentin?" The Brigantium agent had fallen behind. She'd figured, and still did, that he could catch up on his own. "He doesn't need a sitter," she began to argue.

"I need you to lead a team."

Lead. As she absorbed that, she followed his gaze to where a handful of his crew were organizing weapons and climbing equipment near the fireplace. She hadn't noticed them on the way by. She should have.

"Founders Hall?" she asked, leaping ahead.

Murphy nodded.

The Landmark was by far the tallest building around. The

second-tallest was Founders Hall, over in the next block. On the opposite side of Main from Eclectica, it would offer them an excellent position. Unfortunately, because the upper floors were used for rental storage units, security was top-notch.

"The owner couldn't be reached?" she asked. "The on-duty guard?

"There is no guard on site," Murphy said. "Our call went to a remote service. They promised to pass a message on should we leave one. We did not."

Kendra frowned. "What happens if there's a break-in?"

"Roberts asked. Says they told him they'd notify the police. It seems the owner is fairly confident the building can protect itself."

There would be no getting inside, then. Not in time to do any good. That, she knew, was where the climbing equipment came into play. Why bother with "in" when the ultimate goal was "on?"

"Right," Kendra said, her mind already at work on a plan of approach. "Any specific orders?"

Something very much like amusement sparked in Murphy's eyes. His mouth quirked. "I believe you can sort it out."

Kendra grinned. "Yeah. I can."

At the sound of Quentin's arrival, she stepped aside so he could join Murphy in the elevator. The doors slid shut.

Kendra went to join her team, but not before she noticed the elevator was headed down, not up.

● ○ ●

In normal circumstances, Thia was not good at waiting. She was especially bad at it—to the point of physical pain—while Granite Springs was being blown apart around her and people she cared for deeply were out in it, risking their lives. Every fiber of her being ached to move, to do. Something, anything other than just to stand at the base of a ladder and stare up at the night sky through an opening in the roof.

As in so many other moments of waiting, Thia thought of her phone. Not for social media, though, or a mindless game. She called Kendra.

Her hand trembled as dialled, set it on speaker. Two rings. Three. She hadn't seen her friend since before the ambulance had pulled up to the Landmark. Four rings.

"Thia, what's up?"

Her breath left her on a grateful whoosh. "Kendra. You're okay? Where are you? What's going on?"

"—fine."

So much noise came over the line, Thia could barely make out the words.

"I'm across—street going to Founders—" The last bit was lost to a crackling, then, "Sorry. Almost dropped you."

Thia thought she understood some of the trouble with the connection. "Are you running?"

"Yeah. The alley in back of Founders Hall. We're going to climb—oh, shit. Hold on."

"What? Hello? Kendra!"

A loud explosion shook Eclectica.

"Ah, screw it." Phone awkwardly in hand, Thia climbed to the roof. Cormac had told her not to go out until he gave the all-clear, so she didn't.

She stayed on the ladder and poked her head up.

Smoke drifted overhead, a street-lit haze against the night sky. There was a sharp smell to the air. Sounds were much louder; much more directional. She could pick out individual voices. Shouts. Bellows. Cries.

It was all really happening.

Ten feet away, Cormac crouched, peering over the parapet where Eclectica abutted its neighbor. Her low angle and the height of the division limited her view, but it was shocking enough. *Wælfyr* and other projectiles were being exchanged between people at the Landmark—on the roof and through open windows along the top floor—and whoever was on the roof two, maybe three buildings down the line. She wondered what more Cormac could see.

Another street-level explosion rocked Main.

When the noise died down, she realized Kendra's voice was coming through her phone.

"I'm here," she said. "I'm here. What?"

"Cassie's minions arrived from the camp," Kendra told her. "They're going after the people disarming the snowflakes— mostly by blowing the damn things up. If they're hit with any kind of *fýr,* they go off. Are you safe?"

"I'm with Cormac on Eclectica. What should—"

"Good. I have to go. The ropes are set."

The call ended, and Thia was left to put together what she should have understood from the first mention of Founders Hall. Kendra planned to climb it.

Staying as low as she could, Thia scrambled out of the hatch and began an awkward crawl across the roof to Cormac.

He heard her and spun around, still crouched. Alarm made a quick shift to anger. Glaring furiously, he waved at her to go back.

● ○ ●

Blood roared past Cormac's ears. He'd told her to wait, yet there she was, out in the open. Could Eclectica's wards keep out *wælfýr?* They certainly couldn't keep out bullets. No ward in the world could.

At least she had the sense to keep low.

His phone vibrated. He retrieved it, told Thia, "Go back to the hatch," as she came to his side, and then answered the call with a curt, "Yes?"

"My crew on the Landmark"—Murphy, on the other end of

the line, didn't waste time with preliminaries—"spotted you there with Ms. McDaniel. I'm about to take a team onto the corner roof to challenge—"

"This is important," Thia began to speak over him. "Kendra is about to—"

"—Cassandra," Murphy went on. "Kendra is taking a team onto—"

"—climb Founders Hall," finished Thia.

"—the building across the street," Murphy said. "If we keep her focus on us, can you break her wards? Quentin can help on our end."

Thia poked Cormac's shoulder until he paid full attention to what she had to say. "Cassie's people have arrived."

No wonder she was so insistent.

"They're going after the people disarming the snowflakes," she continued. "Using *fýr* to blow them up."

Murphy's repeated "hello," increased in volume and temper.

"Fine, yes," Cormac snapped at him and disconnected the call. Morrigan's cloak, it was easier to work alone.

He thrust the phone at Thia. "You want to be a part of the action? Handle any calls. I'm going after the wards Cassie has around her and need to concentrate."

She took his phone with such an air of determination that he felt a little guilty about the relative meaninglessness of the task.

It would, he figured, satisfy her need to be a part of things and keep her from doing something dangerous on her own. She couldn't possibly get herself into trouble waiting for calls.

He had not lied about the need to concentrate; and while he did, he wouldn't be able to keep tabs on her. With things about to escalate thanks to Murphy and Kendra, there wasn't time to convince—or force—her to return inside. If she kept low her current location was presently safe enough.

"Stay close," he told her for good measure, and then closed

his eyes as he worked to clear his mind of distraction. The protections Cassie was using were devious mix of knowledge gleaned from Idris and the Brigantium both. There would be lures, false trails. Traps and hidden dangers.

With a check to be sure his internal guards were in place, he began.

● ○ ●

The Rekkrs were having a field day, riding street and walkway alike. They fired indiscriminately, targeting people for the fun of it. As Quentin looked through windows by the hotel's side door, he was relieved to find that in the time it had taken to retrieve weapons from the basement stronghold, most of the bystanders had cleared out. Of these blocks, at any rate. He hoped the same could be said for the rest.

Behind him, ten of Murphy's mercenary acquaintance were preparing to make a nuisance of themselves atop the building across the street. This, in theory, was to serve as distraction while Cormac worked to take down the wards Cassandra had placed around herself and those with her there.

Briefly, Quentin wondered how Edith fared. He hadn't been in contact since before the explosions.

"My security staff will cover us from above," Murphy said, referring to those he'd sent to the Landmark's roof and upper floors. "But we'll still need to make a run for it. *Can* you run?"

It was a fair question, but Quentin found that he resented it nonetheless. "I'll manage."

"We can't slow for you." Murphy fixed him with a cold look that he then distributed throughout the gathering. "If anyone falls behind, for any reason, the rest of us must continue on. No stopping, no slowing. And for fuckssake, no going back."

"Understood." Quentin shifted his weight, testing. The pills he had taken earlier were nearly out of his system. He would soon have full use of his faculties for spellwork, but the next minute was going to hurt.

However, he needed only to get from this side of the street to the other—part of the hotel, as it happened. Salon and spa. And as such, locks and security wards would not be an issue.

"A shame that your stronghold lacked bulletproof gear," he remarked as he and Murphy went to the door.

"An oversight," was the reply. "One I mean to rectify as soon as this is done."

One for the Brigantium to consider as well.

Murphy set hands on the push-bar. Paused. "Sooner done, sooner ended." He shoved, flinging the door wide.

Quentin followed him out.

The first running steps were clumsy—how long had it been since he'd so much as tried? His hip was fire. Murphy's team, charging out of the door behind him, caught up immediately, surrounding him. Passing.

The streets were in chaos. Explosions, flashes. Shouts. The roar of a motorbike—the *pft* of a crossbow bolt followed by its sickening impact. The man to Quentin's left collapsed toward him, forcing an awkward leap and a side-step landing. His leg nearly buckled, but the man passing on his right braced him up.

That man's momentum kept him upright, gave him a speed which otherwise would have been impossible.

With the abruptness of waking from a nightmare, what was left of their group was across and running into the stairwell that would take them to the heart of the fight.

Stairs. Bloody hell.

● ○ ●

With everyone else actively fighting or—in Cormac's case—working with magic, Thia was feeling distinctly useless. Oh, sure, she was in charge of his phone and hers too, but that hadn't amounted to anything but waiting. She was terrible at waiting. She peeked over the parapet.

One roof between them. Not a very big one, either.

Cassie and eight others, a mix of her gray-cloaked followers and a few Rekkrs, had taken over the roof only two buildings from Eclectica. Positioned along the front edge, the Rekkrs fired conventional weapons at street-level targets. Cassie was much more mobile, traversing the whole of the roof as she used *wælfýr* to keep Murphy, Quentin, and more pinned down behind HVAC equipment on the corner building. They didn't have wards like she did.

A jagged streak of energy shot from Quentin's cane, lifted above the air handling unit he used as cover.

At the point of impact high above Cassie's head there was a brilliant green flash. Thia's Sight showed the color spread like ripples on water…only to fade out. The wards had absorbed the power. Cassie flung *wælfýr* in retaliation.

How was she able to send magic through the wards? Was it specifically woven into the wards when they were created? Or did it have to do with the energy itself?

Something about that made Thia think of the Brigantium pendants, and how they'd been found to be ineffective against threats from anyone who also wore one. It sensed a trusted… what, frequency? Something like that, maybe. The pendant failed to recognize the threat, so it didn't activate.

Did Cassie's wards recognize her other magics in a similar way? Was there something inherently *hers* about her craft that gave it—gave her—a pass?

Was that why Cassie was the only one wielding magic from within the rooftop wards?

If someone could mimic Cassie's *wælfýr,* could that be used against her?

Surely, if that were possible, it would have been tried before now. Thia was new to all this but Cormac, for one, had been involved with such things for nearly three centuries. If he felt the only way to get to Cassie was to destroy the wards, then that was that.

Except...the snowflakes. They were hers. Her magic.

Intended to harm others, not Cassie or her people. So, they wouldn't be perceived as threats, right? And they were small, lightweight. Easy to handle. To lift.

To call?

Not her, of course, but someone skilled, like Cormac. She turned to ask him if she might be onto something. His eyes were squeezed shut; his brow furrowed with strain. His fingers were working frenetically while he muttered, the words too soft for her to hear above the noise of the world gone mad.

She wouldn't disturb him, or any of the others, either. There was too much going on, too much at stake. She was probably wrong anyway, and nothing would come of it.

Cassie's wards absorbed another energy strike while those of the Landmark flickered orange and purple. The glass of its windows cracked, shot by the Rekkrs with Cassie and, by the sound of the gunfire, the street below.

Over on the roof of Founders Hall, Kendra and what looked to be at least ten more men and women were hurriedly setting up positions and physical weaponry along its wide cornice.

While Thia did nothing.

Dammit.

She could at least test her theory, couldn't she?

With another glance at Cormac—still busy—she set off in a crawl for the front of Eclectica. She hoped to find someone working to disarm the snowflakes and, without anyone else's attention, get them to throw her one.

But, as she discovered when she peeped over the edge, the only people down there were Rekkrs. Tons of broken glass littered the pavement in front of the store.

The plate glass windows.

But Eclectica's wards would keep people out, would they?

Shit. The *nighttime* wards would. It'd take someone as much difficulty as Cormac was having with Cassie's for someone to break those. But Eclectica had closed early. It was still time for the weaker, business-hour wards.

Thia couldn't worry about that now.

She tried not to be distracted by the situation along Main, either, but failed. Rekkrs roamed on foot, vandalizing stores and public fixtures, while more roared their motorcycles up and down streets and sidewalks, both.

Such an array of weapons they had. Guns, pikes, throwing stars, swords.

One of the police officers, it seemed, was fairly adept with a wands as well as rifles. Both were employed in attempts to blow out motorcycle tires. There was police presence, and a few attempts to engage that Thia could see, but the Granite Springs force was small. Theft, disorderly conduct, and ordinance violations were what they dealt with most often. They weren't trained for combat. There was only one SWAT unit in the whole valley, and it was stationed miles away.

Not all of the glistening mess was window glass. Some of it, Thia realized with a sinking dread, had a distinct snowflake shape.

But, sure. Cassie wanted revenge on her in particular, didn't she? Of course she would want to see Eclectica destroyed.

All Thia had to do now was get one of those snowflakes... without help and without leaving the roof. Okay. She'd have to call one to her, that's all.

All the times she'd messed up sprang to mind. The many-times-damaged garage door. The damage done at the Landmark lat night. The raging candle flame. The burning boxes.

She could do this, though. She just needed to relax and not worry about losing control...like she did every time she—Stop it, she ordered herself, and hunkered down, out of sight.

She closed her eyes. This was the point where she needed to

center herself, to calm both her mind and body.

Yeah, right. Pulse pounding, gut clenched, she managed to focus her thoughts enough to envision a crystal snowflake in her mind's eye. Would it matter if the details weren't exact? Hopefully not. She layered a vague, "any will do" notion into her process, then worked to get the "feel" of the imagined crystal—as if she held one in her hand. Cold with complex, sharp facets. Not heavy, but solid. She extended her cupped hands, ready to receive, and pictured it coming to land there.

She concentrated on it, willed it to be so with all she had.

The Cailleach's power woke within her bones to speed like wildfire along her nerves. She didn't realize she was shaking. Her teeth clenched.

Snowflakes. Snowflakes, come to me.

She felt like a fool as she repeated the dull phrase over and over in her head. Spells were supposed to have a certain lyricism, weren't they? Or at least rhyme? She couldn't even do that much.

"Thia." Cormac's voice came from close by. "Thia!"

She opened her eyes, found him crouched before her, his attention on the sky.

"What in bloody *ifrinn*, Thia."

"Oh, wow."

It was beautiful. Crystal snowflakes were coming in from all directions, glinting against the dark of the night sky. Fifty at least, maybe more, and all of them headed straight for her.

Oh, shit. She waved her hands in refusal. Not that many. Go back. "I wanted to get one—*one*—and see if it could pass through Cassie's wards. Like with the Brigantium's pendants. Her magic—"

"—might let in her own magic," Cormac finished, getting the gist. "How did you manage to call all of them to—never mind. They need to be redirected."

Snowflakes had begun to drop onto the roof around them.

They behaved like hail, bouncing with light, bell-like pings. If they were to explode, they'd blow the roof off Eclectica and kill her and Cormac. Thia had done Cassie's work for her.

"How?" Thia asked. "How do I redirect them when I don't even know how I called so many? I shouldn't have tried." All she ever did with magic was make messes.

Two roofs away, Cassie was intent on her *wælfýr* attack, now expanded to include Kendra's group on Founders Hall, who seemed to be making headway against the Rekkrs below.

"How did it start?" Cormac asked as more crystals pinged down. "If it's a vision, change it. Change what you saw as the outcome."

Oh, sure, was *that* all? Thia was going to hyperventilate. Or be sick. Both. Closing her eyes, she pictured Cassie's hands instead of her own. "I'm trying."

Cormac laughed that near-silent huff of his. "Don't make me say it."

She groaned, put her head in her hands. "No try?" she asked. "Only do?"

"That's the one."

She felt him settle in beside her. He took her hand in both of his. That was when she realized she'd been shaking.

"Belief is more than half the trick," he said quietly, and she felt something inside herself settle. He was doing that, she supposed. Helping, somehow. She took the first easy breath in hours.

"That's it. No, don't look," he added quickly. "Concentrate. Imagine that Cassie is a magnet. The crystals can't help but go to her. Lifting from the roof, altering course in the air, they want nothing but to go to her. Magic, returning home."

Sounds changed around her. Thia couldn't *not* look. Snowflakes were rising from Eclectica's roof to join those in the air and fly toward Cassie. Some already fell upon her.

Through the protection wards.

"It's working?" Thia hardly dared to believe it, even as she maintained the idea Cormac had suggested, and fed it with the Cailleach's power.

"Seems to be." Cormac gave her hand a reassuring squeeze. Since neither wore gloves and they were working with power, there was such a heated contrast to the cold air that Thia was surprised not to see steam.

Cassie yelled orders while her people scrambled to pick up snowflakes and throw them off the roof. They'd simply rise again. Seek her again. She was being pelted, the roof around her becoming thick with the glittering, timed explosives. Her orders became a chant. In Latin, Thia thought. The language the Brigantium often worked in, and yet one more thing she'd have to learn if she were to study with them. Assuming she survived the night.

"*Damnad,*" Cormac said. "She's disarming them."

Thia thought he would say more, but his attention shifted and took hers with it to a large, dark object floating up from the alley.

A dumpster. What could have possibly caused *that?* And to what end? It moved toward Cassie.

She and her people noticed too late. Picking up speed, the metal bin sailed across the roof. Several cloaked figures dove out of the way. Others, not so lucky, were knocked down.

Shouting, Cassie extended her arms in what Thia assumed was a magical attempt to hold the thing back, but it was no good. The dumpster slammed into her, mowing her down like she was a deer in the path of a semi. It settled with a horrendous, metallic boom.

"Stay here," Cormac told Thia and, letting go of her hand, sprang up to race across the buildings.

No way would she not go with him.

CHAPTER 22

Main Street, Granite Springs
Winter Solstice

Without leadership, Cassie's people fell into disorder. Some, Cormac saw as he vaulted onto the next building, had gathered around the bin to argue with increasingly dramatic gestures. Others took the opportunity to save themselves and ran for the rear of the building for the set of stairs the Rekkrs used the night before. Only a few thought to continue with the attack. That's what you got when you recruited through compulsion spells: Lose control and your people would be left to think for themselves—rarely for your benefit.

Cassie's wards, weakened by relentless assault, fell when the first of her *thegnas* crossed through to scramble over the back wall (to then be taken out by a *wanfýr*-charged dart shot from high on the Landmark).

While Cormac sprinted across the adjacent roof, a cry went up and Murphy and his people charged. Those atop the tall building across the gave cover, firing a mix of weapons and magics. Most found their targets—Rekkrs and *thegnas*—but a stray arrow whizzing past Cormac's ear had him diving behind an industrial ventilation unit.

"*Ifrinn,*" he said under his breath—then again, louder, when Thia scurried up from behind.

"Are you hit?" Crouched, she began to run her hands over

him.

He grabbed them, gave her a shake. "What did I tell you? Stay. Dammit, I told you to *stay.*" Her mouth parted, but he wasn't done. "Are you hit?" He began looking her over, patting her down.

"I'm fine." She shoved at him. "Stop. *Stop.*"

They both flinched when something heavy struck the side of their cover. The metal trembled.

"What was—" Triumphant cheers drowned out the rest of Thia's question. Their direction told Cormac all he needed to know. On impulse he took Thia's face in his hands. Her eyes went wide.

"This time would you *please*"—he gave her lips a smacking kiss—"stay *here.*" Grinning, he sprang away to run the rest of the distance to the next roof, where Murphy barked orders as his team rounded up what remained of Cassie's people there. The dead, they left where they lay. Cormac paid little notice. To him, only the woman herself mattered.

Her feet stuck out from under the rubbish bin. The rest of her was beneath, saved from being crushed by the height of its wheels. It had come to rest near the roof's center. When Cormac got to it, Quentin was just levering himself down. He shone light from his cane under the bin.

"She won't be unconscious long," Quentin informed him.

Cormac hunkered down to look. Their nemesis lay on her back with her head turned his way. Long tendrils of her hair criss-crossed the blood that ran down her face. Her eyes were closed; her mouth, open. Blanked of expression, she looked almost harmless and so very, very young.

His little half-sister.

What an odd thought to have. He stood, saying, "We'll need to bind her."

He then cleared his throat, having found his voice rougher than expected. The cold air, most likely. He offered his hand when Quentin struggled to rise.

"I'm fine." The man was leaning on his cane so hard that it wobbled.

"Of course."

With a grunt, Quentin lurched against the bin. He remained there, leaning almost drunkenly.

Cormac frowned. In this light, Quentin's pupils should have been dilated; instead, they were pinpoints.

It was none of his business.

Footfalls, rapid and vexingly familiar, heralded Thia's arrival. Anxiety and frustration mixed. He turned on her. "*What* did I ask?"

She dodged both him and his question to come to a stop by Cassie's booted feet. "Is she...dead?" Her voice went soft on the last word.

"No." He wrangled his temper. "You should *not* be here. It isn't safe." The rooftop fight may have been won, but there were still sounds of trouble coming from Main Street. "You should go back to Eclectica."

"No." Thia went to Quentin, who continued to use the bin to hold himself upright. "Are you okay?"

"Fine."

She looked like she might argue but then her focus drifted to the bin. "This is ours. Eclectica's." Frowning, she touched its side. "Why did it come? I didn't do this, did I? It's not a snowflake." She began to lift the lid, making it easier to identify the source of the faint, nearly supersonic hum. Cormac had misidentified it as having to do with building electrics.

His gut turned to ice. The bin was not a snowflake, no, but what was *inside* it...He grabbed Thia's shoulders, spun her to face Eclectica, and gave her a violent shove. "Run."

She stumbled but went no further. "Stop handling me," she said, and then struck at his hands when he reached for her, thinking to carry her off. Fury lit her eyes. "Stop! Just...stop.

I'm sick of not knowing what's going on. If you have something to—"

"You'll not get far enough. Not in time" Quentin said with ominous calm. He was looking in the bin. "None of us will."

"How long?" Cormac went to see for himself. Twenty-odd snowflakes lay inside the otherwise empty bin. The humming grew louder as the crystals' vibrations increased. They began to jitter like corn kernels about to pop.

Not long enough.

"Here," Thia said, and prodded his side. "Here."

Cormac looked down. She held six vials of toadflax.

"Thank Brigid," Quentin said, taking one. He removed the top and shook the liquid out over the snowflakes.

Cormac did the same with another, then another.

"Will it be enough?" Thia asked as the fourth was emptied, but then came to her own conclusion. "We need more." She yelled a request to the rooftop at large.

But Murphy's people here hadn't been tasked with snowflake deactivation. Heads shook. Empty hands were held up.

Beneath the dumpster, Cassie moaned, beginning to rouse.

She could stop the crystals, but would she? She was so hellbent on revenge, she might not care if it killed her.

Cormac caught Murphy's attention across the roof. "That binding spell of yours would come in handy right about now," he called, thinking of the one used on Thia the night before.

Murphy signaled several of his people, sent them over.

"What are the words?" Thia asked, emptying the last bottle herself. "Oh, God, I can't remember the—"

Cormac and Quentin spoke at the same time:

His, "*Ne scyrde,*" with the other man's, "*Non nocere.*"

Shaking her head, Thia backed away. "I don't think so. It was something else, something more...French, maybe. Why can't I remember?" She looked guilt-stricken.

"Same meaning," Cormac assured her, closing the distance. "Different words, that's all."

Behind them, the bin's lid slammed.

"Clear out!" Quentin yelled and began to hobble toward the corner building. "It's not enough."

He was right.

Cormac could hear the high-pitched hum. Not as intense as before, thanks to the toadflax; but that was little consolation, standing as close as they were to what was about to become shrapnel.

"Let's go." He and Thia ran flat-out for Eclectica. A number of people joined them. Others opted to follow Quentin to the corner building or take their chances on the rear stairs.

"Hurry," Murphy shouted. Cormac glanced back to see two men carrying Cassie onto the corner building's roof. Murphy held open its access door.

Cormac vaulted the first of two parapets to come. "Here," he said, reaching. Thia braced her hands on his shoulders. He grabbed her waist and hauled her over.

She hit the ground running.

One of Murphy's men caught up to run alongside.

"Did they finish the binding spell?" Thia asked him.

"No." The man was flushed and breathing hard. "Let's hope she doesn't wake before they do, yeah?"

At Eclectica's parapet, Cormac repeated his vault-then-lift maneuver with Thia. The roofs behind were empty, save for Cassie's dead.

The dumpster was rattling.

"Time's up."

● ○ ●

The explosion propelled Thia forward, like being thrown by a wall. She landed hard and slid, unable to stop even when a substantial weight landed on her. She and whatever it was slid together. Her face and hands burned, scraping across the roof. She would have cried out but the air had been knocked from her, and the weight—Cormac's weight, as she came to recognize the feel of him—was making it difficult to replace.

Sounds were muffled. She thought that was due to Cormac covering her head and therefore her ears, but when he lifted from her and started pulling to get her to roll over (which she then did) she realized she still couldn't hear right.

"Move." That's what she thought he said, anyway. She was looking up at his face, inches from hers, and that's what his lips seemed to shape. *Move.* He looked panicked.

And no wonder. The sky above was thick with smoke that flickered orange with light cast from below. Thia felt her eyes widen. Fire. She shoved Cormac off, rolled to push herself to her feet only to drop back to her hands and knees on a wave of dizziness. Her ears were ringing.

No, that was a siren. The fire department. She hoped it was safe enough on the streets for them to come.

Together, she and Cormac half-crawled to Eclectica's hatch. She went down first. Somehow, the ladder was easier for her than standing. At the bottom she dropped to her knees on the linoleum and stayed there. The three men who had come with them were there too, sitting and holding their heads or even lying down—also holding their heads.

She wasn't alone, then, in the headache department.

Cormac plunked down beside her, his blue eyes intense. His face was white beneath smeared blood and grit.

"What's burning? How bad it is?" Thia asked. Oh, good, she could almost hear herself.

"The roof where the dumpster was." She could almost hear him, too. Much better. Except he hadn't answered her second question.

A phone vibrated in her coat pocket. "Excuse me," she said

politely.

It occurred to her that she was in shock. It wasn't exactly easy to think what to do—what she should do—and her head swam if she moved much. She should move, though, shouldn't she? A building was on fire. That could spread, and quickly. What about natural gas lines and the risk of explosion? And what about the Rekkrs? What was going on outside? There were probably a zillion other things she ought to do in place of answering her phone. And it was her phone. Cormac's was in her other pocket.

"Hello?"

"Thia, thank—"

"Kendra?" She checked the read-out to be sure. "I'm having trouble hearing. Are you okay? What's going on?" She gave a couple of wasted seconds before admitting, "Sorry, I'm going to hand you to Cormac. I can't make out what you're saying." She did so and then tried to gauge what was being said by his expression. It was an exercise in futility; he never gave much of anything away. (And when did, there was a good chance it was deceptive.)

The call didn't last long. He handed back the phone, gave her hand a squeeze before pulling away.

"It's over." Cormac spoke distinctly, as if Thia were hearing impaired. She supposed she was. Please, let it be temporary.

"Over?" she asked.

"Essentially." He leaned in close, which helped a little. She concentrated on his lips. "The fighting is done. It's a matter of running Cassie's *thegnas* and the Rekkrs to ground as they flee."

"And the fire? From the dumpster blowing up. The building caught fire, right?"

"Under control. Or nearly so."

"Oh, good. That's really...good." Such an inadequate word, but it was the best she had to give. Relief, confusion, sorrow, all of it overwhelmed her vocabulary.

She reached out, touched gentle fingers to Cormac's blood-smeared cheek. "We made it, then." Her breaths were shaky. Crying was imminent, but she wasn't ready. Not yet.

But a softness came into his eyes, and as the corner of his mouth lifted in a kind of smile, she felt him try to contain a tremor. She wouldn't say she launched herself at him, exactly, but she must have because suddenly she was there, tucked up against his chest and being pulled onto his lap as he adjusted his legs to accommodate her.

She pressed her face to the crook of his neck and let silent tears flow onto his jacket and into his shirt collar. He smelled faintly of all they'd been through that night. The earth of the tunnel. The tar of the roof. The smoke of that final explosion. Her arms wrapped tight, filling themselves with the solidness of another person. Of his person in particular. What was it, exactly, about Cormac that felt so much...more?

"I do love you, you know," she said and felt his throat work as he swallowed. His grip around her tightened and his head dropped to hers. His warm breath moved through her hair to brush her neck. She thought he said something, but damned if she could hear what it was.

If it was important, he would repeat it.

And she was crying too hard—sobbing, honestly—to make too much of it. So she surrendered to the moment, both of them alive and relatively unharmed.

Too many others had not been as fortunate.

● ○ ●

It could have been worse, Murphy allowed. He had seen—had been responsible for—enough destruction in his life to know. But Granite Springs was his, and as he stood in the middle of Main to survey the results from the ground, he could hardly stomach the rage.

Bloody right it could have been worse, but it should never have happened at all.

From the ground, things looked much as they had from the roofs. Minor building damage: shattered windows; holes or furrows where bullets and other projectiles had struck bricks; torn awnings from the same. Evidence of looting from shops where wards had failed or that had never had any to start.

Insurance ought to cover most of it. Eventually. Tight-fisted bastards being what they were.

Downed streetlamps and signals would need to be replaced, along with a few of the benches set along the walks. A motorbike was embedded in one of the cement-block planters the city maintained. Parade barricades had been knocked all to hell, many of them driven over. Pieces of balloon—the star and the gingerbread man—were every-fucking-where.

He looked to the sky, squinting as he scanned left and right above the buildings, then out toward the mountains. Where, he wondered, would the tree balloon turn up?

Sirens continued to wail distantly, traveling further into the valley. Pursuits, he could assume. Law enforcement agencies across the county were now involved. More would join as the night wore on, not just to track down Rekkrs or Cassandra's people but to assist in the investigation.

Christ, but he was going to have some fancy explaining to do with the city officials. Not so much the police chief—they had an understanding, and while this wouldn't help it any, it shouldn't harm it, either. But the mayor? The council?

All of that would need to be done before the start of the news day. He checked his watch. Granite Springs was about to explode—no pun intended—on the national scene. International, too. Not to mention the Otherwordly.

They would need to have their story straight.

A group of firemen left the alley to return to their engine on Main, parked with its lights flashing. As they passed, one gave

Murphy an acknowledging wave. He nodded back, suddenly conscious of how his clothing reeked of smoke. It was soaked, too, from his assisting with the firefight. He should change.

For the moment, things appeared to be managed. A detailed search was underway for dangerous items. Caution tape was being strung across damaged storefronts, and he'd sent a crew to see about getting the hardware store to open so they could get supplies for boarding up the gaping holes left by broken windows and smashed-in doors.

He walked toward the Landmark's lobby entrance. His staff had removed the detritus left by the EMTs in their effort to save the woman struck down at the start of things, yet the stain of her blood remained on the pavement. His pavement.

Changes would need to be made, more precautions taken. He had plans for this place. Longstanding, far-reaching plans. The set-backs from this would take months to overcome.

Ah, bollocks. He had forgotten about his car, parked where it shouldn't be and in no telling what condition. With a sigh, he turned around. Best see to that now, he figured. *Then* he'd change clothes and deal with city officials.

CHAPTER 23

**Lake of the Woods
21 December**

Kendra left the activity of the barn and began crossing the parking lot. Edith and Quentin were having what looked to be their fifth squabble since their arrival less than an hour before. Lifting her hand, Kendra acknowledged the wry look Edith gave her. Quentin, not even glancing her way, tapped his watch.

"It's a bloody waste of time," he said to Edith while Kendra continued past.

"Fine," Edith responded. "But unless you have something you'd rather I do besides sitting at the airport, it's my time to waste. We'll be ridiculously early if we leave now."

Kendra saw Murphy come around the far side of the lodge. She changed course, cutting across a stretch of fresh, undisturbed snow to arrive at his side.

He had turned around and was eyeing the roof. His stance was alert, his expression one Kendra had come to know well: calculation.

She felt the first bud of a smile. "What are you thinking?"

"Ross," he greeted, his attention never leaving the building. His hands were in his jacket pockets. "Potential."

The smile bloomed. "Won't ownership be a problem?"

They had returned at dawn but there had been no trace of the odd man.

Avery ap Hywel...otherwise known as Avery Powell, owner of record of the land and all its structures and contents.

People were going over every inch. The more they had on Cassie, her minions, the Rekkrs, and Powell, the better.

Especially Cassie. Weeks ago, she had absconded with Idris Cathmor's entire collection of grimoires, relics, and the like. Dangerous stuff to have out in the world, unaccounted for.

Which was why, instead of starting on the massive load of work to be done Granite Springs, so many people were *here*, searching for anything that might suggest the whereabouts of the missing collection or the people themselves. Or could be used as leverage against Cassie during what could otherwise prove to be frustrating interrogation in London.

There was no such thing as "too small." What might on its own seem insignificant could prove vital when added to other details. Sometimes a puzzle picture wasn't clear until all the pieces were laid out.

Murphy had been silent so long that Kendra wondered if he had forgotten her question—too caught up in his developing vision for the place. He was a brilliant warrior, but what he loved was business. The making and the running.

"I'll sort something out," he finally said. "Powell has clearly put in a lot of work. He may not want to abandon it entirely. Should he not resurface, however, I know some...people who know some people."

She hadn't missed the pause.

She wondered if it was significant.

"I'd best be off," he said with a new, unusual energy. If she had not known better, she might've thought he was nervous. "I've got a thing to do before my meeting at the Landmark."

"You're not going to the airport?"

The Brigantium was sending in a team on a private plane to

take Cassie to London. A contingent from hotel security was to make sure she got on board without incident. Kendra had thought Murphy would be part of it.

"You can handle it." His lips quirked. "If the *claimsech* slips the physical leash, you could take her with one hand behind your back. Her power is more than sufficiently bound. Just watch out for her claws. I understand she likes to scratch."

"That's what handcuffs are for." Kendra looked beyond the still-bickering Edith and Quentin to the far edge of the lot, where the Landmark's catering van sat with its engine idling to power the heater for those inside.

● ○ ●

Getting what he needed from her would be easier, Cormac thought, if it was not like looking into Idris's eyes. Cassandra Swinton was their father to a T, from the amber brilliance of her irises all the way down to the hatred that burned deep in her soul.

He assumed the woman had one. A soul. That, too, would make things easier—if he could convince himself that she did not.

She sat perfectly still, cross-legged in the hotel van's cargo area. Her back was to the wall of the driving compartment. Her hands were cuffed at her front. The stillness was due to the binding spell. Cormac had no doubt she strained against it, fighting with all she had to break free.

That was only a matter of time, no matter how excellently the spells had been crafted. When they got to London, he'd talk the Brigantium about extracting her power and binding it in an object. It was a much more secure method, as he'd make sure they understood. What he wouldn't mention was that it would give him something over Cassie, if she thought he could use her power to bargain.

He sat with his back to the rear doors. She had been glaring at him for almost an hour. Seething, at least on her part. He didn't quite know what his part was.

He had not known he'd had a half-sister—emphasis on the half—until Samhain. He had learned of the existence of his half-brother, her twin, at the same time. That man was dead within minutes, having impaled himself (unintentionally) on the knife in Thia's hand. It had set off a chain of events which continued to play out all these weeks later.

And weren't done yet.

"I see none of him in you," Cassandra said abruptly.

"Idris, you mean?" Since that had been the direction of his thoughts, it might have been hers as well. It was only natural, wasn't it, to try to see the progenitor in the result? People did it with newborns, for Morrigan's sake—the most amorphous a person could be outside the womb. Certainly they would do it with the more defined form.

"Yes." The word hissed out as her eyes narrowed to furious slits. "No wonder he abhorred you. You're nothing like him."

It was quite possibly the nicest thing ever said about him. And yet she meant it as an insult.

He laughed.

"*Mera.*" She would spit on him, he thought, if she were able.

"Language," he chided, and laughed all the more. "I'm going to enjoy our time together, sister dear."

It felt good to say as a taunt, and in a way he *was* enjoying himself. But he had no illusions about what lay ahead. Once he began trying to get useful information from her, their time together would be a miserable slog.

Without the Achill Bell, he could not fulfill his part of the bargain with Murphy.

Upon pain of death.

Much as he'd rather stay in the van, he had to go. There was a conversation he had been avoiding, and he was running out of time.

● ○ ●

The Retreat, Granite Springs

"I want to go to Portland," Zoe said, and took a tissue from the box offered by the African-American woman in the deep purple cloak. Alma, she had said her name was. She was older and had a soothing demeanor, and Zoe totally envied her hair.

Not the color so much—white and gray, as was natural for her age—but what could be done with it. All those narrow braids wrapped elaborately on and around her head. Jeweled clips and two of those sticks like Zoe had always wanted to be able to wear (but had never been able to get to stay in) held the collections of braids in place.

"Portland," Zoe found herself saying for emphasis. "I really like Portland."

"There is much to like." Alma had a wonderful voice. Rich and soothing. Zoe envied it, too. Such a powerful instrument for theater.

They had been talking for a long time, just the two of them, although Zoe couldn't put an exact length to it. Ever since she had woken up, and long enough to talk about what little she remembered of her time...her time somewhere else. And no matter how agitated she had become, Alma had remained calm. Comforting, in a distant kind of way.

Zoe blew her nose and dropped the tissue into the waste-basket with the rest. Then she found herself again looking at the lovely crystal.

Alma had been wearing it when she'd first sat beside Zoe's bed in the cozy little room, but soon after that she had taken it off to dangle it from its gold chain, her arthritic hand held high.

The clear crystal really caught the light. Such a pretty thing; not very big at all, but so bright. A German-sounding-word diamond, Alma had said, although it wasn't a diamond at all.

So bright and lovely, and Alma's voice so soothing.

Zoe could feel all her worries, all the confusion just...melt away.

"Portland, you said," Alma gently reminded her. "What is it you would do there?"

"I act." And something else. Zoe felt various thoughts drift by. She managed to catch the right one. "I really love to bake. Desserts, pastries. Pies are fun, too. And easy! So many ways to make them. I was working on a biscotti recipe...before... before...." She let that one go. It didn't matter. "Chocolate. Everyone loved them."

"I know many people in Portland," Alma said. "Would you like me to see if they can find you a nice place there? Somewhere you can bake all those delicious things you enjoy, and maybe do a little acting on the side?"

"Oh, yes," Zoe gushed. "Oh, please. That would be perfect."

Alma smiled a beautiful smile. "Then that's what we'll do."

● ○ ●

Pine Meadow, Granite Springs

"I should get going," Thia said. Over Abby's objections, she collected her coat from the chair. "There are a zillion things to do."

"And I should be helping." Reclined on several pillows and with her legs stretched out on the sofa, Abby plucked at the thick blanket covering her to her chest. A cloth band held her hair back from her face, making it easy to watch the tiredness creep in.

"No, you should be *resting*." Thia fastened her coat. Her own tiredness and the stiffness in her overworked hands made her clumsy. "There will be plenty to do later."

Thia could hardly remember all that she'd done last night. Crying on Cormac's shoulder was poignantly clear...but after that was a blur. Helping to clean up the shards of Eclectica's front windows had led to helping a number of store owners and staff pick up other debris. Then someone had brought in plywood to cover the windows, and Thia had found herself helping with that, too. She had aches everywhere, a terrific collection of bruises and scrapes, and hadn't slept. Hadn't had a chance yet to try.

On the bright side, at some point during it all, her hearing had returned in full.

She went over, gave Abby a careful hug. "I'm so glad you're okay."

Abby hugged back. "Me, too. That you're okay, I mean." She rolled her eyes. "Although I *am* also glad for myself."

Thia smiled. She had needed to come, despite all that was going on, to cancel out the image of Abby, unconscious. She was very glad she had. She pulled out her keys. "You're sure you don't need anything?"

They had been over this before, and Abby's answer was no different. She was fine and perfectly capable of taking care of herself.

Thia then had to refuse—again—to let Abby come with her into town.

"Not even to let me get my car?"

A fair point but, "I'll ask Kendra to drive it out with me later."

"There's a spare key on a hook by the door," Abby said when Thia walked into the entryway. "If you'll be at Eclectica, I can ask one of the coven to get it from you. They're coming out later. Save you and Kendra the effort."

"Really?" Thia found the key, dropped it into her pocket.

"We have the solstice to make up."

"Oh, right." So many holiday plans had been thrown into confusion. "I *will* be at Eclectica. For the afternoon, anyway." A police officer was to meet her there to take her prepared statement. She had spent the morning writing it, as dictated to her by Kendra over the phone.

Thia was to be merely the owner of a damaged store who, like the rest of those on Main Street, had been victimized by a violent motorcycle gang.

The Rekkrs were to be blamed for everything. No mention of Cassie or, indeed, magic whatsoever. Thia hoped her brain could keep the new story straight.

Thinking about that brought to mind Zoe, staying at the Retreat for "counseling," as Kendra had called it. Thia would try to visit her later.

She poked her head back into the sitting room for one last look and a wave. "I'll see you tomorrow...sometime. I'm not sure when I'll be able to come by, but—"

"I'll be at Eclectica." Abby smiled wanly. "Don't argue with me. I'll be perfectly fine by tomorrow."

Thia frowned but recognized that it was pointless. Besides, if their places were reversed, she would probably do the same. She surrendered to the inevitable. "Okay. See you tomorrow, then."

"See you."

Thia took out her car key, checked her watch as she pulled open the door. She startled at Murphy, coming up the front steps.

"Ms. McDaniel." His hands held a white poinsettia, its pot wrapped in red plastic and tied with a matching bow. "I was just up at Lake of the Woods with Quentin and the rest"—he cleared his throat—"and thought I'd, uh, stop by to see how Ab—Collins was faring." He adjusted his grip. "How would that be, then?"

Thia had never thought to see him so...flustered. Something clicked in the back of her mind. How he had been the first to reach Abby after she'd collapsed, how he had been the one to carry her. It didn't fit with their animosity...or did it?

"She says she's fine," Thia said, and watched him take in a

deep breath. As if for the first time in a long while.

"Good," he said, breathing out. "That's...good. Has she the right of it?"

Thia translated the colloquialism: Was Abby correct in her assessment. "I believe so. She's tired—weak, maybe, but fine. Is she expecting you?"

"No, I most certainly am not," Abby called from inside. She had heard through the open door, perhaps also seen through the front window. "But you might as well let him in anyway."

In an undertone, Thia asked him, "Sure you want to?"

His expression was wry. "Might as well, to quote the lady. Such a gracious welcome," he said more loudly.

"You're letting in all the cold."

Sharing a smile, Thia and Murphy exchanged places at the threshold. Once inside, he turned to tell her, "There was no sign of Powell. The man whom Abby attempted to read last night," he added after Thia's frown. "The one who took Zoe."

"He's gone?"

"So it appears. With Cassandra under the binding spell, he should be released from her control, hence no longer a threat in that way—but that doesn't mean he isn't dangerous. And until the Rekkrs and the rest are rounded up, you'd be wise to take extra care."

"Will all of them be found, do you think? All the Rekkrs and Cassie's people."

A muscle in his jaw clenched. "Live in hope." With his hands full of poinsettia, he used his foot to nudge the door. "Good morning, Thia."

She bid him the same and headed down the walk.

It was hard to believe that the day was just getting started, but the proof was in the sky. The sun shone softly down, not yet halfway through its arc.

Thia made her way along the stone path. The jingle of her keys on the wide ring she'd hooked on her finger broke what otherwise would have been anxiety-boosting silence. Abby's property was surrounded by forest. Yes, there was a fence and other protections, but fences could be climbed. Wards could be broken. Anyone, anything could be in there.

No guarantees.

Much of the landscape was blanketed in sparkling, wintry white. It had snowed since she'd been here....all of, what, two days ago. She frowned. One?

After rounding the turn past two giant rhododendrons, she stopped abruptly. Beyond Murphy's sportscar (which looked like someone had taken a crowbar to the hood) and leaning on hers was Cormac.

The cuts and scrapes she'd noted after he had cleaned the blood and grime from his face had healed over and were on their way to fading as if they had never been.

"You rode with Murphy?" she asked, and resumed walking to her car. To him.

He shifted so she could unlock her door. It put them rather close, and she had a hard time not doing away with the rest of the distance.

There was a familiar box on the hood beside his hip. She stared at the patterned paper she had chosen. The bow she had tied. Another lifetime ago.

"You've been under Eclectica's counter," she said.

"I have." He picked up the gift. "For you." He couldn't meet her eyes. "I had you in mind. The whole time." His voice had lost almost all volume.

"I was there at the time, talking with you," she said. "It'd be a bit hard *not* to think of me."

"No." His gaze lifted, found hers. Amazingly blue, his was, and earnest. "From well before that. From the moment I left you on Brodgar until—until never. I haven't stopped having you in mind."

He thrust the gift toward her almost violently; her hands

came up automatically to take it, and then he walked away.

Her heart pounded like a wild thing trapped within the cage of her ribs. "You're leaving?"

He stopped but didn't turn around.

She could hardly believe it. But, of course. That was why he was doing this—that's why he was being open. Honest. She swore loudly. It felt good. "You're leaving *again*."

His sigh was a visible puff in the cold air.

"I thought that we—" On a frustrated sound, Thia started over. "I'd already decided not to spend this Christmas with my family. With the trouble I have with the Cailleach's power, I didn't think it would be safe. So I've been planning a get-together here. With friends. And I thought that since you were here, I would invite you." It sounded silly spoken aloud.

And it didn't matter, anyway.

"Since you're leaving," she continued to talk to his back, "I guess I won't need to. Except I sort of just did." She yanked open the car door. "Never mind. I'm sorry."

"Do not apologize," he snapped, turning around. His eyes flashed cobalt. Thia froze, the hand with her keys on the car, the other cradling the gift to her chest. "Not to anyone," he insisted, returning. The door was between them. "Certainly not to me."

The anger or whatever it was abruptly drained, leaving him to look weary and maybe even a little sad.

"Never apologize for your kind and giving heart, Thia. And do not believe for a moment that I wouldn't"—he struggled visibly—"love to spend Christmas with you. But I can't. I'm going with Cassie and the Brigantium to London. The plane is due at the airport within the hour."

"After that?"

"I made a bargain with Murphy weeks ago. It has to be kept. Please believe me."

"I do. Believe you."

The muscles of his throat worked, but he only nodded.

"Well." Thia pushed past the mess of her emotions, like a swimmer surfacing after a dive. "You'll be back when you've finished whatever it is."

It was not a question.

He made a small sound, then, "Would I be welcome?"

She only just managed to not call him a fool. "Cormac, good grief. Of course you would."

"Oh."

It could've been the way the sunlight reflected off the snow around them or it could've been her imagination entirely, but she thought she saw the sheen of tears in his eyes.

With a small shake of her head, she leaned across the door to plant a quick kiss on his cheek. Then she slid into the car and set his gift on the passenger seat. She grabbed the door, closed it. Rolled down the window.

All with him standing like a statue, his face frozen in shock.

Thia turned the key and, above the sputtering start of the motor, called out, "This time, come as yourself, would you?"

Flashing him a grin, she shifted out of neutral and sent the car down the drive.

EPILOGUE

Founders Hall, Granite Springs
21 December

One of the principle rules of the Rekkrs was to scatter when they needed to lay low. Numbers attracted attention. But with several law enforcement agencies, a group of skilled mercenaries, and a modernized Brigantium now after them, it wasn't like they had a lot of options as far as where to go.

So when nine had chosen to take refuge in the basement of Founders Hall—because sometimes hiding almost literally under someone's nose was the best thing to do—they didn't argue about who had gotten there first; they congratulated one another on their smart thinking and settled in for a long wait.

Unfortunately, Skati did not agree. And, already pissed off about what theyd done for Cathmor's daughter (which wasn't fair, really, since he had been the one who'd told them to do what she asked—but, then, apparently she'd lied to *him* about what she would ask them, so they could see why he had a right to be pissed off, maybe...it was confusing). Anyway, pissed off about that, Skati had cut his trip abroad short.

Which meant that his temper was already blown when he went into his building's basement and found the nine of them together.

Brody got it first.

The ones who were left felt bad about that, since Brody had been a funny guy and a better than average mechanic.

As the day would stretch on, seemingly without end, they would come to envy him. And resent him, too, that he should have got off so easy.

But that was later.

At the moment, with Brody's blood fresh on the wall behind where he'd been standing, they felt bad for the guy and more than a little terrified for themselves.

"I leave town for a few weeks and look what you get up to," the man they called Skati said in That Tone, the quiet one that was somehow the worst. He wiped his blade with a cloth while he raked a particularly chilling gaze over the remaining eight.

"You could have ruined everything."

GLOSSARY OF TERMS

A mhac: (Irish) son; also, slang equivalent of "pal" or "dude"

Black Moon: the second new moon of a month

Blatqnn: (Old Norse) black tooth

Caethiwed: (Welsh) bondage

Cailleach: (from the Old Gaelic, caillech "veiled one") a
    goddess from Celtic mythology

Claimsech: (Old Irish) bitch

Diarfoga: (Welsh; imperative) Disarm

Fè m 'konnen sekrè ou: (Haitian Creole) Let me know your
    secrets

Fýr: (Old English) generic term for magical energy/power in
    visible form
        Wanfýr: non-lethal; white
        Wælfýr: lethal; blue

Geaef: (Welsh) Winter

Gelýcost: (Old English) twin

Geswefe: (Old English; imperative) Sleep

Glamour: spell used to disguise/alter appearance

Gwanwyn: (Welsh) Spring

Ifrinn: (Gaelic) Hell

Kite m 'pou kont li: (Haitian Creole) Let me alone

Mac conlón: (Old Irish) son of canine excrement

Maw!: (Romany) an exclamation

Mera: (Old English) incubus

Miri kushti: (Romany) my happiness

Miri mora: (Romany) my friend

Montre m danje a: (Haitian Creole) Show me the danger

Muileach: (Gaelic) beloved

Ne scyrde: (Old English) Do not harm

Non nocere: (Latin) Do no harm

Pa fè mal: (Haitian Creole) Do no harm

Rekkr: (Old Norse) warrior

Rwyt ti mewn trymgwsg: (Welsh) You are in deep sleep

Sidhe: (Gaelic; also *sídhe, sí, síth*) supernatural race of Irish
    and Scottish mythology (think fairies, elves)

Sumite vires ex lumen: (Latin) Take strength from the light

Thegnas: (Old English) followers

Vánagandr: (Old Norse) a monstrous wolf also known as
    Fenrir, son of Loki

Abby's Circle Casting
    Bless this circle formed today
    To keep all trouble far away
    While safe within its unseen light
    We do our work for good and right
    As above, so below
    Lady of Silence, please hear these words
    And make it so

The Wheel of the Year

    Samhain: 31 October - 1 November
    Midwinter: 21 - 22 December
    Imbolc: 31 January - 1 February
    Vernal Equinox: 20 March
    Beltane: 30 April - 1 May
    Midsummer: 20 - 21 June
    Lughnasadh: 31 July - 1 August
    Autumnal Equinox: 22 - 23 September

ACKNOWLEDGMENTS

Many, many thanks to those who encouraged and supported the making of this book, and also to those who reached out to say that they enjoyed its predecessor and looked forward to more.

Writing is a mostly solitary endeavor...and yet it is done with the intention to entertain others.

Such kind and enthusiastic words mean the world.

Special thanks to Gwen Dandridge and Barbara Messinger for work put toward fixing typos, grammatical confusions, and other potential problems. For whatever remains, I have only myself to blame.

ABOUT THE AUTHOR

R. A. Finley is the author of the three published novels so far; a former animator of technical gizmos and systems which she cannot share due to nondisclosure agreements; an aspiring photographer and artist; a hobbyist knitter; and a graduate of the London Film School, Gnomon School of Visual Effects, and Southern Oregon University (not in that order).

A self-described middling adventurer, terminal eccentric, and gardening enthusiast, she is surprised to now reside in the Midwest. She may be found searching for a coffee shop to favorite, familiarizing herself with the local parks, and (sometimes) posting on www.rafinleybooks.com and various social media (as @rafinley).

EXPECTED IN 2024

THE VALE OF SILENCE

The Wheel of the Year: Book 3

For news and updates: www.rafinleybooks.com

Read on for an excerpt:

Sunset should have blazed over the meadow in brilliant, fiery hues. Reds, oranges, golds. Colors as spectacular as the woman herself had been. That would have been no less than she deserved—which was nothing of this. She should be here; but then none of them would be in this particular location, now, if she were. Thia was aware that this made little sense. So little did, lately.

The time had been chosen to coincide with the setting sun, but unlike some people (one, specifically, had come to mind), no one involved in the planning could do anything about the thick canopy of cloud.

Ladened with threat of yet more snow, it hung low over the long meadow to turn winter's early sunset into an even earlier dusk. There would be no full dark, not with so much reflective white on the ground and surrounding woods. A mix of pines and firs, that was, all of them motionless for the absence of wind. Their needled branches were bowed, burdened by days of excessive, late season storm. Thia felt a sympathetic ache as she studied them with distracted concern. She knew what it meant to carry such a cold, relentless weight; to have more and more piled on until one either bent with it or broke.

Taking a slow, difficult breath, she stepped from the woods to make her way to the gathering set in the meadow's approximate center. Preparations had finished while she'd held back. She hadn't meant to be the last to arrive; she just hadn't been ready. She still wasn't. She kept her eyes downcast, watching her booted feet along the path. Mason jars lined both sides. The candle flames within danced, shining on the clear glass and sparkling on the snow. Snow that muffled and absorbed sound. She heard only the soft, frozen crunch of her steps. The soft rasp of her breath through her scarf. The soft thrum of her blood behind her ears, of her heart in her chest.

Heavy with sorrow, raw with grief. Clichés, but no less accurate. That was how the aftermath of this loss felt, as if the usual buffers from the world's full impact—its overwhelming complexity and fragile impermanence—had been torn away, leaving Thia exposed to a pressure so immense that simply putting one foot before the other felt like an almost impossible slog.

At her approach, the circle of mourners shifted, opening a place between her friend Abby and a man she recognized as a Landmark parking attendant. She stepped in, murmured a greeting. Now that she stood closer, most faces were familiar, with one notable absence. Given the family's opinion of him, though, it was understandable.

Abby, with her gaze fixed on what lay at the circle's heart, reached out her hand. Gloved though it was, this was nonetheless a speaking gesture for someone who, as a rule, shied away from contact. Thia clasped it. Her mitten made the grip awkward.

Instead of the expected withdrawal, Abby kept hold. "This is so hard," she said in the way of a plea, although there was nothing Thia could do. Nothing anyone could do.

Or say.

She gave Abby's hand a gentle squeeze. This *was* hard—yet how much harder for a *best* friend. Abby's eyes, red-rimmed and haunted, were dry. That was a result of effort, Thia knew, because she was making the same. So many tears had already been shed. So many more were to come.

It was time.

A single, solemn ring of a bell had her turn to face forward, into the circle. She could no longer avoid what had brought them all here: The timber and brushwood pyre and what had been laid so carefully upon it. Even now her mind balked and her eyes wanted to rebel. But looking away would not change what had happened. As impossible as it continued to seem, this was reality. Unacceptable yet undeniable.

The body had been wrapped in undyed silk and laid upon cedar branches.

Thia's gaze went unerringly to the top, where the familiar face would be and she braced herself, afraid of both what she would see and of her response . . . but nothing was visible beneath the shroud.

That made for a different kind of trauma and, irrational as she knew it to be, she couldn't help worrying that not enough air could pass through the cloth, that the artfully bound strips were too tight. Stifling. But of course none of that mattered.

What lay there so impossibly still did not breathe, did not feel. It was merely what remained.

Five days earlier...

As the lone occupant of the pub's front corner table, Cormac had a wall at his back and a clear view of the door. The Cobbler's Findings was that sort of establishment—the sort where such precaution was advisable. And because his was that sort of life, potential exit routes had been scouted before his first trip to the carved, oaken bar. By the time his pint had been pulled, those routes plus two more had been assessed for convenience and likelihood of success. Ranked thusly, they sat in the back of his mind much in the way he sat now, waiting for the action to start.

Patience had been a painful lesson of his youth. Well over two centuries later, it remained more a matter of determination than inclination. An inherently impatient man playing a role.

He allowed himself an inward smile. Technically, he played the role of a man as well, since his blood and talents contained a vital inheritance from his Otherworldly mother. Man and *leanan sidhe,* he was. Both yet neither. It made him adept at pretense—and at identifying the like in others.

Good thing, considering why he had come all this way to County Kerry.

His timing could have been better. Torrential rain and gale

force winds had battered the whole of the western coast for two days.

Through the bank of mullioned windows on his right, he kept an eye on the flooding street and beyond, where Dingle's mid-sized harbor was crowded with trawlers of all sizes and conditions, all bobbing wildly on the bay's dark, choppy water. Even the most intrepid fishermen had been forced ashore, for which the pub could credit the brisk mid-afternoon business along with the pervading odors.

The front door opened on a rush of sound, letting in such a force of cold, briny air that empty packets of crisps blew off the nearest tables. Three more fishermen—large ones— stomped inside. Water cascaded down their yellow slickers as if they had come from the sea itself.

They fought the wind to get the door shut. It took all three together along with a stream of profane bickering. Croatian, Cormac thought it was. Afterwards they laughed, wide smiles splitting the wet shag of their beards. The brawniest took a good-natured punch to the shoulder and then, intent on the bar, they began to wend their way between overfilled tables. The noise level, having dropped when wary interest shifted to their arrival, rose again.

Tension remained high.

With deliberate unconcern, Cormac returned his outward gaze to the newspaper crossword on his table and penned an answer. He kept his inward gaze—his Sight, it was called— directed at his surroundings.

Where the winter storm took away opportunity in the form of fishing, it put in place another that was potentially more lucrative: Smuggling.

He had spent countless hours in places nearly identical to this. He knew there were three types of players present. The first and largest in number were fishermen who could be had if the money was right—and it almost always was. With the climate's future proving to be inescapably volatile for north

Atlantic fisheries, the numbers of ships-for-hire had swelled exponentially.

Next were the thrill seekers, those who thrived on danger. Maybe they had started out with good intentions; maybe a criminal record made finding other work too difficult. Maybe they had learned the trade when The Troubles were at their peak and this was how they kept their glory days alive.

Cormac knew how potent a drug danger could be. Raised to be of service to Idris Cathmor, when he had come of age, he had been put toward "acquisitions." Objects, information, people—all by any means necessary. He had spent the greater part of his Otherworldly-extended life being both thief and confidence artist, in and out of some level of danger on the regular.

It was who and what he was.

He had, in the shock and lengthy aftermath of Idris's death, lost sight of that. He was returned to it now, like slipping back into a familiar autumn coat after a long, bewildering summer.

The third type, present here as surely as one or two had been present in the other places visited in his search, were not like him. They were worse.

He lifted the pint to his lips, used the act as another chance to survey the room. The winter ale—this was his third—was surprisingly pleasant. Smooth with a complex finish.

The back of his neck prickled.

Idly, he set down the glass and, angling his head, met the bartender's dark-eyed stare. The latter wiped hands the size of hams on the apron tied around his barrel of a middle and turned away to pull more ales for the Croatians. But Cormac did not miss the subtle tip of the chin given to another dark-eyed watcher across the room. This one was seated much as he was: back to a wall; half-finished glass and newspaper on his table.

The prickling of Cormac's neck became a buzz. Full alert.

He eased his grip on the glass and, with deceptive calm, took up his pen to resume working the puzzle. The man across the room pulled out a smartphone. One touch of the screen and a call was placed.

It did not last long. A few words spoken with lips too stiff to be read. Another touch of the screen and the mobile was set down beside the folded paper. The bulge in the latter could have been anything: a pack of cigarettes; a gun.

Cormac, having left off using any glamours or other means of disguise, had no doubt that he'd been recognized—either from prior awareness or a database accessed from that very phone. In these modern times with CCTV and widespread addiction to posting on social media, he continued to do his best to limit exposure. Likely, few images of his true appearance existed, despite his recent lapses. But exist they did and he used that deliberately here.

He lifted his head, met the other man's stare full on. Amber flickered in it, a show of power too quick to be a threat. More like an acknowledgement. Cormac didn't bother with a show of his own; the man was a gatekeeper only. Outside, as framed by the windows, a sleek luxury sedan pulled to a halt.

The arrival did not go unnoticed throughout the pub. Talk dropped to a low, nervous hush or ceased altogether. No one looked directly at the door, yet all waited for it to open.

It did, easily despite the storm, and was then just as easily closed. The small man it had admitted wore no raincoat, but not so much as a drop had touched his crimson pinstriped suit.

His diminutive stature and bright red hair in combination with the golden buckles on his heeled leather shoes left no question as to his identity. More gold gleamed on the buttons of his coat and, given how it acted in the light, in the fabric itself.

Cormac had expected someone higher up to be called, but not *this* high. It was both intriguing and troubling.

The room was stillness itself while the O'Shannon wended his way to the bar. Once there, he greeted the bartender with simple familiarity.

"Rory." His high-pitched voice fit his size—five feet at the most—but was nevertheless discordant given the amount of power he carried.

"O'Shannon." The bartender turned to his left and, from a special shelf, took down a bottle of whiskey and a cut crystal tumbler. He set them on the bar, pushed them to the front edge. The O'Shannon took both—the gold of multiple rings glinting on his blunt-tipped fingers—and with a quick pivot, headed directly for Cormac.

Bright green eyes sparkled beneath bushy, ginger brows as, above the Donegal-style beard, a smile began to creep its way into being.

"My, my," came that treble, sing-song voice and a chill skittered down Cormac's spine. To cover for it, he used his foot to push out the table's other chair, opposite. His hands remained as they had been since the O'Shannon had entered: flat on the table in the accepted gesture of "no threat intended." When lethal magic could be called to one's hands in an instant, it certainly wouldn't do to raise them.

The O'Shannon nimbly sat. His smile widened to reveal a shiny gold tooth. "You're looking quite . . . *yourself* on this fine afternoon, Idris Cathmor's son."

Cormac's jaw clenched on a flare of resentment. Ever in his father's shadow. Ever his instrument.

The O'Shannon chortled, having so easily won a reaction. Nudging aside Cormac's newspaper and pen, he put his glass down to then deftly unscrew cap from bottle. "I'd offer condolences on your loss," he said, pouring himself two generous fingers of whiskey. "But as I'm thinking you found it no loss at all, I'll save the breath." He recapped the bottle, set it aside. Then, with a pointed glance at Cormac's hands, he raised the glass in toast. "*Sláinte.*"

Taking that as a grant of permission, Cormac took up his pint for a welcome swallow.

"Well, now." The O'Shannon set his glass beside the bottle. Crossing his arms, he leaned forward. No fewer than seven gold buttons ornamented each cuff. "Never did I think you'd be sitting plain as day here in my own place of business. So when word of that very thing reached me, I said to meself— O'Shannon, I said, there's bound to be good reason, for the boy isn't stupid—not like your cousin Diarmuid or the *eejit* your sister married. No, I said, Idris Cathmor's *Cormac* wants something, he does, and you'd best get down there to find out what that is."

The joviality was a mask, Cormac well knew. Everyone did, which was why the tone of conversation in the pub remained hushed if not outright cowed.

Slowly, Cormac withdrew a leather pouch from his jacket, draped over the arm of his chair. He held his hand out, over the table, and let the pouch drop. It hit the table with a thud. The metal within clinked faintly.

The O'Shannon swept it up with the speed of a dibstones champion. He gave it a little shake, his head cocked. "Brass?"

"Naturally."

The flash of the O'Shannon's grin revealed two more of his infamous gold teeth. With quick, avaricious tugs, he loosened the drawstring, then shook the pouch over his cupped hand. Several of the twelve dozen cobbler's nails dropped out. He made a hum of appreciation. "You have more of these?"

"I do."

"Ah. Well, then." With a wave of one hand above the other, nails and pouch vanished. "Let's step into my office, shall we?" Giving no time for objection, he rapped two knuckles on the tabletop.

Everything around Cormac and the O'Shannon froze like a paused television show. People had been caught mid-gesture, some with pint glasses tipped to their mouths, the beer they had intended to drink no longer flowing. On the hearth, the flames stood as if sculpted. Outside, raindrops hung like beads on invisible threads. Not a single ship moved in the harbor. The waves, the storm, all of it suspended. All of it, silent.

The O'Shannon's office, as it were. Not so much a where as a when. A place outside of time.

When one was caught up in this particular Otherworldly trick, the hardest adjustment to make was not to the disconcerting visuals and absence of sound outside the—well, it was referred to as a "fairy circle," but that was a bit of a misnomer; for one, it was spherical, surrounding its occupants in every extent.

It took away the *feel* of all that lay beyond. *That* was what made adjustment difficult—the absence, and the conflicting sensations which resulted: One of the world closing in; the other of being entirely adrift.

The O'Shannon took up the whiskey bottle. The scrape of the metal cap seemed overly loud. The clink of glass against glass. The splash of liquid.

"I hope you won't be wanting another just yet," he said with a nod toward Cormac's nearly finished pint.

It wasn't that Cormac couldn't pick it up and drink—he was as free to move as the O'Shannon—but he could not leave the circle. There would be no refill.

"I'm fine."

That got a merry laugh. "If you were fine, boy, you'd not be calling out the likes of me. You aren't usually so obvious." A greedy light entered his eyes. "You must want whatever it is very much indeed."

Usually these things were an intricate dance of allusion and subterfuge. But, as had just been observed, Cormac had been unusually obvious. Might as well keep to it.

"The Achill Bell."

Smile gone, the O'Shannon tipped back in his chair.

"For a start," Cormac added, and then finished his ale. It did nothing for the dryness of his throat. His hand was steady, at least. He schooled his expression to one of amusement. The bitter kind. "I assume you've heard about Idris's collection."

"About it not being where it ought? Mm." The O'Shannon's fingers drummed the table. "To hear it told, all of Fiend's Fell sits empty." He referred to Idris's mountain stronghold, used for centuries to house the man himself and the main of his unnaturally extended (and abruptly ended) life's work. Relics, grimoires—any and everything that might be of use in ritual magics.

It had been Cormac's life's work as well. Work he had been raised to do. *Made* to do, with the expectation of inheritance serving as the only light in times of extreme dark.

Earned through his labors and his blood, the collection was rightfully his.

"'Tis the general notion that you're behind the clearance," the O'Shannon said, offhand. "After all, you killed the man."

Cormac jerked hard on the reins of his temper. He would not give the O'Shannon the satisfaction of having provoked another response. Strictly speaking, Cormac had not been in control of the power that had flowed through him as he and Idris fought. The Society of Brigantium had. They had used him as a conduit.

Yet the O'Shannon was technically correct, and in Cormac's line of work, to be seen as capable of patricide was a plus.

"For myself," the O'Shannon offered into the stillness, "I'd wondered what took you so long."

"Risk assessment."

"Sure, fair enough." A twinkle in his eyes, he swigged his whiskey. "Did you really call down a storm—and on *Insi Orc,* no less?"

"On Samhain?" Cormac scoffed. "That would be a foolish

thing to do." And just as foolish to admit to it.

"Indeed." Grinning, the O'Shannon steepled his beringed hands. "Ah, but I do enjoy dealing with you, Cormac son of Idris. Should anyone hear of such doings that night, it won't have come from me." He winked. "Not for a time, yet. Longer, if you make it worth my while."

Information with a side of blackmail.

"The Achill Bell," Cormac insisted. "Whatever you have on it. Then we can discuss compensation. For the *assistance*." To suggest payment was for anything else would be tantamount to an admission—as the O'Shannon had intended.

Never trust a leprechaun.

"I'd be wanting it in the form of a good turn," the latter said. "Your skills in . . . *procurement*, shall we say."

Never trust a leprechaun and—above all—never owe one a good turn. Unless the alternative was worse.

"All right—*if*," Cormac emphasized, "your information is of equal value."

Glee immediately suffused the O'Shannon's face. "Oh, t'is grand, that is! Absolutely grand." Clapping, he bounced child-like on his seat. "What I can offer holds great value. A great deal, indeed."

Dread was a warning Cormac had no choice but to disregard; he was here because he was running out of options and time, both. He needed the Achill Bell to fulfill a bargain made weeks ago. A bargain made upon pain of death.

He arched a brow.

So it was done. The O'Shannon lifted one hand. A slim red book materialized in his grasp. He set it on the table and with one ringed finger, slid it forward.

Cormac picked it up. The weight of the good turn owed was made manifest, borne on sheets of vellum bound in crimson leather.

A great deal, indeed.

Pub sounds flooded in. Conversation. Thuds of glass upon wood. The outside roar of the storm. Cormac looked up from the book. All around, activity had resumed.

The O'Shannon stood, and the tumbler and whiskey bottle vanished from the table. A glance showed them to be back on their special shelf.

"It has been a pleasure, Idris's *Cormac,*" the O'Shannon said, again putting malicious stress on the name. With a laugh, he spun on the heels of his fancy shoes and headed for the door.

Across the room, the man who had been watching rushed to get there first. He held it open.

"I'll be in touch," the O'Shannon said over his shoulder, and left. His lackey followed.

With door's closing, the atmosphere lightened. The book in Cormac's hand did not. It remained damnably, menacingly heavy. He laid it on the table.

Only after the O'Shannon's car drove away did he open to the first page of barely legible scribbles. As if Gaelic was not challenging enough in written form, the dialect was Munster Irish. An intentional choice, no doubt, to make things more difficult.

Leprechauns.

Cormac wanted another pint.

THE VALE OF SILENCE

The Wheel of the Year: Book 3

For more information: www.rafinleybooks.com